GHOST DANCE: A PLAY OF VOICES

A NOVEL BY ~~GLADYS SWAN~~

Gladys Swan (signature)

LOUISIANA STATE UNIVERSITY PRESS
Baton Rouge and London   1992

Designer: Laura Roubique Gleason
Typeface: Trump Mediaeval
Typesetter: G & S Typesetters, Inc.
Printer and binder: Thomson-Shore, Inc.

Library of Congress Cataloging-in-Publication Data

Swan, Gladys, date.
    Ghost dance : a play of voices : a novel / by Gladys Swan.
        p.   cm.
    ISBN 0-8071-1706-4 (alk. paper)
    I. Title.
    PS3569.W247G48   1992
    813'.54—dc20   91-20123
                                                                  CIP

For Dale and Burt
And for all the others who have entered the Wilderness

It is indeed a Wandering in the Wilderness
that I am undergoing.

—Kafka

CONTENTS

Ghost Dance: A Play of Voices

I   SCENE: THE TOWN

Things were in a slump. That much everybody knew, since the fortunes of the town were tied to the price of copper. As they'd once been to silver, and before that to gold. The golden dawn, the silver day, now the copper evening, dimming, it seemed, into night. Boom or bust, hanging on by a gasp—hail or farewell?—from the end of one cycle to the beginning of the next: Chloride. For the bottom had dropped out, leaving the town on the verge of becoming part of the broken-windowed past, while desperation clung to the notion of a future. Waiting for the next strike of inspiration or richest ore.

Meanwhile, the big mine was shut down—for how long was anybody's guess—and months before they'd handed round the last paychecks and chained the gates at the smaller lead and zinc mines in the area. A crop of signs sprang up among the cacti on the rocky slopes in front of the houses in the newer subdivisions, sudden as desert poppies after a rain: For Sale. Picking up stakes and moving on, a migration, gathering as steadily as rainwater into a flash flood sweeping down from the mountains. And who can measure the losses?

There was a mystery in all this, like a secret hand prying a wedge loose here, breaking a strand there, leaving a gap in the defenses. During the same period a fire broke out, gutting a warehouse that had once been the town's main hotel. A rumor went round that a certain half-witted boy had set the fire. Then a bakery burned to the ground. This time people said it was for the insurance and grimly wished they'd thought to do the same. A kind of paralysis gripped the town: no one knew what to do.

Those who didn't leave seemed to walk in a dream, as if they couldn't bear to wake to what was happening.

For some never leave—those destined to slip down beneath the present, bobbing and floating in a time-stilled limbo; others who find in the debris of one life the scraps for another and make do; and finally those rare and perhaps lucky few who seem to stand somehow outside circumstance, as though they hold some powerful secret of their own that, outwardly observed, might be called their genius, or else their destiny.

Among these, perhaps, are the ones who can either stay or go, more rarely those who can return.

"By God, turn things upside down enough and you shake out everything in the goddam corners including the lint," Virgil Langtry announced by way of prelude to the steadfast coffee hounds of the Cactus Cafe, who gathered every morning just about ten.

"What've you got on your mind, Virge?" the mayor asked, as Millie filled his cup and went round the table.

"Bird's come back." The man had crossed his vision as he stood looking out the window of his real estate office at the boarded-up windows of an appliance store across the street. One more business gone under. And who'd be next? You just woke up one morning, all the starch gone out of you, knowing you couldn't make it. Nothing more under your feet, nothing to hold on to. Maybe nothing on this green earth. Only, this morning there was one thing you hadn't banked on: A. J. ("Bird") Peacock was back in town.

"So he's come back," Emmet Early, the jeweler, said—as though from the tiny jewels of interest you might pick up from listening to gossip came the irony of holding nothing of worth.

"I thought he was dead," Lester Pruitt, of the Frontier Bank, said. "Never expected to lay eyes on him again, not in this life."

Neither had the mayor. Something uncanny in that. Had Bird caught the smell of bad news, a sniff of what the town he'd neglected for so long was planning to do to him? For his spread was about to be snatched out from under him, auctioned off for taxes. Some, not to mention any names, were just waiting to see it happen. Motions were already astir, plans in the air. The

2

banker and few others were in on it. A note of promise to take their minds off their headaches, the piling-up of debt and loss. How many foreclosures? Ordinarily a man who acted as though he'd cheerfully load the bank's money onto the back of your truck, who knew and once could have predicted the balance in nearly every account, Lester Pruitt now pulled his earlobe or bit his thumbnail. The pockets of the town were being turned inside out. First the mines, and then the fires and what promised to be the worst drought in five years.

"You suppose he's got the loot to pay off all the back taxes?" the banker wanted to know. There was an exchange of looks: the key question.

"Maybe he'll bring out his money machine," someone suggested.

"Sounds good to me," the insurance man, a relative newcomer, put in. "Be glad enough to have one of them myself. What the hell is it?"

And they told how Bird put a good one over on a bunch of local-history buffs he'd invited out to see his spread and his collection of Indian relics. Just before they left, parading them in front of a gadget that looked like the cockeyed offspring of a player piano mated with a jukebox and telling them that was how he really made his money. "This ranching business just don't pay off." That's what he tells them. "I've done my time playing with God and the weather." And takes out his wallet, pulls out a single and sticks it into the slot. Then the lights flash on and gears whir and the whole thing starts humming and shaking and the musical part strikes up "La Cucaracha." A solid minute of beeping, flashing, and noise, and out pops a ten-dollar bill. "Here," he says, to a tall, thin fellow who works for the newspaper, "you try it." All the rest have a turn. And trot off home with three, four hundred dollars. Only then they get a big idea: counterfeit money. And call in the FBI. Agents swarming all over the place. And Bird laughing fit to kill. All perfectly legal tender. His little joke.

The insurance man roared with laughter. "That's a good one," he said. "Sounds like somebody I'd like to meet." You'd think, he considered, that somewhere in the world there'd be the real thing. The money tree always growing fresh leaves—thousand-dollar bills you'd have to climb farthest for, all the way to the top; five hundreds in the middle; and nothing smaller than a fifty on the lower branches.

"Yeah," the banker said. "Only wait till you're the one he's making a fool out of. Which seems to be mightily his pleasure. Only it's not just jokes. There's a kind of mischief, I don't know. What d'you say, Mayor? You know him."

"You got me," Curry Gatlin admitted. "He's a tough one to figure out. Neither hide nor hair of him for God knows how long, and now he's here. Like a bad wind blew him in. Maybe he caught the smell of trouble in the air." So continued the mayor, who'd watched him come and go. And who meanwhile had made a good thing of the zoning in the town and the bids for contracts, had come to know the sweet profit that can follow the routes of roads and the laying-out of streets. And who had it all set up to get the best of Bird's being away. The way he figured it, he was in the way of doing the town a favor.

"I say he's a menace," Lester Pruitt said.

"Oh, come on," the real estate agent said. "A few practical jokes . . ."

"No, you wait . . . There's something behind all that. When he gets that glint in his eye, there's no more stopping him than a force of nature. Then, when it's over, he can sit back and laugh at the born fools that get taken in." It was perverse, to Lester Pruitt's mind. Not just showing people up but continually poking them from the rear, as though they'd better never forget to look around at what was behind them; catching them at the curve behind the eyeball where things go a little aslant.

Emmett Early remained silent. He didn't like to think in the direction of ill omens, of what might arrive to make bad things worse. But the man violated the morality of the works of clocks and the straightforward gleam of silverplate, things that expressed to the jeweler the polished surface of civilized life. He saw hands hard with cunning, always about to break something delicate and valuable. Looking at gold and silver and copper in their state of utmost refinement, he could only wonder at the larger workings that would keep his stock from sitting there on the shelves. The present turmoil had already given him an ulcer. Later that night, he would have a vision of dark wings and sit up suddenly remembering.

"So you think he'll pull things out for himself?"

4

"Always has before," someone suggested. "I wonder how he does it. The way he riles people up. That time with the strikers. And then with the Commies. A wonder the things he stirs up don't turn on him. Lucky sonofabitch. He's got more ways out than a Houdini."

The real estate agent could have used a few himself. And how long would the houses sit, signs in front, waiting for a buyer? Months lengthening into years—the desert of the future sifting down, while the stucco darkened and roof tiles fell and yards turned to cactus thorn. "I wouldn't shake hands with the bastard. Wouldn't know what was up his sleeve."

"Always going against the town. Never marrying, only sitting still till the craziness catches him; then he's on his way like a man on a bender." Harry Monroe shook his head—the furniture dealer, whose hair grew white at the temples as he sat over his gray account books, unable to tear himself away, feverish combinations of figures dancing his brain to rags. What a mistake to carry his own credit. Repossessions: mattresses he'd have to throw in the ditch and sofas with stains and vermin, and broken appliances. The future turning into junk . . . At some point he'd sit with an old Smith & Wesson in his lap, one he kept in the case of robbery and had never used, and wonder if it might not take him an easier route.

"What does he want, do you think?" the insurance man said. He hadn't heard anything yet that could clear his confusion. And he liked the money-machine joke. They were getting worked up about the man, maybe because he was handy to pin something on. He'd been away and out of it. And things were bad and getting worse. Though it didn't sound like this Bird fellow was in for any picnic.

"Well, I don't know," the mayor said. "I think he likes being where trouble is, picking it up and turning it his own way, whatever that is. Otherwise he wouldn't be satisfied. It's a restlessness in the genes," he said, clapping O'Conner, the insurance man, on his back. "Some people hanker for it, got to stir it up where it doesn't exist. Hell, I can still remember what happened back around '51 when he let all those Communists out on his place to make that film. That was after the strike."

"I'll bet he's still a Communist," the undertaker said.

"That's because he's a maverick. Only he doesn't believe in

nothing." You believe one thing and folks can get their hooks into you: he could remember him saying that, back when they were younger and lent each other books. Pour your mind into a religion or an ideology and you live in one room all your life. He had ideas, that one. And rolled around like loose change. No loyalty. No, too quick, too clever—just step to the side, sidle out of the way, sidewinder that he is. "Likes to get folks to quarreling and sit back and watch the fun . . ." He didn't mention the old embarrassment, the way Bird had sicced Ginger on the town when Ramirez tried to close her up. And it still rankled him when he thought of it. The madam rattling him, bearding him in his own den. He'd come out okay, the council all gung ho for a clean town. Maybe for the sake of hiding a few of their own peccadilloes. All except for the one good puritan, who had only his principles, by God. Even so. But the town itself he couldn't bank on. Though he'd put down his roots and made his connections and turned all the tricks of a man in his position. Treacherous—twist one way and roll back the other. Lift you to their shoulders one minute and toss you into a cactus clump the next. Cattle—blank and stupid, or else on the stampede. A mystery.

"Peculiar." Which could have been the voice of anybody there. The insurance man shook his head. Five years in Chloride, every morning at the Cactus Cafe, member of the Elks, and he still couldn't stand around and talk politics with the boys at the courthouse. Hadn't dipped deeply enough, got hold of the experience to pass muster. But he'd get there yet. And all this was taking him somewhere new. It didn't make sense, all the lather they'd worked up, and the fellow not in town two days.

"That old Mexican woman used to cook for him told me he's got ways of talking to the dead."

"He can talk to them," the undertaker said, "but that doesn't mean they'll answer back." He himself whistled around the dead, and sometimes talked to himself, but no corpse had violated the sanctity of his privacy. This side of the grave the dead had nothing to say.

"Throws his voice, that's what he does. Half ventriloquist and half hypnotist. I've watched him," the mayor said. "Convinces people he can do séances."

"I hate all that kind of superstition," said the jeweler, coming out of his brown study, his voice like a whistle blown too hard. "Just let times get bad and people go wild, seize on the worst kind of superstition."

"We'll see what happens," Curry Gatlin said. "I'll keep an eye on him. Just let him step out of bounds . . ." The mayor smiled. Out-coyote the coyote. Do in the old bird. Maybe he'd have some fun of his own. But he was worried. If Bird had the money to salvage his place, what then?

"Talking to the dead. People haunted by their troubles— hearing things and seeing things. Ready to run to the next prophet, pour money down a rathole." The jeweler's fingers twitched. Sometimes ideas obsessed him.

"You don't think he'll try any stuff like that?" the insurance man scoffed.

"It's all nonsense," Lester Pruitt said. "Just what some Mexican or some old woman would say. They believe that kind of stuff."

"I've heard some tale about money being buried . . ."

"Let him dig it up then."

"Trouble enough in this town without . . ."

". . . they say his mother . . ."

"Spending all this energy . . ."

"And why is he so ornery then?"

"Comes by it natural."

"Four generations of Peacocks in this town. And killing was good enough for one of them anyway." The banker laughed.

"The old West had a few advantages. Let a man make mischief and . . ." Virgil Langtry made the gesture of a noose around the neck.

The insurance man looked around in amazement. He didn't understand it. He had to envy this Bird: he could sure as hell call attention to himself. He looked over at the mayor.

"Killing's good for . . ."

". . . being a general damned nuisance." The banker laughed again.

"It would take people's minds off a few things."

So the mayor said. And was he serious? He didn't know himself, but the old coyote was back, and he wouldn't mind putting one over on him if he could beat him to it.

". . . the old woman was trying to . . ."

7

"Trouble-making sonofabitch . . ."

"He getting you worked up, Virge?"

"What is this? What sort of man?"

The jeweler put his hands over his ears. A small vein in his forehead throbbed. His mind was momentarily crossed by a vision that almost made him cry out, Wait, wait, don't everybody talk at once.

A flood of words. Lines of thought broken past present future rushing together at some dangerous crossroads. Sweeping things away in a gathering emotion, the waters breaking down through the arroyos, sweeping away trees, breaking up branches. Confusion and a mouthful of sand. Chaos in the town. On the last day words breaking apart into syllables and the din of voices in their final howls of dismay. A drama of the unimaginable. But now those individual dramas: what do we do when the money's gone, and where is tomorrow? Soup kitchens during the week. Drunken men reeling home, out of work. Children whining and tempers flaring. A smack of the hand, a blow of the fist. Black eyes and blue-edged bruises. A gathering chaos of voices. Hard work to hear yourself think in the din, to catch hold of something before the wind scatters the facts of your life like scraps of paper. What can you catch? What branch is there to cling to like belief? What can you do to make the old horse go?

Chloride, the town. Hanging there in the mountains, isolated, off the beaten track. And the voices of the town, taken up with the ring of copper in the marketplace, the reverberations setting the teeth on edge. Events will tell you now and then that something hangs in the balance, that nothing will ever be the same. A fateful moment, when you might conclude that the past was better than the present.

Step back then into the darkness of origins: a wilderness before the town ever came to be. And did the explorer, picking his way over mountain after mountain, finally gaining a vantage point from the heights, only to see wave after wave of peaks disappearing into the distance, think then his journey might be endless? Or that he should never have started? At first, a place where the footfalls of the Indians left no track, and the grizzly bear roamed without let or hindrance. Then the Spaniards came up north hunting for El Dorado, the golden phantom. Later, fur trappers and prospectors wandered in. And then it happened, a rich gold strike in the mountains to the north, and the light of an era flared up, drawing men to this wild place to tear the land away from the Apaches and the grizzlies, *Ursulus horribilis.*

Among them, Bird Peacock's great-grandfather, mustered out of the Union forces with a twelve-dollar-a-month pension, enough for flour and salt pork and provisions for his mule. Harrison Peacock, who staked a claim he was nearly killed for holding. Some folks had gotten wind of his good fortune, and eyes fixed on him and followed him every time he saddled his horse to ride off to work his claim. And one citizen lay in wait for him, when he thought he'd given them all the slip, taking false trails, doubling back, traveling by night. But that sharper spied him out, set on him when he led his ore-laden mule toward Chloride. Shot him in the shoulder. But Peacock killed the man, and took it as a sign. Sold his claim, took his gold, and let the dust slip through his fingers.

He took his fortune to San Francisco, discovered the theater, and flung himself into a great good time. Went every night and threw gold nuggets on the stage while Lotta Crabtree lifted her skirts and showed her legs, all in provocative innocence. Oh, naughty girl. And he yelled her name and clamored for more. Would have carried her off, at least in his fantasies, if her mother had let a man come near her. Meanwhile, fling the money into the air, let it go in a golden stream. Drink up and set them round for the boys. Dreams grow in its place. And a good time is worth the gleam of yellow any day. Lots more where that came from. All around California and Arizona he wandered with fresh schemes. But nothing panned out. What did it matter? By the time one dream had fled, he'd already started dreaming of the next big adventure. So he'd never been to see the elephant, as they say, never came away disappointed.

Finally, back in Chloride, health shot and money spent, he found a saloonkeeper's widow who liked him well enough to keep him, feed him, and give him a son. She'd had visions when she crossed the prairie, of great cities on the plain, and she sometimes wondered what all that meant. As for her man, he never killed anyone and died with the light of expectation in his eyes.

In the saloon across from the hotel that civilized the main street of Chloride before a flash flood turned that street into a ditch and the hotel into a ruin, Jonathan Peacock won half the Lucky Star silver mine in a poker game. That would have been enough for most men. But his passion was land, the good ranch-land along the Gila River. And he bought it up cheap. To the settlers already there, he gave the choice of selling or being killed by one of his gunmen. With the land, he took the water rights and extended his empire over ninety thousand acres. How much land did the man want? "I just want all the land that borders on mine," he said once.

He built a fine house in the Spanish style with adobe walls a foot thick and wooden vigas across the ceilings. Craftsmen from Mexico carved the tables and chairs and bedsteads. And he imported glassware and china and crystal chandeliers and carpets from Europe, bought a library and paintings for the walls and a grand piano. Then he could hobnob with eastern capitalists and entertain them royally. Teddy Roosevelt was invited to come and hunt on his land.

But he had his troubles. Not with the settlers who cleared out, helpless and bitter, after two or three had been found dead in the arroyos. Nor with his henchmen, to whom he gave land and cattle. But with his bookkeeper, who was being too friendly with his wife. He gave him fair warning—so he swore afterward. Came home one day and shot him dead. And told them all how he'd been wronged by the man he'd treated like a son, trusted, given every opportunity, including the one he never should have taken: to violate his bed and corrupt his wife. Oh yes, he had to tell it to his shame, how he'd found the two of them in bed together when he came home a day early from a business trip up to Santa Fe. The story blazed from the headlines all around the state. The wife, of course, was ruined. She disappeared, leaving her young son to the care of the Mexican cook. Though the furor died down, some never believed Peacock but figured he had some other reason for wanting the man dead: a bookkeeper knew a lot.

All the important men from the East continued to be guests

in the great house on the Peacock ranch. And he was a power in the town and in the state, all that land and all those cattle multiplying and being sold and bringing in a fortune. Till the day he went down to El Paso to arrange the sale of some of those steers. A letter had come to him, making the offer, naming the place of meeting. He was last seen getting into a car. That night he didn't return to his hotel and was found the next day shot to death in an alley—by whoever had lured him there to kill him. PEACOCK MURDERED, the headlines declared. TOWN'S LEADING CITIZEN DIES AT HAND OF UNKNOWN ASSAILANT. "With a funeral procession that included friends and associates from all parts of our noble state and the august presence of dignitaries from the East, the greatly lamented loss of one of the town's leading citizens was observed with due ceremony." It was a bigger story than the adultery.

The copper mine had always been there, going back to the time the Mexicans mined it, working the peons till the Indians drove them off. Now with the Indians gone, the Mexicans defeated, the Yankees in ascendance, copper brought the company, changed the landscape. And like a huge magnet, drew everything to it. The great stack of the smelter rising into the sky, with a curl of smoke that extended against the backdrop of the mountains; and the growing slag heap that in later days looked like a peculiar geological formation. The great pit dug into the earth, deeper, wider, spiraling down through the layers of many-colored earth, lined with train tracks for the ore cars to get to the bottom. Ideas of production and efficiency, a growing modernity. Mexican workers in the mines, living in unstuccoed adobe huts on the rutted dirt streets of the hills surrounding the town. As in the past—the only difference being a new boss. Then the union coming in with its stoppages and strikes. Sometimes the company shut down the mine under the threat of strike or when the market fell. Then the bars were crowded and the goods in the stores remained on the shelves and everyone waited in the atmosphere of rumor.

But hold on. Somewhere in the middle of that, Bartley Peacock, grown to manhood, rescued what was left of his inheritance and became president of the local bank. When the crash came, he disappeared into Mexico with the funds and remained till it was safe for him to come back. Some say he made a deal. Across the border he opened up a club, took a dollar a head from the girls who came and sold their favors, took a percentage of the gamblers' winnings, and made a killing off the liquor. Back in Chloride, he opened a liquor store, built a hotel, served as mayor, and fathered a son, Bird.

The last fledgling of the local dynasty. Always in the public eye. No, they were never done talking about the Peacocks, father and grandfather—all the way back to where rumor outreaches the memory of the living and becomes legend. Bird, they said, was the worst. For though his forebears had been hated, even as they had been admired for their guts, at least they had been understood. They'd wanted gold and land and power and women, out of the simple lust natural to men willing to admit it. And they'd seized upon what they wanted with a certain style and lived with a certain flair. But this one—all he wanted, at least all they could figure out, was to turn things upside down.

So that's what you get when you pull a thread and see where it goes: the line of Peacocks woven into the fabric of the town. All this is history. As for Bird himself, he seemed in a way always outside it, though he was as much a part as anybody else. Couldn't help it, carrying the town with him as he did, whatever the town was. For it was hard to tell, he'd been away so long and traveled so far, and people he knew had gone elsewhere or died and others had come in their stead. But at times their voices spoke in his head as he walked the streets of whatever foreign city he happened to be in: words that had been lost and stories left untold of those who'd been before him. As a boy he'd heard them, sometimes had been under the impression he was carrying a whole history in his head that he didn't know about. When the town wanted to create a museum, he'd surprised everybody by putting a lot of money into it and left them wondering what sort of trick he was trying to pull this time. And they marveled at the sight of him looking long at old tintypes and daguerreotypes and reading in old newspaper files and books he found in the library.

At the same time he himself wondered whether anybody could know a town, could claim to capture its reality. Or if it mattered whether you lived as though the past had never been. But one way or another, he'd decided that the lot of men could mostly make do with toys, scrape off the surface of the useful, turn it into cash, and sleep with numbers ticking in their brains.

There were others too coming back to Chloride, just when good sense dictated leaving. So Bird himself discovered one morning soon after his arrival. He'd walked into the lobby of the Frontier Bank with a man no one had laid eyes on before, a Mexican, a squat sausage of a man with bushy eyebrows and a disconcerting maplike scar over his left cheek. He stood by the window scowling at those who stared at him, and brought to mind sudden thoughts of the evil eye, even as people scoffed at the idea. But more than one customer took the trouble to exit by the door farthest from him when walking out.

After Bird turned away from the teller's window, he found himself confronted by an image he wasn't expecting to see, one that hit him squarely. A poster of a woman both seductive and somehow ethereal. Clearly past the first bloom. Look beyond youth, the photograph insisted, promise still beckons. Toward what? And how recent a photograph? Bird wondered. Something provocative in the white curve of neck and shoulder, also suggested by the smile. If it were only the erotic, powerful and arresting enough, she might have been easier to take in. Ah, let the body play. But the eyes. They knew too much. Haunted and haunting. What had they seen? Would you have to see it too? No, seize on one feature. But under your gaze even the smile turned enigmatic.

The man in the leather jacket and beaten-up western hat appeared to have a great deal to study in the picture. Why not? He had claims. He'd known her as she'd grown up in the town, though he was nearly half a dozen years older than she. Had watched her act in plays and looked at her and known something about her then he had no way of telling except as a tingle in the blood that set off a certain disturbance of the mind.

At one point he'd made an oath to follow her the rest of his life; he was that romantic. A wonder he hadn't written out the oath and signed it with his own blood.

Young fool, he judged himself now. But then there were worse things to occupy your time. He hadn't forgotten her, despite the passage of time and the overlay of circumstance. Now he looked

13

at her as though trying to define and fathom the experience that gave the particular look to her eyes. She was going to be in Chloride.

"Well, Bird."

He frowned at the man who'd interrupted him, shook hands with Lester Pruitt, the good old boy who'd been there forever.

"What brings you to these parts?"

"Fired my foreman and kicked out my lawyer. You can't imagine how things go to wrack and ruin just when you turn your back and think to get a little peace."

"You've been gone a mighty long time, Bird."

"That meaning you can't count on anybody when they're not under your eye or thumb." He gave the banker a sharp look, as though *he* could tell a few of the things that had been going on.

"You aim to be with us for a while?"

"You want to know how long you're going to have to put up with me?" Bird said, with a laugh. "About nine days. Just long enough to fix things up."

Lester had no idea if Bird was putting him on.

"That's my new man over there."

The banker turned and saw the ugliest man who'd ever crossed his vision. You wanted to laugh at this stump of a man, whose chest put the buttons of his fancy western shirt to a test, the rest of him equally stuffed into the black pants he wore, silver studs as big as flowers along the sides. The banker could imagine him with gunbelt and pearl-handled revolvers stepping up to the teller's cage demanding the cash. "But who's down there?" the teller saying, looking over the edge of the cage. He almost laughed, but was caught abruptly in the midst of his fantasy. Too much suspicion, or meanness, there in the eyes— sharp as the edges of black obsidian—and the little set mouth. Then, as he stared, the fellow grinned, paraded a mouthful of uneven teeth, a kind of idiot simplicity in his face. The banker was disarmed.

"He can ride and rope with the best," Bird said. "And he's a crack shot with a pistol. Likes to shoot rabbits with one hand, while steering the Jeep with the other, right out over the range."

"No shit?" The banker felt sure he was being strung along, led to some unaccountable place not located on any map, where he'd be left without food and water or a single clue as to direction. "Where'd you find him, Bird?" Under a rock, he wanted to add, in the middle of a cactus patch?

"He's come up from Chihuahua, got some kin up here."

An illegal alien, the banker came leaping to the conclusion. He'd remember that.

"He was born up North," Bird said, as though to forestall him. "Don't know much about his background. You let go of the whys and wherefores when you're looking for competence. When you can't account for cattle sold . . . When tax statements go astray and lawyers don't do what they're paid for and there's all sorts of ravens and vultures swooping down to feed on you, you start looking for competence."

"That's right," Lester Pruitt agreed soberly. Every card a trick card. And Bird with the whole pack.

"It's a fact," Bird went on. "For the most part, stupidity rules, when it's not downright malice. Now I've got me a man here who'll take care of things—mend a fence, keep the cattle from straying. Not afraid of work. Strong as a horse and quick as a fly. And when the wind's right, he can hear voices. I've listened for them, but he can hear them."

The banker shifted uneasily. You might expect him to throw some such nonsense into the midst of a conversation. Throw you off, get the upper hand. The inscrutable face of the one— the grin was gone—the mumbo jumbo of the other. They both ought to be put where they could hear voices all the time, he thought; let folks get on with their business.

"Was thinking of starting my own church," Bird said, "considering the state of inspiration he can get into, but I've decided against it."

Bird was putting him on, Lester was convinced. Just like him. Half an hour with him in the building and you couldn't think straight. "We got lots of churches," the banker asserted. "And some fine people in them."

"Can't say I've been experiencing any great overflow of sanctity. The way I see it, people's minds have got all junked up and they can't tell what's in the air from what's in the bottom of the pit."

"Well, I got my wife to set me straight," the banker said, with

15

a laugh. "That's about the only voice I can take in." He couldn't stomach any more of such nonsense. Dangerous talk. He looked at the dark figure that stood in the middle of his bank as if it were a visitation. Like some piece of the fantastic caught in the light of the ordinary, a stubborn piece of rind between the teeth. There to make the day go lopsided and the night a broken puzzle. As though an elaborate set of numbers and formulas would turn into a cake recipe or the cracks on the sidewalk spell out the date of the second coming and provide the guest list. No wonder Bird had found him: they belonged together, both of them an insult to the day you were trying to get through. When you needed a large supply of the normal just to get to suppertime.

"I think he's going to scare away the customers," Lester said jocularly.

As if in response the man turned on his heel and went outside, leaving the banker stupefied.

"Huerfano will do all right," Bird said casually, as if he hadn't noticed anything unusual. Actually, he was waiting for Pruitt to leave him alone so that he could study the poster some more. But the man hung on him like a plaster; couldn't seem to tear himself away or else didn't want to let him off without some scrap of assurance that he could go back to his desk and find the print on the page hadn't turned into gibberish.

Actually, the banker was simply curious and though he would be no more satisfied after Bird left, he kept up the conversation. He gave a nod in the direction of the photograph. "Knew her, didn't you?"

"Yep. Great little gal." That was enough for public sentiment, though in the fifties they'd probably have stoned her if she'd come back to town. Now just before the decade turned into the eighties, she could be the local heroine. You had to choose the right moment for sentiment. If there was more than one mystery, allowing for transubstantiation, then it was the public. A matter of timing. Certainly his father and grandfather were onto the trick. Maybe that's how they'd done so well with theft and murder. Except for his old sinner of a grandfather proving faulty of judgment and letting himself get killed. In the process, though, he'd given the town some excitement and considerably improved his public image. Killing him had doubtless improved his character. The town required its images.

"A great thing for the town," the banker said, the poster between them like a piece of merchandise. "Good to remind folks there's something else besides their troubles."

"Using the old psychology," Bird allowed. Nothing like a little distraction in this dark time, when the stores were empty and the bars were full. Another image to keep a little hope warming in the pan.

"Course, it could just make people angry," Bird said, out of pure meanness. Surely the man had a few mortgages to foreclose. "Make them jealous."

"Well, I don't think so," the banker said. "I think folks'll be real proud."

Yes, here was a hometown girl who'd gone to Hollywood and become a film star. And they'd be snared again the way he was once. Though he'd kept secret the reason for his going to L.A., where he'd groomed horses for one of the studios, and tried to put off his father, who kept sending him ultimatums to come home and take up his responsibilities. Bird figured he was getting a better education than he'd gotten at the university: all the politics whirling around him late in the forties, what with the Red scare and the union troubles. And a few other things, like trying to beat off a homosexual photographer and an athletic ex-Wave, both of whom wanted his body.

Meanwhile he curried horses and observed Roselle's career: not one of your starstruck languishers who wear themselves out as waitresses or barmaids or leap into bed with producers. Her rise to fame had been a stroke of luck. She'd come to Hollywood in 1949, when she was just nineteen and made a series of films that were tops at the box office. Typical Hollywood love stories. He wondered now if she had been any good at love. The films took the promise that, to his young man's eyes, beckoned toward a mystery that was also leaping in his own blood, turned it into the old tapioca pudding, and sold it to the public. Under the name of love. Nothing more. Didn't want anything more; it would have been too volatile. Give them the least thing they can imagine for themselves, and they'll swarm to it like wasps to the wisteria. As the notices raved, TRUE LOVE, FLAMING PASSION.

17

An invitation into the *forbidden.* The safely forbidden. Even so, he'd kept a box full of clippings, all turned brittle and yellow if not to dust by now.

"Bet you had a crush on her," the banker said, though Peacock had turned away, ignoring him.

"Looking at her picture gets me right here," Bird said, clutching his stomach. He could have struck the fool.

The banker held his ground. "Come on, Bird. You know what's happening in the town."

So Roselle was coming back. He didn't know what had happened to her. Maybe she'd gotten disgusted, or really fallen in love. She'd done the wrong thing anyway if she wanted the patrons to line up at the box office. Got hooked up three or four years later with a director they claimed was a Communist. He'd stuck around long enough to see the studios drop her like hot grease and went back home. She was all through. Her films would have been picketed, so they claimed. Well, he'd gotten in one for her, or tried. The bunch of radicals that had come out wanting to make a film on the miners, he'd let them have his land for the production. Till the local folks ran them off with stones and pitchforks and his father, who'd been off in Kansas selling cattle, had had a fit. His name was mud. Good for him. He'd had a wonderful time watching all the nonsense.

"She's making a real comeback." The banker insisted on how lucky they were to have the film previewed here, with all the fanfare, lots of people in the town. "She's going to help us out. A real boost to business." And things would've been better yet if Bird hadn't turned up.

"Yep, it figures." Bird gave a chuckle. They'd milk her for all she was worth. He could see somebody lighting up with the idea, perhaps in the teeth of desperation. Some slick press agent or some local go-getter. Maybe the twin ends of desperation coming together. And they'd bring the little girl back, rescue her from time and oblivion. Dress up the failure in the colors of success. To be worshiped once more. And let the town take a lesson: rise up out of the ashes, and things will go humping along like a cripple with a new stick.

Aha! So this was what he was back for. He owed the banker a favor for giving him his inspiration. It hadn't occurred to him till then that he was coming back for the greater good of the town. Now he could get in his little contribution as well. He glanced at his watch. He had just enough time to drop in and have a little chat with the mayor. Curry Gatlin, the old grafter. No doubt he'd be glad to see the prodigal. They had a few things in common, including a certain suspicious regard. He wondered what the old cuss was up to. Yes indeed. Just for the sake of curiosity.

And he was eager to see the restored queen, a part of his past, to see what time had done to her. To take her measure and his own. It would be a challenge. And the town would have its own as well: a mirror to see itself in. Amusing. He couldn't wait. He'd been in various parts of the world and, having eyed its fascinations, had not been convinced but that some of what's most intriguing lies in your own backyard. At the moment he was itching for something to do, to pass the time while accountants and assessors and lawyers tied themselves up in knots. To hell with them. As long as there was money, and even when there wasn't. The main thing was never to be bored. He'd invite the whole crew out to his place and do it up brown. If they'd let him . . .

"Wouldn't miss a thing," he told the banker before he finally got rid of him.

By the time he'd made his second trip into town, banners were strung along the main street, flapping their red letters in the breeze above the thrift shops and bars:

Welcome back, Roselle. Our own Roselle More.

It was hard to judge exactly what Roselle meant to the town, beyond the collective satisfaction in her name and in the short-lived fame she'd once enjoyed and might achieve again. But meanwhile, except for a few like Bird, and Jessie Biddeford, her former drama coach, the town had had time to forget her completely. Even now, while her name fluttered in the air, her future was not all that clear. People were ready to ask questions like, Wasn't she a Communist back then? And didn't she go about as far down as you can go? Dope? Alcohol? Some possibility for sympathy lay in that, even admiration for struggle and triumph. At any rate, here she was coming back, and whatever had happened to her, she'd at least made it out of her obscurity —to the point of being interesting. But for Jessie Biddeford the real miracle, which had occurred long ago and had since been lost sight of, was that Roselle had amounted to anything at all.

"Whatever Roselle was, she certainly didn't owe a diddly damn to her family for it," Jessie had been fond of saying, back when her connection with Roselle was in people's minds. The Mores, an ignorant lot, who distrusted everything except the automobile, loud music, and a certain animal vitality that never got any farther than the back roads. It was a wonder to Jessie that Roselle had survived her childhood in the public schools, that great laboratory of failed good intentions, much less had the ambition "to make something of herself." As an actress, of all things. Ordinarily, though she taught dramatics and directed the plays in the little college that in a limited and, at times, pathetic way opened for some the doorways to the future, she almost never encouraged anyone to make a future of acting. Even if the talent was there. But with Roselle it was different. If she hadn't helped the girl on, she couldn't have faced herself in the mirror in the morning. (Not that she was given a lot of encouragement by the expression she found there.) If nothing else, to escape the wretched town and lifetime employment at the gas company.

Even so, she'd said to her lo those many years ago, experience looking upon untried youth, "You don't know what you're asking for." Afterward she blamed herself. Ambition was a two-edged blade, and whichever way you walked, you were likely to hit into one of the edges. Maybe that was why Roselle had finally quit writing to her. The blush of success was how many shades of red? From that, she could only go on to even more ambitious forms of humiliation. She'd run the gamut, till politics defeated her. So much for ambition. Took you by the hand to see the elephant: the world stripped bare and without illusion. But without ambition? Here I am, Jessie thought from time to time. Only, once I had it too.

Now she had her garden, a few rosebushes and assorted annuals she coaxed to grow in the rocky soil. She'd always lived alone, being, she said, of a temper not to want anybody underfoot. Lately she'd been having trouble with her eyes—some days could barely see to watch television or even to get around

—and seldom left the house. She'd had to give up reading almost entirely. But she still spent a lot of time in her garden.

That morning, Thelma Germain, her only really close friend, if she could be said to have any, was coming by to drive her to the doctor. She'd asked Thelma to come early to have a glass of iced tea and some bakery cake she'd bought. She hadn't seen Thelma for a while; they'd had a falling out, she couldn't remember over what, but she knew she'd hurt Thelma's feelings. The cake was a gesture of conciliation.

When Thelma drove up and emerged from her ancient Ford, she found Jessie watering her flowerbeds. Without looking up, Jessie said, "I always did favor pansies. Especially the ones with the little dark centers. Remind me of pickaninnies back home. You're not supposed to say things like that nowadays. But that doesn't change the fact they're around, probably still suffering with pellagra. Anyway, pansies are pretty little things, don't you think?"

She didn't give Thelma a chance to respond, gave no hint that they hadn't spoken for nearly a month. "Of course, pansies in a bed give you a sense of things being orderly and right but not fussy. I don't like a tangle and I don't like preciousness. I do like sunflowers for the birds. Got those along the back fence. As for roses . . ."

Thelma risked an interruption. "Did you see in the paper who's going to be in town?"

"Well, if it's that actor who thinks he's president-elect, I wouldn't bother to raise the blinds. I haven't bent that far to the right since the fifties. Taste of gall and ashes." She straightened up. "Trouble is, I'm getting too old to bend over, and too blind to see anything when I get there."

"I thought you still got the paper."

"It comes, but I don't read it. Mostly, I don't want to take the trouble. And the paper boy does some little jobs for me. Pretty soon it'll be that if I even get downtown I won't remember any of it. The way they keep tearing things up and burning things down."

"Then you don't know who's coming?"

"Well, who is it?" She never raised her voice, but by emphasis alone she had been able to get the immediate attention of her students all the years she taught English and drama. As an actress herself, she had valued the understated. Nor did anyone ever see her lose her temper. Now quite stooped, Jessie Biddeford, who'd once been tall, was still imperious-looking. Her hair, piled elegantly on her head when she was younger, was now short white wisps around a face in which the large eyes, prominent nose, and full lips seemed to form the simple elements of a sculpture or a mask. But the skin had shrunk around the cheekbones and the full throaty laugh had turned sharp. Irony, she felt, had saved her. No wonder the great dramatists had been so keen on it.

"Why, Roselle More," Thelma said, without a shade of triumph for knowing it ahead of her. She was used to Jessie. Used to a certain quickness of wit that sometimes left her like a hooked fish on the ground. Her own mind was more reflective. And she had a view of Jessie that might have surprised her: complicated, tough in a way, and quick. But Thelma, not in the least sentimental, would not have hesitated to add, fragile. Thelma would also have admitted that even after all these years, she didn't really know Jessie. She didn't know anybody who'd made it past Jessie's formidable reserve, probably not even Roselle.

Jessie had her view of things as well. "Thelma," she liked to say, "has the opinion that everybody has some redeeming feature. Anyone with that quaint view of things can hardly be said to live a life."

So they had kept up their banter, got back at each other—at times lightly, even playfully. But they wounded each other as well, like cats who don't know the sharpness of their claws.

"Roselle More," Jessie said. "Hmm." She took off her gardening gloves. "But then what's that to me?" she said.

Your star? Thelma started to say, then with her usual tact, caught herself. Jessie, she suspected, had bound up a good deal of herself in Roselle.

"That was what—thirty years ago? And a goodly amount of water has flowed over the dam."

"You made her what she is," Thelma said, meaning it.

"Oh, I hope not," Jessie said. "I hope they can't lay that at my feet."

She'd done it quite wrong, Thelma saw, and tried to salvage the moment. "She'll come to see you, of course."

22

"What makies you think so? What's she here for anyway?"

"There's going to be a special preview. I thought you knew about her new film—just being released."

"Well, after all these years. Well . . ."

Ordinarily, she loved to gossip, loved anecdote, enjoyed the contrast between action and motive, beginnings and resolutions, what people came to. She'd had a good time that morning speculating on the domestic life of one of the local ministers, who'd shocked his congregation by marrying and divorcing twice in the last year, the second marriage lasting only a dozen weeks. She quite relished the dismay of Mr. Sanders, who brought her her groceries. But the news of Roselle's return caught her up short. She hadn't thought about her for a long time, hadn't allowed herself to. In fact, when she was going through her things, on a day when her eyes werc good enough to read a little, she'd come across some old letters from Roselle. She'd read them through and then wondered why she still kept them. She felt, as she always had with Roselle, greatly disturbed. Now she'd find it impossible not to think about her.

"It's right hot here," she said. She swept a hand across her forehead. Suddenly she was weary of her life. "No point letting the sun beat on us when we could go inside and have a glass of something cold."

Thelma, fanning herself with her hand, was ready for the shade. "It's a funny thing," she said, "the way the past is always popping up when you least expect it."

Yes, Jessie agreed wryly. She let Thelma go in first. She didn't really want to talk about Roselle; gratefully she discovered Thelma had something else on her mind.

"You remember the Collingwood boy? I don't know if you had him."

"Yes, poor crazy, mixed-up fellow."

"He moved back here after his father died."

"I remember you told me that," Jessie said. "I'd forgotten. I read about his father."

"He left all those paintings, you know, all the work he'd done the last few years. Once he let me see some of them. I tried to buy a painting, but he'd never sell a single one. All those canvases, and himself shut up in that huge house."

"Peculiar man. A genius, I guess." Jessie said, interested and relieved. She set out a pitcher of iced tea and the chocolate cake, reminding herself to relish it slowly. She didn't allow herself sweet things very often, but it was a comfort to eat them occasionally. She loved chocolate cake.

"Oh, he was."

He'd had a lot of attention when he was young, Thelma reminded her: his work in all the galleries up in Taos and Santa Fe. Prizes, exhibits all over—California, New York. He'd made a lot of money too. Then his style changed; the critics didn't like his work; and the public turned against him as well. After that, he wouldn't sell anything. Not even to the galleries. For a long time, in Thelma's opinion, the work wasn't very good. After his wife died, he just holed himself up in the old house. Then something must have happened.

"You've seen the boy? What am I saying? He and Roselle were in school together."

"I've seen him," Thelma said. "He's sole heir, of course. Those paintings are worth a fortune now. And I've been dying to see them. But he's very strange. You can't talk to him."

"He'll sell them?"

"Oh, I'm sure. He's going to have an exhibit. A couple of weeks ago he told me he was getting it ready. He's trying to take advantage of the publicity around Roselle. It'll open while she's here, part of the celebration."

"Enterprising of him."

"But he wouldn't say anything about himself—what he's been doing all these years or where he's been."

"Obviously he didn't have much success as a painter."

"Jessie, the poor fellow didn't have, well, I won't say he didn't have talent. Maybe a lot, and I tried to get something out of him. Afraid of himself, I think, afraid of not being great. But somehow with it all a terrible ambition. And he's very strange."

Well, Jessie thought, things have a way of working out different from what you planned. "I got my living from teaching the drama," she said. "But I'd just as soon never see any of my students." And turned to the chocolate cake.

The banners announcing Roselle More's return to town aroused a certain anger in Lauren Collingwood. He would have liked to go out at night and set fire to them. All that attention for somebody who'd pandered to the lowest level of public taste, writhing in the most obscene way to public applause. But he wasn't being fair exactly. He'd known Roselle from long ago, and she was harmless. A victim. He would honor the past by going to her reception that night. And besides she was actually doing him a favor. Because of her, people would come thronging to the exhibit. And sit up and take notice. So would she, whatever sort of woman she was. They'd all take notice. They were beginning to. He'd gotten his exhibit without a hitch, and with all sorts of publicity surrounding it. Gallery owners, critics, artists were flocking to Chloride from all over the country as well as from up North.

Since he'd been back in town, people kept pestering him, trying to get a response from him, asking to view the paintings, offering to buy them. He'd be able to sell the whole collection. On his own terms. No one would see the paintings until the exhibit. Everyone would have the same chance. Let the expectation build. Let them itch to see who could write the largest figures in their checkbooks. It made him laugh; they were so eager to see paintings they would have ignored years ago.

And he'd spent days and nights working on them: cleaning off the dust, sorting and framing them. Meanwhile entertaining himself with the public impatience. In a spirit quite different from the awe that had palled upon him when he first came back: that his father could die. And the sheer magnitude of the work. Along with the dizzying voices in his ears, of buyers and gallery owners and magazines wanting interviews.

"I want to arrange a small exhibition of my own." The idea hit him, the perfect thing, at a meeting his lawyer had arranged with a gallery owner. "The impact on the art world will be such," he said, lowering his voice, "that the collection will be worth a fortune."

"I don't doubt it, Mr. Collingwood. But if you wish to arrange the exhibit through us—you know people come to us from all over the country."

Yes, he'd thought, and give you control and a healthy slice of the pie. "I'll consider it," he said, greatly enjoying himself. Watching the fellow calculating his chances. And now he was having the exhibit his own way.

He was vindicated. They were coming to him, as they had never done in the past. From the very first, his efforts had met with either condescension, from his father, or ridicule, from his fellow students. His father had given him more scolding than encouragement: "You've got to forget all about me and strike out on your own." But had never taken him seriously. But then his father could never bear any sort of competition. And because of his father, no one had ever been able to see him. His father's name hung over him like a curse, and his light eclipsed him like a fate.

He'd been conspired against. Deprived of the chance to live out his own talents. Driven to the gutters—to drawing people's portraits at fairs, to commercial advertising, and even, when things got bad, to working as a house painter. Even though he changed his name and wandered from one town to the next, a dark futility shadowed him.

Once, some half-dozen years ago, he'd come back—he wasn't sure why—and found his father alone in the great house, the paper peeling off the walls, the rugs rolled up into the corners, and everything coated with dust. His mother many years dead. They'd been unable to locate him to give him the news. He had been fond of his mother.

His father met him in paint-stained clothes he probably hadn't changed for days, a thin, bony, shrunken figure who threatened to disintegrate in the sunlight. Who looked him over not as an object to be kicked out of the way but as part of a world that no longer mattered to him. "I'm finally onto something," he told Lauren with an excitement that made his eyes glitter. "For the first time! All the other stuff is junk."

Junk. All the paintings that hung around the country, bought by museums, privately commissioned works, pieces in collections. Junk. The man was mad, of course, but he couldn't help envying him. And even if he was mad, was in pursuit of some will-o'-the-wisp, it wouldn't matter. His father had always existed in some other dimension. And here was one more door closed to him. "And your work—" his father asked, "what have you been doing?"

"Traveling the country. Thought I'd get back in one place and start in again."

"Look at this," his father said, indicating the accumulation of canvases. "After all the years, my greatest work is coming."

For his father, he wasn't even there.

"I hope there's time," his father said. "God," he said, clenching his fists, "I hate every moment away from my palette. I sleep three or four hours a night—it's all I need."

The thing unborn in himself coiled more tightly; he felt its juices drying out. His father had stolen his soul, perhaps at birth. Even as the old man said, "You'll have your chance now. You'll have money. You can paint till the end of the world." His father went on, eagerly, eyes on the future where he would stake his claims, "I'll tell you what to do. When I go, you'll be executor. Take what I leave you and sell it. It'll make you a fortune."

At first, after the news of the old man's death, his return felt as tentative as if he were growing new skin. No one would recognize him. He was there to claim exactly what? He approached the iron railing that gave onto the yard choked with waist-high weeds, and struggled with the gate. And stood before the great Victorian monstrosity that went back to the early settlement of the town—Gothic windows and gables and gingerbread. And went inside, his footsteps echoing through the rooms; now and again pausing as he listened for his father's voice, urgent and triumphant: See, see what I've done; see what it'll do for you.

Every room was littered with falling plaster, filled with paintings. Canvases rolled up. Canvases still on the easels. A bed in one corner of the dining room with a pile of rags and blankets his father fell into each night, spent with exhaustion. And a table overflowing with empty cans and bottles, others stacked or rolling on the floor. Unspeakable, the filth his father had lived in. Painting, painting while the house fell down around him.

The first night, Lauren went out to buy bread and cheese and a bottle of whiskey. He found a broom and swept out a space. He set himself up in the abandoned bedroom, where, though the carved wooden headboard was split down the middle and mice had left holes in the mattress, he could sleep with some comfort. He was beginning to feel more cheerful. The old man was gone after all. The sounds in the walls belonged to the invisible life that takes over old houses; the creaking floors were complaining of age. And if the house held something of his own past, now decayed, something was left over imminent and shining: his future.

During the next days he pulled out the various canvases and hung them on the walls, set them up on the floor. He was amazed. Deserting the abstract expressionism that had created his early fame, his father had turned in his last years to a new mode of painting that put him in another era, not the past but the future. It was both epic and symbolic. In one painting depicting the encounter between white man and Indian, called simply "Geronimo," a wounded, agonized horse, Indian feathers with eyes painted on them and certain twisted faces, blending and emerging, the violence changing the forms into something indefinable. He caught the influence of Picasso, but the work was very different in conception and style. In another, that of a western town, all very solid and real, ghostly figures peered through the windows, their shapes, both benign and sinister, emerging from cactus and rock. All the colors burned with the same intensity, as though everything glowed with a furious inner life that would not be denied, even those things no longer present. It seemed to annihilate him as he looked.

For a time he stood spellbound. Then he said, "Crazy, that's what. They'll never accept it." It tore things open, crushed and distorted appearances, wrenched them apart, and let another world spill out. He knew what he must do.

For Jeanetta Barton, the interview she'd had with Roselle More was the high point of her career doing a series of weekly interviews for the local radio station, KCHL. She had pretty well mined the personalities in the area: the descendants of ranchers who'd gotten their start rustling cattle; daughters of pioneers; Mexicans whose forebears had settled the area before the Anglos, one of whom had built the first church in the town; an aging cowboy who, from a combination of oddity and flamboyance, had made himself into a local character. They'd all been there too long, she thought, had forgotten there was a world outside. And she had been longing for a new voice, the mystique of a new personality. During the interview with Roselle, she kept wishing she could hit upon just the right question to unlock some secret, hidden spring. It was there. And Roselle had brought something to life in her, a great yearning and a powerful sympathy. It was the best interview she'd ever done, even though she had come away from it with the sense of something missing, she couldn't tell what. She had wanted more.

At one point she had looked uncomfortably around the studio and felt its impersonality: the blank, colorless walls, and the engineer behind the glass window with his headphones on, scarcely a human presence. Roselle didn't belong there. She wished the two of them could be in some quiet place, perhaps out of doors, so that the unspoken word she was reaching for might suddenly emanate. Perhaps even a tape recorder would have stood in the way. She'd have to be content.

Possibly she could interview Jessie Biddeford, though the old woman had practically turned into a recluse. A phone call never hurt. She never allowed herself to be discouraged, though she'd been put off by that fellow Peacock, who belonged to one of the town's oldest families and who'd returned after an absence of years. Somebody'd told her his chief talent was raising people's hackles. She'd tried to get hold of him on the telephone, and was told he'd rather she interviewed his grandfather. In the silence in which she decided this was a joke, and was about to say, "Well, I'm sure if you can arrange it," the voice had politely thanked her for her interest and hung up. She hadn't worked up the nerve to call him again.

Now, though, the morning before she was to run the interview of Roselle, she'd run into some wretched luck. The tape had somehow been damaged by the tape recorder when she tried to play it back and was completely garbled. Frantically, she tried to get hold of Roselle, so that they could simply do the broadcast live, as she sometimes did. But she couldn't reach her. And it was lost, that wonderful exchange. Had there been time, she would have burst into tears.

Fortunately old Merle Fullmer would be on hand that morning, whose interview she'd planned to use whenever she had nothing better to offer. The garrulous old man was a mine of stories, when he could remember them—the sort you could always bring out in a pinch. Nothing timely or, to her mind, terribly interesting. Local color.

He had been born while New Mexico was still a territory and could remember when Bear Hawkins, a prospector out in the Wilderness, had been clawed by a grizzly. He had listened to his mother tell stories about the marauding Apaches. But all the old hunters and trappers back then had bear stories or Indian stories. Whoever didn't have one would have been put to the task of inventing one merely to keep in the running, and she suspected the embellishments and lies were at least as interesting as the truth. For her, it didn't much matter.

At the moment, though, she was grateful for whatever she could get.

When the old man entered the studio, silky white hair to his shirt collar, a long fringe circling the bald pink scalp, white beard somewhat unkempt, he acted as though he'd been roused from sleep and wasn't sure where he was. After she led him to a chair in the studio and the engineer had given the signal to begin, she had a hard time making him understand her questions. She couldn't tell whether it was his hearing or his understanding that had gone on failing since her last interview with him. She repeated the questions, raising her voice. A number of times they had to stop, back up, fill in. Fortunately all of the gaffes would be edited out, but her nerves felt like hot wires before she was done.

"You say he'd never come back to town."

"No, ma'am. He lived out in the Wilderness all by hisself. Bad scarred up. Face all twisted. Couldn't bear for anybody to see him. That grizzly bit him right through the jaw."

"How did he live?"

"Yes, he lived, he didn't die . . ." The old man seemed to have the hermit before his eyes.

"And you saw . . ."

"I saw. Once when he was sick: they went out looking for him in the Wilderness. Oh, the Wilderness then, it was a wild place, I tell you. Mountain lions and bears. Indians wanting your scalp. I went with my father. He was the only one Bear would ever talk to. If he seen anybody else he'd just go hide. But I got up real close, and he said, 'Hello, glad to see you, little fellow.' Only it was hard to understand him."

"I hear he was later killed by the Apaches."

He paused, lost in thought: "They killed old Ben Lilly."

30

"You remember that?"

"Just a boy, just opening his eyes to see the world around him . . ."

Once again he appeared lost in confusion. She tried another tack. "Did you see the Apaches, Mr. Fullmer?"

"They got him, little Everett Collins."

"Can you tell us something about the Collins boy, Mr. Fullmer? Everybody knows that story."

That had been one of the headlines of the day: Judge Collins and his family, prominent citizens of the town, taken off the stage in which they were traveling, the father and mother killed on the spot, and the boy carried off, never to be seen again despite the rewards for his recapture. Their portraits hung in the museum. And their house had stood beyond its day, becoming the local whorehouse on the edge of town, finally torn down to make room for a new post office when the town spread. Everybody wanted a brick from that house—and paid good money for it. Lots of men who'd known Ginger in one capacity or another. She should have interviewed them all, Jeanetta thought now. Let them talk about progress.

"They forced the coach to stop and made us all get out . . . Killed my father and mother." He was becoming excited.

How strange, she thought. This is going off the map.

"But they never found the Collins boy."

"Of course, they never found him. Carried him off to Mexico," the old man insisted. "And living to this day."

He'd lost all sense of time. "But he never came forward, Mr. Fullmer. Perhaps he died young among his captors."

"I am sure he is alive," he said, striking the table in front of them, making her wince—she'd have to edit that out—"and in the flesh."

"It's part of an era, isn't it?" she said, trying to placate the old man. "Part of the sacrifice of settling the West."

The old man was seized by a cough. She didn't signal the engineer; it was too complicated with the old man. Another bit of editing to be done later. She wondered if she could salvage anything. Then it occurred to her she could just talk about Roselle More that afternoon. Let the old man say anything he wanted, nobody was going to hear it anyway.

When he recovered from the fit of coughing, he said in a

31

choking voice, "Didn't tell anybody, not anybody. Lived with old Mrs. McGee."

She had no time to speculate about whether some part of his life might have been secret, buried. Rather she felt a little inward laugh: she could talk about anything. What would happen if the radio suddenly went crazy?

"And many were left widowed and orphaned," she extemporized. "Killed by hardship and disease, as well as the Indians. Do you think the pioneer spirit has survived, Mr. Fullmer?" She felt rather proud of the statement; she felt inspired. Perhaps if she kept on, something might just pop into her head, and she'd say something that would surprise her and everybody else. Only suppose it was the wrong thing. She had a sudden vision of people stampeding the station, a chorus of accusations and curses as they hauled her out to string her up. What a thought! And what could she possibly say with such an effect? It was quite beyond her. She felt a little giddy.

"Chief adopted me and taught me their lingo and dances. Taught me to hunt and shoot. Made me join in their powwows and take an Indian wife, but I was too wily for 'em. I kept looking out."

"And how long did you live among the Indians?" she asked, as if it were fact. For you could always see the Indians somewhere out of the corner of your eye, those people so different, alien, yet still present, their strange speech and dark skins. And the terror. Maybe if you weren't careful it could still get into your head. She looked at the old man. What had happened to him? Maybe he was a hundred and twenty years old and had lived two lives.

"Many and many a year. Thieving from the Mexican ranchers, raising all kind of havoc."

His eyes were fixed as though he were watching an absorbing spectacle of the past. And drawing her in as well. You get so you almost believe, she whispered to herself later. She was strangely affected, as though she'd been drinking or had sat up in the middle of a dream. She had to keep hold of herself, remember where she was.

Fortunately, the moment came to sum up: "And just consider, ladies and gentlemen, how the past has come alive for Merle Fullmer this morning. How often he must have heard the story of that family so brutally slaughtered, the young boy never to be seen again. So glad you joined us this morning, and when we meet again, we'll have that lovely lady you'll want so much to hear, our very own Roselle More." And she'd better come, she thought, or I'll look more foolish than usual. But afterward, in a moment unusual to her, she thought, But it won't make the slightest difference whether she comes or doesn't come, whether I play this tape or not. Who was out there listening? And considering what was happening in the town . . . A week from now nobody will remember.

It was as though she stood outside herself, outside the thick glass of the studio window, watching herself ask questions, watching people talk, but understanding none of the words. "I think I need to get out of this place," she said aloud.

The mayor's office too had a poster of Roselle More on the wall, the first thing you saw when you entered the door—looking down like a patron saint, except that the eyes, though they might lead you beyond yourself, suggested an uneasy realm of the spirit. In any case, the three men sitting beneath her gaze were paying no attention to her.

"It's true," the mayor was saying. "A maverick is something by definition that you can't tame or change. But that doesn't mean there aren't stumbling blocks built into his nature like everybody else's, doesn't mean he can't stub a toe like the rest of us. Nobody's foolproof."

This was encouraging. And Lester Pruitt and Virgil Langtry were waiting to be relieved of pestering doubt. They were on guard, as if they might be overheard, as they sat with the mayor, Langtry in the very chair that Bird Peacock had occupied only a couple of hours before. They had already experienced the grand dismay of balked intentions. By his very presence—or at least his extraordinary timing—Bird had put an end to a little scheme that was so close to hatching they'd imagined it finished and done. All the men agreeing it would have done the town a considerable favor—done away with a nuisance and given a boost to the local prosperity all in one fell swoop. Without a single regret. And there he was—very likely onto them.

"How do you suppose he got wind of it?" the banker said.

"You don't suppose old Spicer was playing both sides?"

"He's too smart for that," the mayor insisted. "He's already risked getting disbarred, if Bird wants to go after him. And he'd better have a few friends around."

"Uncanny," Langtry said. "Snatched the whole thing right out of the fire. Paid off the taxes—just sitting on top of the world."

"Who'd think he'd have hired somebody else to check into things?"

"Shows he has good sense," Langtry said with a laugh. "Think he knows what we had in mind?"

"Even if he did," Curry Gatlin said, "he couldn't fix anything illegal on us. Interested in the property, that's all. Business partners."

"Well, it's a damn shame," the banker said. "That place sitting empty for years, when it could make a real resort and tourist attraction—all that history clinging to it. Get enough tourists here and you could save this place. By rights it oughtn't be his. What's he ever done for the town?"

"Don't give up yet," the mayor said. "There's a lot of things can happen. An idea is an idea. Meanwhile you just play along."

"You mean you're actually going to let the whole lot of them go out there?"

"Why not? You got any better ideas? It's one of the show-places of the county, and Bird said he'd wine and dine them—and us too."

"Where does he get his loot?" the banker said. "That's what I want to know."

The mayor shrugged. "He knew Roselle way back when . . . I never did; my folks moved up to Albuquerque when I was in high school. But anyway, I heard there was something between them."

"No shit?"

"It's all rumor," the mayor said, with a gesture of impatience. "I'm not going to make a lot out of it. But maybe he's like everybody else—wants to give her a show, for old time's sake."

"My God, Curry, that sounds downright normal," Langtry said. "Aren't you getting carried away?"

"Besides," the mayor continued. "It'll keep him occupied.

34

Turn him down and you'll give him a reason for mucking up the works—a challenge. I know him."

"And how do you know that's not what he has in mind anyway?"

The mayor was getting a bit testy. Try to keep a piece of ground you could stand on, and the apostates were ready to grab it from under you. He still couldn't reconcile himself to Bird's sudden appearance. Or the reality of a good thing slipping away from the town, from himself in particular. For he had caught a glimpse of himself in a new role. He'd always envied Bird in a way he couldn't quite define: he could do the outlandish, the unexpected—and not seem to care how people took it. Enjoying himself at the expense of the gawkers and the fools. Whereas he, Curry Gatlin, always had to pretend his right hand didn't know what his left was doing, to conceal his deviousness. He recognized that he was small-time. Too small to win a place in the public eye that the Peacocks, not just through theft and murder but through the sheer willingness to flout public opinion, had held for four generations. If Bird hated the exploits of his family, he certainly inherited that part of their talent.

"Listen," the mayor said, "you get to thinking that way and you're defeated before you start. At least we got a way of keeping an eye on him. And don't forget, all this power people think he has, they're the ones that give it to him. He's a charlatan—that's the fact. Let him throw his voice as much as he pleases, conjure up all the dead he wants. All you got to do is sit still and watch for the loophole. I know him that much."

"Whatever you say," Lester Pruitt said, and Virgil Langtry agreed with a shrug. "We don't have any better bets."

"Keep a lookout," the mayor said. "Things are going to happen. Roselle's here, the son of that crazy artist, all kinds of people in town. And Bird's going to do us a helluva favor. See if I'm not right."

And they left it at that.

As soon as Roselle had written to her that she was going back to Chloride, her friend from high school, Mary ("Mair") Voorhees had, with a determination of spirit unusual to her, decided to

35

take her vacation and meet her there. They hadn't seen each other for nearly thirty years. She arrived in El Paso that afternoon. It was hot, the light in the middle of the day blank and merciless, the sky bleached in its intensity, far from blue and very close to white. No clouds to offer cooling shadows. Coming back, she had imagined, hoped for, something different.

Perhaps if she had come in the morning, the light would have been fresh and sweet, allowing the mountains to rise into presence like the shape of promise. Or in the evening, when the blue shadows stand against the orange glow of the sun on the horizon, softening the hard edges of things. But now houses, animals, people stood trapped in the glare. She too. She had stopped for a light lunch, gotten back into her rental car, and left the city as quickly as possible, thinking, It is best to rise and seize one's chances early in the sun. I didn't do that.

She lit a cigarette. She would smoke half. She wanted to quit, to get rid of her smoker's hack and lighten her head. It was her last chance. She was going back to Chloride because her mother, whom she'd taken care of for years, had died and left her a little money. She was going to see if the town could be home for her. And she'd see Roselle after all these years. Amazing how they'd kept in touch. She had a little bundle of letters that she would never show to anyone, hidden away in a drawer. The two of them had started out together, full of hope and wonderful schemes, and both had sunk into failure. Roselle at least was a star. And she? She had never been anything, never risen beyond failure. A secretary, divorced, no family.

She drove north, out of the city that had claimed such a vast stretch of desert during her absence, and through the valley, where water was becoming more precious every year. The land opened up, the mountains shaped the horizon. It looked different somehow; she had been away so long. Could she return and make a fitting ending for her life, gather her energies and rise again out of the past?

The stack of the smelter, at first a slender pencil against the sky, brought her up sharply: she had indeed lived here. And the slag heap had grown with the passing years, stretching for a mile or more, a permanent scar on the desert. She drove on toward Chloride, thinking, even as people were fleeing from the town, Last chance, last chance.

Despite the elaborate preparations, there were those in the town, perhaps the majority, entirely unaffected by the presence of a film star. On this particular evening, while the festivities were getting under way Dr. Frank Lucero was preparing to leave his office. He was on his way to see one of his patients, Bernardo Gomez. Usually there were several he looked in on at home. Most of his patients he saw in the hospital or in his office, where he carried on a family practice. But at times, something remained to be done outside either place, not in terms of only the patient but himself. Gomez, in his midfifties, a man who'd never been sick, was a special concern of his, suffering from an elusive wasting disease since he had been laid off at the mines.

Frank was troubled about him. Several months before, he'd put him into the hospital for observation and rest, but the interruptions, the noise, and the lack of privacy exasperated the patient, and Frank had sent him home. He had been trying to reach something in the man's spirit that would initiate the healing, draw it out, elicit it by convincing him that certain medications would help him. But Frank found himself saying, I am working against despair. What is the medicine for that?

And before the enigmas of the spirit itself, the doctor felt exhausted and impotent.

"It's all over with me, like it's all over for the town," Gomez said to him during their visit.

"But Bernardo, nothing says it's the end."

"Only look at it. In the old days, silver, gold, copper, zinc. Now it's all closing up. Nobody can make any money. First the silver goes. Okay, lots of copper. Now they do it cheaper in South America, Japan. All over. You see what happened to Red Rock: a ghost town. Now here."

"You can do something else," Frank said.

A momentary animation came into the man, a gleam as from rotting wood. "What other things? I spent my whole life in the

mines. For me, what? This town has no reason to be here anymore. No reason to exist. What for?"

It was useless to argue. Gomez would die; Frank knew it
as well as Gomez knew. The will was gone, and without the
will . . . nothing remained to be done.

He felt stymied, totally at a loss. Now that it was gone,
people were looking for an approach to the spirit they'd trodden
into the ground. And whatever he himself had been looking for,
whatever had remained hidden from him for so long, still beckoned him uselessly: the roots of the past, what the Indian, the
Mexican he'd come from had once known. It was too late. When
his eyes had opened, it was only to the loss of that, and to squa-
lor. And though he'd gone on to the medicine that, with its miracles of surgery, the wonder cures of its drugs, would put tradi-
tion to rest, yet there was an element missing he'd never been
able to find. Let him believe that doctor and patient worked together to engage the energies of the healing process. Let him say
that all that had been possible in the past was now to be discovered again. In the early years, when some of his patients had
come from Mexico, if they became ill, they turned their minds
immediately to death. Or else to the curandero, an old man now
dead himself, who would sweep his patients with lemons and
eggs, with black chickens or sweet basil, all the while uttering
prayers, his own special incantations. And some got well again.
Perhaps because he convinced them that life was possible. And
Frank always felt that through his own work he must do the
same. If only it were possible with Gomez . . .

When he first came to Chloride, he had gone to the homes of
his patients to track down their illnesses in their surroundings.
Certain realities stood in the way of healing: the crowded adobe
huts with dirt floors, where patients lay on piles of rags. Germs,
lack of sanitation. Let him work against these. Let him work
ever so hard that now his wife had left him. Let him go without
sleep, walking dazedly from office to hospital; let him continue
to visit his patients, searching for the source of sickness and the
elusive thing that still hid from him. All the obstacles he had
tried to work past over the years: dirt, ignorance, alcohol. Now
there was another, even more formidable. Gomez was the final
reflection of his failure.

Maybe it was true, the town no longer had a reason to exist. So things came and went. Some would pick up and find their future elsewhere. Yet there were those who would stay, who must live. And he himself? His life had been different when Linda was there; he was sure of it, though he hadn't made her happy. He'd worked too hard then too, fighting against the world. Now he was too tired to think about it. The years had wearied him. And Linda's absence was a constant reminder of what had never been settled between them.

He took his mail and newspaper out of the box and climbed the stairs to the apartment above his office, his cat following him, rubbing against his leg. Inside, he fed the yellow tiger cat and took out a bowl of chili to heat up. He was really too exhausted to eat. He glanced idly over the newspaper while he sat at the table; then he read with a certain interest an article about the film star. He looked at her picture and for a moment was reminded of the expression in Linda's eyes. Then he turned off the light and sat in the dark. Because of a faint glow from the streetlight at the corner, he could catch his reflection in the glass. The face was so torn to rags, he found himself examining it, as though it belonged to one of his patients. "Why are you so miserable?" he asked it. And almost as if it were a voice speaking outside himself, the words came to him: Because you're sick of it.

In the years since Roselle More had been in the town the old Palace Hotel at the corner of Bullard Street, named for the man who had discovered silver in the surrounding flats, thereby giving the town a reason to be, ceased to exist. By the time she was growing up, the hotel had already become seedy, occupied by transients, some of them families who came for a few months looking for a second chance, the first one having rusted out, then moved on, in the meantime living in the cheap rooms with their scarred bureaus and antique wallpaper. At that time, it bore a closer resemblance to the original hotel, where those who came to settle in the town shared a room and fleas with a dozen others—men sleeping on one side, women on the other, while the wind whipped through the cracks in the walls—than to the palace it was to suggest in its heyday. Then the lobby was adazzle with crystal chandeliers beneath which the guests could sit on brocaded sofas with carved walnut frames. And the dining room drew the townsfolk to the hotel for Sunday dinner. But all that had degenerated into the tiredness of another era.

At some point in recent memory the ancient sun-faded rugs, the sagging mattresses, and beat-up furniture had been cleared out and the place turned into a warehouse. Now it was gone. A fire had turned it into a blackened shell enclosed by planes of plywood pasted up with notices and posters, including one about Roselle.

Another small hotel around the corner and up the street sat among the empty buildings on either side, several with their windows boarded. On the outskirts, away from the deteriorating center, three motels, along with a shopping mall, had sprung up in a sudden burst of expectation—concrete and plastic pushing away the desert—when the town became convinced that the newly widened highway would be a major route to Los Angeles. These offered modest rooms, a bar, and at one, a small indoor swimming pool. None of these would have served for Roselle and her retinue.

Fortunately, there was a guest ranch several miles from town, where they could be alone with a view of the mountains and enjoy a certain rustic comfort. The rooms of the lodge were simply done, all in rough-hewn timber. Roselle had been given the largest suite. After the preview there was to be a big party at the Peacock ranch, where Bird—so he'd convinced the mayor— would put out a real spread and foot the bill. And the visitors could spend a few days resting up before they flew back to Los Angeles.

The day of their arrival, the town gave a barbecue at the guest lodge for those who'd done all the work and planning for events of the week. A side of beef was roasted over a bed of coals and served with beans and coleslaw and kegs of beer. The mayor, members of the town council and their wives, executives from the copper company, and various ranchers and local businessmen were there, both invited guests and all those willing to pay the price of a ticket. Altogether, a large crowd, friendly and informal.

Roselle was one of their own, though there was always something a little strange about those who take off in the direction of fame. They never seem quite real, the image and the person, like two cards in the stereopticon that don't quite merge. Roselle More. Even the sound of her name had to be tested against her presence, for she'd been born with something Slavic, and therefore alien. On the other hand, there were those who remembered her films and couldn't quite separate the role from the actress. And others who remembered her from high school or college and had no idea what to make of her. For her life had grown beyond them. Some speculated on her downfall, as though that alone made her human. Though it was pretty vague to most minds. Mixed up with politics. McCarthy and the Red scare. Too bad getting mixed up in politics; now all the old issues were dust in the carpet. And where were youth and glamour now? Here she was, fighting for a comeback. Well, some stars aged well, became grandmothers, and were still going strong. Look at Liz Taylor. Now they stared at Roselle More and tried to fix an opinion.

"She really holds her age well," Netta Gatlin said. If there was envy, she didn't betray it. There were those who could afford face-lifts and expensive beauticians and cosmetics with secret formulas. And since they were in the public eye, she couldn't blame them for keeping young. The mayor's wife was a small, rotund woman, with four grown children, and she had to think of herself as a grandmother. She wouldn't hold Roselle's slender figure and long hair against her. Unless she was bitchy and conceited and treated folks like dirt under her feet. That kind of woman she could stick pins into, especially since they were the ones men usually admired, even though they got chewed up and spit out in the process. And there was the secret knowing that she'd take your man too, if she wanted him.

But Roselle was not so fatal. "Considering what she's been through," Margy Pruitt added. They murmured sympathetically, knowing what she'd been through. It gave them a common ground. She was only human after all. There was comfort in knowing that not all the million-dollar homes and face-lifts and alluring men and public attention could avert what Roselle had been through.

The mayor was meanwhile indulging in a brief moment of self-congratulation. As he was keenly aware, people were gener-

41

ally criticizing him behind his back, as though he were personally responsible for what was going on in the town, like some
big muckety-muck. Though they didn't really believe that.
Sometimes he felt as tense as a virgin, especially since he'd been
caught once or twice standing naked on one foot, so to speak.
But right now he was making a good impression, and he was
soaking up the glow. And if the whole thing put money in
people's pockets, if they could build . . . who knows what . . .
He had been thinking lately about trying his luck in the state
races. If this film thing could do something for the town . . .
That was Roselle's interest for him. Nothing to excite his fantasies. He had in mind a younger, more playful type that neither
his wife nor Roselle embodied. A little wicked. He had met up
with one or two like that when he'd gone to Denver and San
Antonio for Rotary conventions. To him, Roselle was nothing
more than a local girl good for a little mileage. That was the
limit of his imagination.

And as he saw Bird watching her, he had a real curiosity to
know what might be going on in his mind. Memories of a youthful crush? Flimsy as milkweed. Whatever Bird was thinking, it
wasn't likely he'd give anything away. But he'd try to gig him a
little when the chance came.

Bird had indeed been observing her, a welter of impressions
crowding his mind. She still had the effect, even though he was
older, of jarring him into a heightened state of sensitivity that
he refused to identify simply as lust, neither then or now. Even
if you started out under the banner of its confusions, something
lived beyond the original impulse. She was like an actress in an
inward drama that had never quite left his mind. In his youth
she'd spoken to him directly: Get the hell out of town. And look
at me. Look every woman full in the face and if there's anything
left over after you see her skin . . .

On the screen, she could only tell him she was a paper doll, a
piece of sawdust, a cute little trick. And he'd turned away in
disgust, not so much at her but at the uses to which she'd been
put. She deserved better.

He'd gone on, and if she'd called him to action, it wasn't nec-
essarily noble or even courageous—maybe only a waste of time.
She'd called him to a certain recklessness and a certain cunning. He did not suffer fools patiently. He was not to be pinned

42

down. He took refuge in elusiveness, in surprising the enemy. And he'd gotten by well enough—he was still alive—considering how he'd behaved, the enemies he'd made. Yet somehow he blamed her. For he'd been sure that if he followed her long enough, he would discover something. He did discover he was a fool, that much.

Well, she'd haunted and teased him once upon a time, he was thinking. He'd lived with her in his brain, till all of what her image called up got buried with her under the rubbish. Only now she had changed. And he had a hard time remembering whether she had been anything real, or something he'd imagined. Meanwhile he'd bounced around till he'd been so many things he wasn't sure they all added up to one human being or were just the scattered parts of several. One way or another he had followed her. For here they both were. But what he was to her was no doubt less distinct. This time, though, he wouldn't give her a chance to forget him. That much he had in mind.

"Well, what do you think, A. J.?" the mayor asked him.

Wouldn't he like to know? "You've seen one, you've seen them all," he said. He knew Gatlin was very likely waiting for some good word about the arrangements, the cleverness of the idea, even though it probably hadn't been delivered out of his own brain. He had no intention of giving the mayor that kind of satisfaction.

"Why, you old cynic. Can't you ever let your hair down?"

"You need me to give a touch of reality to all this. Otherwise you'd throw yourself at her feet and Netta here would die of grief."

They laughed. He let them coax out of him that she was a woman he'd walk across the room to meet, just so long as he didn't have to give up an afternoon of the Cowboys to do it. He remained, however, an interested spectator; too many people around her just now, he'd meet her some other time. Besides, he was almost as much interested in the reactions of the guests as he was in Roselle. After he went to refresh his drink, he stood apart and tried to catch a glimpse of Roselle as she shook hands and greeted her public. The touch of celebrity, the glitter; they wanted to put their hands to it, as though you could come away with the revitalizing spark.

Someone identified the director for him, a high-voltage type, who threw himself into conversations with a rush of words and emphatic gestures. He took up a great deal of room. Bird wondered if he had been able to do right by her. None of the others had. He liked the energy in the man.

She must have seen Bird, for she looked several times in his direction, as though she was trying to find a path out of the throng. But whether or not she recognized him, he didn't wait to find out. He slipped out of the crowded room, paused outside to smoke a cigarette and enjoy the evening. He'd had enough of the press of bodies for one evening; he wasn't in a hurry. Maybe he still had to figure out what he wanted from her. And something about her was bothering him, had given him a sort of chill. Something he'd first caught from the photograph, that made her seem as though she weren't there at all.

"Have you asked her for her autograph?" He couldn't imagine anybody putting this to him as a serious question. But it came from just a kid standing next to him. Then he recognized the reporter who'd been hanging around the edges all evening, snapping pictures, annoying everybody with his flashbulb. But all the idiots probably wanted their pictures taken. He muttered something unintelligible, and the young man strolled back inside. The reporter had already written up his article, a spread that would have his by-line in the local paper the next day, and he was exceedingly proud of it. He expected the piece to be picked up by the Associated Press and distributed. On an inside page of the local paper would be an interview. The actress had answered his questions forthrightly, he thought, had made him feel she might not say the same things to someone else. It was a special gift she had given, only to him. And how graciously. Now he watched her almost jealously, a tall woman, who moved like a beautiful animal, whose spirit suggested the mountains and secret hollows. He could imagine her black hair, which she wore in a French roll, loose, an undulating wave down her back, or caught in the wind like curls of dark smoke. But she had strong hands and eyes that at first had made him uncomfortable, as though he were just a little boy with a notebook. She scared him, but then as she talked to him, she had taken him over in a way that made him more real to himself. Now all he could think about was that she was his story.

He'd downplay what had happened to her, he decided. Let her

rise triumphantly out of the past. That would be his gift to her. There were shadows still cast over her expression. As just now. She was speaking with a baggy, ruddy-faced man, with a shock of hair over his forehead, who looked like he'd slept in the gutter. At first an eager smile, then an element of constraint. He'd have been glad to punch the guy out. He knew who he was, the son of a local artist recently dead. Some kind of nut, like his father. He'd tried to interview the guy, who'd waved him off like a fly. Too busy to be bothered with him. He couldn't believe Roselle would give him two words. Indeed, she looked annoyed or perhaps weary. He was ready to go to her aid when someone else pressed forward to greet her. The awkwardness passed; she was smiling.

She was wonderful. Brave. And regal, yes queenly. He would use that word. He wanted everybody to see what he saw. She was human, she'd suffered and triumphed. And lost nothing in the process. He was sure of it, in the confidence of his youth. Now, though, she was beginning to look used up, the lines deepening to show her age. He watched her say good-night; people kissed her, took her hand. She had to work her way out of the room. He saw Walter McKay, her publicity agent, bend over to give her a peck on the cheek—enviable dog. Probably didn't mean a thing to him. A brief exchange took place between Roselle and her secretary just before she stepped into the hall. Then she was gone.

For him, the light had gone out of the room.

II   DIRECTOR

Energy: it seemed to make the air crackle around the man, charge the atmosphere of the room, the inner source unceasing and resistless—leg swinging, fingers drumming as the words came tumbling out. He could not sit still; his standing seemed a prelude for flight. He was on the run through ideas, people, things—life. Snatching, grabbing, shouting, then pulling himself up into a single knot of concentration, a glowing center. Small wonder his crew complained. He worked them till they dropped, himself along with them. Yet they worked beyond exhaustion, because, they said, it was a real experience to work with Bill Brodkey. They wouldn't have missed it for anything. They loved him, tall shaggy tyrant that he was.

And there'd be this lousy piece of shit the studio had assigned him, the plot as predictable as a see-through blouse, but he'd take special pains with a scene, get an effect nobody'd banked on. And there in the midst of that dog of a film you'd come across the same craftsmanship you'd find in a significant movie. They loved him all right.

He'd slacked off some since his youth, when he could work all day, carouse all night, come back to the set the next morning shaking off sleep and booze, ready to throw himself into the next punishing day. Now parties bored him, had for a long time, though they still got him wound up enough that he couldn't sleep. After this one, he'd probably lie awake for hours, his mind racing.

At home he would go to the refrigerator, sit at the kitchen table writing and eating cheese, ham, cold chicken, drinking beer, never gaining an ounce. During their early years together, his wife, Helen, used to struggle up sleepily out of bed and demand what he was doing there at three in the morning. After a time, she left him alone. He'd come back to bed at dawn, find her curled up like a small child, her chestnut hair tangled on the pillow. And with a rush of tenderness he felt the pull of guilt. Then he sank into sleep like a stone, without waking her. When he allowed himself the luxury of such reflections, he wondered if his self-absorption hadn't put a wedge into their marriage from the beginning. But he couldn't help himself. He might as well have quit breathing.

Then it had been ideas that kept his brain going round all night. Now he had fewer of them, but he still couldn't sleep after an evening filled with people. Bits of conversation, mostly inanities, kept him awake, maddeningly so, the old mill taking any grist. He'd have been grateful for a night's sleep, but he knew it was impossible.

After Roselle had left and the crowd thinned, he went over to Walter McKay, supposedly making every promising ray into the glare of publicity but looking bored out of his mind, and suggested a nightcap.

"Thank God," Walter said. "Anything to get out of here. Make it my room. I've got some Chivas Regal I can't wait to drink up—alone. Sally," he said, beckoning Roselle's secretary, "come have a wee drop. An exquisite drop that will fill you with love for all men—even me."

She laughed. "First let me see how Roselle's doing."

"Christ, you don't have to tuck her in, do you? She's a big girl."

"She said she had a headache. I just got hold of some aspirin. I'll be along in a jiff."

"Do you want ice?" Walter said. "I hate to let anything get between the nectar and me. Agreed then," he went on as Bill dismissed the ice.

"I always heard about the ends of the earth," he said, as the two men walked upstairs. "Now I know what they mean. No wonder they're so friendly here: otherwise they'd be killing each other."

"This is only Friday," Bill said. "They save that for Saturday. In the bars."

"A comfort to know," Walter said. "Makes me long for a good

traffic jam on the freeway." He'd grown up in Los Angeles. It was his city and there wasn't any other, not even San Francisco. Let him complain about the noise, traffic, dope, crime, and the fact that you couldn't see it for the smog; it was still the most beautiful city in the States. And small towns he hated with unconcealed contempt. "Deprived" he called them. "Beyond deprived" he called this one.

"Well, I grew up in a couple just like it," Bill said. "Little town in Illinois. Then . . ."

"Not like this," Walter insisted. "I'll bet you had a neat white house with grass in the yard and shade trees. And Chicago up the road."

"What the hell are you talking about? Coal mines and dirt in the air. First Carbondale, then Dawson. I never saw Chicago till I was grown. And that was after my dad died in the coal mines up in the northern part of this state. Bet you didn't even know they had coal mines in New Mexico. Hell, I know this place."

"Sorry, sorry. Forget I said anything."

"What are you complaining about anyway? They've certainly given us the treatment."

"Yeah, all the local big shots strutting out their little day in the sun. Trying to pretend this town's not the hole it so obviously is."

"My God," Bill said, amazed. "A whole industry out there bumping egos and cutting throats, and you're complaining about this."

"At least there are people. I mean people who've been to the next town. Not just empty space with two hundred miles of cactus and lizard in every direction."

"Why, you're lonely," Bill kidded him, thinking it was very likely true. Walter without his city, without his usual haunts. A man without his habits. He was used to it, loved it, fractious and unmanageable though it was. For once, Bill was glad to get away from it. Glad for an excuse. When he was working on a film, he never saw where he was except for the space the film occupied. He took his vacation afterward, if he took one at all. "When you've got all this magnificent country. I want to do a film here," he said, almost to himself.

"Come on. Another goddam Western?"

48

Bill ignored him. He was thinking aloud, trying to get something in mind. "It's been a myth, and people got stuck on it. Only it doesn't work anymore. That great romance, the great stage for good and evil everybody can understand. The outlaw captured, the cattle baron done in. All gone. Only you can't get rid of the hunger for it. And there's nothing . . . And even under the great romance, what was it? Greed and ruthlessness parading under the name of ambition. Land hunger. Whoring and drinking and killing . . ."

"So you're itching to make another grim little gem. What else is new?"

"Because all the same stuff is still going on. The exploitation of the Mexicans, the Indians, the land," Bill continued, fired up. "Think of all the stuff happening. The big mining companies, the developers. It's all so fragile—and once we lose it . . ."

". . . we might get something more interesting."

"Sure. Mobile homes and traffic jams from coast to coast."

"Christ, I just wanted a little pleasant nightcap."

"Since you can't escape to L.A. . . . Look away, look away," he sang.

"Look, I'm not getting into idealism on the landing. If you want to talk, come on. I want a drink." He went ahead, opened the door of his room, stood aside for Bill to enter. The room, on the second floor, with a balcony looking out over the pine-covered hills, smelled pleasantly of old wood. Light from electrified kerosene lamps left a glow on the walls that brought up the grain of the wood and created wells of shadow in the room. "You can have it all," Walter said. "My folks came out to Arizona. And they'll die there in the sun, bankroll in hand. They love it there."

They always goaded one another. Nothing could faze Walter, bring on more than a shrug. At times Bill wondered how they could say what they did to each other and remain friends, if they were friends.

"No," Walter said. "You can get all wound up if you want to. It fits your character. But my advice is, keep to simple stuff. Less sweat. Roselle, for instance. Small-town girl makes good. That they love. Come on, Bill, cut the crap; you know what it takes," he said, giving him a friendly poke.

"Yeah," he said. "What ever happened to your social conscience, Walter? I thought you were a child of the sixties."

"I've just gone the way of my brothers."

With the door closed on the noise below, the sounds of the summer night entered the windows, the insistent grinding of locusts, the last twitterings of birds. The sky was thick with stars, which Walter seldom saw in L.A. or thought to look at now. He opened the bottle, poured liberally for them both, sat down, stretched out his long legs, and relaxed expansively, like a cat.

Bill was ready to tie into him. "I know you, you hack. You've been telling lies, faking public images for so long, you've forgotten there's anything else. Why don't you write for real?" He meant it. He kept trying to convince him to do a screenplay. He knew he must be getting drunk; when he'd had enough to drink, he always tried to convince Walter to write a screenplay. Walter never got drunk enough to consider it.

"Not me, boy. I learned that one long ago. Break your ass over something good and watch it get cut to pieces. Or if it does actually make it out there, you get to watch it die at the box office. No thanks. Give me lies any old day. I like the money they pad you with." He leaned forward. "And I like what it can buy, including love," he said, raising his glass. "Good old fickle public infatuation, free-floating, trying to find an object. Hunk or sexpot. Give me that any day. I don't have to break my heart over what's on the cutting-room floor."

"That's why you took on Roselle?"

"A challenge," he insisted. "Don't go sentimental on me. I know about your tricks. The way you slip in and out."

"Survival techniques," Bill said. Wooing the box office so he could get past the junk, he'd learned to live with that. The stuff he'd had to do because he was under contract to the studios. All the way back to the beginning. All the disasters. Knowing most of them wouldn't even go with the public.

"You still pay your dues to the moneymen."

Often enough, and not happily. "It's been worse. That's when all you can do is think of a wonderful creative angle for a scene in a piece of junk. Otherwise, you'd go crazy."

"You see why I couldn't do it. I laugh at you guys."

"And the good stuff," Bill went on. "That rape scene I did; I told you about it. One of the best goddam performances I ever got from an actress. The way she played with the men, and then suddenly the violence. And the public needed to see it. We were in Korea then. They needed to look at what we were doing. What we do."

Walter had heard about that rape scene a dozen times. Let the alcohol hit a certain level in the blood, and out came the rape scene. Obsessive, those guys, remembering the things they couldn't let go of. Christ, it had been twenty-odd years ago. He quit listening, submerging in the scotch. Let the fool get it out of his system, if he ever could.

"It's still one of the best sequences I ever filmed. And I think, Why do they do it, that kind of cowardice? Just betraying the culture. Keeping the public from seeing itself. Just jingoism and escape. And what does it do to us all not to have . . ."

Walter's face was softening before his eyes, the features blurring somewhat yet keeping a certain hard line, the expression difficult to read. Bill could feel himself reaching the danger point, an old anguish rising up like nausea to turn him inside out, make a fool of him. He was stuck there. And all he'd been able to do was go on making films. So as not to be defeated. Act before you get torn apart. And yes, he'd played the game; he'd done that. Looking for a chink, a place to weasel into, get a foothold. Take a little risk, then another. Sometimes it worked. But he was always dissatisfied, hungry for more. He hadn't done it yet, whatever *it* was.

Lost in his own train of thought, Walter couldn't move from some dim scenario of Bill's career. A prayer coalesced in his head: Lord, protect me from folly. "And then when they gave you your head," he muttered, "you had all those 'critical successes.'"

"Thank God."

"It's a wonder the studios still bankroll you. I admit this latest thing has got something to it . . . and it'll probably go."

"You're goddam right it'll go." His voice echoed in his ear like a shout across the lake, someone else's. "Or I'll goddam leave the States and go to Europe, Africa. They've got things going in Africa. The hell with the sons of bitches."

Walter gave a snort of laughter. "Hello, white man, you

make film for us," in high-pitched caricature of a black accent. "White man hero show black man way into twentieth century. You can do it, buddy."

"It'll go," Bill said groggily. Somewhere, he felt, he'd lost the force of the argument. What were they arguing about?

"On its own steam? Come on," Walter said, nastily. "It's the image in the public eye; that's what'll sell it."

"Not all of it's trash," Bill insisted, catching on to something. "Not all of it's hype. The public just *can* once every other blue moon like something good."

"Here, you need another one. May as well kill this bottle before the night's over. There's not a fucking other thing to do. Not even a decent-looking female in the rout. I could almost go for Sally except she doesn't have any boobs." Now if he were home, with a few topless starlets decorating his swimming pool . . . "Now tell me something . . . I've been curious, but I've been biding my time. Waiting and telling myself, Patience, Wally, one of these days the moment will come, and you'll be satisfied."

"So spit it out," Bill said. "Nice buildup. I love your style. You've got the right touch for comedy, Walter. Sure as anything."

Walter looked at Bill narrowly, as though he didn't want to lose any subtlety of his expression. "Tell me: Why did you think of Roselle for this film? Suddenly this actress, who's been out of it, really out. So far down, you've got to reach into the back pocket below the lint just to fish up her name. Oh, I know, they say your best stuff is all with women. But the place is crawling with women, young things to satisfy the pubescent itch, mature types, rising talents, even the girl next door ready to be popped by the boy next door. The works. Are you in love with her or something?"

"Of course," Bill said, unconcernedly. "I love the women. And Roselle. And who are you to be talking anyway? Who's your latest?" He needed air, but it was too much trouble to stand up to get it.

"Seriously," Walter said, "why her, why now?"

"There's a debt," Bill said. "To her, to the past. I don't know. I didn't want her to disappear. I didn't want her just to go without a trace . . . let people just forget."

52

"Forget?" Walter said. "I'd think it was an act of charity. Those godawful potboilers back in the fifties. And then she got cut out because of the McCarthy thing . . . She was one actress he did a favor to. What are you trying to resurrect?" Suddenly, struck by an idea, he said, "Oh no. You wouldn't be idiot enough for that?"

"She didn't have a chance," Bill said bitterly. "I watched the whole thing. Even in those disasters she was in, you could tell there was a real talent there. The things she did in little theater: brilliant. And then when it all fell in on her and she hit bottom, I couldn't believe she was done for. I was afraid"—he couldn't help saying it—"that even with that much real talent, or should I say, especially with that much talent, she'd gotten the life crushed out of her. Maybe I had to see," he said slowly, "just for my own sake."

"Christ," Walter said. "Oh Christ." He paused, shook his head to clear his brain. "You've made a terrible mistake, Bill. She's not tough enough." He sat over his glass for a moment but didn't drink. "And you know what I think? My guess is, she won't do anything after this."

"You don't mean it?"

"I'm dead serious," he said. "She can't take it. All this: coming back, shaking hands with the folks, being treated like a celebrity. She hates it. Didn't want to do it. I told her, 'You've been out of things for a long time. If you want this one to go you need to make a few concessions.' And you know what she told me?"

Told Walter but not him. Spared him; was that it? His head was one large ache.

"I'll tell you what she said. 'It's no good. Just a big phony gimmick.'"

"She didn't mean the film, did she?" Bill said, aghast.

But Walter was slow to answer. "I blew up. 'What d'you have me around for? Of course, it's a gimmick. We want everybody to look at that small town out in the sticks, so all the folks in small towns all over this great nation will make a beeline for the nearest box office. Look at what we're competing with. Just try to wrench the viewer away from the TV set. It's damned hard.'"

Bill felt he was being asked to concede something, but

damned if he would. Yet he was deeply shocked. The film a gimmick? Surely she couldn't . . .

"And you're maundering around about virtues of public taste." Walter's face felt warm, but the scotch, if anything, made him more articulate. Bill was staring at some spot on the floor and very likely anything that smacked of good sense was being lost on him. Once he got a wild hare up his ass, there wasn't any talking to him. He was surprised he'd found a producer in the first place. Now he'd slowed down a little and deserved some shaking up. Walter was the man to do it for him. "Like I say, it's what you put into the public mind. But anyway, she's not interested. And there's something sad about her, the way she can't brush past the nonsense. She's off thinking how it ought to be and never is. And she's got to pay attention, be a bit manic. It's a manic kind of culture; you think I don't know anything? Play along—if you're going to make it worthwhile. But more than that, she can't throw off the past. That's the killer."

"No," Bill said angrily. "That's the problem. Bury all the garbage. Forget anything ever happened. A whole conspiracy of silence, that's what it was for so long."

"Christ, Bill. You make me sick."

"I know. The industry's no more corrupt than any other. Look at who's running the country. But it's all politics. What happened to her happened to all of us. And still is. Bullies and fascists and people on the make."

"I knew it," Walter said. "You're crazy. You want a symbol, a public monument. You want to fight the Great Forgetfulness. Dust under the rug. You want to pull away the security blanket and watch us break out in boils. What a joke. Why the kids out there, our biggest audience, can't remember back past Vietnam. And who wants to think about that?"

He dropped it there. In his way, he was a modest man. He credited himself with not only surviving but enjoying himself like hell. He hadn't asked more of himself than he had reason to expect. He had a salable skill. And he had no contempt for people who made trash and knew they were doing it. Let the others keep running into barbed-wire fences, if they were so inclined.

Bill was turning his glass in his hands, as though he didn't know it was there, his mind not in too much of a fog for him to feel strangely exposed. "It'll go," he said, as if to assure himself. He'd talked her into it. Cajoled and pleaded till he'd cornered her. It took no end of talk, even though she needed the money. He was responsible.

"You've loved your women, Bill," Walter said in a low voice. "But wouldn't it scare the hell out of you if you found one that wasn't your creation?"

Bill looked up and tried to focus on Walter's face. The mouth seemed to widen like a wound and the eyes bored into him. It was hard to keep down whatever was threatening to rise. What was he saying? The words carried such brutality. He couldn't think what they meant. Love them. Of course, love. His creations, creatures. Using them. Oh God, what was he saying?

There was a long silence that Walter finally broke, realizing that he'd come too close to the bone. "God, I had a real start today."

"What's that?" Bill said dully. Right now he wanted only silence, pained though it was, as if it were a new place he had stumbled upon, or a place he himself had forgotten and had to rediscover.

"A woman found me. Somebody must've put her onto me. She walked in the door and I thought, *What's Roselle doing here? She's supposed to be doing some kind of interview with the locals.* Enough like her to be her twin. She's come down to get a story. Conned some little rag of a paper out in the tules to send her. Boy, she sure blew my cool. And she laughed."

"I'll be damned."

"When Roselle was big, she told me, people used to ask for her autograph. Stopped her on the street. Once in Albuquerque she went around telling everybody she was Roselle, just for kicks. I thought of doing something with her, but I figured it'd take away from the main scene. Maybe later, after this thing goes. And I've got enough to do."

The fog was gradually clearing, and whatever threatened was beginning to subside, at least for the moment. "Wonder if they're anything alike."

"I'd say this gal is feistier, but that's a matter of opinion."

"Hell, I don't care," Bill said. "I've got to get some sleep."

When he opened the door, he nearly ran into Sally, who had just come running down the hall. "Roselle—has she been here?"

"What d'you mean?" Walter said. "Why should she be?"

"I don't know," Sally said, flustered. "I can't find her. I've looked everywhere."

"Hold on. Maybe she went out for a walk."

"Have a drink," Bill said, "if there's still anything left in the bottle. I've got to get to bed."

She didn't sit down immediately but looked about her, as though she expected a voice to call her. Then Bill handed her a drink and she collapsed into a chair. "God, I'm exhausted," she said. "I hope she's okay."

"You're not paid to worry that much. You'll be old before your time."

She shook her head. "It's funny, that's all. I can't get rid of this feeling . . . that she's gone."

Bill Brodkey was awakened from a dream that seemed to follow him into consciousness. Then he was unable to sleep. His stomach seemed painfully connected with his head. He sat up, regretting everything—the evening, the conversation afterward, perhaps his whole career. He'd had a hard enough time getting to sleep as it was. Now he was staring into the dark, wide-awake. Bits of conversation came drifting back, particularly what Walter had said about Roselle. Certain old dissatisfactions he had with himself combined unhappily with the food and drink he'd had too much of, and the heaviness of stomach and spirit he felt were enough to sink him to the bottom.

In the dream he'd been trying to get a shot of Roselle, but just when he got the camera set, she drifted away. He found her in another attitude, and again, when he approached, she eluded him.

And her voice drifted to him. "Bill," she said, "it's too late."

He'd been trying to persuade her then to make another film. Others had done it, had vindicated themselves. And so could she. A great blight on the national character. One couldn't let it lie there.

"The damage is done."

"Roselle," he had tried to tell her, "there is more than one story."

"I've lived too many," she said. "None of them worth the candle."

He was trying to write another story, but kept crumpling the pages.

"Bill," she remonstrated, "I try to forget myself as much as possible."

"I know. How about entirely?" He didn't mean any sarcasm. "To get rich you have to be poor first." Idiot laughter.

Sitting up in bed, he couldn't separate the dream from actual conversations they'd had. Sure, the early films were nothing to brag about. But they weren't all bad. Apprentice work. She'd learned, and now and then you caught glimpses of the actress waiting to be born. She couldn't blame herself for the stuff they were doing those days, most of it. A few actors, actresses, who managed to create a character and make a career of it: the kindly butler, the gangster, the inept maid. Enough for a certain style, constraining though it was. Maybe they came off the best. And Bogart and Bacall, and a few others. But Roselle hadn't gotten that far along. At first she was too young to figure out what she might be able to wangle from the system, and then she was defeated. But to let it all go, the energy, the delight. It still had to be there.

He'd thought of her the moment the idea for the film first struck him. And that was a long time after her recovery. She hadn't done anything for years. Not after watching David go under. He'd made that one film, an embarrassment, in the early sixties after he'd come back from England. And when it bombed, he was all through. Gone where alcoholism and depression had taken him. She'd worked for a time for a small press, and did some coaching for one of the acting schools.

Now he wondered, Had she done the film just for him— when he was trying to make up to her for something. The enthusiasm he read from her face: his own? Not wanting to disappoint him, was that it? Like the one time . . . Create her? No, see what you can do with this. Every encouragement. Her own part. And yet? The film itself. He wasn't sure now. He wanted a certain quality from her. If he could evoke it, see it, it might be so original, so compelling, nothing would ever be the same again. Something distinctly new brought to life. Only now, just when he'd convinced himself he'd made one of the best films of his whole career, he was racked by doubt. What had he done? What had he really done? He did not fall asleep until just before dawn.

III   ACTRESS

Couldn't fool her. Shopping center and gas stations and motels to the contrary—sprawl of business. Banks are taking over the world —money fortresses. Car wash, what not. A place to make you eat your heart out, devour you to the dust. She knew towns, grew up in one just like it. The one Joan Gallant came from sprawled for a longer distance along the highway. More package stores and salvage shops with silver hubcaps in rows along the sheds like buttons, more drive-ins and used-car outfits. Here, the usual highway junk, then a downtown that must have been there forever, dingy and depressed, the life leaking out of it drip by drop. Stores sitting empty, the names of the owners fading into the sides of the buildings. And here a star is born. Welcome back, Roselle, batting the breeze. Well, they were trying. And Roselle was coming back for reasons best known to herself. To all the little boys and girls who'd settled down here to raise their brats and make a go of it selling auto parts and clothing and gifts for the entire family. Joan could see it.

Could see Roselle throwing off the Chloride of the mind, isolation and ugliness and the numbness of routine and the hard lines of practicality—the real world, that is—and going off to glory, the eyes of the town following her, glued to her career. Watching her failure. See what it gets you: climbing up there on the rooftops, thinking you're such hot stuff. That's what people always said after the fact. But they liked feeling sorry for you. Now that she'd been through the school of hard knocks and drawn down to scale, they'd hug her to their bosoms. Welcome to the prodigal. Then release her back into the clouds once more, their fantasies a halo around her, envy and desire a burning dust, as they imagined mansions and wild parties around swimming pools and all the tinsel of fame.

Joan knew all about it. Pin your fantasies to the stars. The glittering galaxy. All the affairs, marriages, jealousies, divorces. You wove your stories out of their imagined excesses. Screaming up a fact till it stood black in headlines above a photograph that took up the rest of the page, a little article buried below. But that wasn't what she'd come for. She wanted to look at the real thing. Come on, Roselle, we've got an old score to settle.

And here she was, poking around the town as if she herself had grown up in it. She might as well have. Changed, of course—things you wouldn't recognize if you'd been away. See that shopping center, Roselle. New since your time. What d'you think? Progress? And they've paved the streets, put the highway through all the way to Cal-i-for-ni-ay. But the cars still park up on the hill where the first boy pulled down your panties. Only you don't dare turn your back on anything, because once you do, it all goes up in smoke.

She parked her car near the end of the main street across from a deserted bank building. A café stood catty-corner. Next to it a bookstore. Racks of magazines, used paperbacks. She walked in—the place was empty—picked up a local paper from the counter. From behind it a man rose up from where he'd been roosting, barely visible. His eyes held a certain vagueness, as though he'd just been recalled from another plane. He could have been sitting there for hours. At the back, the slightly parted curtain suggested a living space beyond. Joan imagined a hot plate and a cot—nothing fancy—a couple of hooks for clothes, a shelf.

"New in town?" he asked her, looking at her in a puzzled way, as though he should know her.

"You might say." She paid for the paper.

"Seems like I've seen you around."

Pale like the salamanders that live in caves. Did he ever venture out into the sunlight? Lanky—thin arms and skinny hips and no more butt than a pencil. Long, stringy hair in a kind of ponytail at the back. But something intense in his expression. Too much for the exchange of paperbacks or the sale of magazines. Throwback to the sixties. You still saw a few. And he'd found this little corner where nobody'd bother him. "You don't look like the kind that sits inside a store all day," she said, curious.

He smiled, looked at her. "It tides me over," he said, "while I do my research."

She was interested. "What about?"

He took her measure again, decided to take her into his confidence: "Plants, mushrooms." He turned around to the counter behind him. "It's all in here," he said, taking out a slender, paper-covered booklet. "Goes all the way back, only people have forgotten. The sacred mushroom, the root of all religions. The way to god-vision. That's why the name of god comes from the same root as *mushroom*." He was pushing the book at her, pointing out the syllables of root words, showing connections, turning pages before she had a chance to read. "And now they're trying to poison the world, poison the mind, cross out all the ways of getting back, so the moneymen can carry on their wars."

"Read this," he said, triumphantly, pointing to a paragraph:

And when they ate the sacred mushroom, they were brought to the face of god and knew him. But once the powermongers were in charge, they hid the knowledge from the people, because it would make them dangerous. Only listen how we have been cheated of our birthright, even now in the conspiracy of Wall Street and the Pentagon—left to paw around in the trash of dead religions. Rascals and varmints. Garbagizing land and sea. We breathe the poison of their deadly fumes, and forget what we should know. Wake and rise.

She liked the ring of exhortation and bought a copy of the book. He'd published it himself, he told her, and was working on another. He'd come to life and would have gone on talking, having found Joan a kindred spirit. But it was time for her to get on.

She walked back out into the sunlight. People on the fringes, hanging on the edges in a place like this, dozens of them, she could imagine. Theories spinning like tops while things went downhill, split apart, nothing to hold them together, so everybody was going hunting, herself included. She'd come hunting for a story.

"Wait," he said, leaning out his doorway. "You're the actress, aren't you?"

She smiled, waved and turned into the café.

A story. There was always a story, but usually not the one that made the headlines. Chalk it up to fate: nature up to its tricks, giving her somebody else's face. Explain that one. When she was younger, and Roselle More was all the rage, there she was too, a living copy. And she made the most of it. The face was a mask she could look out from, hide behind. Let them mistake her for somebody else; it gave her the edge. She composed a set of gestures, a little wiggle of the shoulders, a tilt of the head, and a set of expressions, her own act. Every once in a while she was brought up short, as though she'd borrowed someone else's skin, and it gave her the willies. Other times she watched herself with a curious detachment: *I'm saying it, but I don't mean it. Somebody else is speaking.* She was almost convinced. She could slide through certain crevices into a space she couldn't define. She had escaped . . . exactly what?

She saw all of Roselle's pictures a dozen times, till she had the lines memorized, and then she went home and in the privacy of her own room—how carefully she locked the door, even when her folks were gone—acted out all the parts. Fifteen then, perhaps four or five years younger than the real star. She could be the young German girl pursued by the Communists, trying to escape the country to freedom, having to leave her lover behind. For some time a German accent colored her speech. Then the young Russian composer she'd met before the Cold War set in. She had to give him up too. With her allowance, Joan bought a symphony of Tchaikovsky's, the only Russian she'd heard of, and the first classical music she'd ever sat still for, and sang "None but the lonely heart" until her mother asked her please to sing something else for a change. "And now, my darling, I have composed my greatest symphony. In it is all our love, our separations—what will never die. Here they will never know. Good-bye, my darling."

"Oh, Vladimir. Your memory will live in my heart forever. For ours is a great love—beyond nationality . . . beyond politics." Actually, it was a film that would get Roselle into trouble later on, because, along with other things, it supposedly branded her as a radical. But when it came out, Joan thought it was wonderful. Those private dramas that she could act out all the parts of. After a while, Joan found herself inventing her own scenarios, making the films come out differently. And it gave her a crafty pleasure to manipulate the plots.

Always love against the obstacles of the world, its rocky course: lovers going off to war, wife or sweetheart remaining to suffer and sacrifice; or else someone giving up a lover or a child, or a woman dying after choosing a new wife for her husband. Lovers too dangerous to choose. Lovers in exotic places, that you loved and left for a steadier man. Lovers rich, but criminal. So much to sacrifice of immediate satisfaction for the sake of a higher principle. Just the little attractive brush with illusion— that it could somehow work out. What was life but giving things up? One way or another the name of love was invoked whether Roselle got the man or didn't.

But it was not the parts, not even the glamour of the actress that compelled her: it was the desire to be set apart and distinguished. She grabbed at the only distinction she could find, which, ironically, came from looking like someone else.

After a time, when Roselle had dropped from sight, people forgot her resemblance to the actress and she was cast back upon herself, faced with being Joan Gallant, whoever that was. A thankless task.

In the films the choices were made clear, even though Joan indulged in a few rearrangements. But for herself, nothing captured her imagination. She blundered down a series of alleys: college, crummy jobs, marriage. And after each she discovered she couldn't find her way back to the beginning. Circumstances had twisted her here, turned her about there, borne down upon her, left her seared or smudged. It all took something out of her. Expectation opened the doors, but the rooms and passages she entered seemed narrow, badly planned, tastelessly decorated. They led her on to something worse. I've had experience, she could say to herself, but what does it mean? This was reality: the way she had chosen had shaped her life—to what end?

Now she was, in her own terms, open for employment. To fit her talents, whatever they were. Nowhere to go. She'd had too many men, too many kids around, even too many dogs and cats.

The men she'd seized upon along the way were supposed to show her where to go. And for a time they gave her imagination a certain impetus as she tried to invent a decent scenario. "Don't you love anyone?" her third and last husband asked her, as the plot once again went awry, and the play closed. Love. Hadn't she tried to give her heart away? Maybe she'd been drawn by too many prospects, always imagining the greater possibility. She should have been a kitchen drudge, scrubbing floors day and night just to survive; it would have kept her busy. Too tired to think. She'd had too much time on her hands. And she'd held on to the luxury of dissatisfaction, without having to go beg in the streets, her life hanging on the coin in the basket. Frivolous and sordid this waste, her energy spilling over the sides. Even when she'd worked like a horse and kids were underfoot, there was some left over she couldn't get rid of. She made up scenarios in her head. Roselle had ruined her.

Now she'd come down to Chloride for a lark. Why not? Roselle owed her something, seeing that she'd had to carry around her face. And had enjoyed it once, when people used to stop her on the street or turn to stare at her. But you can't get fat on that. Worst of all, Roselle had afflicted her with a fatal curiosity about people. Maybe that was why she'd never had a life of her own, nothing that had stuck or satisfied. She had a book full of half-sketched lives, observations and comments that never found their way into her stories. She had no idea what she would ever do with them. No matter where you turned, it seemed, they always asked you for the least.

She wanted to write some kind of story, give the wandering spirit a body. Okay, so she had to make things up as she went along; still she needed a tag, something to go on. At times she wondered if she hadn't been looking for her own story, the right part in it, all her life. At first thinking the story was down at the fire or the police station. And she'd gone tearing down there, stepping into the excitement. Till she drank her full measure of boredom. Some people you still couldn't convince it wasn't down there or on the sports page or in the society news. She'd been the society page—fashion shows, weddings, formal parties. Duller than ditch water. She did love an occasional big Mexican wedding. All the family in church, the little boys stiff in their suits and the little girls careful in their pink-and-white

64

dresses. The delicate-waisted bride lost in folds of lace. And the slender groom in his tuxedo—black hair, black eyes, and the flash of a smile. The feast afterward, the music and dancing. The ritual of family and church. Festivity. She could get excited on such occasions, dance till she dropped from exhaustion. Even though she was only a spectator.

Otherwise you looked for the story down the dark corners of the bizarre. The ultimate story, the impossible. The story pushed beyond the limits: "Woman Chased by Talking Bear"; or "Eighty-Seven-Year-Old Woman Gives Birth to Live Child After Sixty Years." Even here, she was bored. Whatever the fact, it was never enough.

Goodness knows, she had a taste for oddity, bred perhaps by her own peculiar circumstances. What she noticed and remembered were the little twists of the ordinary, things caught in a sidelong glance, the meeting place of coincidences at the corner of the eye, where things fade out of focus. Where did it begin, all this? When Roselle was born, when she came into the world? The world was already there, a zillion oddities playing behind the scene. Maybe there were only a few threads you could pick up. Heaven knows facts didn't explain anything.

She knew only that Roselle More had cast a shadow over her life. That she couldn't help looking at herself through the actress' image, even though the person herself lay behind all those saccharine roles, unknown. All her overblown sense of importance had come to her from Roselle's face. She was marked out for something special. Foolishness. When things started going bad for Roselle, Joan hated her. The cheat. She'd been taken in. And all the while *she* didn't even know of her existence. Somehow it had to be Roselle's fault. And if she couldn't play the part properly, the one Joan had somehow assigned her, she was going to have to answer for it. She'd get hers. Have her fun. If nothing else, play a few games. Let them think Roselle had been in two places at once. They still looked enough alike to be mistaken for each other. She'd get some kind of story.

The first thing she thought of was calling up the old girl who'd put Roselle on her way, to see what she could get out of her. Jessie Biddeford—she'd found the name in a recent clipping.

65

Called her from the café before she sat down for a bite of lunch. It took the woman one hell of a time to get to the phone. No, she didn't care to give an interview, thank you. Whatever she was to Roselle was nobody's business but her own. Came the click of the phone.

Joan went back to her table. Couldn't help smiling. Just the way she might react herself. She wouldn't mind knowing the old girl; she had spirit.

The waitress came up with the light of recognition in her eye. "Aren't you Roselle More?" The girl was all in a quiver.

With something of perverse pleasure—Roselle popping up everywhere, she could see it—Joan put on an expression of dismay. "I forgot my dark glasses. Please don't tell anyone."

"Oh, but I wouldn't," the girl reassured her.

The delectation of having Roselle all to herself. But the moment she was out the door, the kid would scoot back to the kitchen, overflowing with the news, and tell all, because it was too much to be kept in the bounds of adolescent emotion.

"It's a big secret because I sneaked out," she said in a conspiratorial tone. "You know, like the caliphs of Baghdad in the old days, out in the streets. I wanted to go back and look at the house where I grew up."

"How exciting!"

The girl's eyes were fixed on her as though she might turn into an elephant or disappear in a puff of smoke. There was awe, there was uncritical admiration. Soak it up like a sponge, it comes rarely enough. The girl fumbled with her order pad, dropped her pencil, looked embarrassed. "You have a sharp eye," Joan said kindly.

"I saw your picture in the paper. And they had all your old yearbook pictures out in the display case at school, and news articles. I was in the class play last year," she said, "and I'm studying drama . . ."

Oh God, another one. Joan had spared herself all that trouble, by merely dreaming and watching herself in the mirror. "Good to get it out of your system," Joan said. How terrible youth was: all glowing, silly with hope, a green lion ready to devour the world. The future as nothing-but. The past only a small nuisance over the shoulder as you lingered outside history, and faced the bright mirage. No wonder you craved unreality: Hollywood, theater, a life at sea or among the cannibals. Nothing was quite real anyway.

"But you did it," the girl insisted. "You got through that awful school."

Never forget that. Joan wanted to ask her if she knew about the rest of Roselle's career, the scary part. But of course that was water under the bridge, the same things would never happen to her: the confidence of youth. "Well, if you believe and trust in yourself . . ." What nonsense, she thought. How terrible of her.

"Oh yes," the girl said, waiting.

What did she care anyway? The kid was going off to get burned like the rest; that's what it was all about, wasn't it?

"Let's see, I'll have the salad with french dressing and a glass of iced tea." She had to get rid of her. But the kid was looking to her for something else. "At least take a few bookkeeping courses on the side. You need something to live on when you don't have a role."

The girl seemed to take that as encouragement. Don't forget babies, she started to say, then thought better of it. Roselle hadn't had any; and though she'd mothered over seven or eight, only one of them had been her own. Anyway it wasn't exactly cricket to use them as a bolster against your own failures. But the only time she'd felt complete was when she'd had the child growing inside her. She'd felt in harmony with the life working through her. She could hug the earth then in the mindlessness of the body, in the slow contemplation of ripening fruit. And she loved the smell of infant skin and hair, the smell of young animals. Afterward, though, what did you do with them, or yourself?

"Could I have your autograph?" the girl asked after she'd set down the salad and tea in front of her. She held out a paper napkin.

"That'll be in shreds in five minutes. Besides the pens don't work on them."

The girl rushed off to find a sheet of paper. And Joan wrote out Roselle More with a wonderful flourish. There, she thought, I haven't done too much damage, have I? She'd given the kid a thrill even if she'd been taken in. And Joan'd get her kicks watching people's faces, seeing how startled they could get being interviewed by a reporter who looked like the actress. She was harmless enough after all. But she was going to get hers. Fate owed her something: old Mama Nature with her tricks. Who else should be doing the story anyway?

She checked into the hotel without incident. The clerk looked too indifferent to care who stood there in the dim light of the lobby. In her room she threw her suitcase onto the bed, changed her clothes, and went into action. She found out the name of Roselle's publicity agent. She called him, saying she was from a major newspaper. And actually got to see him. He'd been startled for perhaps half a minute. As she sat across from him, she tried to calculate the exact level of his interest. A smoothie, she decided, almost able to watch his thoughts materialize: *Maybe we can use her. What would be the angle? How much return?* The wheels whirred for a moment, as he played with the odds, and delivered up two oranges and a lemon. Waning of interest. Charming, animated, he answered her questions, gave her some prepared material, expressed enthusiasm about her talking to Roselle herself after the preview. Maybe they could do a feature on the two of them. But she knew he had already decided against it.

That was all right. But they might regret it: she was out of their control and who knows but that she might run amuck? She savored the idea. But the next morning when she returned to the hotel after a couple of hours of looking up articles about Roselle's high-school and college activities, she found various telephone messages. They'd tried to get her a number of times. Half an hour later Walter McKay was in her room.

"She's gone?" Joan said, her turn now to be startled.

"Simply disappeared. We have no idea where she went." Dismayed, impatient. "Of course, we have people looking—here, back in Los Angeles. We just don't know. But we haven't let out any word."

"She's gone?" she said stupidly, as though Roselle had no right to do such a thing.

"It's just damned strange," he said. "When everything was going along . . ." He stopped himself.

Order and predictability violated. Which he counted on as

much as a freshly ironed shirt and a row of ties to choose from on the rack. She was seeing him, she realized, in a rare moment.

"It'll ruin everything, you see, if suddenly she's not there." And then, reluctantly, he added, "And ruin her."

"Yes," she agreed, while her mind moved among eventualities. Disappearing on the verge of a new start. The one shot. Throwing it all away. Her head whirled. It was so . . . extraordinary. Did she have enemies? Suddenly kidnapped by the radical right or the Ku Klux Klan or a jealous lover—like something from one of her films? Absurd.

"So you see, we don't want to let the whole thing out—not with all the publicity."

"I thought that was your business," she said. If they wanted to publicize the film, the reality offered better than the film itself. Better than anything he could invent.

"Exactly," he said. "And if it were left to me . . ."

She looked at him narrowly. What was his game? A conspiracy? To hide exactly what? And if she got into it, by what twig would she be caught?

He paused. "We're just trying to find out . . ."

"I understand." She didn't understand a thing. She could just have sat in her present stupor waiting for light to enter. But it could have taken all day. It was one thing to give a little waitress an autograph, making up things as she went along. She'd done that kind of thing. But this? Really stepping into her skin—even if it was just for a few days. Not one of Roselle's roles, but Roselle herself. If she got into it, could she get back out? A ridiculous question?

"You'll be paid for your trouble—suitably."

Money even. Her first real role. "Okay, I'm game," she said impulsively. Considering where she was at the moment, what did she have to lose?

Once-over, twice-over: the look-alike remained, a life-sized doll created from patched resemblances. A sidelong glance among themselves to catch one another's reactions. Startling, yes. And then, when she spoke, the listening for tone, for inflection. If Bill closed his eyes, the younger Roselle would have been there, the residue of all the old roles, the parts played over and over.

But she was not Roselle. Even though she'd gone through all the motions and lifted something of Roselle from the surface, she hadn't located the source. The recognizable gestures, the emotions revealed through a voice something like, struck him as out of whack; her movements, the jerking of an old film, quirky and ill timed. A caricature, both comic and pathetic. And for him, an anguish. He'd known Roselle for almost the whole of his career. The longer he listened to her, studied her, this cheap imitation brought in to be an understudy for a life, the harder it was for Bill to hold himself in. He wanted to leap up and shout, "Enough of this obscenity."

She wasn't trying to put anything on, he was convinced: some fundamental confusion lay at the root of what she was doing, as if she were a child trying to get it right. The play at the corner of her mouth gave her away, the expression of habitual self-deprecating irony. She struck him as totally transparent. Tough though she might act, she'd taken her knocks. Probably a loser, adrift, playing on guesswork and surmise. She was doing them a favor, he supposed. He hated it.

Sally and Walter were strong in their amazement.

"Why you two could be taken for twins," Lila said.

Bill smiled wryly. Could she see the insult in that? As if the woman had no existence of her own. No doubt Lila intended a compliment. Who wouldn't choose to look like Roselle? But then she and Walter dealt with appearances. Perhaps the woman did too.

"She has a tendency to lean her head a little to the left when she's talking," Sally said, "or listening. I think it's because she doesn't see well with her left eye. She doesn't like the dark meat on any fowl."

"But noboody is going to notice that sort of thing," Walter interrupted. "The main thing is some background on the people she knew here, so that Joan can respond to them."

"Of course," Sally said. "She doesn't have any family here. Her parents divorced when she was in high school. And her mother died a couple of years ago in California. That leaves only the people who were around here before she left."

"An old drama coach for one," Bill said. "She was always talking about her. And the fellow who's having the exhibit. You can avoid most of them—and hell, just look a little sorry and say you don't remember. I've forgot half my life already."

"I have a couple of her old high-school yearbooks," Walter said. "I was using one of the pictures for a press release."

"And—I wonder if it's all right to show it to her—" Sally said, "there's a notebook. She was writing down some of her impressions coming back to the town."

"Surely that won't be necessary," Bill said testily.

"Oh, but it would help me," the woman said.

He was taken aback. A different note, something erupting spontaneously, almost imploring. Joan, yes; curiously he had trouble remembering her name. What was she asking him with such eagerness? Voyeuristic bitch. Some sort of dybbuk trying to take over another soul? All of it was getting to him. He felt suddenly ashamed: his hostility must seem to her quite personal.

He'd wanted to drop everything and go looking for Roselle; he'd already spent hours on the telephone before they managed to persuade him everything possible was being done. He was still racking his brain: Where had she gone, and why?

"It's a matter of privacy."

"But she's probably mentioned the names of some people," Sally said. "I could just look it over, and if there are a few spots . . ."

"It belongs to her," he insisted. "And I consider it spying."

A silence built among them. He was determined to have his way in this.

"Sorry. I was just trying to help," Sally said. "Anyway," she went on, "I'll show you the dress she was going to wear to the party. You must be about the same size."

Her diary and her clothes. The most intimate details exposed to the eye and touch of strangers. Better not leave behind any unfinished business. Better an unfinished symphony than an unfinished life. Someone stepping in to finish it for you. For better or worse. He was getting melodramatic.

God! If he didn't watch himself, the whole idea was going to intrigue him. He felt trapped in a nightmare. And the woman too was bringing something of her own to haunt him. Not any kind of direct appeal; she was too guarded for that. But he could tell she wanted at least an assurance he was on her side.

And his role? The director. He was deeply implicated, after

all—this was his idea—and he was going to have to help her out. "But the main thing," he said, forcing himself, "is to act naturally; I should say, be natural. Improvise. There's only so much you can know about a character, a role; then you have to let go and be that person, imagine yourself Roselle so fully you forget . . . everything."

"There's not much to forget," she said wryly.

"Roselle was a good person," he said. He could see her wince. "I mean . . ." What did he mean? "A lot went wrong but . . ." He let it go.

"I think we've got things nailed down. Go ahead," Walter said, rescuing him. "Sally and I'll give her some coaching for the interviews coming up."

"We appreciate your help," he said stiffly, as he rose from the sofa in Roselle's suite.

"Thank you," the woman said. For what, he couldn't possibly imagine.

Younger, she'd imagined herself being called Roselle instead of Joan, that hard, commonplace syllable. Roselle, Roselle: the nymph running through the woods, tall, swift, doe-eyed, with gazelle-legged grace. Roselle, like a call to the unknown and distant parts of her nature. An invitation to be extraordinary, climb from the bottom rung to a new and uncommon fate. But she was stuck. Joan: a little stone hurled by mean kids, or husbands who couldn't find the aspirin, or lovers checking out in the middle of the night.

Unfortunately, she'd grown used to it: name as fate. Now Roselle sounded strange to her ear. A mistake. She was still on the bottom rung. Had botched things up. Now she had to wonder what the two of them had in common. They might look alike, but there the resemblance ended. Roselle's eyes looked out of the photograph with something Joan couldn't recognize in herself. She hated the confusion.

Roselle! Calling *her* Roselle! It was all she could do to prevent a startled look, hold down a sudden jerk of the body. She had to keep herself from drifting back into the tough, slack creature she'd become, with the bad mouth and the heavy sarcasm. Throw all that out and remember her role. As yet she didn't know her character, what Roselle meant. She'd had only scenarios. What was she to do?

It had been horrible, all of them sitting there while she, stuck in her own person, was trying to provide answers for unknown questions. At least Sally and Walter were on her side, but Bill Brodkey was an adversary; she knew that much. She wanted to woo him as if he were father or lover, make him look on her approvingly as she made her debut in the world. But there was no playing up to him; he'd rejected her not only as an idea but as a person. As if she had no right to be what she was. It made her bristle. There wasn't a whole lot she could say for herself, but she wasn't about to concede anything—not to him anyway.

Now she turned around in front of the mirror in Roselle's bedroom. What was this, the fairy godmother coming or just an impostor in borrowed dress? Elegance? Gold and white—what a laugh. She'd borrowed a costume, was slipping into somebody's skin for a while. Princess or witch.

"You look wonderful," Sally said.

Going all out with the enthusiasm. Well, she'd play along. Glamour girl. Speak, vanity. Actually, it was surprising how good she looked.

"Remember your shoulders. I don't know what to do about your hair—yours is a lot shorter. I think Ginnie can put it up so that it looks more full. I'll see what wigs she brought."

They could do that, give her everything. Dress her up, transform her. Make her gorgeous. Make her sporty or elegant, chic or daring. Give her back youth, the dream of becoming. Let silk slide over all her faults, all her mistakes. Her going from one man to the next, always looking for the missing part. Which one?—as she went grieving out into the suburbs. The Egyptian women gathered up the parts of Osiris, all but his penis, which they couldn't find. Joan's men all had one of those, so she didn't know what she was looking for.

Ginnie came in with several wigs. They did one up in a French roll. More elegance. Christ, they took ten years off her age by the time they got done with the makeup.

She pulled off the interviews well enough. One sarcastic crack escaped from her, just slipped out. But mostly she behaved herself. Let them talk all they wanted about Roselle's films; she could jabber away better than the original. "Roselle'd just as soon forget them," Lila had told her. Why they're more mine than hers, Joan thought. I got stuck with them.

"They were a bunch of dogs all right," she told somebody. "But you've got to start somewhere. So I did. When you're young, you don't know beans anyway."

She and Walter had rehearsed. He'd shown her the publicity file he'd brought with him, limned in the past, brought her up to date. That much was easy: the facts. But in the heat of conversation, things just came out on their own; she didn't know where she got them. Or how they were taken, if they stuck in the craw or went down like butter. Maybe they'd swallow anything, they were all so eager.

It wasn't as if she were making it up. Well, she was. But it was peculiar. Just coming like that. The bad years. "Well, they were bad all right. I mean I didn't know which end was up. And I did bad things to myself." So what else was new? Roselle's man had died. She too had loved one once, and when he left, it was just like a death. She knew all about it. One loss or another. "I depended on him. When he was gone, I didn't know where to turn." Roselle's man had wanted to rebuild his career, poor guy. Drank himself to death. Politics—no point in talking about them. Lives had been ruined. People blacklisted, graylisted. Get them by the wallet, she might have said but didn't, and you've got them by the balls. Her future: she was looking for the right part. *The* one.

They were full of admiration, Walter and Sally. She'd done it. The first round anyway. God, she was tired to death; it took a lot out of her. Even though they weren't asking much. To play a superficial role so that they could quit the scene without being caught and still keep the future open for Roselle—if Roselle wanted a future. Half the world was looking for her: private detectives, the FBI. She wished them luck.

The day whirled around her. Stardust? More like ordinary dust, unless you cared that people were asking you a lot of questions. When she had a moment, she tried to catch a glimpse of herself in the mirror.

"You are Roselle More," she said to her image. "You are Roselle. Don't forget. Everything else in the background. Little Joan and all the nonsense."

Someone named Mair was coming that afternoon. Strange name, worse than Joan. A high-school friend, Lila told her: she'd acted in plays with Roselle, then gone on to two bad marriages. Now she worked for a savings and loan. They'd kept in touch over the years. Friendship. She tried to remember friendship. Close but at a distance. She'd had Maggie. That was in the coffee-all-morning phase after the kids got shipped off to school, when the dishes never got done but you got to piss and moan about all the things gone rotten in your life. They'd both ended up divorced. All her high-school friends were scattered to the winds. She couldn't think back to anybody she'd like now, if she did then. She'd have to wing it. Roselle and the friend from the past had exchanged letters all these years. A marvel of constancy, Joan thought. Well, something must've linked them up. Only one brief visit during all that time, years ago. They were to have lunch together. This was going to be a tough one. One more piece of Roselle's life she was going to pick up and handle, then find a place to set down.

A blue suit came toward her, with a ruffled blouse. But the woman underneath was rather sagging, depended on good cloth to hold things together. She'd put on her best face too, pancake makeup to fill in the lines worked by time and disappointment, blue eye shadow and crimson lipstick for glamour. A halo of dark curls surrounded her head, softening somewhat the heaviness of the jaw. But through the mask, the soft, dark eyes made an apology: she was trying, she'd have been glad to offer something better had it been in her power.

Joan recognized this the moment she saw her, butterflies in her stomach. Well, honey, don't feel pregnant, she thought as they hugged one another. We all do a little reneging. Let it be a comfort to you. But we've got to get that jacket off. The woman looked so warm the heat waves seemed to surround her face. Perhaps from a rush of excitement, or the hurry to get there. As she hugged Roselle, she was trying to keep hold of a thick folder.

"Oh, look at you," she said. "You look terrific. I can't believe I'm seeing you."

Making our first appearance, Joan thought. "Right here at the source," she said, "where we both started out." Role of the old friend, meeting after long separation. Joy, nostalgia, a certain wry humor. Go to it, kid. "Strange—and wonderful. The way it all works. Even when you don't plan a thing." The lines sounded hollow, no good at all. If she didn't quit standing there as spectator and critic, she'd be a real flop. But who'd notice? She would.

"Oh, I know," Mair said. "Over thirty years. Imagine, it's the first time I've been back here since high school."

"I hardly recognize the place," Joan said. "The downtown's just fading out. The streets are paved. But come upstairs," Joan said. "There's a table set up for us on the balcony. No one'll bother us."

"Roselle," she said, wiping her eyes. "I can't believe this."

Joan took her arm.

"And you must be so busy . . ."

"What do you mean?" Joan said, leading her upstairs. "Too busy for you?"

"I've been so looking forward . . . you just can't imagine. When you wrote you'd be coming, I couldn't believe it." She paused on the stairs to look into Joan's face. "I've been planning this every waking moment. And do you know," she gave a little laugh, "I even tried to imagine conversations we'd have?"

Good grief, Joan thought. Everybody was in on it. Making up scenarios.

"Still writing plays, eh?"

"Oh, Roselle, how long ago that's been."

How the woman devoured her with her eyes. She was being stripped bare. What did this call for anyway? She couldn't think. Play on, nothing to do but let it unfold. The play's the thing . . . But how to avoid sinking into the commonplace—mindless chitchat. No way to get through anything without exaction. The ordeal of impersonation more difficult than life?

"It's nice out here," Mair said, as they stood out on the balcony. "The smell of pine." She breathed in deeply.

She'd take that home too, Joan thought. Every sensation, every crumb of conversation, to be enshrined. She pushed down a feeling of revulsion. They sat down across from each other at the table.

"And you know," Mair said, laying her folder on the table, her hands trembling as she unfolded the napkin, "I think I left the best part of myself here. I look at you and I know it."

"What nonsense," Joan said lightly. This woman needed to be saved from herself, but it was probably impossible. And wanted something from her, God knows what.

"No, not at all," Mair insisted. "I know." Her hands lay defeated at the edge of the place setting. She'd painted her nails, Joan noticed. Took all the trouble. But the nail of her index finger was torn; perhaps it'd happened on her way there. "I'm being impossible," Mair apologized. "And we've scarcely seen one another ten minutes." A glisten had risen to the surface of her makeup.

"Oh, Mair," Joan said. "You haven't changed a bit." She was sure it was true, and hoped it wasn't an insult. "But aren't you warm?" she went on quickly. "You must take off your jacket, let yourself go." The good hostess, a voice suggested. Quit that, Joan told herself.

Mair smiled, took off her jacket and put it around the back of her chair. "Do you mind if I smoke?" The state of her nerves, Joan could see, required it. She reached for her purse, took out her cigarettes, lit one and inhaled deeply. "I'm trying to knock the habit and get rid of this awful hack," she said, "but this is a special occasion. I allow myself half." She coughed and cleared her throat.

"So how are things?" Joan said, concentrating, trying to throw off spectator and critic.

"Everybody thinks I'm nuts," she told her. "My sister said, 'You're crazy, Mary. Why do you want to go back? You haven't lived there since you were a kid. What makes you think you'd like it now?' Well, that's what I want to find out, I told her. And what's so wrong about that?" Her eyes flashed. She'd done it, she'd stood up for herself. But it left her in a tremble.

"Would you like a drink?" Joan asked her, going for the telephone to dial room service.

"I'm trying to cut back. Too much of that, well, you know."

"Yes," Joan said, "I know all about it. I'm going to have a glass of sherry."

Mair brightened. "So will I," she said, given the encouragement. "I tell you, Roselle. I worried about you. I could never believe, you know,"—her voice dropped almost to a whisper—"you'd go under. I just knew."

She'd depended on her, in some obscure way clung to her image. "You never know," Joan said. Now the words came easily. "You come so close to the bottom, it seems like you'll go all the way and stay there."

"You don't have to tell *me*." Mair looked at her gratefully. "You don't know how glad, just how . . . It's hard, you know. Everybody thinking they know what's best for you. My mother, my sister. It isn't like they haven't had their own lives to botch up, they think they've got to have a crack at mine."

"Some people have more talent than they can use."

"I just want to hug you. You're just so . . . I just knew . . . I mean, you're in a different class."

"Who says?" Joan scoffed. "What was so wonderful? A few godawful films."

"Yes, but that's all past. And now you've got another chance. A new life."

Joan smiled. Let her keep the illusion. "Yes, that's true."

"And I want one too," Mair said fiercely.

"And you'll have it," Joan assured her. "I know you will." At that moment she wished she smoked.

"Do you really think so?" she asked. "I've been trying to lose some weight," she said, looking down at the bulge at her waist. "If I can get off fifteen pounds or so, that would be a start. And give up my bad habits. I'm trying to tell myself there's something left," she said, "now that it's all over. I look at you . . ."

So that's what she wants from me, Joan thought. She'd have to put on the act, all the way.

"I'd like to find a little spot of my own. I came back to look for a house, to see if I'd like it here."

"You're thinking of moving back?" Joan said. To a dying town. Looking for life back among the cinders of the past. Well, an odd way to go: you couldn't call it less than a challenge, she supposed. Hair of the dog, or something.

"Does it surprise you? Well, I've had too much of the city. And what's there to hold me?" She gave a shrug. "He's gone, thank God. I just finished throwing out all his junk. No kids, fortunately. It's all my stuff now. Mother's gone too. I have a little money. And no ties."

The sherry came. "To your future," Joan said, and they clinked glasses.

"Thank you," Mair said. "And to your overwhelming success." She beamed. "Just seeing you . . . what it's done for me." But then her expression changed. "My sister thinks I'm crazy," she said, going back to that. "She tried like the devil to talk me out of this. 'Well, Mother's gone,' I said. 'I did my share. Steve's got a new girl friend. So what's to prevent me?'" She snuffed out her cigarette, half-smoked, and lit another. "You know," she said, "I haven't gone anywhere like this for years."

It had taken all her courage to do it, Joan could tell.

"But I made up my mind," she said. "I arranged the flight, and got the car. I arranged it all. And I didn't even tell Esther where I was going."

"Good for you," Joan said. "Sometimes you've got to run for your life and lie like crazy." She looked around almost as if she were expecting Roselle to be there looking over her shoulder. She ought to be there. But whether to inspire her or judge her or what, she had no idea. Joan felt a strange vertigo: all the ground rules had been switched on her and she couldn't count on a thing. The words that came out kept surprising her. Something was moving inside, trying to push its way out, almost in spite of her, as if she were simply there to watch and let it happen. If it did, where would she be? Did it matter, since the whole thing was going to be snatched away from her in a few days? She had to stop herself in the middle of a shudder. Mair was before her, still fighting her way past her sister. Perhaps Mair's sister stood behind her chair.

"She doesn't like anything I do, not even the church I go to. It's too liberal for her. She thinks I've wandered from the fold."

"Why, it's none of her business, is it?" Joan said.

"That's what I think too. But I'm so used to it," Mair said. "It's hard for me to speak up. But you see," she said, triumphantly, "I made it here. Knowing what you've done . . . I just admire you . . ."

"Sometimes it's luck," Joan broke in. "Don't forget that."

"No." She was insistent. "You can't get away with that.

Look," she said, reaching for her folder and removing a scrapbook. "I've kept everything. Do you remember this?" she said, showing her the program for a high-school play. "That was the first one we were in together."

"Ah yes," Joan said, "and you've kept it all this time."

"It was the only play I had the main part in," Mair said, without envy. "And here's the play I tried to write myself. I didn't get far." She smiled. "And *Gas Light* . . . you were so wonderful. Even in high school everybody knew." There were clippings of articles Mair had written for the school newspaper and programs from all the plays she'd been in. She mentioned names of people she still kept in touch with. Even a couple she planned to look up in Chloride. She was into it now, a glow in her eyes. It was the past she had come back for.

Their lunch came, and the conversation turned to Roselle's future. "I'm hoping for another film," Joan said. "The right part this time." They embraced as Mair left.

When Roselle was young, the city hall, now standing empty in the center of town, had been a place for the old men to gather. They stood leaning against the huge round pillars, jawing and spitting on the sidewalk. Often one of the policemen from their headquarters next door joined them. Now the building stood empty, waiting for a state agency to use the offices. The brass spitoons had been removed from inside.

For the time being, the hall had been turned into a gallery. The walls of the main entrance had been given a coat of paint; the long hallway and some of the offices were now hung with paintings. Off to one side were tubs of California champagne on ice, and the mayor's secretary, Isabel, who was on top of everything in the office and knew everybody in the town besides, was pouring the champagne for the guests, with the assistance of two of her friends. A large crowd had come, more out of curiosity than any abiding interest in art. A number of dealers of southwestern art were in town for the occasion, as well as several major art critics and even a few patrons who had bought Collingwood's paintings early in his career. And Roselle was there.

For the occasion Lauren Collingwood had rented a tuxedo

and gotten his hair cut and styled. Even so, he was feeling a little thin around the edges, owing to the demands of the last weeks. He'd worked feverishly, snatching only an hour or two of sleep some nights, much like his father. But he'd done it. Not a large exhibit. The main body of the work still lay in some disorder in the derelict house. But here at least was a sampling of the feast. There remained literally hundreds of drawings and paintings to clean and sort and frame. Months, possibly years, of work. He refused to let anyone see them until he was ready. People were continually making their way to where he stood, full of questions.

Doris Broadbeck, who'd seen more of his father during the past years than anyone else in town had, was enjoying the public spotlight as well. Cashier at the store where his father had regularly bought his ration of bread and cheese, she'd been telling Lauren and a few other listeners how it was.

"He didn't eat regular," she was saying. "I used to worry over him. Coming late in the evening to grab something from the shelf. Used to paint till all hours. I'd see the light on at midnight when I went home. And him in there just working away. The dirt so thick on the windows you could barely see. He was one of your geniuses, I would say."

Looking past her, Lauren tried to gauge the reactions to the paintings. He'd put no prices on them. He was ready to negotiate with the galleries when the time came, sell one of them the whole collection. Pit them off one against the other. He'd be set up for life. All the years of scrounging left behind, when he'd drifted around, living from hand to mouth. Finding some little Mexican whore to sleep with for a few bucks. Going on a bender on some foul rotgut. His father had opened a door for him.

Once he got the paintings taken care of, he would leave Chloride behind forever. His father could have lived anywhere he chose. Only to hole himself up in a slum. Existing on air. Not even booze.

But he had his mind on a house in L.A. and an apartment in New York. He wanted to travel in Europe. He wanted to surround himself with people, especially the young, magnetize them as Warhol had done; he wanted a circle.

"Lauren, how well you're looking tonight." The thin bony little woman gave him her hand: Thelma Germain, who'd taught him perspective with a vengeance. All her spinsterish needling. All her tyrannical little exercises. Now ready to give him his due.

"Miss Germain," he said, condescending to her, "I hope you're enjoying the exhibit."

"Yes," she said, "but it puzzles me."

"Really? In what way?" He was being polite.

"The one big painting. The town, and all the faces. Ghosts, I assume. They're so extraordinary, those faces. Like you'd see in a dream, if you could dream the history . . ."

He was given a handful of telegrams from well-wishers and asked to shake hands with a writer for an important art magazine. When he looked around again, Thelma was talking with an art critic, who was expressing a similar enthusiasm.

He saw Roselle. Photographers were taking her picture as she entered and moved into the hall. When he'd tried to talk to her the night before at the reception, she acted as though he were someone she'd just as soon forget. In school he used to tease her, pick on her for some reason. Once she'd chased him down the hall and torn his shirt when she grabbed hold of it. "Well, Miss Queen," he would say to her, "Well, Miss MacIntosh," depending on the part she had played. He didn't know why he had done those things. Perhaps to get her attention. And he wanted it now.

A great deal of attention was being generated by the picture Thelma had commented on.

"It's magnificent," someone said. "Surpasses everything."

He was waiting for Roselle to come over in his direction, whereupon he would lead her to the refreshment table and hand her a glass of champagne. He would tell her about his plans to settle in California. Perhaps they would meet. He was enjoying himself, savoring both fat and marrow, the way things had turned out. He thought of the artist who had made his living forging Vermeers after having been rejected for years for his own work. The credulous public. Always the same. They'd swallow anything, even talent if you gave them the right lie. Several people had already made offers on some of the paintings.

"Could you tell me anything about the rest of the work," Bannister, the art critic, now at his elbow, was asking him.

"A great deal of it is taken from the old sources," Lauren

said. "Christ among the disciples, but also Indian myths." His father had dipped into everything.

"Very curious," the man remarked. *The Ghost Dance* is splendid. I've never seen anything like it. A masterpiece."

"And the others?" Lauren said. "What about the others? You're not going to seize on one canvas out of a man's lifework," he said heatedly.

"I'm sorry, I didn't mean to offend you," the critic said, and emphasizing the interest of certain of the subjects, he left Lauren and lost himself among the viewers.

He was trying to take this in. The big painting, the others. But aware of something missing, he found himself searching the room. Roselle, where was she? She couldn't have gone, she couldn't have. Her rudeness struck him like a blow.

Running scared, that's what. She couldn't help it, couldn't put down the trembling she felt, even when she was back in her room. The events of the evening kept replaying in her mind. The strain of encounter had left her numbed, this time totally falsified. She'd had to keep looking into people's faces, concentrating on their words in order to keep from floating away. Her attention kept wandering, and she'd had to draw herself back sharply. Afraid the mask would be ripped from her face, as it had nearly been.

She had the sense that the artist's son, who had been identified for her, was in a similar fix. He looked unaccustomed to wearing a suit, much less a tuxedo. He stood awkwardly. His animation seemed forced, and his habit of continually glancing around, listening to conversations to either side of the one he was in, gave him a certain furtiveness. Whenever someone stood in front of him, he leaned almost into his face. Obviously not doing too well either. But she would approach him, and they would each speak out of their respective falsehoods, whatever his happened to be. She would fabricate some enthusiasm about their high-school days. But it was crowded, and too many people were clustered around each of them.

To wait until the press thinned, she moved with those looking at the paintings, following a pair of men who were commenting on them.

"But see, the same amateurishness. I don't understand it. There was a brilliance there, the whole conception. And then all these raw edges. Like putting a bucket over the light."

"It's the same in every one. Do you think—I mean the paint looks fresher—he could have had the insanity to come back and . . ."

"I don't know. Hard to say what happened to him in those last months. But look at this. My God!"

They were standing in front of a town that gave one the impression both of coming into being and fading into a mysterious background, while faces played in and out of their surroundings, equally mysterious. Some were Indians. Also pioneer women, a black man, a Chinese. The two viewers stood in front of the painting for some time, stepping back, moving up.

"Magnificent," they agreed.

"So totally different. Like another man painted it."

"I can hardly believe it. There are things in the rest, struggling to come out . . ."

"But this one—it's really the only fully realized work."

"You think he knows that?"

Joan stood just at their elbow. They were pointing out certain details. The town also seemed to have its levels. A fading luster, on the one hand, but also a raw and rather mean aspect. A multitude of faces, the expressions of all impulses: fear-ridden, greedy, and depraved; hopeful, hardheaded, spirited. Vice and recklessness, pity and courage vied with one another. Her eye was drawn to where a group of dancers leapt and flung themselves in a circle.

"The new heaven and the new earth." She turned to the man who had made the announcement. Rail-thin, sharp-eyed, weathered.

"That's what they were trying to dance into existence," he said, with a shake of the head. "Took about nine days, trying to dance flesh into spirit. Danced till they fell to the ground, but didn't feel a thing. Past hunger and thirst—dead to fatigue. Gone beyond it for the sake of vision."

She looked around. No one was standing near them, and the momentary lull, the murmur of voices from near the refreshment table or from the rooms beyond, made it seem as though she stood outside everything—space and time, and the crowd of people. And who was this man who'd so suddenly materialized? She wanted to move on, but he stood in her way as though his presence alone held her there. An unreasoning panic seized her: this man would strip her bare and put a knife to her throat.

"They hoped to be delivered from the white devil," he went on. "The messiah would come, bring back the buffalo and all the dead. But it never happened."

In self-defense she turned back to the painting. The town itself appeared ghostly, as though fading into the mist.

"Dancing at the edge of desperation and damnation," he went on, as if he were intoning a chant. Maybe he was a preacher of some out-of-the-way sect, it occurred to her, as his voice sent an involuntary shudder through her. Both his eyes and his voice held her. "Damned to live in a world turning upside down. Poor fools died for dancing. And left the rest of the fools to fool themselves. And what do you think of it, Roselle? Is it all worth remembering?"

The tone was suddenly personal, even intimate, as though something lay between them. And she was drawn by that, at the same time that it seemed the most threatening thing she'd yet come upon. Did he know her?

She glanced at him. "Maybe better to let it go," she said in a low voice, "if it's past cure."

"Just let it lie then, past cure and past memory?" He considered. "Everywhere you go, blood cries out from the ground. Maybe it's as well you mostly can't hear it. And whatever you catch hold of, pull out, can you get the truth of it anyway?"

"Do you really want it?" she found herself asking. "Maybe what you get is only what you can use anyway?" she said, not sure what she meant.

"Meanwhile let the dance of illusion go on," he said. "Why they make up forgeries of man himself," he said, with a laugh. "Just plant some bones and talk about a few million years. Wish I'd thought of it myself."

And he'd be capable of it, she thought. "You like to fool people?" she said.

"Why, you got to," he said. "Or you'd never survive. Most folks want to be fooled anyway."

"You believe that?"

"Absolutely. And right here's their chance. This painting here is the genuine article: the rest are fakes."

She looked at him. "How do you know?" She was locked now into the conversation. Other people approached and moved away as though the two of them stood inside an electric fence.

"I just do. Sometimes you're forced to learn a thing or two," he said. "Maybe I owe it to my family."

She was intrigued.

"It's my great talent."

"Picking out the fakes?"

"And creating them. I've learned a few tricks."

Maybe he could teach her then. She was just now in need of some help. His eyes, yellow with dark rings, had an almost hypnotic effect. She had to will against him to hold her own. Otherwise every secret she owned would be pulled out of her.

"It's one way of spending your time."

"You got anything special in mind?" she asked him.

"Just might. You can never tell."

The idea appealed to her, though she had to get away from him. Why had he selected her for his audience? Should she know him? He must know her if he could address her so familiarly. And yet he might do that with anyone. He didn't strike her as the sort of man who stood on ceremony. Now he was telling her that he knew a fellow once who'd rigged up an outfit that turned out money, changed ones into tens. Told folks that was how he made his money. "Almost got himself arrested," he said, with a laugh. "Only it was a joke. Most people can't tell the phony from the real thing," he said, with a tilt of the head, as though even now he were examining an article. "And if you haven't got a sharp eye, you get taken in."

She looked at him squarely. "But you're safe," she said. "I can tell that."

He grinned, bore down on her. "Who are you?" he demanded.

"Who do you think?" The words just came.

He shook his head. "Well, I'm not sure," he said.

"The real thing," she said brazening it out.

He looked at her, the quizzical expression giving way to humor, even appreciation.

"I believe it."

"Well," she said, ironically, "for a man who sees through everything, you're quick to take my word."

"I like your style," he said. "A. J. Peacock," he said, holding out his hand. "We'll know each other better." And he melted into the crowd.

She watched him go. He could see through her: she was that transparent—as thin as a strip of celluloid. It was a sensation different from what she felt that afternoon with Bill or with Mair. Altogether frightening, as though she had no substance whatever, were indeed falling through space, past life even, no longer flesh and blood, falling into the shadows. I have watched myself too long, she thought, been a spectator of things. She had a sudden flash of all the events of her life skimming past her vision, unable to hold on to any of them. The men, cats, and even the children had all fled away. Herself lost as well. What has been my experience? she wondered. Haven't I had any?

The closeness of people, the heat, made her feel faint. She turned to concentrate on the painting. She didn't understand it. There were too many things violently present all at once, vibrating in front of her eyes. Indians and settlers, the ghostly faces of ruffians in the trees. Her head began to spin.

Now she was alone. Or nearly. She'd had a drink, and smoked a joint Walter had given her. Her head scarcely belonged to her. She put on Roselle's robe and sat at the desk trying to write down an impression that eluded her. Something had happened and she could no longer locate herself. She had lost the thread of the story and wasn't sure she could get it back. Giddy, almost nauseated, she seemed to float about the evening, above everything she could remember. She was someone else's face and clothes. Nothing was her own, nothing she could claim. She couldn't write anything down. She kept seeing the spaces between the lines, shaped by the letters of the words she'd written. They grew and shrank beneath the words, then ran into the margins. She scratched out the sentences she'd written. They meant nothing. A jumble of fragments, with space hanging from them.

She should stick to news articles. Stay with facts. She shoved the notebook aside. Another book was lying on the desk, which she hadn't paid any attention to. Now as she opened it and read the first few sentences, she saw that it was Roselle's journal.

Sally hadn't taken it away. A terrible curiosity seized her, and also a great fear, as though reading it might implicate her more deeply in what she was doing.

"Do you want to know what's in there?" A voice spoke just above her ear. She looked around in confusion.

She wanted to protest, But it was an accident—a book just lying there.

"It's yours to read."

She couldn't bring herself to touch it. "And if I read it?"

"Then it's yours, all yours, and you'll have to take it on."

"I don't know what you mean."

"I can't help you there. No, I can't let you. It's too much. Run while there's still time."

"Oh, where can I go? It frightens me. All I wanted was a little play. A few good meals, some free drinks, and even a little flirtation. The clothes looked good, and when you put on somebody's clothes, you can forget . . ."

"Or remember. You might have to remember all that's underneath. And take it on. All that's under the surface of gold-and-white brocade—what lies beyond the shimmer and flirtations. And have to glance over the shoulder."

"Oh, what am I doing? Are you ever coming back?"

"Too much is twisted out of shape."

"Never, then?"

"Who knows? I need to watch for a while."

"Watch me be you?"

"Why not? Sometimes you watch another actress play a role you've had."

"But that's not the same. Your life, you live that."

"Sometimes you don't. I'm not real. I scarcely had the chance—till it all fell apart."

"But they worshiped you. Something leaked through. I know it did. I caught something."

"The illusion sliding past on the screen. Empty as air."

"And my past, my impressions, what good would they do you?"

"Let anything suffice. You'll have to take it on."

"What do you mean? My life isn't yours. It's too ridiculous."

"And will you take on mine? Will you do that? Dive into the forgetfulness I can't forget, the old prison I stand in. The past that draws me back and swallows me. The past that cannot change. It's like a death. If one could be delivered . . ."

How? What was she supposed to do?

"Roselle!"

"That's you, now."

"And what about my past?"

"That's yours, too."

"Roselle!" She could hear someone in the hall.

"Fool," she wept, putting her face in her arms. "Fool!"

IV   FLASHBACKS

Where, how did people get lost? Missing children, gone
without a trace: where did they disappear, leaving only
their loss—a portrait in the newspaper, a poster in a public
building, the offer of a reward? Or those last seen crossing the
street in the most casual way, just leaving work or the grocery
store and never arriving home, never to be seen again. Foul play?
Or was it that they couldn't find their way home again, like a
cat disoriented in a new neighborhood—theirs the loss of some
thread, some connection? A forgetfulness as they somehow
misplaced the moment, losing its contents and its link with
past moments. Or was it a shedding, a stepping out of a life, letting go of all its possessions, structures, meaning and standing
once again naked as the day they were born. Gone. Having
slipped out of a skin or fallen off the edge of the planet. Lost
only to the ones who sought them or to themselves as well? Unaccountable. And who knew their lives or deaths? To Bill, it was
terrible, the secrecy buried in things. To disappear as though
you'd never been. Maybe a landscape somewhere held the memory of struggle, final protest, acquiescence. But meanwhile the
anguish leapt from every pore: you jumped around, swore,
grabbed telephones.

"What do you think we're doing?" Walter demanded. "Every
minute we sit here, we're reducing the chances." What possible
value lay in hiding a disappearance? To protect whom exactly?
Stupidity ruled, in the name of some impossible moral delicacy.
It filled him with disgust. "Why not get everybody looking? The
more the better. What are we but accessories?"

"To what? Her disappearance?" Bill said, bristling. "There's no sign she was kidnapped, no indication of a struggle. The way they've been through these woods—dogs, the works—it's a wonder the whole world doesn't know. What more can we do?"

"Really look. Find her, and end this charade."

"You just want to capitalize on all this."

"Goddam you." His face flushed with the effort to hold himself in. "Sweet Jesus, how I wish I'd never got into this. Just trusted my instincts instead. It's been trouble from the start. I've got a ton of stuff to do, I've hated being here, every moment . . ."

"Goddam you and your ugly self-indulgence."

It was a wonder they didn't come to blows. He'd all but goaded Walter into hitting him, and would have been glad to hit somebody himself, tearing rage that he was in. "Look, you've contacted the L.A. folks and the FBI. What more do you want?"

"But if her picture were in the papers, someone might recognize her."

"Yeah, fifty people, and all of them cranks looking for publicity and a few kicks. And then what? Look, I'm convinced she walked out of here of her own free will—okay, maybe with some sort of mental aberration."

"All the more reason . . ."

"But then, would it help really . . . I mean, to have the whole public diving in on her? When she's right on the edge? To be exposed? Would she want that?"

Walter shrugged. Okay, let him have his own variety of craziness.

"It's better this way." In his own ears his voice sounded flat. A sense of blame had already begun to take him over, and he couldn't sit still with it. They had eaten breakfast—Joan and Lila were off to some engagement—and for once there was a lull between now and the afternoon, when things would start building for the preview. He hated it, felt time dying all around him.

"Besides, we're in too deep now." He had to argue his way out of it, hitting out in all directions. "We acted, on the spur of the moment, but we did it."

"Yeah, and we're going to come out looking like a bunch of assholes." Walter lit a cigarette and picked up what he considered a poor excuse for a newspaper. He wanted L.A. He wanted his Sunday paper.

Bill got up and went back to his room, where he stared moodily into the trees. Assholes? That would be the least of it. Scoundrels or criminals more than likely. The question of whether or not she was still alive lay unspoken between him and the others. That she might be dead was unthinkable. Yet he was afflicted with the uneasy premonition that he would never see her again. Even as they tried to find her, she was slipping away from them, her reality fading as their flailings and sputterings filled the screen, creating the drama that obscured her. It was merely a matter of technique: create the roles to fit the circumstances, let the dialogue grow out of the characters. In time it would seem more real than Roselle herself.

And who would know her? Even now he was convinced he had lost hold of something, or failed to grasp it from the very beginning—especially now that the whole scheme could be weighed against the present disaster. Trying to find her was the great effort, the center their energies flowed from at the same time they were creating the fiction of her presence. The convenient lie, for the sake of what truth, if any?

In his room he continued to drink the coffee he'd had sent up, resisting the impulse to get drunk and go to sleep—escape from the conviction that he was somehow responsible. He took her disappearance personally; he couldn't help it: a message to him that he failed to understand. "You've loved your women, Bill. But wouldn't it scare the hell out of you if you found one that wasn't your creation?"—it still rankled, Walter's comment, a hook in his hide.

It was too much to grant that Walter might be right, that Roselle had hated it all from the beginning. The hoopla in her hometown. A put-up job. Pure gimmickry. If they'd done the filming here, a story that came from the heart of the place, expressed its existence, that might have been different. A different story. For Roselle, for him, for everybody with a stake in the thing. A real reason to preview it here. But he'd not only gone along with all the flimflam, he'd been enthusiastic as hell. Even though he'd had a niggling feeling from the start that what the folks would see on the screen would give offense anyway.

But let's say it was the best he could come up with, that he'd pushed himself as far as he could go. Somewhere in the back of his mind, no matter what trash he'd had to earn his living by, he'd gone for the most that was in him, the most that film had to offer. Even with that, in his absolute insistence on her for the part, his own motives were becoming less and less clear.

That Roselle was a woman of talent, certainly he'd been convinced of that. He meant it when he justified himself on that ground. Grant that it had been a challenging part: he'd thought so. And that he'd not wanted to let the great gift go to waste. And loyalty, add that—to her, as he watched her approach the cliff's edge, held his breath, and wondered if she'd make it. Personal loyalty, talent, and possibility—give them their due. But what Walter had hinted at . . . Let us not take refuge in easy illusions. The grinning Walter. Who had jerked the line so hard Bill had felt the hook go in all the way.

But why bring her back? Her name didn't mean a rat turd to the youth that now took their lusts and boredom to the theater, wanting the newest upcoming sexpot, the latest thrill while they felt up their girls and handed round the popcorn. And those of her era might just prefer to forget her. Why look back to the grayness of the fifties? It was hard for him to see himself now as the white knight taking arms against a sea of forgetfulness. A sea without a ripple, only something deadly under the surface.

But the film was the great medium of the century. And if you couldn't do it there . . . Kill that conviction and he might as well stop breathing. As a kid, he'd been an addict for anything on the screen, the Saturday serials, Westerns, gangster films, musicals. After his father had died and his mother moved to L.A., he not only haunted the theaters, he trekked over to the studios to try to get on as an extra. It never occurred to him he wouldn't go into film. He worked at odd jobs, picked up what he could find in order to get through UCLA, where he showed a talent for screenwriting. He also had the beginnings of a novel in the drawer, but if writing would take him into film, then screenplays it would be. During his senior year, he was put in touch with one of the studios, for whom he worked on the rewrite of a dog of a script. He didn't get a screen credit, but at least they gave him more work. And paid him good money. He could let go of the car-wash and hash-slinging jobs. Till he was one of a horde of nobodies grinding out material for the studios. Mindless comedy, and what passed for drama. Most of it godawful. A bad knee kept him out of World War II. He stayed behind trying to find a way into significance. He worked on a couple of gung ho patriotic films that at least had some excitement to them. Mostly he was involved in a studio project making win-the-war films for the army.

Two things had gnawed at him for a long time: the film industry and politics. If he had a good idea, if it gave even a faint whiff of anything of social consequence, by the time it hit the screen it was either gone or so watered down he couldn't recognize it. And you always knew what wouldn't get past the producers. What a ruckus had come up over *Blockade,* with its allusions to the Spanish civil war, its suggestions that war killed women and children, victimized everyone. Demonstrations against it—imagine! And the one film about racism that did make it to the screen had been, he felt, dishonest.

An awesome power lay in the cinema: it reached millions, spoke to them, shaped their imaginations. Most of it harmless enough: Betty Grable's legs and Fred Astaire's dancing and Nelson Eddy's voice. Something to take in after you got the kids' noses wiped, brought the last drink of water, got them to quit bellyaching and go to sleep. So you could forget the unpaid bills and the leak in the roof. Why not some inflated heroics? Or romance among the well-heeled. Or an extravaganza: chariots and the clash of swords. Or cheesecake and fancy costumes. Escape. Something to dream on. But maybe that was the harm. Bread and circuses. Being given just enough to get you to stay in the rut, live on scraps. Without ever rising to any occasion, much less struggling to climb out of the pit. It robbed the imagination of its gleam of the possible, fed it on pap.

But what if you could call up something—he couldn't even give it a name—a shape of things to come. A new idea. Change. A change of life, when you were sick of it.

No wonder he was seized quite early with the passion to direct. If you could write and direct your own material, have a say over the editing . . . A dream. Why not? He wangled a couple of a.d. jobs on a horror film and a "serious drama"—just for the experience, he told people. For the sake of his writing. So he served his apprenticeship, a long one. In his thirties, he was considered a bright young light, even if he was still just a writer.

It was frustrating. His readiness was at its height when times were at their worst. He'd had it best during the war. Some good work came out. *A Walk in the Sun,* and a couple of others he could look at with admiration, with the thought that there was something significant to say in film. But even then, a germ, something unaccountable, was growing in their midst, spreading sickness, creating a miasma. A couple of years later the House Un-American Activities Committee swooped down, and the fear became palpable. In that atmosphere of suspicion and accusation, the people he most counted on went under, at first with shouts of protest from their supporters, who were the next to have the finger pointed at them. Down to the survivors, silenced, alone. He continually heard rumors that certain people would get the ax, and they did. The air was never still. And the stink of it! The bitterness of betrayal, of lives gone sour. He expected to be the next. He no longer spoke of his admiration for Eisenstein's work; things were that bad. The Russians were the enemy now.

He was confused: Elia Kazan and Robert Taylor before the committee, naming names, saving their skins. And more. Ugly, criminal. And some of the best talent fled to England, to Mexico. Wrote screenplays under pseudonyms. Got jobs in factories. Wait it out, he thought. It can't go on.

Meanwhile, all the vipers came to the surface. Till Eisenhower came along and McCarthy was all through. People were ready to forget him then, relieved to sweep the whole mess under the rug. Though those who'd been ruined still couldn't get work. And the last exiles didn't make it back until the sixties.

He'd survived. Lucky? Of course he was. He'd lived in the continual fear of the subpoena or else of being quietly graylisted and banished from the industry. For some reason it didn't happen. Cowardly? So Helen, his first wife, called him. Okay, he'd grant her that. He'd kept his mouth shut, put his liberal notions into the background, bided his time while he looked for some crevice to slip into. Devious? Ambitious? You'd better believe it. But not just that. He knew what was good: something that could leap beyond the moment even as it spoke of this time, this place. He had two chances, one to help direct a film in New Mexico being made by some blacklisted Hollywood people, the other to join forces with a director he admired, David Weimar. Instinctively he knew what he wanted, someone to show him the way: David, recently married to his protégé, Roselle More.

His film, which attracted Bill because it was set in Korea, had begun as an ironic account of what happens to people in the process of war. Toward the end of the film, the two officers in command, having sent their men into an ambush, end up shooting the terrified villagers of the town they're trying to capture, including a number of women and children caught in a crossfire. The officers were portrayed as neither cruel nor violent but rather as confused men under pressure. In the ambiguity of their situation they are able only to act out of instinct, killing as they go. Some of the infantrymen were presented as equally bewildered, and horrified by their actions.

Bill had been excited by the film. It was a good film, it tried for something. It was Weimar's conception and script; he wouldn't let anyone muck around with it. And Bill knew what was there. Not cheap heroics, not a slick glorification of national interests. But something hard won and true about how people act. It would be controversial: people would love it or hate it, but they couldn't dismiss it.

He watched Weimar get into a battle with the studio heads as more and more of the film got cut. Ugly, unpatriotic, they called it. By the time the slaughter at the studio ended, the officers in the film were, if not exactly heroes, never in the least called into question, and the killing of the villagers was passed off as a necessary tactical maneuver. Weimar was incensed. He had fought hard. And for his pains, it was clear he'd never have the chance to direct another film.

His loyalty was already suspect. During the hearings, a fellow director and good friend, had, Weimar felt, betrayed him. Had groveled before the committee. Had explained how all his own films had been free of any taint of Communist propaganda but that there were others who, he presumed to say, were under Communist influence. He named names, Weimar's being one of them. Weimar had never belonged to the Party, had kept himself from all political affiliations. Still he was under a cloud, even though he cleared himself. After the latest effort, he was finished.

But he'd had to do battle for his film. Take on all his enemies on this one ground. Whether he really thought he could win, he never said. Perhaps he knew he was doomed, even though he was a director of some stature and his films had done well at the box office. Money talked as eloquently then as now. But maybe he was fed up too. He'd finally made the film he wanted to be remembered for, the one that would speak for him. How carefully he had set things up, hovered over his casting director, passed on the technical people. He'd staked his career on the film.

"Somebody's got to do something," he kept saying. "This whole country's turning to shit. If it's not the Reds, it's the fascists."

"Can you get away with it?" Bill asked, perhaps hoping for some assurance for himself. Self-conscious, though hardly in his first youth, still being put to the test. Afraid Weimar wouldn't fight, and thus betray something Bill counted on; afraid of what would happen if he did.

"Can't people see the way things are going? We're so busy imitating those we're afraid of, we're destroying ourselves. Unbearable." He balled his fist. "You've got to keep trying, hope you can slip by. Try everything." He sounded weary.

And Bill had the opportunity to watch him go to his death, so to speak. Not immediately. Roselle was still working on a picture, so they stayed around Hollywood. But things would catch up with her too. Guilt by marriage. They went to England, where David directed a film—a bad film, and he knew it. He made one more before he was finished for good. That was after he came back to Hollywood, where he was to die of cancer after a long bout of depression.

And what had Roselle been to him all this time? At first no more than a big name in the box office, an image on the screen. With her long hair and high cheekbones and a look in her eyes and a huskiness in her voice that all came together as a blow between the eyes. You could fantasize about that one. And for all that suggested the erotic, something teased and excited and never quite emerged. For she was also the Hollywood image of fulfilled womanhood. Came out fighting but went home loving, ready to reproduce the basic economic unit. We need you in the kitchen, honey, to tackle those dishes and in the bedroom to hmm hmm hmm. Get out of that dirty factory: the war, hooray! is over.

She didn't like any of her films. "All junk. One after another. Can you ever get past it, playing up to people, turning yourself into a child on the screen or off? When I tell them I want something serious, they think I want to play a killer, a man-eater."

Bill didn't know what she meant either. Though he did look at her and try to figure it out. And wondered at times where the energy could go. She fascinated him.

He went over to her and David's house a lot, to dinners, to parties, sometimes alone. One of the family. With Roselle he talked about himself. It was a wonder she didn't throw him out, he was going all the time. Had she seen this or that film? What did she think of so-and-so as a director? He tried to impress her with his plans.

One evening when he came up to the house unannounced, he thought he heard voices in the living room. He wondered if he'd forgotten some party he'd been invited to; he was, as far as he knew, always invited. Curious, he worked his way around to a window on the side of the house where he could catch a glimpse. In the living room he saw a swing moving back and forth and on it a couple, nude. The man sat with the woman on top of him, her legs sticking out behind him. Fucking in a swing! He'd never seen anything like it, but then his experience was not all that large. He tried to make out who they were. The man was an actor he recognized, but the woman's back was toward him. He was convinced it was Roselle. And others were sitting around on cushions on the floor watching. Fascinated, horrified, he could not take his eyes away. Then ashamed of his spying, he sneaked off and went home.

But he couldn't get the scene out of his head. If it was Roselle, and yet would David . . . And the people watching . . . But if it was Roselle . . . And after that he couldn't look at her without the impression of that scene in his head.

Perhaps that's why it happened. At a party some weeks later, he'd gotten rather drunk, and Roselle was concerned about him.

"You're sure you can get home okay?" she said. "Why don't you leave your car here and take a taxi? Or just stay the night."

They were standing in the bedroom trying to find his jacket

under various coats and shawls. "Kiss me," he said, putting his arms around her. "One for the road."

She kissed him lightly on the lips.

"Not that kind of kiss. Like a bitty child getting a kiss from his momma before she tucks him in." He put his arms around her. "You think I don't know you? Come on. Something deeper— like only you can put out. This kind." He mashed his mouth against hers, fell over with her onto the bed.

"Bill . . ."

"You can do better than that," he insisted, tearing at her clothes, reaching her breast with his mouth. He pulled at her garter belt, let go, found her panties, and pulled till they ripped.

"Bill!" she pushed at his chest. "What the hell do you think you're doing?"

"Raise your legs higher," he demanded.

"Please, Bill, anyone could come in here."

"Is it in?" he said, uncertainly, searching for entry, afraid of going limp. He had the sense of hands flailing, striking at his face. He went on, maddened, pressing her hands back for an instant, pushing against her. "Is it in? Now tell me to fuck you."

"Are you crazy?" she said in a choking voice, finally tearing loose, twisting out from under him. They both got up unsteadily, panting, looking each other over like two strange beasts. "Get out," she told him. She pushed the hair out of her eyes, tried to catch her breath. "Get out."

How he made it home was the wonder of the evening. When he woke the next morning, sprawled out on the couch, he had no clear memory of what had happened. But later it all came together, surfacing like a bad dream.

Apparently she never said a word about it, because a week or so later David invited him to come for dinner. Fortunately, he had an excuse. But when David asked him again, he couldn't refuse; otherwise it would appear that he was playing the coward politically. But it took all his effort to face Roselle, who treated him as if nothing had happened.

After David's death, Roselle slipped away. Heavily in debt, she sold their house in Beverly Hills and rented an apartment. She was on the board of several charities. A few times she was a hostess at benefits, though she didn't perform herself. She did do some little theater. She even worked as a waitress. Bill was sure she didn't have to do that. In fact, he offered her money, which she refused. He wondered if she wasn't doing it to punish herself, for reasons that weren't clear to him. He used to visit her between productions, risked the jealousy of his wife; he'd married when his future seemed secure. As time went on, he could see that Roselle was drinking heavily. There were periods in a sanitarium. Now that he was directing, writing his own material, now that he had some control, he tried to persuade her to act in one of his films. Every chance he got he brought her a script to read. At first he got nowhere. But he kept at her. And when he saw he was making headway, he kept pushing.

"But I haven't done anything for so long, not anything good."

"Give yourself a chance," he insisted. "Nobody's asking for instant brilliance. Trust me a little. I know what I see in you."

"And what's that?" she demanded.

It came out lamely enough, "I see you as a talented, lovely woman . . ."

She looked at him almost scornfully, as though he'd missed some obvious point. "Oh Christ," she said.

He got angry. "I can see it, damn it. I see potential. What more do you want?"

"I want a role . . ." she said, pausing to think.

"Okay, that's not hard to do. What has to be so goddam special?"

She ignored him. " . . . that will make me do something different, think in a different way."

"What does that mean?"

"I thought you knew."

"You think I don't?"

"I didn't say that. At least let me try to explain. You know Hedda Gabler. It's a wonderful part. And I'd love to do something like that. And that's necessary. But all she can do is destroy."

What had Roselle been doing but destroying herself?

"For once I'd like the other side, whatever that is."

"So would I, damn it."

As it was, it took all your energy just to fight your way to the threshold. You never seemed to have any left to make the leap across. It had happened to David. Watching his last great testimony come to nothing. And maybe to Roselle herself. Bill hadn't been put to the test, not yet; he'd watched from the sidelines. He could have gone for the thing in New Mexico. But he didn't. Whatever else that film was, it couldn't have been his masterpiece.

But he'd escaped real confrontation, because the climate changed. In the late sixties and early seventies, a fresh wind swept through, and the control of the big studios was broken. Independent producers on the scene, a new excitement. He'd been able to make some good films, he liked to think, even if they didn't answer to what Roselle wanted. But at least with real characters, trenchant social criticism. Now that money was tighter and the costs so terrific, things were thrown into question again. He could think of two or three people who had a free hand, but for a while you'd had the proof you could do something truly significant and do well at the box office in the bargain. He caught something in the air again that he wanted to deny, a sweetish smell like something rotting, a whiff of the fifties. Let me be wrong, he said to himself.

In every generation, as he saw it, you had to fight the evil. Cut off one head and up pops another. And maybe that's all you could do. But this time he wasn't going to be able to dodge. Backlash, self-righteousness, a new conservatism looked to be moving in. A generation with blinders on. Now with this film, he'd gone to Roselle and pushed as hard as he could. "Come on. Will you do it? What are you afraid of? It's your last chance. Will you do it?" He'd gone to Roselle with the best he could offer. And what did it offer Roselle? "I want a role . . . that will make me do something different, think in a different way."

She'd done it for his sake, he knew now, because she didn't believe . . . He leaned down and held his head in his hands. My God, what had he done? And what had he made her do?

To her great relief, nothing was scheduled until Sunday evening—in deference to the churchgoers, she supposed—and Joan could linger over coffee with a whole morning to herself. She intended to read Roselle's notebook—to discover exactly what? She hadn't expected to find it still there in her room. Bill had pored over it hoping for some clue to explain her disappearance, and Lila had brought it back to leave with the rest of her things. Joan took it out of the drawer where she'd put it out of sight. Perhaps things had come round in a circle, beginning in Chloride and ending there. Or was that too pessimistic? Or perhaps it was a spiral, and Roselle had shot beyond the point of origin. She opened the book to the first page. There was no date.

I wanted to write something now that I've come back, because I've walked into a strangeness and I don't know what to do about it. It rises up like heat from the pavement, and I feel giddy. I have come back, but what am I seeing? I don't know. It's like bandages have been removed from my eyes and the things that stand in front of me have no name. As though I'd touched them in the dark, grown familiar with them, and now can't recognize them. Fragments, bits of chaos that hang over me and threaten.

Curious. This isn't the place I left. I can't smell the fear. Then I was walled in by it. The air was thick with what people said. Good and bad were painted on the sidewalks like daily headlines. You had to always watch out that your slip didn't show, pretend you had no sex. Otherwise you were cheap, a whore. But put on the lipstick, and the tight sweater. Give off the scent, then deny and deny.

I can barely see myself. Or anybody else. It's like watching figures moving behind a scrim or in the mist. And when I was down inside that creature I was, I couldn't see myself either. Held in, held in, afraid to make a move. And yet always hitting against fences, not even knowing that I would. Something inside trying to get out, a wild thing I couldn't pretend wasn't there. Always it betrayed me, and that was what Jessie called my talent. On the stage I could escape myself—in another person I could live. I have always wanted to live.

Most of the people I knew then were much less vivid than those whose lines I spoke. Real suffering, real desire, real humor—where was it to go? It went farther than Chloride but fared no better. And why have I come back?

Now the town sprawls up to meet me: gas stations, motels, discount stores, the works—metal and glass and gold glitter—all the shoddy making out to be spanking new. For a moment, you are caught, and you almost forget it was any other way. I looked around in the jumble for the one lone café that used to sit out on a hill, nothing around it but the parked cars and the coyotes. The Hilltop Cafe. Gone, of course. And maybe the hill too. At least, I couldn't pick it out. This hill, or maybe the next. One moment I was sure, then I was confused. I can't even be sure of what I do remember. Or who's remembering it. Does it matter?

Maybe none of it's here anymore. Not even all the ugliness. Maybe that's gone too. But it lived in my imagination then. Then it was mud and dust and strikes in the mines and grubbing for a livelihood. Jack Benny on the radio. It sent me flying out of here, thinking, If I don't leave, I'll die—turn to bone bleaching in the sun, wind blowing through the eye sockets; or wither and break loose in the wind and go tumbling like baling wire lost in the dust and confusion forever. The dramatic turn of mind. I look at those who stayed while the voice whispered to me, Run. Run for your life. Grab what you can get before it slinks away and somebody luckier than you takes the lot and makes off to paradise—with money love power men and peace of mind. All the splendid glitter of it. They've stayed on and lived their lives—and what have I done? Oh, I was young then, and the blood was in my veins, and dreams were cheap.

And there was Jessie saying, You can do it—don't waste your talent. Or it'll leak into the ground like it never was. There's a whole population settling for the least of nothing much.

That was a long time ago, Jessie. And there's a certain natural snobbery in the idea. What would you say to me now—if you're still around? That I tried. Oh, no, not you. I know what you're thinking. That first I sold out, then paid the price. You'd be unsparing, Jessie. I can see you looking at those films, thinking: That's what it's come to, has it? Well . . .

And will I be redeemed even now? Bill's all excited, thinks he got it this time. I remember how he tried to get it once, though maybe he didn't know that's what he was trying to do. Poor Bill, catching hold of shadows.

So much for me. Well, one of us made it to the moon and another to the legislature—that's something for this town. As for the rest—Frank Lucero and Lauren Collingwood, the melancholy genius, and Mair, who kept in touch, in and out of failure just like me. And we will meet, two old survivors, just barely that. Coming back to start over. As if anyone can. We'll see each other after all this time, but God knows why. Maybe because she seems like flesh-and-blood evidence that I must have been real once.

The others, if they are alive, are still here. They seem thin as smoke. Ghosts—all ghosts. And I'm one too, walking among them. My own ghost. I keep walking the streets, where everything has turned strange, as strange as the moon in a cowl, as strange as the very earth, though the mud beetle goes on moving the same ball of dirt. I can't help it. I come back to find what I couldn't escape from then. Something ugly still. A chill, an old horror. I think of something trapped and trying to escape . . .

That was all, and after Joan read it, she closed the book and put it back in the drawer. I should have left it alone, she thought. That's what comes of prying.

The trouble was, she was drawn to it. Once she discovered the little packet of letters in her husband's drawer, love letters from his woman, she'd spent a good many entertaining moments reading them: Yeah, that's what she thinks. Just let her live with him. Joy and rapture. You should always look at the hands first. If they're small, watch out.

She took a cheap thrill in knowing more than they thought she knew, meanwhile preparing herself: holding out money, ceasing to pay bills. Taking her revenge.

And her love of gossip must have been inborn. For her, the small-town paper was license to peer and poke and pry. Insinuate herself into places, pick up their secret life. So much was hidden. If she could figure percentages, she'd say that 90 percent of what went on played in the shadows. Every now and then you turned something upside down and there was revelation, scandal. Illicit love and bribery and blackmail and treason. All the good stuff. Still most of it remained buried, for all you turned over the rocks, and you never got the full story—how Marilyn Monroe died or Kennedy was assassinated. The facts dissolved into motives, and motives reached down to the secret springs of impulse, the unspoken and undefined. So what thread did you follow, and what would bring you safely back from the labyrinth? A dangerous game, being drawn to hidden things.

She had no idea now what she was looking for. A secret that lay behind coincidence? The fortune of her face? This time, though, she couldn't run back to the feature column. "It's yours and you'll have to take it on." So she'd opened a door and got her foot caught for her pains. This time she wouldn't be able to shake loose. Roselle was with her now, inside her. From the moment the voice had spoken in her ear—as though she'd invited it, put herself in the way of being spoken to. It had given her fair warning too. It was no longer a question of playing the little role they wanted her to, making her little motions through the preview and the party, then disappearing. For now the role had expanded and taken her in. And she wouldn't get out of it till something had been exacted of her, satisfied. "You'll have to take it on." The past, the suffering. All that was in it; it went with the role, didn't it? If you were a character, you were her past. Otherwise you could never understand the life you were trying to play. But why, why have to do that? For what?

And if she stayed, there was the future. Mair she'd got through, blundered her way past. But the fellow in the gallery, he'd be hovering around. He knew something and wouldn't be put off so easily. To Bill she'd always be trying to prove something and it would never be enough. As for old Jessie, who must be formidable, they were going to meet too. She'd have to wrestle with them all.

This is stupid, she thought. Let me just get in my car and go home. Make a quick getaway. Rescue myself. But who's that anymore?

When you reached a certain age, Jessie considered, there's a fading of importance; the present lost a certain vividness. Youth had the advantage of passion continually ignited and a sublime ignorance of the complexity of things. If the younger generation was making the world any worse, it wasn't because hers hadn't had its innings. It struck her as odd that some of the leftovers of her generation, including perhaps the most successful actor in the world, were now appealing somehow to youth. He should have been a better actor, she thought; then he wouldn't require a second career. Well, she was an old woman, and she couldn't help matters. Not that she ever had. Meanwhile her enthusiasms had burnt out, save for an occasional short-lived flare.

I'm an empty bucket all the same, she admitted to herself. All she really wanted out of the past was to gossip about it in a way that didn't force her to think. And to feel a little superior for knowing the way things ought to have been done. An old woman, after all, had earned her place as elder goddess for at least a few moments every month or so. Just now, though, she was happy to hear Thelma rattle on.

"Roselle was there, of course. Jessie, she's still splendid. I think Lauren expected something of her. He kept looking out of his conversations in her direction."

Jessie laughed. "That impulse to try to improve on the dullness that's around you. I killed that illusion years ago."

"But she didn't go up to him. I saw her talking to Bird Peacock. And the next moment she was gone. If you want to go to the preview . . ."

"Bird?" Jessie said, surprised. "He's still around these parts? I thought he'd disappeared long ago."

"Well, he's here. Some kind of legal tangle this time. But when wasn't he in some sort of tangle?"

"He's the one person who can make me laugh. Wherever trouble is, Bird's sure to find it. Always liked Bird. Never thought he had any malice in him."

"Riles people up, though."

"Fortunately. Yes, he's the one person I might abandon a conversation for. He keeps the juice flowing."

Thelma let Bird go. He wasn't what she wanted to talk about. "She was the big attraction, of course. Surely she'll come around before she leaves."

"So she says."

"You mean you've talked to her?"

"Of course. I keep up the telephone."

"And not a word out of you. You sly dog."

"I'm telling you now."

"That telephone you're keeping up; it works in more than one direction."

"I wasn't aware of your burning interest," she teased her.

"When is she coming?"

"Maybe next week, provided I'm having a good day."

"How exciting."

For Thelma it would be exciting.

"You know, I've always thought Roselle was like your daughter. You giving her her chance in life."

"Perish the thought," Jessie said testily. "Look what it turned out to be."

"She had her success."

"Flimsy. Cheap. Hardly a shred of her talent could make it through any of that writing. Not that I blame her . . . Some-

106

times it's trash or nothing. I knew that, and she didn't. And didn't bother to tell her. But she ought to've kept to the stage."

"They say the new film . . ."

"They're always saying . . ."

"So you think she's let you down," Thelma said.

"She didn't let me down, because I couldn't be let down," Jessie said. "What she did was her own business." No, Roselle hadn't let her down. When you lived in the twentieth century, you figured just about everything was going to let you down. Maybe any century.

"You planning on being disillusioned by the Collingwood boy?" Jessie said to change the subject.

"That's different. I think he's done something worse than throw himself away."

"Why, dear me," Jessie said, with her usual irony, "drama in all of this."

"Yes," Thelma said, close to anger, for there were times when Jessie exasperated her. She never came out and actually accused Jessie of having turned into all but bleached bone, but right now she was tempted. "I think he's not only a fraud; I think he's a criminal."

"Really?" She had to be careful; Thelma was not to be taken lightly.

"I was too busy being polite," Thelma said, wryly. "God knows why. But I sensed something all the while—that he was trying to pull something off and it wasn't working."

"Probably hasn't had enough practice," Jessie said. "Now if it's genuine fraud, there's something in me that admires the grand effort, provided it's the right sort of lie." She meant it, but she'd have to think about it.

Thelma didn't challenge her. "So peculiar. Of course I was sure the paintings would be spectacular. And they were trying to be. But it was like a film had congealed over the surface."

"Well . . ." Jessie said. She had respect for Thelma's opinion. It seemed to her everybody was in the game, throwing out a set of appearances, hollowness ringing behind them. And behind the cardboard? Pure instinct, she thought. Mostly greed or fear. The old animal playing with its shadow. Wreckage. Crime in the streets. The language itself going back to the apes and hyenas.

"And the one, absolutely magnificent. I can't tell you how it held me. Chills all up and down my spine. I've been back to see it two or three times. And it strikes me different each time, the way the faces fade in and out. As though you're watching a merry-go-round go past, with all the horses and the fixtures tarnished. Only one of the horses, you can't tell if it's even real, is lying on its side, face twisted up, a look in its eyes. I can't tell you . . ."

"Well," Jessie said, visualizing it as Thelma spoke. Oh, I don't want this, she thought. She felt her heart being squeezed. I'm too old. Let me just think about my garden.

"It makes you think something's happening in the world, trying to be born . . ." Thelma couldn't contain herself. "And Lauren standing there in a suit, all gussied up. I'll bet he hasn't had a suit on in years. To make a grand debut. I suppose he did. The mayor and all the biddies loved it. And the gallery owners are ready to snap everything up and make a fortune. But it's all gone wrong, Jessie. I think of old Russell, during these last years, painting till dawn. He was a man inspired. What happened to it?"

"Maybe just crazy," Jessie said, cruelly, trying to spare herself.

"No!" Thelma insisted. "Lauren's the crazy one."

Oh stop, she wanted to cry out. Don't tell me about things wasted and lost. Her hand shook as she held her glass of iced tea. She put it down and breathed deeply. Slowly she rocked back and forth. Nothing was worth getting into a lather about; besides it was too late. All that youthful energy and promise under her hands and Thelma's. The kids grew up and came back to visit her, all as wise as any man baked in an oven. They had wives or husbands and kids and managed department stores and worked computers. And they brought their nostalgia.

And now Roselle. What on earth would they say to each other?

She'd never seen Thelma in such a state: the old rage and impotence. She wanted to feel sorry for her, but she had no business to be condescending. "Well, it's a shame," she said. It was the best she could offer.

"More than a shame," Thelma cried. "It's a disaster. It's dead, it's dying, then suddenly there's a place you can look, only some madman comes along . . ."

She was hearing eloquence, something you can't even teach. For this one moment. The power of it. Once she'd known that power. Neither of them spoke for a time. Oh, Thelma, she thought. What have you done to me? I'll never be able to die a quiet death.

Frank Lucero was allowing himself a rare day off. He was going fishing with an old friend of his, Henry ("Bootleg") Martinez. The past couple of years Henry had practically lived in the Gila Wilderness, wandering the mountains like one of the animals that inhabited them, panning for gold. For the past three months he had been in town, living in his mother's house. Frank had never known him to sit still that long.

Henry came by for him in the beat-up truck he drove, tackle box and poles in the back.

"You've not been sick?" Frank asked as he got into the truck.

"Why? When do I get sick? I live outside. On the ground in my sleeping bag in my little tent. In the rain, in the snow. I never even catch a cold." He was flexing his arms, parading his health.

"But you've been in town three months. You'll get so soft you won't want to go back."

"Maybe," Henry said, and smiled. "Who knows? Maybe I'll get rich anyway."

Rich? Panning gold? Frank wondered if he seriously believed there was gold to find. Or whether it was a fantasy he lived, along with his others, this time casting himself as prospector. For he was always talking about getting rich, always had some scheme in his head, and just when you thought he was pulling your leg, a certain grimness would come into his expression. Whatever scheme he had going this time was obviously enough to keep him in town. Frank was never sure when he'd see Henry; he might turn up after a couple of weeks in the bush, or be gone a couple of months to California. Back in town he'd get a new tattoo—the last time, a fox chasing a rabbit into the hole nature had provided. And he boasted that next he would get a torpedo on his penis. He had a woman tattooed on his arm, and he'd make her hips shimmy when he flexed his muscles. And a large snake circling his thigh.

Nights he spent closing up the Buffalo Bar, where the girls were treated to drinks and tales of his feats of strength or cunning and his triumphs in love. His brother Angelo would collect him in whatever state the evening left him—laughing, weeping, or ready for a fight—and haul him out to his truck and up the hill to his mother's house. In the afternoon, when he woke, he would fortify himself with some of her excellent chili and tortillas, disappear for some hours, then plunge through the swinging doors of the bar. "Hello again. Hello. I'm back and very thirsty." And he was given a loud welcome.

When he got bored, or his money ran out, he took off again, no one knew quite where.

"And what is it this time?" Frank questioned him.

The gold fever was even more fantastic than his previous scheme: bootlegging liquor into Oklahoma. That had ended when he'd been beaten to within an inch of his life for venturing into territory already staked out. He still walked with a slight limp. But that was like Henry: he snatched ideas out of the blue, and with a wonderful devil-may-care walked right into where he expected his luck to be waiting.

"A secret. But when the time comes . . ."

"But you have a fortune in pans," Frank kidded him. For he had the gravity pan, the Wilson pan, the Flaherty pan. One of them had cost five hundred dollars. "I think," Frank had told him, "you'd be richer if you'd kept the five hundred dollars." He had a little vial of gold he carried around with him—"flyshit," as the locals called it.

This time Henry gave the impression that he was simply hanging around and enjoying himself. But he was, had to be, hatching some scheme. For he was never idle. And he had an endless fertility of invention. "What d'you think," he'd asked Frank, "of a mass-produced saddle? I've thought of a way you could do it, and horse shoes of rubber that would go over the horses' hooves and then shrink. Save a lot of money. You got to shoe a horse every six months. Worse than a kid. But with these . . ."

Frank would laugh.

"You laugh, but wait. You think everyone has to be a nut who comes up with a new idea. And one of these days, I'll do some-

110

thing nobody has ever done before, think of something so wild and full of miracles, it'll rock you back on your heels." He was dead serious, of course.

"You'll be a hero, Henry."

"And rich. Rolling in dough." A strange gleam came into his eyes.

But that morning they were going fishing; Frank didn't have to think. He fell into the swaying of the truck on the curves through the hills, looked off into the trees, and as they climbed, looked out over peak after peak of the Mogollon Mountains. They parked the truck and hiked for a mile or so down to the middle fork of the Gila. Henry led him along the shallow river, crossing back and forth as they headed into the canyon. The river had flooded early in the year, raging up past its banks. Trees lay scattered along the old course. They paused finally where the river moved among some large boulders before it rushed down over the rocks. They did well, moving from one spot to another that Henry knew, where the trout hid in the deep pools. Before noon Henry had caught eight fish, and Frank had gotten four.

He watched, admiring, as Henry built a fire, set up a series of forked sticks, impaled the trout on sticks with pointed ends, and cooked them. Frank sat against the trunk of a cottonwood, the sun on his face, and leaned back for the first suggestion of contentment he had felt in months. He allowed his eye to follow the line of the canyon, bluffs of red rock rising above the river.

"I can see why you come out here," he said to Henry. "Gold is just an excuse."

"Man, one of these days you'll see a real strike. These hills are crawling with wealth. You know, lots of people have been here and found good mineral deposits—zinc, iron, copper. Only the government won't let them bring in equipment."

"You want to tear up the last piece of Wilderness? They haven't torn up enough?"

"But think, man. There's a fortune here."

He'd never believed gold fever was something real until he'd known Martinez. When he talked about gold, his eyes glazed and an unearthly glow surrounded him, as though he had entered a different space. As long as the talk was about money, the fever held him. When the subject changed, he became inert, almost sullen until he came back to himself, amiable, cheerful. Then he acted as if he'd been under a spell.

"What would you do if you got rich?" Frank asked him.

"Play the horses. Chase the girls."

"You do that already."

"But, man, with some loot, you could do it in style. That's what I want, style. Picture it. You walk into a store, get this. Say it's clothes. You just pick up ten, twelve shirts, all fancy. Silver buttons, embroidery, different colors. And the salesman, he just falls all over himself, because you've got a wad, man, and he's going to be nice to you. And shoes—you could have a hundred pair of shoes—handmade, fit your feet like velvet."

"When would you wear them all?"

But he was all caught up. "And rings. Gold rings, with big diamonds. Flash and dazzle all the way. And cars, man. I'd have a whole fleet of buggies. All the big names. Ferrari, Mercedes, Rolls-Royce. And when I wanted to take a chick out, I'd say, 'Okay, sweetie, pick your wheels.'"

"You've got all the girls running after you as it is."

He shrugged. "It's a start."

He was a handsome man, lean and well built. His time in the Wilderness had hardened the muscles in his arms and legs and back. He looked very strong even though he was slender, relatively small. He had a quick smile, somewhat teasing, and flashing eyes that did him well by the women.

"You should have been an actor, Henry," Frank said.

"You think so?"

"Then you could always play yourself on the screen or off."

"I'd like that," he said. "Out there in Hollywood. A big house and a swimming pool, all the booze you could drink and girls and . . . That movie crew that's here in town . . ."

"Everybody's got the same idea."

Henry shook his head. "And the actress. A little old for me, but still a woman. She's rich, and beautiful."

"Don't forget the fish. If you dream them into cinders, I'll gnaw your arm."

Henry laughed good-humoredly. "I never forget the food. The belly comes first." He took the fish off the sticks, put them on tin plates, and they ate, speaking only in grunts of satisfaction. It was good, the fresh air and the taste of food, the river moving along beside them, gurgling around rocks, forming little whirl-pools, then becoming subdued and slowing past. They sat without speaking, idly watching the current.

From where he lay, Frank could see what looked like a red arrow painted on the cliff just above him, and part of a square, a pictograph. They had been here, the long-vanished tribes, all through the area. His ancestors perhaps. Lives that had dimmed out of memory. One of his grandmothers was Navajo, so he was told—and there were Ute and Apache in his blood. At times he wondered if that blood in his veins made a difference. For a summer, he'd worked for the Park Service at one of the Indian ruins, and afterward he'd gone around the state looking at other sites, making sure the places were run right. He read books about Indians and gave his opinions freely to those in charge. But nearly all his knowledge was secondhand. Perhaps if he knew more of a certain kind of healing, of putting a man in touch with the source of his disease, opening up a certain part of the mind . . . perhaps old Gomez could be healed. His father had given up the old ways, moved far away from his people, married into another culture. He had grown up with Mexicans and Anglos. It didn't seem to matter to his childhood. Whatever he lost, it was gone before he could know what it was. He would never be able to put himself back into it—into that: opening up the moment, stamping it open in dance, drawing out whatever lay coiled within, going down to the mysterious depths where the gods took charge and led a man to where he would live or die.

He had gone the way of science, and that had its value. He did not regret that. Science could set a bone and remove a kidney stone and straighten some of the twists of nature. And every method had its casualties. But what of the disease that was a wasting of the spirit? Cureless? That week he hadn't seen old Gomez. But on his return he would have to go back, dreading what he would find.

Henry had been sleeping, but now he moved and sat up. "You

know what I dreamed," he said, excitedly. "I dreamt I saw a whole mountain of gold. Solid, man. It makes me want to gather my stuff and come right out here."

"At least you're rich in your dreams," Frank said.

"Got to get back out here pretty damn quick," he said. "You got to believe those things. You know, I heard about a woman who dreamed she hit the jackpot in Las Vegas. She got up and went there and won a million dollars. It can happen."

Disgusted, Frank got up and walked down by the riverbank, over the stretch that had been the old river bed. No doubt the river had been shifting around for centuries.

"But think, man, what it would do," Henry said, following him. "A big gold strike. Or silver. Put the place on the map again. Jobs. People with money to spend. Everything booming. Everybody happy."

Frank turned. He recognized the glazed look. Henry could have been in a trance watching mysterious figures in another world. All pointing the way to wealth.

"It could happen," Henry insisted. "It happened before. All you got to do is believe."

"Well, I'm a practical man," Frank said.

"So am I."

Frank laughed.

"Listen. We've got something good. Me and Angelo." He leaned over to whisper. "Choice stuff, planted and growing— ready to harvest the end of the summer. In California they pay tops."

So that was it, the big secret, the reason he was back in town. Overseeing the crop, waiting for the harvest. "They beat you up in California too—and worse."

"You're like my mother," Henry said, dismissing him. "And where they'd never think to look."

"Here?"

"With all the rangers? Are you crazy? No, land not far from here, where no one goes. Lots of woods. Peacock's ranch."

Frank couldn't help laughing. A joke on the old Bird, and one he'd appreciate. "I once heard there's a treasure buried on that land," Frank said. "Geronimo's gold."

"You mean the old chief?"

"Don't fall for that one. Hell, the Indians had no gold."

"I bet he did," Henry said, excited. "Got it off the white man, buried it on the land. I'd believe it."

"You're crazy, man."

"But who told you?"

"Maybe my mother, maybe somebody else." Hijo, he thought, I've put another idea in his head.

V THE FILM

Entertainment: where all the world's a stage, and all the players merely men and women. But not to the public; it loves, envies, emulates them so. Larger than life it casts them. Like the images on the screen. And away from studio and screen, the high drama must continue: marriage in headlines, divorce in photographs. And so they become their images. Then something under the surface breaks through. The "real" story. A story of child abuse. A woman dead with a coke bottle stuffed up her vagina. A court trial over a virgin supposedly seduced. A death by drugs. A cult murder. Suicide. And even then, what is the real story?

How much, Bill wondered, does the public create us? They had help certainly. And if all the fragments were put together, would they make any sense or just a single large distortion, like a prefab house put together by Buster Keaton with all the instructions mixed up.

They are waiting, he and Joan, alone together in the theater before the real preview that evening, waiting for the film to begin. Joan has insisted: How can she play her role otherwise? Though it leaves him queasy in the stomach, her demand is reasonable. He can't knock it, when everybody else is playing a role. Both on and off the screen. All the tough guys he's known who've found their image on the movie set and continue to play it the rest of their lives. More real than anything else. And he is thinking of an old actress, face half-paralyzed, gowned for television, painted up for glamour. Youth and the perfect face, though age and time rebel.

116

And the director? He is there to lead you into the dream. Let the lights dim and artifice will take you by the hand.

"It must be strange for you," Joan says, out of the silence of the empty theater. "Strange for you to be looking at this with me."

So rub it in. Roselle, both absent and present; this woman next to him neither here nor there. She doesn't look directly at him when they're together, but sometimes he catches her watching him when she thinks he's not looking.

"Maybe stranger for you to watch," he says sharply.

"Oh, I'm a good charlatan," she says.

She makes herself into a joke, wanting you to laugh or somehow make allowances. She's asking for sympathy, he's quite sure. And he has none to give.

"Then you may as well sit back and enjoy it." He can feel her bristle. He'll give her no quarter. She got her role at Roselle's expense; she has no right to triumph.

Nor does he. The last time he saw the film, just after he'd overseen the final editing, Roselle was with him, everyone telling him what a fantastic job he'd done, Roselle too. He'd got himself a film, after a long dry spell and disgust with himself. And still he wasn't sure what to think of it.

Sit up in bed thinking you've been called by a voice out of a dream, it is that remote. And reach for pad and pencil and go after that glimmer of an idea fast and furiously, nagging at you like your mama's voice—beyond the borders of consciousness, the vague itch you're forever trying to scratch. Coming to you in the middle of the night, just before you get up to answer the first call. So it came to you. Lured you into thinking you could do it. The midnight madness. The thirst, the fever, the itch. For which you'll spend your life looking for the balm. Elusive as moonglow, the mirage leading you on. And you, you stupid sonofabitch, you'll go after it. Empty your pockets, sacrifice wife and kin. Toss peace of mind to the birds with the bread crumbs. And you'll perish all the same.

Now that it is finished, you don't even know what you've got.

The lights go down. The film opens: a long shot of the desert and a train moving across it, a small black worm cutting through the vastness. Becoming larger, more fiercely metallic, blowing smoke, driving, clattering down the tracks. Arriving at a small western town, settled into the landscape, certain of its modernity. The steam engine. The railroad. Progress—the taming of the West. For the day of the frontier has passed, and it is no longer the solitary western hero who rides into town. As the credits roll, the train pulls into the station with a flush of steam, and a man rises from a seat by the window, young but not young, balding, rather overweight. A little seedy. He puts on a dark hat, picks up his cloth bag. He is wearing a clerical collar. Piety emerging from the train. To be met by a tall, lean, and impeccably dressed merchant, dark hair and sideburns, a handsome man, on his hand a diamond of impressive carat. Mr. Culver. You know the stereotype when you see it. And his sidekick, wide-eyed and obsequious, the willing tool.

"A Western," Bill says to Joan, as though she can't see for herself, "but not exactly. I love the stuff." It is not an apology. For the Western is a truly American creation. The great arena where the forces of evil enter and temporarily meet their match. A great ritual drama, and maybe the best we can do, though he doesn't want to concede that. Out of the need for the one who can do what we never can: clean up the mess and ride into the sunset. And that is why he is the hero.

Only things are too messy now; you can't make that kind of flick any more. At least he can't. Not even for the sake of entertainment.

So now it's somebody else coming into town. Not the rustlers or the lawman. It is later in the century. A new era. The West is settled. Finally, there will be nowhere else to go, except to the moon. The energy it took to cross a continent, to clear the land, and defeat the Indian is now being turned toward the civilizing order. And most folks are interested merely in carrying on their lives. Only, once again there are the contending forces. And threats. The railroads versus the cattlemen, one driving up the prices, the other grabbing up the land. Into this comes an evangelist exhorting the townsfolk to think of their sins, which have been causing the evils being brought on the town. For disease has hit the cattle, and even the town is stricken. Some say it's the water. Some say the answer is to get rid of the cattlemen, who have overgrazed the range and polluted the water. One of the cattlemen is killed by night. Posters all around the town promise good jobs on the railroad. The newspaper editor has been writing editorials against both the railroads and the cattlemen. He discovers that the evangelist is in the service of the railroad, trying to get the townspeople worked up against the cattlemen who, in turn, are squeezing out the small ranchers. He is getting threats from both sides. In that atmosphere of obsession and fear, there is the threat of violence. The townspeople are in a frenzy. People are leaving the town, dying from disease, losing their land. The editor is shot one afternoon as he stands reading a newspaper.

Bill looks over at his audience, to see how she's taking it. Joan is sitting forward like a cat watching a bird. She isn't bored; that's a comfort. But she can't be your average moviegoer. With Roselle, he'd been too absorbed with effects, camera angles to pay much attention to anything else. He'd done well there. And Roselle came through strongly; he kept telling her so. She'd had to look at herself up there, watch herself in a new role.

Now the camera focuses on the woman, not young, who works in the editor's office, who has in her face something of the stranger. Alone in the town, she has the company of neither men nor women. She does not attend church, and her only friend is the schoolteacher, who tells her she is no longer safe there. When notices begin appearing, tacked up on doorways and pillars, with the editorials that have been published in the paper, the townsfolk start getting ugly. The evangelist calls her a witch, and there is just enough in her dark looks to sic them on. They talk about running her out of town. People throw rocks in her window, pound on the door. The sheriff arrests her for disturbing the peace. But Mr. Culver saves the town any further trouble. Under the cover of darkness and of official connivance, he carries her out to the desert, rapes her, and leaves her to wander alone. There the film ends.

After all these years he'd finally got his rape scene. With sex you could do just anything now. So did it mean anything? He could justify it artistically . . .

Abruptly Joan rises and starts to leave before the lights go on.

"You didn't like it?" He follows her out, having to speed up to catch her.

They blink against the glare of the street.

She turns to face him. "It's too easy," she says.

He looks at her, knowing he's found himself in a contest and that she'll never avoid his eyes again.

"It can happen," he says. "Just look around you. It's a political statement."

"I have looked around me," she snaps. "I know all about it and I'm sick of it. The vomit on the floor, the greasy rag in the sink, and the cockroaches crawling over it. Political statement! Everything's a political statement."

"So?"

"I want something else."

"Terrific. Just send in your order. Another world. Man the spacecraft. Well, sweetheart, I didn't write the Great Script in the Sky."

She grimaces at the cliché, and he feels weakened.

"You left her worse off than when you found her," she accuses him. "It's not even tragic, just ugly. If you couldn't do better than that, you should have left her alone."

He blinks at her in the street, as if she were a child who'd just kicked him in the vitals. "Hey, what are you trying to do? The actress isn't the picture." He would have liked to strike out at her, at least break open the state of her confusion. "What do you want, a goddam message? A piece of therapy for the cast? Like peach pie? If you don't know what art is, go back to reality, friend."

"You think that's all there is?" She turns on him and starts off down the street.

"What the hell do you want anyway?"

"Discovery!" she yells.

"So discover America."

She doesn't dignify him with a reply but keeps on walking. And how the hell did she expect to get back to the lodge? What the hell does she know anyway, about the voice that finally spoke to him in the middle of the night, the obscure itch always driving him? His role and sense of mission. Who does she think she is anyway? A goddam critic? He'd like to ask her that. And he wishes like hell that it was Roselle who'd been sitting next to him, who'd turned to him after it was over and said, "Fantastic, Bill. Some of your best directing."

A queer little jolt shook her out there in the sunlight, and Jessie had to reach out for the fence to keep from falling. Steady, she told herself. Perhaps she'd had too much sun. Before her eyes, the petals of her roses blurred and trembled, swimming in the light. She tried to catch her breath, which came in little gasps, as though something snagged it on the way down, and waited for the spell to pass. If it was going to pass. For a moment she closed her eyes, as if to give herself to darkness. To make an exit. When she opened her eyes again, she was still there. Not yet, not this minute. Her vision cleared to an unusual sharpness and the snapdragons and roses became almost painfully brilliant. Crimson and pink and yellow and cream. It had all come to flowers. Striking her like needles. She couldn't tell if the spell had passed or was coming round again.

After another moment she made her way indoors, just left her trowel lying on the ground. She sat for a long time without moving. When she'd gathered her strength, she went to a cupboard she kept locked and took out a box. She didn't want to be caught short. She had secrets she'd just as soon keep. And she wanted to mull things over once again. Now that her vision was clearer, she'd be able to read a little.

It was a large box that contained her past: clippings and theater programs and articles about her acting career. Up to the year she'd left Hollywood. On the top of the pile was a letter from a director she'd had an affair with early on:

Well, you left at a good time. I guess you saw it coming. I remember those days we were together in the meetings talking about whether all art had to have a socialist message and what could be done to affect the conscience of the audience. Freedom and equality. The race question, the woman question, all the burning issues of the popular front. You got out in time, before they could find you and crucify you. Some of the rest of us weren't so lucky.

I managed to hang on, but it took some groveling. That or never do another piece of work. Look at what happened to Marsha, and she was

121

never a Party member. I went to Brewer and he told me to write a letter admitting past mistakes and he would see what he could do. See what you escaped.

Escaped. Partly because things began to scare her not long after the war: rumors about Reds, noise about rooting out the menace, something ugly in the air. And partly because her career had come to a halt. She'd had only minor roles at best, with bouts in the theater between. And she'd come to the recognition that hers was not a large talent for the stage nor the sort to make it to the top in film. She was thirty-five years old and had better find a place for herself. It might as well be obscure. Well it was, at the little college lost in the mountains of New Mexico. And there she'd stayed.

She wondered why she'd kept that letter. To remind her of her cowardice, or what? Her getting out. Quietly leaving, going to Mexico for a few months. Carrying the burden of the future. Maybe she should have stayed, fought, built a life. Now it didn't matter . . .

She paused, made herself get up and gather two or three newspapers from the kitchen, then started a little fire in the grate. The folly of keeping such rot. She should have burnt it all a long time ago. Well, Herman, she said, tossing in the letter. You did get to make pictures. I hope it was worth it. Who knew if he was alive? She didn't keep track anymore. Let oblivion have him. She watched the letter flare up and disappear. Faces danced and words came back. All that had smoldered under the surface. Political ferments and loyalties, buried accusations. The worst of times, the best buried so deep you thought nothing from them would ever surface again. That was what fear did. Changed people into wolves and dogs. Made you cringe and cower and find the worst in yourself. She didn't stick around for it, though for a while she knew what her friends were suffering. Had run while there was still time.

Only . . . She held up a picture close to her eyes. She didn't know if he was alive either. Gabe. Not a bad actor then. Might have done something decent. Finished in the wash. But that happened in the fifties. He had the looks; that's what they wanted then. And he hadn't got to do much except show them off. If she'd gone ahead and had the child: Should I have told you, Gabe? Would it have mattered? When you think of bringing a child into that world. Anyway, I was leaving it all behind, and I had to earn my way. Nobody would have hired me. Cowardice too? Once she'd written him a long letter, telling him what she'd done. But she'd never mailed it. Though the compulsion would come over her, rise up like a lump in the throat: write him and tell him. For what? To put another knot into his life? She threw the picture into the fire. The flame bit a brown hole in the center, where his smile had been.

All past and gone. Their child hovering over her, a dim possibility. And really she hadn't wanted children. Not cut out for the mother role. She'd have hated the dollhouse and equally hated competing with a man for a career. Hollywood was too much for wives and mothers. That's what she'd told herself, though, in fact, she knew when she left she couldn't have stayed in Hollywood. Finished with all that. And spared herself the rest. Cowardice too.

She threw in the old theater programs. The parts no longer interested her: Nora. Katherine, the shrew. Clytemnestra. She'd had some good ones. All of it better than being a drama teacher in a one-horse town. Well, she'd played that one out too, created the role for herself. Crusty spinster from an old southern family, though in fact she hailed from Illinois. A genteel lover of the theater. A believer in the old values. Straight and stiff. She'd done the part especially well. They treated her like a lady. She gave them class, with her aristocratic pose and her high view of the drama. In this raw town it was easy to impress the locals. She directed their wretched plays showing off their aspiring and talentless youth, taught the drama, and got by. Nobody bothered her.

Except Roselle. Talent bothered her. Should you let it go down the drain? Or watch it get crushed to death by the machinery? Scylla and Charybdis. She had to give it a chance. Selfishly even—to give herself a chance. Win a way past her own mediocrity. Let someone carry the impulse forward. Her only future after all. And she still had a few connections. She got Roselle out of that wretched place and sent her to people who could do something for her. And they did. And kept her secret.

Even so, Roselle had got caught, the fool. As she was bound to do one way or another, even if she hadn't married so fatally. No wonder she'd caved in. The roles for a woman then. Trivial. Say what you would about the stars. The old conflicts about role were all settled finally in the bedroom and kitchen. As though a woman couldn't have any sense of who she was, any destiny worth thinking about. Thank God for the theater, she thought. Not much there now, but at least for a time there'd been the legacy of the past. Her career: certain graspings at possibility. Losses. ("What price salvation now, Major Barbara?")

And ironies. There in the box were still some letters from Roselle she hadn't been able to throw away—thanking her with the ebullience of the young, describing her friends, her training, in a single breathless rush. The little girl in the big town . . . Old notices from *Variety*. Pictures of Roselle. The charm was still there, the intensity. No, she hadn't been wrong about that. She set them aside. The other stuff she fed to the fire, one thing after another. But Roselle she kept. Of whom the images in her memory were clearer than the ones before her eyes. Even so, she had to have her a little longer. A few scraps saved out of the rubble.

She poked out the fire.

Once again he returned, stood looking over the dark shadows that sat against the dark. For a moment, Lauren listened to the crickets chirring in the grass. A house falling apart. And he'd been holed up there alone in the heat of summer, breathing the choking dust. He'd pulled out the rags stuffed into the broken windowpanes, for the windows themselves wouldn't budge, and lived with the flies buzzing in. Only his father could have shut everything out: the plaster that fell around him, the groan of the floorboards, the bugs. Just living his dream, taken over by it. Scarcely living in the house. The dream had eaten out his insides, left him gaunt and wild, not even in the world anymore.

If anything, the paintings belonged there in that house of spiders, where in the mingling of the smells of turpentine and linseed oil and dust, his father's work had come to its final flowering. They spoke of an old order crumbling, the fabric rent, as though a familiar ground had shifted. But that wasn't all.

Through the cracks ghostly figures entered, things forgotten but present coming from the realm of what had been and would always be. They were drawn with elongated bodies and unearthly colors and expressions, haunting Lauren with their presence. At first they strung out his nerves, made him look around when the house creaked. Gave him a perpetual unease with their twisted bodies. He wanted to smash something in their expression, threatening, like the bad wind from another planet. He'd moved into the bedroom with the hope of comfort, for he could never have slept in the same room with them. Even so, he kept waking in the middle of the night, with the sensation that they'd been looking into his sleep, about to find entry there. And he'd stayed awake, trying to shake off the feeling that they'd take over the nightscape of his mind and haunt his dreams forever.

During the day their eyes were on him. They must have come upon his father, these figures, invaded him, taken over the decaying house. Hallucinations. Waiting to enter his mind as well. He knew from the first he'd never give them to the public.

With an inspiration worthy of his father, he'd done what he had to do. Changed everything: toned down the figures, relieved the expressions of their violence, assured the viewer that when he turned back to his everyday world, it would still be there, safe, and he could go about his business.

An incredible number of paintings still surrounded him, too many, the efforts of these past few years. As though his father's mind turned molten with his visions, taking him in thrall, pouring out faster than he could put them to canvas. To put them into shape, Lauren determined, would require the rest of his life. But they'd keep the money rolling in. For the exhibit he'd done just enough to satisfy the public curiosity, even though he'd worked to exhaustion. Now they were his paintings, the thirty he'd chosen to work on. Only one of these he didn't change: the large canvas of the town with its ghostly faces. Every time he went toward it with intention in his brush, he felt a resistance as though he were facing an angry mob. He couldn't touch it, though at one point he'd picked up a knife to slash it. Curiously, whatever prevented him became an impulse to include the painting in the exhibit. To expose it to public scorn. He expected the fury that had first greeted the impressionists. Instead the townsfolks had been drawn to it with astonishment and wonder, clustering in front of it like a swarm of ants. As though it spoke to some obscure instinct. He should have known how despicable they were. Too stupid for their own good. He'd have liked to string them up and watch their little legs twitch and dangle.

Now with the exhibit over, he was back to celebrate his secret triumph. He pulled off his tie and tore open his collar. Eased off his new shoes and slipped on a pair of ancient huaraches his father had worn. He'd bought a bottle of whiskey, which he opened, pouring some into a grimy cup. He drank and leaned into the heat that burned from his throat into his stomach.

"In time they'll know," he said, as to a roomful of listeners. "When the day of reckoning comes, the betrayers will be struck down."

He held up his glass. "To the master of light and dark," he said, and drank. "Rembrandt!"

The masters of dark had apparently triumphed that night, for outside a black, moonless sky obliterated the mountains, and a wind blew across the desert. Such light as he could see by came from a single bulb in the copper chandelier, a weak light that left the walls dark and the corners in shadow. It should have left the figures in the canvases dim, the colors without tone. Yet a strange light seemed to emanate from within them: a bluish white hue, a diamond light, from one; the glowing blood red of garnets from another; an opalescent luster in a third, a flash of fire under the blue light. He got up to turn the canvases against the wall. A moment's pause and he turned away a young woman whose look threatened to unman him at the same time she beckoned him against his will.

"Are you afraid, Lauren? It's only life, you know."

"For God's sake, Lilly. You know I have my career. When I'm known, when I'm famous . . ."

"Is that what you're living for?"

"Christ, what else is there?"

The reproach in her voice, the line of her head as she turned away—she had given these things to memory, to paint, if he cared to paint them. Fortunately, he didn't. It was too trivial a subject. He should have taken her; it was what she wanted, holding out her hand to him like that. He should have bent her back, given her what she was asking for. Something to remember him by.

It wasn't enough for him, the play of lights and darks on the surface of things, though revealing the inward. His father had taken in everything. Had looked for the light that lives in gems or stained-glass windows. Greater thickness of paint . . . "To Rouault," he said, with a flourish of his glass, and drank. No, let him take that back. Let him keep his clowns and Christ figures. Rouault hadn't done anything for his father or for him. The thicker the paint, they told him, the more gross the expression . . .

"But don't you see, there's something flat there? The emotional tone, it isn't coming through."

"I don't understand. I've worked on this for weeks. I haven't slept, scarcely eaten."

"It's not a matter of mortifying the flesh, you idiot; it's a matter of giving yourself to the feeling. It's not just flat, it's dead."

Oh, they wanted you to believe that, with their petty notions of what talent is. They think you can't see the envy living at the heart of it. They want to make you over to fit what's trendy. Say my work is flat, or mawkish. Liars and hypocrites. Go fall in love with craziness instead. To goggle at. It's interesting to you, the craziness. Let the fellow go mad; then he can paint.

Van Gogh. And now Collingwood, père. Crazy father, waiting to destroy the world.

He poured himself another tumbler of whiskey. No toasts to them either. "To the real artist," he said, raising his glass.

"Why did you do it, Lauren?"

He sat for a moment listening to the noises in the walls. He had nothing to be afraid of.

"Why? Well, Daddy, because I could. My talent."

"Traitor!"

"Oh, you'd think so. Wanting to have it all your way."

"Your talent? Bringing things down to your own level. Not even flying with somebody else's wings. Just shooting them to the ground."

"It's too much."

"Excess? Of course, excess. And you can't stand it. Crawling on your belly though life. Coward and traitor!"

He started to giggle. "It didn't get you anywhere, did it? Now you have to get there through me. You want to sweep everything away. Leonardo's deluge."

"Only things gone dead, to make room for what can live. I could *see*."

"You can't have it, Daddy."

Hand unsteady now, he poured more whiskey into the cup. Guardian of the public mind, protector of the real. He had suppressed what threatened to tear the seams apart. Even as he looked at the figures of the paintings on the walls, they seemed to grow taller, more formidable. If he didn't stop them, they would rush into the room, spill out into the streets, and take over. The deluge would sweep everything away, gas stations and motels, housing tracts and shopping malls, TVs and motorcycles. He would have to stop them. He staggered up from the broken chair and found the broom, poured turpentine over the end and lit it. He set the burning end to a stack of canvases. *Perish in flames.*

The fire seemed to sweep into his head, and as it came he could see a greater conflagration. And now let the earth become a bath of fire, so that all the trees are burning, the wood crackling and blazing, so that the birds fly up and the air is black with wings. And now the elephants trumpet from the jungles and the lions roar and all the animals flee in the brush as the fire rages. *Get back. Never come into the world.* The fire rages. And now the towns and cities are overcome, and great crowds of people rush to the edges of the sea, as behind them the black skeletons of trees stand over the blackened earth. And now let the birds drop from the sky, falling bits of char as the clouds sizzle and steam till they are ghosts in the blackening air. And see how a great beast emerges from wood, with human head and lion's body, trampling the dying creatures, tossing them into the air, tearing their limbs from their bodies. And all the ores of the earth are melted and pour over the dying earth, silver and gold and iron, a stream of metal hardening into veins like twisted roots.

Better to destroy all.

The whole earth. On the promontories and islands stand human beings huddled together, their smoke-begrimed faces streaked with tears. But the fire is coming to them too. Some throw themselves in agony into the sea, tossing their children

128

before them. Animals crazed by fire attack those that are left and rend them apart, while all around the smoke fills the sky. Pockets of gas explode and shatter the mountains, great clouds rising into the air.

Destroy the creation. The paintings were all burning now, and now the fire had seized upon the old, dry wood and flames were shooting up the walls. He stood for a moment watching the burning canvases. They would no longer haunt him. He looked around astonished. Fire circling the room. Where would he go? Saints and angels, I am here.

The heat was terrible and the smoke filled his lungs. He felt suddenly weak, the fire in his head. He couldn't see anymore. He reached out, arms flailing, tried to remember where the door was. Stumbled and fell before he reached it. Then the flames rolled over him, caressed him, and passed beyond.

They kept coming, the crowd materializing there in the night. People all around her. Standing. Breathing hard. Those who had poured out of the theater, those the sirens had brought. The town aroused, turned out of doors, watching as the smoke and flames billowed upward and the wail of sirens brought out the fire trucks. The buildings on either side of the theater were burning too, though how far the fire had spread no one could tell. Joan's eyes smarted from the smoke, and she could feel the heat. She was still trembling. Fire! When it comes, you go crazy. You have to get out, you and everybody else. You'll trample your kind like a herd of animals. She stared in front of her, looking at no one. They all stood anonymously in the crowd. Mexican women from the nearby houses stood around her in the street, their children jabbering excitedly. All watching with those who had fled up the hill to look down at the burning midsection of town.

Fire—and you are shaken, your whole sense of things. And you're left to stare at where things were. Fire sweeping through the theater and across the old section of town, blackening everything in its path. Tomorrow they would stare at ruins. She could scarcely remember what had happened. Everything lost in the panic. Unreal. The local master of ceremonies starting things off so grandly, taking his time, stretching his moment in the sun till the audience grew restless. "Now, Curry Gatlin, I've known him since Hector was a pup and now he's mayor of our fair town." Then the mayor, who thanked half the town, one by one, everybody standing up for applause. The election was coming up. ". . . our fair town . . . achievement . . . pride . . . the eyes of the state and nation . . ." Something to cling to, something to make much of. Here you needed it. Then the fire swept it away. Halfway through: a closeup of Roselle, then smoke. And panic.

The race toward the exits. Where had it started, this blaze suddenly on them, their lives in jeopardy? It ran through her mind again, the hurtling of bodies, pushing, elbows jabbing, the same images, the same events. Stuck in the same place. Fear and running. Get out. Don't push. The herd of frightened animals.

And now, looking down at the scene from the hill above, the questions: Was anybody hurt? Are you all right? Ambulances had come and gone.

The fire appeared to be moving farther back into the section of old houses and decrepit buildings where it must have originated. The town, burned out in the center. A great gaping hole.

No place is ever a flat photograph in two dimensions. Not this town, nor any other. The town across the screen of the mind hurls the present into your eyes, but it never lies still. Nor the past lying there in wait.

She saw . . . what did she see there in the darkness? Shapes caught in the light of the flames. Figures dancing in the hell of smoke and fire. And tomorrow, look out at ruins, no longer smoking, but soaked with water, giving off the sharp, acrid smell of burning. Things gone up in smoke. *That's time, that's all things burning. This town, any town—it goes on. You break your connection and go your way. And take only the last frames that moved across your eyes. They become your dream, the actors going on, coming off. And you, the spectator, watching it happen over and over, till what happened and what you've created become a blur. Where is the story then? Pinch your wrist: flesh and blood. But you have come back a ghost.*

Now all the people were coming down to look, standing there as she was doing, not really seeing anything, not even thinking of the blackened walls, but only talking about what was happening. "I can remember when they put in that old theater," someone near her said. "The first silent films. When I was just a kid." But for Joan, there was no past, nothing really for her to remember of this town. But it didn't matter. All towns were one to her: in each she had buried her losses.

Gene, where are you? You loved me once. And we could have been on top of things. I know I made you miserable; I was so restless. I didn't know what I wanted. I wanted you to do it for me, write the splendid book to bring you fame and fortune. God knows you tried hard enough. Sitting in front of that machine, poking at the keys, piling up the pages. But so much was blank. I'd pick them up and read—I shouldn't have done that— and say, "But is she the sort of woman who'd just walk into the house and take over that way? Why is he always walking naked through the rooms?" Oh, Gene, I'm a blunderer. I just barge into things, knocking half of them over.

When everything broke up, and you left and your kids were sent away to school, Molly died of grief. Too much for a mere dog. Remember how she always peed on the carpet when any of us came home, she was so full of joy. She had to have all of us. And we broke her heart . . .

. . . that tried to hold too much. Tried to do what we couldn't. That's dangerous, to stake your life on that. Or to stake your life on any passion. Such blunderers. And blundering is my best talent. Into marriage and out of it again.

I'd not have married Dan but for a mix-up, an assignation at the motel with a man I didn't like all that much. Sex that time, sweetie. A little quickie. And I ran into Dan, who was out for the same thing. The four of us—I was ready to dump Henry— were all still with our mates, four separate hells. But his date didn't show, and neither did mine. How's that for coincidence? Meant for each other . . . hah! I think I loved his mustache and his anecdotes. The way he could pour out drinks and troubles and give you the breath of them in bed. Speak of passion.

He had the most incredible underwear of any man who has stripped down to the skivvies for me: stripes, spotted leopard jobs. Proud of his muscles. No, the rest wasn't terrific. A man for weights and jogging, for fitness. Hiking and skiing. Outdoor type. I blundered around after him, scarring my knees, getting cut and bruised and scratched. We had a houseful of children between us, all but one his. Growing onward and upward. Well, Gene, it ended like it began. Back from a trip to Florida in time for his new sweetie, the au pair girl—from Corsica at that.

The others? No marriages, nothing permanent. A psychic, who knew what I wanted to do before I wanted to do it myself. Intolerable. Then a building contractor. A physicist. A folk singer. I alienated all their mothers. I'm terrible with the mamas. Ladies' clubs and Sunday church: no thanks. Nor all the cant of self-denial. Even when I've groveled in excuses for doing badly. Well, Gene, that about sums it up. I could put it all in a letter, send it special delivery. I have written you hundreds of letters and never sent any of them. Do I delude myself that I still love you? No. But we could talk. And you still live in the spaces of my head.

"Miss More, would you care to say anything about the fire?"

"I think it's a poor idea."

A young man holding pad and pencil looked at her strangely. "I've been interviewing some people who were in it."

"It was terrible," she said suddenly, as though she just now realized she'd escaped from a fire. Her knees began to buckle. She could barely remember anything. Only the maddened crowd, the fear. "Did anybody . . . is anybody missing?"

"We're not sure yet. One old man overcome by smoke . . . took him off to the hospital. Kept yelling about the Apaches. Gone out of his head."

Suppose I had died, Gene, she thought, unable to stop shaking. Would it have mattered? All the failures gone up in smoke.

"Here, now. You're going to catch your death in this night air."

She looked in the direction of the voice, which she recognized but couldn't place. Then she knew him: the man who'd scared her at the exhibit. Peacock. Where had he materialized from? He put his jacket over her shoulders and stood beside her, a dark shadow in the red light. "I'm relieved to see you safe."

A marginal safety she was barely clinging to. "Something's burning," she cried. "It's like an old skin. I left it all back there," she babbled.

"Does it feel all right?"

"I don't know."

"You're safe," he assured her.

Did he know what he was saying? She dared not trust him. "No," she wept. Joan Gallant had died in the fire. Suppose her name appeared in the newspaper as one of the casualties. But if Roselle came back . . . Her mind raced ahead into a chaos of possibilities. Joan, a ghost to her own life. Like Roselle. But she wouldn't come back . . .

"I'm fine now," she said, uncertainly. There was nothing to be afraid of, she told herself. Who was this man? She stood uneasily with him at her side as she concentrated on the fiery glow unsettling the darkness. Her skin prickled, as though in response to some communication he was sending her. She found herself leaning against him. She must put her mind elsewhere. She was sure he was a danger to her. And if Roselle came back . . . Her mind raced round with that. It wouldn't matter. It would just be another blunder to worry about: Will the real Roselle More please step forward? Back at the theater she watched herself get caught in the flames. She remembered now; the man standing next to her, she had clung to his arm in the panic of the burning theater.

"Am I dead or alive?" she asked hollowly.

"I think you need to get out of here. Come," he said. "I'll take you home." He began to lead her through the throng.

Where was Bill? Where were the others? Why wasn't he there to take care of her?

"Nothing is destroyed," she heard Peacock saying. "It's just left a hole in things. But then something else will show up. It generally does."

She looked at him. Suppose she'd died and taken on another form. A sacrifice, dying in the fire. An accidental sacrifice, to her curiosity or something even more obscure. And if she took on Roselle's . . . what would she now make of herself? Take on another role, another fate?

"Thank you for . . ."

"Nothing at all," he said.

She looked at him again. In his face she found an expression, an attitude of knowing that suggested a mastery of the lie in which she was engaged at the beginning. A man who knew her secret. Perhaps she had drawn him to her on just such an account. Friend or enemy? It was as though he'd led her back to life. And he had seen her in her terror. But she couldn't let him rattle her. Whatever challenge he presented, she had to take it on.

This is my town now, she thought. No, she wasn't able to make that claim. Not yet. She was still too shaky.

VI   PERFORMANCES

The fire had struck the heart of the town, leaving a blackened core: the theater and the old Greek's candy store alongside, the high-school hangout, and buildings on both sides. Destroying a furniture store and a men's shop, then depriving the Benevolent and Protective Order of Elks of a meeting place, as well as the poker players who'd met, supposedly in secret, upstairs above the Buffalo Bar and sometimes lost a thousand dollars at a sitting. The fire blazed through the bar, bottles of spirits popping in the heat and spraying glass in all directions. A rough place on Saturday nights, with a fight or a stabbing to puncture the general drunkenness, now and then some fellow having to hold his guts in with his hands till they got him to the hospital. Then the fire moved on, roaring through the houses on the streets behind the theater, the old frame and brick Victorian houses with gingerbread along the porches and columns in front, the fancy houses built when respectable folks were settling in and there was money and the future lay coiled like a copper spring. Before the combined efforts of two fire departments had finally subdued the blaze, one wall of the old city hall had collapsed, laying the building open to the elements.

So that now as the townspeople came to look at the damage, they found the broken walls and splintered boards that enclosed the charred interiors still reeking and smoking from the water poured over them. It was a street filled with wanderers, as disoriented as amnesiacs. Those who'd lost their houses or businesses could not believe it but kept staring at the ruins as though they held the mystery. Occasionally someone bent over to pick up an object that had escaped the flames—a piece of chain, a pan, a shoe—as one might pick up an arrowhead. Several dogs wandered along the streets, looking for their owners.

For the time being, those dispossessed were quartered in the homes of friends or relatives or in the motels on the edge of town till they had somewhere else to go. The insurance companies were being notified and now came the business of assessing losses, filing claims. The town council met the following day in emergency session. Meanwhile the sites were blocked off and trucks and men came to cart away the debris. For a long time they would live with boarded buildings or fenced-in foundations, an eyesore that you'd first stare at and then grow accustomed to. You'd think about how the town had been going down, wonder if the theater would be rebuilt, there was so little to keep it going. Or the city hall. That white elephant. High ceilings and wasted space, the burden of another era. And what about the furniture store? Would the old man open up again or just retire?

"Well, there are plenty of empty houses around," Virgil Langtry commented, staring into his coffee, as though it might prove oracular and reveal the fortunes of the town. What did it all add up to? He was not accustomed to such thoughts, but now that things were going from bad to worse, he was unable to sleep nights. And even under the fluorescent lights of the Cactus Cafe, he saw his life going by and ending up . . . where? Would it matter if the whole town went up in smoke? Might as well go to wrack and ruin for all the buyers lining up for his real estate. Real, only if you believed you could make a future out of it. He dreamed of Arizona, of moving west to fresh opportunity.

And plenty of graves, the undertaker thought gloomily. He'd never run out of business until the town itself was done with. What a consolation: to batten off death.

The jeweler who'd looked up to the great powers of copper and silver and gold did not know what to make of fire. He had squinted up his eyes all morning looking into watchworks.

"What can you make of a burned-out town?" The mayor put the question.

"Fire, flood—things fall and rise again. Good morning, gentlemen."

"Didn't see you come in, Bird."

"How are you, Lester, Emmett, Mayor, everybody? Got to see the sparks dance, didn't we?"

He could be cheerful about it; he had nothing to lose. Envy the man who has nothing to lose.

"You don't have to live here," Lester told him, "or at least you don't do a helluva lot of it. We've got to put up with the whole mess. What do you do with a burned-out town?"

"Where's your enterprise, gentlemen? You're the leaders, the ones to spur things on, get it to rise up out of the flames. The old pioneer spirit. What brought us out here in the first place?"

"You got any suggestions?" They looked at him, cocksure bastard. He'd have his ideas all right, only who'd want to hear them?

"Why, you've got one film here. Make another. Make a dozen. Think of the employment."

He was pulling their leg, standing there, smiling down at them. No one asked him to join them.

"Like the one they made on your land, Bird. Why, they chased that crew out with rocks and pitchforks. Lots of people got upset . . . You selling out to the Commies that way."

"Hell, I've got no politics. But nobody's forced to look at the damned thing. Haven't seen it myself. Though they claim it's still going round speaking of the dignity of your Mexican miner and his woman."

"A pack of lies. The miners themselves laughed it down."

Bird shrugged. "Well, like I say, I got nothing at stake. People can figure it out for themselves. And if there's a grain of truth in it, probably it'll get threshed out one way or another."

"For all you care."

"Tell me, do you think it did any more harm than most things? Considering the lies that get passed around for truth."

"You're the one to talk, Bird."

"Well, if you're thinking of my daddy or my granddaddy, their talents weren't lost on the town."

The mayor found Bird looking straight at him. "They probably found a few imitators."

"Is that a fact?"

"I think it's a truth. I'll tell you what to do with a burned-out town. Look at its insides. Go down into the hole. Good morning, gentlemen."

"That sonofabitch," Virgil said, after they watched him go out the door and cross the street. "Standing there, making fun of us. I wouldn't mind . . ."

"Half the people in this town have some grudge against him," the undertaker said. "His family slickered with the best; no wonder he's come out of that."

"I can't figure it out, though," Lester said. "Things go his way. He's got that property all in hand now. Nothing's gonna snatch it from him."

"But nothing's foolproof," the mayor reminded them. "Look what happened to his grandfather. The worst thing is to assume he doesn't have a chink in the armor. It takes fire to fight fire."

"What have you got in mind?"

"Nothing yet," the mayor said. "But I know this: we're wasting our time sitting on our butts staring into the cinders. He's given me an idea, maybe two or three."

"Well, let's hear it."

"We still have the film people. We'll still have the celebration. With things falling apart, people have to get together. We'll have a rally. I'll put it out over the radio. And call Ed Link at the paper. Have them put out an extra edition, all about the fire."

They were of two minds. He might have something; then again, he might not. Would it bring in any money, do anything for business? You couldn't bleed a stone.

"Fight fire with fire," the mayor said. "Come on. We got work to do."

That night Emmett Early would have a vision of fire, voices speaking out of the flames. The voice of Bird and the voice of Curry Gatlin, two figures emerging, both on horses galloping across the screen. He couldn't remember the colors of the horses.

The old man, Merle Fullmer, whose hold on the present had become increasingly tenuous, was swept away in the confusion of the fire. No one knew whether he had been in the theater during the panic, but he was found not long afterward wandering the streets, not knowing where he was going, saying that all his family had been killed. He was taken to the hospital for observation, and Frank Lucero, who had been tending those overcome by smoke, saw to him as well. In the hospital the old man was full of terror.

"There they are, coming at us. Daddy, oh, Daddy—taking his gun and trying to fend them off, Mother turning the coach. Oh, he's falling. They've killed him. Mama, trying to grab me up . . ."

The fire had unstrung him, Frank concluded. It could be a night's sleep would restore him to clarity. He had the nurse give the old man a sedative and in the morning found him calm and in a way lucid. It was clear, though, that the name Merle Fullmer meant nothing to him. He was Everett Collins, who'd been taken by the Apaches and then had escaped. He spoke of the capture of Geronimo and living on the reservation. The events of the past forty years had dropped out of his mind.

The scenes before the old man's eyes were more vivid than Frank's own memories. The Indian part of Frank Lucero was vague and remote. His boyhood in the adobe shack on the edge of town, where his family had lived while his father worked in the Arizona mining operations, wasn't all that strong a link to what filled the old man's head. His interrupted sessions of schooling, his efforts to go to college. His travels around the state looking at artifacts and ruins of ancient Indian life, trying to figure out something about his past. The objects in the glass cases, their beauty and utility belonging to other hands, were all but lost to him. Not even his time on the reservation when he and Linda went back to doctor the Indians, his people, had given him what he was looking for.

Here was one more he doubted that he knew how to cure. Gomez afflicted by the present, old Fullmer afflicted by the past. Maybe the sickness was larger than both of them, greater even than the town. What was he supposed to do about them?

When he left the hospital, he went by old man Fullmer's house and asked the neighbor, Mrs. Streater, about him.

"He's just gone funny," she told him. "Right out of his head. Comes of sitting there all by himself just reading and reading those old books. I kept saying to Dawson—that's my husband— that man is going clean out of his mind. Why, I'd see his light on up to all hours at night, and he'd be marching back and forth up and down, yelling all such stuff. "General, there's been an attack on the settlers. Marshal the troops." And about half the time, seemed like he was an Indian too. All kind of yelling and whooping around. He kept telling me about the Collins boy. Now he's got that in his head. You might better phone up his daughter in Glenwood."

The old man had lived alone for years. Though he'd had a wife, no one remembered her or when she'd died or left. The interior of his little house was crammed with stacks of *New Mexico* magazine, and copies of *The American West*. He had cut pictures from some of these and tacked them all over the walls. Frank paused to look at them. In one, a cavalry officer in a tattered uniform, one arm in a sling, surveyed a deserted settler's cabin. In another, he recognized Geronimo, the tough old face impassive, hands manacled. They'd never figured out what to think about him, Frank thought, old renegade that he was. Roaring around like a force of nature. Recalcitrant as the desert that bred him.

He walked back over the cracked linoleum into the kitchen. More pictures on the walls. Old calendars. Newspaper clippings. Stacks of magazines on the floor. A faucet dripped. The kitchen smelled of lard and fried potatoes and bacon. There was a spider on which the old man did his cooking, a couple of saucepans and a skillet hanging on the wall above. Three plates, two cups, and several glasses had set him up for housekeeping.

Stuck on the wall was an envelope with the name of the daughter, and when he went back to his office, Frank called her up. She said she was too badly crippled with arthritis to get down, they'd have to see to the old man themselves. Frank wasn't sure what to do with him. If he could get along on his own—buy his food at the store and cash his Social Security checks at the bank—maybe there was no harm in his thinking he had escaped from the Apaches. A dose of reality didn't always improve matters. The old man had been a survivor after a fashion, could perhaps go on surviving.

He might be better off his way; who knows? Frank thought. Everything was so complicated. You could survive, but sometimes it wasn't enough. He himself was walking a pretty thin line.

A Los Angeles reporter had caught a rumor that Roselle More had disappeared, and made a call to Walter McKay, who was able to tell him he could speak to Roselle herself if he wanted to. The private investigation being carried on had yielded conflicting and puzzling results: a woman answering Roselle's description had bought a plane ticket in Albuquerque for Mexico City. A body discovered in the Rio Grande provoked some speculation, but it had been in the river too long. He received a report that someone fitting Roselle's description had entered a sanitarium in the mountains. No names would be given out. Walter was at a loss.

"So now what?" he said to Bill. "Either she's gone for good or she's in bad shape."

"God," Bill said. "The more we get into it, the messier it is. I'd like to fly out to L.A. and check the sanitarium."

"Even if it is Roselle," Walter argued, "it sounds like she doesn't want to see any of us."

"Damn it all. And I did it to her."

"Horseshit. You're not *that* important. You're just one thing that happened to her. It was a mistake bringing her back. Face it. Something died during those years."

"I don't buy it. And I'm not willing to write her off. Criminal, that's what it would be. Especially now. Go ahead and check out; you're going to do it anyway."

"Hold on. Just a minute."

But Bill waved him off. He'd already convinced himself Walter was going to wash his hands of the whole mess. Let him. He'd stick with it. More and more, the whole thing took on a moral twist. Walter had accused him of a certain self-righteousness from the very beginning. Making himself into a conscience. That had bothered him. And Joan's reaction to the film was a set of needles in his skin. He could not get her off his mind, or Roselle and his part. He'd never wanted to betray her. That was the word that sat on him: *betray*. He'd done his best. But that best . . .

"I wonder if we can persuade Joan," he said, thinking aloud.

"To do what?"

"To go on with it."

"You mean even after we leave here?"

"Exactly."

"Preposterous. Why, they'd see right through it. And what would be the point?"

"You're the publicity expert. I didn't think I'd have to draw you a map. With Joan, we can give Roselle the time she needs."

"Christ! You still believe you can turn this around? You're crazy. Boy, I mean . . . Just remember, I was against the whole idea from the beginning. It's made a mockery out of a disaster. But to go on with it. Bouncing both of them back and forth . . . that's absolutely crazy."

He didn't care. Obsessed and crazy. "What the hell are you suggesting? That I'm exploiting her? Is that what you think?"

"Well, aren't you?"

Bill stared at him. "Hell, I don't know," he said, letting go. "I really don't know. Say it was a cheap trick to begin with . . . But now . . ."

"It won't help Roselle; you've gotta know that. And the whole thing's so goddam bizarre. But it'll make a story." He shrugged. "Go ahead, if you're all so set on it. Might even help the film."

"Good old Walter. Can't help smelling a publicity angle down the road," Bill said nastily.

"You think you can avoid it?" Walter said, with a laugh.

"Go to hell."

"Anyway, I'll be on a plane out of here in less than forty-eight hours. Then you can take this whole goddam . . ."

They were interrupted by a knock, and when Joan, who'd stood outside the door hesitant at first, entered, she received such a welcome from both men that she was momentarily confused and flattered. "Nobody's been this glad to see me for ten years," she said.

"So I get to keep on playing?" Joan said, sobered by the prospect, even though she'd seen herself die in the fire—had shed her old life and watched the dead skin burn. The fire was still vivid in her mind. She'd walked out of it half alive, glad to lean on the arm offered her. And Peacock had given her a certain nerve, she couldn't say how. He'd been there, and she'd come unsteadily through the flames. Nothing that dramatic, but the image wouldn't leave her mind. Now she had to go on with it.

She had even imagined bluffing Walter into letting her have

her way. Practiced the part, the fatal woman, knowing she had all the cards in her hand, ready to blackmail or betray him in public.

"You mean you intend to go on with it?" she could hear him saying in the scenario she was making up.

"Why quit when you're just getting good at it?"

He would look at her. "You've got some nerve." She'd won a certain admiration. "And besides, who knows but that she'll turn up eventually?"

"She won't."

"What makes you so sure?"

"Because I am. Besides, wouldn't it make you look foolish, suddenly to announce that you've been fooling everybody? They wouldn't like that, would they?" She'd tilt her head, look him right in the eye.

"But that's not how it works, hon. She turns up and you quietly fade away."

"Suppose I don't. I didn't sign a contract for the part. It was a desperation move. Well, the part's not over."

"And how would you like to get in real trouble?"

"You can't blackmail me. You're an accessory."

"And I'll swear, and the others will swear, that you're accessory to Roselle's disappearance and created a fraud all on your own."

That threat came out quite without her premeditation. Calling her bluff. Quite enough to scare her unless she had some help with the logic of the whole thing. But if people could be bought off—these folks had loot—who was she to defend herself? The fatal woman wasn't exactly her forte, though she'd have liked to give it a whirl. She'd have to keep it at simple fraud.

Perhaps it would work best to tease him into it. Archness might do what threats would undo.

"I like the part so well I thought I'd go on playing it the rest of my life."

"Think you could pull it off, do you?" he'd say, not without astonishment. "With all those who know Roselle? Come on."

"Who knows what I can do? And why not take the gamble? After all, what've I got to lose?"

"Ah, the little girl wants money and fame."

"Is that news to you?" She would look into his eyes.

He was the sort of man accustomed to being charming; she'd learned that in the first five minutes she knew him. So practiced and skilled he was in the art that even when his immediate aim was neither physical nor material, he could not but be charming. And from the tidbits he let drop, he was the great lover. Bragging, of course. She suspected that he never entered into an affair with any thought of permanence but always with the attitude that a woman was rather the luckier for the encounter. And though, as she imagined it, she might catch him short for a moment, he was accustomed to sudden shifts of emphasis. Perhaps he might ponder where a moment's clutching at advantage had led him. But he couldn't claim that deception was altogether new to him. He'd spent his time with images, and though a man of taste, he'd made his money from the tasteless and the vulgar and thought no worse of himself or his clients for doing so. In effect, she'd hinted they were both shams.

He'd smile. "At any rate, you've got guts. I like that. Perhaps you could say I opened a door for you."

"You might say that." The shade of irony would be delicate.

And he could appreciate that irony. The back side of his talents, a slip, an inadvertence almost, here was, you might say, his creation. Standing there, perhaps to haunt him, exert a power of some kind.

"So what do you want of me?" Standing, hands outstretched, palms open, as though he'd just handed her a sword to use on him, without really expecting her to do it.

Then she'd hesitate a moment, as if she herself might not be clear about her own feelings. "I'll think about it."

"Oh, not fair. When you ask a woman what she wants, you better hold her to the moment."

"Too easy," she'd say and look at him as though to see him more clearly.

Then he'd walk up to her and put his hands on her shoulders. "Listen, Joan, I'm all for you."

End of scenario. One of the hokier ones, but . . .

Only, now it happened that her imaginings hadn't taken in what Bill, not Walter, was saying to her:

"You see, we thought the past couple of days would take care of things. Only now if there's a chance for Roselle . . . if something's happened . . . We've got to buy some time."

And she startled herself by saying, "Roselle, Roselle, everything for Roselle. And what about me?"

A long moment of silence delivered no answer. Bill was still sore at her over the film. And her words of attack wouldn't leave his mind. She was becoming too important. At first comparing her to Roselle had been like watching two images simultaneously that could never come together, no matter what their similarities. Now it was like having one superimposed on the other, as if they deepened and enriched each other. More energetic this one, less tired. True, Roselle had been a ball of fire when she was young. But this one, though she'd taken her knocks, seemed eager for more. Now she appeared to be grabbing at something, even ready to cling tenaciously. Pushing her way into the space. He didn't like it, but he was forced to answer her.

"What about you, Joan?" he asked.

"Who do you think I am?" she demanded.

"I don't know," he said softly. "How about you?" He watched her draw back as though he'd slapped her.

What did the woman want? Bill Brodkey wondered. When he posed the question for Walter, Walter had responded with a shrug, a laugh, and a dismissal: "You're going to worry about that too, are you? Take her on as well. Unlucky Pierre. Don't ask me, friend. I know when I've got troubles enough." But he'd never be caught short. He'd forget both Joan and Roselle. And if the subject ever came up, he'd shrug once again: the joke was on everybody else. He had other fish to fry.

After Bill had raised the question, irritably, in fact, he allowed it to drift to the margins, at least for the time being. It was Roselle who took up all his anguish. Overtaken by her demons, he was sure of it, driven back into chaos and passivity.

He went back to his room, ordered a pot of coffee sent up, and got on the telephone. Now that he had a clue that Roselle was in California, he could do a little discreet inquiry on his own.

He called his former wife, who still wrote material for him, and asked her to look up an analyst who had once worked with Roselle. She said she'd call him back.

Once he was certain of Roselle's whereabouts, he'd take the next step, whatever that might be. If it was too soon to see her, he'd at least keep an eye on her progress. God, he thought, what a rotten shame. What he really wanted to do was to fly out to L.A. that very afternoon. But it was hard to get to Albuquerque for a flight out, and by the time he did get there . . . He waited until lunchtime for his ex-wife to call back. The analyst had not been able to find out anything. According to the sanitarium, no such person as Roselle had entered. He slammed down the phone. Were they lying? Had they set a wall around her privacy? Why would she cut herself off from everyone she knew? He thought of calling the director and trying to get the truth out of him, but that would virtually broadcast it to the public and make the guy sore into the bargain.

At lunch he told Walter what he had done, adding, "I just don't understand. Not any of it."

"Well, maybe they're all false leads," Walter said helpfully. "Don't they have somebody worrying about you?" Walter asked Joan, changing the subject. "Somebody looking for you?"

"I think they're mostly hoping I'll get lost," Joan said.

Bill sat down across from her at the table set up in her suite. She stared at him moodily as though she'd rather not talk to him. Holding something against him, he could see, but he wasn't sure what. The film? Their exchange that morning?

"We're getting nowhere," he said to her. "Are you still in the game?"

"Game?" she said sourly.

"Okay, call it what you like. It's all yours."

"Thanks a lot, I appreciate it."

He was too angry to say anything. He drove his fork through a tomato and put it into his mouth. His hand was trembling. He glanced in Walter's direction, but Walter looked abstracted, above it all.

"Suppose she comes back," Joan said. "What then?"

"Isn't that a bridge we can cross when we come to it?" His anger made his voice deadly calm.

"Sure," she said, "like everything else we've been doing. I suppose you'll just drop me the way you picked me up."

What did she expect? He looked at her, with astonishment, waiting for the accusation to move into some sort of threat: *Just you wait . . .* She was running scared, but why? Dangerous. A small animal with bared teeth. "We're not paying you enough, is that it?"

"You bastard," she said.

Walter had been sitting there smoothing the little blond mustache above his lip, a nervous gesture. "Look," he said to Joan, "nobody forced you. You leapt in quick enough when the door was open."

"To save your hide," Joan snapped.

"Shit," Walter said, putting down his napkin. He was about to stand up, but apparently thought better of it.

"No, Roselle's," Bill said, determined not to lose his temper. "He was against it."

"That's right," Walter said. "And I still am."

She looked from one to the other, having to readjust her fantasies.

"And meanwhile?"

"Are we going to sit here and rave like a bunch of goddam lunatics?" Walter said. "Actually, sweetie, all the publicity would do wonders for the film. And you'd probably cash in too."

"Do you think that's what I want?" Joan said.

For some reason Bill felt tremendous relief.

"Please," she said. "Don't you understand? I mean, it's hard for me now."

"Join the club," Walter said glumly.

Bill felt the whole atmosphere change. Frozen into their separate postures, separated from and alien to one another, they'd been forced together for something that finally none of them really wanted. There was a plaint in her voice. Now, after all the dissembling, he felt something being drawn to the surface—it had been coming for a while—almost against his will. Perhaps with her too.

"I admit I wanted to do it. At first it was a lark. I wasn't even thinking about her being gone . . ."

As Bill looked at her, she seemed to change before his eyes.

He couldn't tell what he was looking at. Her face had lost its tightness; she didn't seem to be defending herself anymore.

"It keeps getting stranger," she said. "Even though I can do it." A note of excitement came through. "You haven't seen me. You don't know. It's like something else takes me over—a power. I'm not myself."

It was hard for her to say this, he could tell. "That's what makes good acting," he said. She wanted assurance, he thought, to be told she wasn't crazy. She was beholding the mystery of it and thought she'd grown wings or an extra set of teeth.

She stared at him as though he didn't understand at all. "But you see, it's not just a part."

And once again she left him with a peculiar sensation, as though her face were floating. He couldn't pin her down, say what she was. And if he tried to look through her to see Roselle, he was baffled there too. Roselle seemed to be slipping away from her too. It struck him that he needed her as much as he'd insisted Roselle did—needed Joan to carry his memories of Roselle, all that entwined their lives: his efforts, failure, guilt. His hopes too. First a gimmick, then a necessity. Filling up a space he couldn't bear to have empty; otherwise something in him would draw a blank.

But he couldn't tell Joan that. She'd hate him for it.

She paused. "I'm probably not making any sense at all."

"You're under a lot of pressure," Walter said, conceding something, but probably not satisfying her either.

"And it's more than just a role," Bill said. More like a borrowed life. Sometime, it occurred to him, he might be called upon to face the mystery of that life. Not just now; he was much too ragged.

She looked from one to the other and gave a little shrug. "Well, I'll do what I can for her."

And for me? Bill could almost hear the echo. What would it do for her, to let her go around manipulating appearances? Till she believed she was Roselle and everybody else did too? And if she did it with enough verve, then award her an Oscar and let Roselle stand on the sidelines applauding. Maybe he could use her in his next film. My God, he thought, was it sheer cynicism that could push him this far? What was going to be *his* relation to her? He was forced to think of that now. Everything had turned to sham before his eyes yet demanded to be lived at all costs—and truly. But what was he anyway but a creator of illusions?

No doubt it would be her most difficult performance, her visit with Jessie Biddeford. She couldn't imagine any other more demanding. The real test for an actress whose teacher supposedly taught her everything she knows. Joan felt she'd been set down in a foreign country where she didn't know the language and just been accused of something illegal or forbidden. "I'm a thief," she said aloud. "This time I've stolen a life."

But you can't steal somebody's life. Whatever it is, they're inside it; it's wholly theirs.

But if I pretend to be somebody else, what's mine?

She had stolen other things. From a sort of jealousy in herself. In high school she'd stolen ideas. Tried to make herself like the winners: paraded confidence, femininity, mindless sociability, all stolen from the nearest popular girl. Or she'd stolen out of revenge. A ring of her mother's, because it had been given to her by a man who'd also made a pass at her. Her brother's navy hat, because he was such a self-important, cocky bastard in it: it gave him prerogatives. Like turning their mother into putty in his hands, and all the little girls who wanted to play grab-ass in the bushes. And her third husband's knife, she'd stolen that too.

A black-handled hunting knife, with a fine edge and a shape she liked to slide her fingers over, back and forth. A knife he always carried in a little holster he wore on his belt. It made him different, carrying that knife, and she could see his pleasure when he took it out to skin a deer or carve up a rabbit. She could feel his pride, his mastery. She couldn't bear it.

Women didn't belong out in the woods; they got in the way. He went alone with other men. He admired her for her cooking, for moving well beneath him in bed. Though he was seasonally out of work, he never quite admired her for holding down a good job. Though at the time she couldn't explain why, she stole his knife, quit her job, and sat around the house in a red bathrobe letting the dishes pile up—till he left. She still had the knife, the ring, and her brother's hat, three stolen treasures, but whose magic she could never learn. All but the knife she'd left behind with her other belongings, never to return to them. Now she had stolen a life.

And in borrowed clothes she went to visit Jessie Biddeford. On the old woman's front porch she fought down the impulse to flee. A note pinned to the screen awaited her there, telling her to come inside. She read the note several times, putting off the action of taking the door handle and pulling it toward her. Come in, come in, the note insisted. She obeyed. She found Jessie in the bedroom lying down.

"I was feeling a little under the weather today," she explained, "but I don't let things like that stand in my way if I can help it."

Joan had brought a bouquet of roses, and with trembling hands she put them in a vase Jessie directed her to, filled it with water, and set it on the nightstand.

"Well, child, that's right nice of you," Jessie said, in the voice that nearly all her life had been dedicated to understatement. Joan leaned over and touched her lips to the old woman's cheek. A chill went down her spine, and she felt butterflies in her stomach: stage fright.

The two women looked at each other.

"Well, you're not worse for the wear," Jessie said, "though I don't see as well as I used to."

Joan fished for the next line. There was in Jessie's tone something that immediately forestalled insincerity. Yet everything was false. "I'm afraid we've both changed," she said. "I can't speak for you. For myself, I can't say it's for the better."

"I was brought up to believe that all things were a matter of will," Jessie said. "You were responsible, that's all there was to it. But I'm not so sure any more. I can't seem to do much about lying here," she said, with a little smile. "I found there were a lot of things I couldn't do much about."

"Jessie," Joan said, feeling altogether dazed, "I just wanted you to know . . ."

"Heavens, that's all right," the old woman said, as though Joan had overdramatized. "I did well enough. I'm just impatient with this . . ." She stretched out her hand as if to take in not only the room and her situation in it but a larger territory.

"You're not one to be flat on your back," Joan was certain she could say with some accuracy.

150

"But you didn't come here to listen to my complaints," Jessie said, leaning up on her elbow, folding a pillow under her head so that she could look at her visitor. "I'm just so happy about your film," she said, with real brightness in her expression, "that you finally got something worthy of your talent and could put all the old mess behind."

"Yes," Joan said. "I hope so," she said, meaning it. "I wanted you to know how much I owe you. I think you taught me what I most needed to know," Joan said. The old woman deserved that much.

"Pooh. Whatever would that be?"

"To survive," she said, finding the words on her tongue.

Jessie gave a little laugh. "Well," she said. "Does that take more talent than acting?" She laughed again.

"At least you've got to have the one for the sake of the other."

"Nothing's taken away your liveliness," Jessie said. "I'm glad of that."

The events of Roselle's life were too well known for her not to allude to them. "For a while," Joan said, "it could have been either way."

"Only it wasn't. My dear," Jessie said, tenderly, "you can't imagine how delighted I am."

Joan felt ashamed.

"I thought you were buried," Jessie said. "Only worse than I was. I took defeat and came here. I didn't do battle with the world, or wait for the new millennium. Though the times did change finally. I left Hollywood partly because I'd never get beyond the bit part, except for little theater. And I didn't go back, because of my politics. There were too many rumors and too many names in the air. If I'd stayed I'd have known only fear and hatred and a sense of betrayal. I was afraid I couldn't live. So I guess I chose the easy way."

Joan was confused. She knew only that Jessie had been in the town for years.

"You didn't know that, did you?" Jessie said, picking up on Joan's silence. "I never told you. As it was . . ." She paused. "So I knew what I was sending you into. Some favor. And I hoped the climate would change for the new generation. You were young. But I had no right to send you into that mess. It got worse for a long time before it ever got better. You had no real warning."

A different tone had entered her voice, breaking through the surface Joan had seen. She could sense a rare moment. Once again she felt ashamed. But she had to go on.

"And I, I allowed myself," Joan said in a low voice, "to feel despair." Even as she said this, she knew it was true, as much for herself as Roselle.

"Yes, the worst thing," Jessie said. "Even though," she said, with a little ironic laugh, "I can't say I've done anything to deserve the feeling. More or less bided my time."

"But that's not true," Joan protested. "If it weren't for you . . ." Roselle would have said it.

". . . you'd probably be a happy woman somewhere," Jessie said.

"You don't believe that either," Joan insisted.

"No, I guess I don't."

There was again a moment's silence. "Jessie," she said, and paused. Careful there, an inner voice warned her. It's your last chance too.

"Yes."

"I've a confession to make."

"No, dear," she said. "There's nothing of that sort you owe me."

Not even the truth? she wanted to say. You've been life's bum all your life, the voice nagged in her ear. Don't throw it away.

"But I have to tell you," she said. "I was scared to come here. To face you after all this."

"You owe me nothing," Jessie said. "And I'm right glad you came. Just keep on, and the right part'll come." The old woman closed her eyes, apparently exhausted.

And suppose she had told her, Joan thought once she'd made her exit, the truth, the honest-to-God truth. Strip away one last illusion. Maybe Jessie didn't need the truth. Could she say that of anybody? Opportunist, she thought. Well, the opportunity had come and handed her the role. Now that she'd picked it up, she dared not put it down. It was becoming part of the fabric of things, woven in, more and more difficult to rip out. Like any other action, pretended or real. For they all got woven in, didn't they? Everything that looked so solid, one great shimmering veil. And she was stuck with her part in it, with secrets she would carry to her grave. As sharp as the knife she had stolen.

The mayor, they said, was going to give a speech about the fire. "Why?" someone asked. "He gonna tell us we've had one?" Everywhere you turned, you heard about it. People could talk about nothing else. What had happened, how it had come about. Like a sudden attack: the shock, the reality, the aftermath of speculation. No one really knew how it began. Faulty wiring in the theater? But then the blaze must have had another source. Someone had seen the old house aflame before the theater caught fire. Rumor had it that a body had been found.

The boy cared nothing about any of that. The flames still leapt in his mind as though he were seeing for the first time all that he had caught during the long hours of the night. When he'd heard the roar of flames and watched as they roiled up to melt the clouds and blacken the sky, snatching the buildings away. With the cracking of timbers, the crash of collapsing floors, the splintering of windows. The town burning, he kept saying to himself. Who said that could happen? The mayor wouldn't have said yes, nor the priest. Was it God—or the devil? He wondered if the priest would know, or tell him he was bad for asking? He'd got as close as he could to the front of the crowd standing behind the fire trucks, the police having roped off the area. Then he moved around the fire, around the whole burning center.

Hours later, when he went home, he knew he would get a beating. His sister tried to slap him. "You, I could kill you," she said. But he ducked away and said that if she wouldn't, he'd show her something. "I was looking for you everywhere," she said furious, ready to cry. "I didn't go tell Mama I couldn't find you. I didn't know what to do." She wouldn't listen to him about the fire, she'd seen enough of it, and she didn't care about the gift the fire had given him. "You're gone for hours and worry me to death." He slunk away. At least his dad wasn't there to beat him; he was part of the skeleton crew they kept on at the big mine, a watchman. And his mother was spending the night sitting with Gomez, for his daughter had her own family to tend to.

He raced off then to Gomez' after his sister thought he'd gone to bed. His mother wouldn't beat him either, not in front of others, and he could tell her what he'd seen of the fire. When he broke into the room, his mother, head bent forward, hands folded across her belly, was sitting in a doze. His entrance startled her. The sick man sighed and turned over. "Look, you've wakened him," she said.

"I'm always awake," Gomez said. "I never sleep anymore."

The boy looked at Gomez lying inert on the bed, his body giving off a sickly glow as though from the glitter in his eyes. His voice seemed to come from somewhere beyond his body.

"I saw the fire," he said, going up to Gomez' bed.

"Wait. Leave him be," his mother said. "Here is a sick man, and there must be quiet. Leave him in peace."

The boy backed away, as a chill went through him. He could see the death in him.

But Gomez reached out a hand, brushing the boy's leg. "No, come close. Tell me the story. I haven't been out of this bed for weeks. Tell me about that world out there."

"It is burning," the boy said.

"Ramon," said his mother.

Gomez held up his hand to assure her.

"Ah yes," Gomez said, "it is sick like me."

The boy was uneasy about approaching again. The bones of the sick man's face were like sharp edges ready to break through the skin, and his cheeks fell into dark hollows. But it was the eyes that frightened him, as though he could look past them into the depths of burning and not know how to get back.

"Come, sit beside me, and tell me."

Ramon approached the bed, holding what he'd brought, the gift, wrapped up in his jacket. The smell of staleness and medicine hit his nostrils; for a moment he could barely breathe. But he sat down.

"Now tell me about the fire."

It was all too much; he didn't know where to find a beginning. Then the excitement welled up again. "You should have seen," he began. "So many running from the theater, all crowding one another, and screaming. It was like todos los diablos running loose. Do you think maybe the demons wait for fire and then come to dance? And everybody's frightened and runs in all

154

directions? And the devils just laugh and say, 'That's just a taste of it. Wait till we give you a real welcome. You can run and scream all you want'?"

"Where did you get that?" his mother asked.

Gomez smiled. "All the devils," he mused. "Running loose..."

"And the houses catching fire," the boy went on, as the telling made him breathless. "People running from the flames, leaving everything behind. They were crying, some of them." He had seen a woman, sobbing hysterically while her husband tried to comfort her. Her children stood around her, tugging at her skirt, staring up at her with wide eyes, as though she were doing the crying for all of them.

"The town was all in smoke so thick you couldn't see where to go."

"When I looked out," his mother said, "I could see nothing. All the noise. You were down there all that time, running in and out? Madre mía." She crossed herself.

Ramon paid no attention. "All the sirens. You heard the sirens? I had to put my fingers in my ears." He imitated the fire trucks streaming in, sirens piercing the smoke and noise. "But the fire, it was so big then, going everywhere. When they turned on their hoses, the flames just ate up the water, just roaring and roaring. The firemen got very tired, and their faces were black. I don't know how long it was before the water started to win. I got tired and came home. Many injured, too—you heard the sirens of the ambulance—and many lost in the flames." He was inspired beyond the event. He shook his head. "It is our hill where they came for safety. The fire would not come up the hill."

And all the time he held his gift, cradled it in his arms, saying nothing of it till the moment came. "And you see what I've brought," he said, holding it out. "I saved it from the fire." For as he'd stood just at the edge of the street, he saw a half-grown kitten limping down the alley, the fire not far behind it. And he'd dashed down the alley and grabbed it up. "You see," he said. "It came out of the fire."

Gomez smiled at the boy, and took the cat and stroked its head. "Poor little animal," he said.

"And what do you think you'll do with it?" the mother wanted to know.

"Keep it," the boy said. "We have to keep it."

"No, we don't," his mother said. "I have all I can take care of now."

Gomez said, "Let it stay here." And to the boy, "Come when you like."

"Now go," his mother said. "Let him sleep."

The boy went home then, but Gomez lay awake. Sleeping and waking were the same to him. If he fell into a doze, it was so light that under its surface played the events that could have been taking place outside him. People spoke. Sometimes his mother and father, long since dead, were speaking to him, and people he didn't know. Now he watched the fire, saw it consuming the center of the town—where he'd walked as a boy and gone to the picture show—and going beyond. No one was there to put it out. The fire was free to eat up everything in its path, and it would go, consuming, consuming.

When Frank Lucero came round to see how he was faring, he too could speak of nothing else. Frank was startled to see him. He looked more gaunt than ever, as though he was losing his substance, drying up. And yet there was almost a feverish gaiety in him.

"It may as well end," he said. "Nothing will bring back copper. All the rest is gone—gold, silver, all of it. And now the town itself."

"It's still here," Frank said.

Gomez shrugged, as if to say, Think what you like.

The center of the town, it was true, had suffered a good deal of damage in an area of several blocks, but in Gomez' mind nothing remained except a few houses standing in the rubble which the fire had mysteriously divided around and left untouched. That amused him. Yes, fire, you've been gracious. You've left us something.

Frank could see into his mind: The town is dead; now I will die too.

"You don't have to stay here," Frank said. "There are other towns."

"Where would I go? What would I do?"

"There are other mines," Frank said.

Gomez shook his head.

He was dying. He wanted to die, and there was no standing in the way of his going. Frank knew the moment he saw him. And the people there saw it too, the visitors he found. The recognition was in their faces as well. Nothing he could do. Perhaps his grandfather, purified through ritual and bearing his ceremonial headdress, could have performed the dance to break the spell. And the spirit would have moved in Gomez again, lifting him from the despair that left him paralyzed in the moment. Frank could imagine the figure, summoning the forces, the spirit helpers. For at times what a man was asked to do he could not do alone. Something had to come from outside, some power, even though it moved within. For it to work, you had to be inspired.

"Don't you see?" Gomez said. "When I was younger, there was a spirit. Even when the conditions for the miners were very bad. But there was Velasquez, there was Juan Chacon. They fought for us, when we were weak, too beaten down to fight for ourselves. And we learned . . . to fight for a chance to live." For a moment his eyes came alive with the old fights and victories; then the light subsided again. "They won, they won against the company. Now they are gone. And the ones left, even though they try, the company is too powerful. It can always close down, always take the ore from Chile. Nothing to do about it, and the miners don't fight anymore."

"But they taught you," Frank insisted. "For the sake of continuing. They are here as you speak of them."

"All dust," Gomez said. "So many laid off now, the mines closed again. What they fought for"—he waved his hand, in the direction of a vanished world—"gone like that. As if it had never been. Everything's changed, and I don't understand."

Like the old life, and the battles fought against the white man. The settling of the West. And the loss of the old culture. Inevitable. Despite the great rush of messianic fervor. Waiting for the messiah to come . . . The Arapahoes and the Cheyennes, the Kiowas and Sioux had taken up the new religion from the Utes. Had tried to dance into existence the new heaven and the new earth. But not the Apaches. The great skeptics. Never believers. Better to fight and die. The desert had taught them to expect no favors from the land or the invaders. No, better fight until the last. But for Gomez, there was nothing left to fight for.

When Frank left him, he returned to his apartment to feed the yellow tomcat and eat a late supper. Afterward he fell into a doze over the newspaper he had opened to read.

The fire was in the headlines. And he tried to remember where he'd been the night before. There with the ambulance rushing to the hospital, not knowing what the flames had consumed, whether the whole town was going up in smoke. Surely not everything would be lost. The past, he was thinking, that's gone. He had lost something in the fire, though he couldn't identify what it was. Or when it happened. Now or long ago. Linda, she was gone. And was it anything he could find again? He had tried once there with her, a long time ago. Where should he look now? Suppose he gathered herbs and learned their virtues, tried again for the knowledge that had once existed? But there was more: everything he had learned since. Forget all that, cut out a part of his life? He thought of the young Indian boys being initiated into the tribe, isolating and starving themselves for days to discover the vision that would give them a name and a calling. He had undergone no such ceremony as he entered medicine. Would it have made a difference?

Did anything remain to be plucked from the flames?

Merle Fullmer was down in a darkness of fire raging and figures fleeing past him. He was trying to seize hold of one of the shapes that flickered just beyond him, to recognize the face of someone he knew. The features seemed to come together, to hover just at the edge of recognition, then to recede and disappear. He woke knowing that someone was leaning over him, a man, with dark skin and black hair; and he cried out, for this was his destroyer. Then out of the darkness a light appeared that was a woman looking down at him, and this was his savior; and he cried out to her not to leave him. For when she did, the darkness closed in again, the red glow of some burning horror.

The Apaches were everywhere. Behind boulders, lying in ambush, their scouts along the routes. A raid at Sibkins. A bullet tearing open the flesh of his shoulder. His brother running across the yard for the cabin. Shot in the back as he ran. Heavy and limp, the still-warm body, as he dragged him into the cabin. Then trying to fire his rifle, as the Indians moved in, encircling the house. The sudden weakness. Looking down at his bleeding shoulder. He could smell the fire. And heard the pounding feet of horses that had been let out of the stables and were being galloped off as the shots rang out. Then silence, his ears ringing in the silence. Failure of hearing. And still the silence. They were gone. Then the faces looking down at him, as he expected the blow that would kill him. The army had found him. Wounded, he lay in the darkness . . .

Sinking . . . faces heaving in front of him, as giddily he walked out into space. He was standing on the planet's edge, watching a conjurer's trick, as now the images were dancing before him: "Oh Noch-ay-del-Kinne, it is known to us that those of our people who have died are still living, but only invisible. If you are the great one we believe you, go call to those of our great leaders who have died. Ask them to help us."

Fasting and dancing, dancing and fasting, they prayed: "Come to us. Show yourself to us again."

And then the shadows came, rising out of the ground, very slowly, coming no farther than the knees. All about them they looked: "Why do you call upon us? Why do you disturb us? We do not wish to come back. The buffalo are gone. White people are everywhere in the land that was ours. We do not wish to come back."

"But tell us what we must do!"

Sinking into the ground again: "Let us rest."

Then the faces disappeared. As he looked around, the bed was heaving, the walls and the room. A savage moon hanging over all. Killer moon. The moon that falls into water and shatters will drive you mad. Now he will stand there and try to put together the pieces of the broken moon, watch the water grow calm and the round, fat globe of light come together like milk on the surface. Until struck by some new violence, exploding, shattering again, and all the pieces galloping in different directions.

"But they brought you back, in chains," he said to the sullen old chief. "You had them running theirselves ragged, chasing you acrost this country, Mexico too. Caught you and brought you down. Into the basement of the old Fleming house." All the Apaches stood silent, as they waited to be shuttled off to the reservation. All the red faces . . .

And they were gone too. Flooding through his mind, his

whole mind a flood, where the night roared and oceans heaved and every living thing was afloat or drowning. Like the ancient oceans that covered the mountains and submerged the world. And he himself. He tried to speak. "Give me back . . . ," he gasped. But he could not find the words that would put a shape around what he wanted. As the faces that bent over him receded, it seemed that no one had heard, that he would be left there to drown in the darkness.

By virtue of the fire a sudden inspiration had struck Curry Gatlin: he was mayor of a town stricken and burned. And that made a difference. All the meetings of the city council he'd sat through, all the discussions with city planners, all the various official functions he'd attended—a mere pantomime. Now that he'd come to the edge of a cliff, the past having fallen away left the drop at his feet. It had been coming all the time. He'd had his one idea that he'd been cheated of: to get hold of Peacock's ranch and turn part of it into a sort of rogue's gallery of the West, bring people to Chloride and keep the wolf from the door, meanwhile putting a nice piece of change into his own pocket. For it was his idea. And folks would have thanked him for it, because the best Bird had come up with was light-minded mischief, whereas here lay the chance to turn a sow's ear into a silk purse full of big bucks. The old Bird had given them the slip this round, yet that day in the Cactus he'd given something after all. Step to the edge and you are hit by the things that matter. Curry Gatlin would give the old Bird his due.

Now for the town, the old dame changeable as a salamander, fickle as young politico looking for bedfellows. He'd taken her on eighteen years ago: a long marriage, growing into dulled domesticity. He'd paved her streets and provided for summer recreation, helped enlist state aid when things got bad. Rooted out the whorehouse and kept her respectable. Got the Chamber of Commerce to put out new brochures that spoke of enterprise and the pioneer spirit and painted a picture of the future with the town's sons and daughters. He went to Sunday church and all the social gatherings and belonged to Rotary and the C of C. Eighteen years of service to the town. Stuck by her for better or worse, not done all that badly by her, he'd say so anytime. He'd maybe cheated on her a bit now and then, taken a few goodies on the side. Like a good husband might in any marriage. But it didn't mean a thing. Considering what you had to put up with: being constantly interrupted at the supper table, having your private life always on public display. He didn't have any qualms, could take a pride that was owing to him. Only now, he felt he'd been summoned for what might be his finest hour. Folks were downhearted, as who wouldn't be? And if somebody didn't look out, they'd be done in, shoved off into despair. Something was needed, something called for: a voice speaking out of the wilderness.

So he spoke. Netta was in the front row and the high-school gymnasium was full. The size of the crowd cheered him. He'd often imagined himself running for the state legislature, speaking to even larger crowds. His eye lingered on the rows of faces all looking in his direction. He ran over his speech in his mind— the bad news and the good news. He'd have to lay the one right out before they could shoot into the second. He couldn't gloss things over. They'd lost a theater and the city hall, several stores and homes, as well as all the work of a celebrated artist and the life of Lauren Collingwood in the fire.

A gasp from the audience revealed that they weren't aware of that fact. He'd seen to it that he got to keep the news for his speech, for he wanted to pull all the stops if he could: shock and grief, hope and expectation. The losses had been great, right when they were expecting a time of celebration. That had made hard things harder still. You worked up all your energy to get out of the rut, and then found you'd spun your wheels and got in deeper yet. He spoke of the great blow to their civic pride, not to mention their personal losses.

He paused after these opening remarks to see how he was doing. They were still with him. He felt a surge of energy. In fact, he laid aside his speech, to look right at Harry Monroe, whose furniture store had gone up in the blaze. "Now, you all know Harry," he said, "and he's lost everything that he worked a lifetime to build up. He's here, though, ready to pick up where he left off."

The furniture dealer, though pale, was actually in a state of euphoria. The fire had released him of a burden; he was going to collect the insurance and retire in Florida. Otherwise he'd have

161

gone broke. People murmured around him while he sat stoically in his place. He was about to shake off his years in the town and forget it; Curry Gatlin was welcome to the burned carcass of his store. He smiled magnanimously.

The personal touch got a reaction. He made the most of it; it was hard for those who'd suffered to remember they weren't alone. There were miners and ranchers who'd lost too. People who'd lost their houses, who were all tied up in mortgages and debts, sweating to stay even. He wouldn't even try to list off the names.

There was a little restlessness. They knew all about it: it was written in Braille for the blind. Let him come up with something else. He picked up his speech, riffled through the pages, then looked beyond the audience waiting for the voice that would call them beyond the facts. It was very quiet. Suddenly he caught a glimpse of Joan. He'd asked the actress to come. She was part of this town. And she was part of his strategy.

A stout Mexican stood glumly next to her. Out of work probably. He saw that a number of the Mexicans had come.

"And maybe some of you are thinking, To hell with this place, I'm moving on. That's what a lot of folks have done. Pulled up stakes and gone elsewhere."

"Sure if you've got money," someone threw out.

"But a lot of us have our lives here, this is the only town we know."

He saw a woman dab at her eyes. Another one put her arm around her.

"There are those who stay and build for tomorrow."

He let that sink in, making a virtue of it. Most of them were doomed to stay anyway. Where would they go?

"We're going to build this town again," he said, "make it rise again out of the flames."

A few cheered.

He was heartened. He had lots to say now. The town was like a mother, who'd given them a place of shelter, a place to grow up. And you had to remember what happened when your mother got old or sick, how you had to take care of her, rally round her. They all had mothers, didn't they?—that was one string he could pull—and you didn't just abandon your mother.

Maybe he struck a chord; at least they weren't getting up and leaving. He raised his voice, with an emotion that took him a bit by surprise. They were with him now; he could feel it. Maybe it was the throb in his voice. They'd held back, but they were coming. Now he'd have to give them the kicker.

The word was *opportunity*. A golden word. He was sure that opportunity was lying all around them. Only you didn't find it, like you couldn't find gold unless you believed it was there. That idea had just struck him: first the idea, the belief before anything could happen. Instead of thinking of burned buildings and wreckage they had to think of the future. The farsighted ones would not perish, or move out, but stay right there to build up a new town and a future.

After all, disaster had come before. He reminded them of the flash flood that had swept through Chloride and torn out the main street. How could they forget? True, it had happened a helluva long time ago. It was a piece of local color now, something to wonder at in the town museum. But there was another door to the businesses on that street, right out the back, and our merchants just opened it and just went on their way. That was enterprise, quick thinking.

Enterprise. Another good word. Opportunity and enterprise. Couldn't get the first without the second. When opportunity knocked, you had to open the back door if the front door was gone. Even if the whole building had gone up in smoke . . . He didn't stop to figure out that one, but plunged ahead. The key thing was the town itself. It had a past; let them make a present of that. Folks were interested in the West. They had film people right there from Hollywood, sitting in the audience this minute to show the town their support. And one of them belonged to the town. Think of that. And think of the money they could bring to the town if they could get a film made right there.

He paused to let it sink in. There was the preview, and something could come from that. Not that it was a sure thing, and he didn't mean to string people along. But you had to go with ideas, even when the ground wasn't solid underneath. And everybody got excited about a film, got stars in their eyes.

And that wasn't all. Some places in this state drew thousands of tourists every year. Think of the resources: Indian dances and crafts, western celebrations, the staging of famous bank robberies and Indian battles. They too had history they could turn into cash. Lots of it.

(Too bad there were so few Indians around, he'd thought, when he was trying to put words together. The town could use their jewelry making and pots and rugs, all the stuff people were so keen on buying these days. But maybe they could import some Indians, lure back some of the Apaches and have them do dances. He couldn't remember whether they were so hot on the jewelry making and the rugs.)

But—forget the Indians—he had to paint a picture for them to carry away. He started with the grave of Billy the Kid's mother. People still came for that. But in addition there were gold miners, Indian fighters, and desperadoes who'd put their mark on Chloride. "The past is worth a fortune," he told them, "a gold mine."

He was still madder than hell about Peacock coming back and rescuing his ranch. Some of his best moments had been spent on the rogue's-gallery idea. Why, you had it all there in one family: gold miner, murdering land baron killed out of revenge, and genteel bank robber. And he could see folks coming from all over, staying in the motels, eating in the town's restaurants, buying gifts in the stores and gas in the service stations. A regular gold mine. And he hadn't given up yet. He still allowed himself the fantasy of trapping the old slicker.

"My fellow citizens, we are not lost. All we have to do is turn round and open the other door."

The crowd clapped and cheered. Afterward a good many stayed around to drink the free beer the town had provided and to dance to a fiddle and an accordion making music in the space roped off in the street. The mayor lingered for a time as people kept coming up to him and shaking his hand, telling him what a fine speech he'd given. "You've put the heart back in all of us," one of the ranchers told him. "Just when you think you're down to your last dollar, you got to figure something will turn up." A woman came up to him with tears in her eyes. "You said the right things, Mayor. We've got to put this town back on its feet." He looked around him. The clouds were hanging low over the mountains, their bellies sagging onto the peaks, but it hadn't rained. The air was dry, and the smell of burning hung over them, mingling with the smell of dust, as the evening softened the edges of the exhausted town.

The mayor stood at the edge, Netta beside him, holding his hand, giving it a little squeeze now and then. They were both watching the crowd. Parts of his speech kept reverberating in his head, certain happily chosen phrases. He could still see the faces in the audience, their eyes looking up to him. Most of them he'd recognized, of course: people who'd lived there all their lives. People he stopped to chat with on the street, give a smile to and a howdy. But this time they'd come to him, waiting to be fed new hope. And he hadn't sent them away emptyhearted. He'd risen to the occasion, found his mission. Mayor of Chloride. It was the best thing he'd ever done. All for the town. And mighty things would come to pass. He could see the town spreading out over the desert, new subdivisions in the hills, mobile homes and shopping malls and housing developments. A new season of prosperity.

Where was Peacock now? he wondered. The old buzzard.

VII   CERTAIN PASSIONS

Risk. In enterprises of great pitch and moment there were casualties. And that, said Bird Peacock, is the law of taking off on your own. And the question always nagging at you, for which you could never get an answer to satisfy you was what made folks take the gamble anyway. Think of them all, he said, with a peculiar light in his eye, as though he were watching the passing of multitudes who'd thrown caution to the winds, left the past behind, all their family connections and bric-a-brac, and thrown themselves into the future. From Independence, Missouri, into the blank on the map. To be killed by Indians, or cut down by cholera or measles, or to find death in childbirth, drown crossing rivers, or starve in the desert. No wonder some had turned right around and come on back. Busted. They'd come to see the elephant all right, had the dream stripped from their eyes, and were going back to the known disasters. Who could blame them?

But that didn't stop the rest. Not the danger, nor the trail of bones across the continent. They streamed out West like cattle on a stampede. They beat down the grass, wore a trail into a road, and kept on coming.

"He's got going," Curry Gatlin leaned over to whisper to his wife. But she had her eyes on him too. As did several others in the huge living room, little conversations dropping into silence as one and another paused to listen. "He'd make a great politician," Netta Gatlin said. "I wonder why it's never crossed his mind."

"Can't sit still long enough," her husband said. Fortunately, he thought. Plus you had to have at least some stake beyond

166

your own self-interest, no matter how consuming that interest was. He didn't say this aloud.

A certain quality in his voice, Joan thought, for Peacock had directed his attention to her—or maybe the chitchat around the room had gone dull. And something in his eyes too. You couldn't help getting caught up. Fascinated like the bird watching the snake. Maybe there was something to the rumor that he could hypnotize you. And she wondered if the same picture was in her mind that was in his. Was he putting something on for her benefit? She looked around the room.

Was it the dream of the land, blotting out everything in sight, Bird was asking, the gleam of gold dazzling the eye? The lust for adventure? Who could tell? That passion to live beyond your life, to break its boundaries and let in the giddiness of circumstance? Bill could see him acting out one of the greater dramas of the West. No, he was too much of a loner for that, but not entirely. Maybe he had only one horse to ride, and he could carry a certain craziness only so far. The rest of the time he was tripping people up for the sake of a little attention, or entertainment.

Bird had a theory: passion was what created the casualties, both living and dead. Land or gold or the desire to strike out on your own. Everybody grew out of the object of his passion, had his life shaped by it. You became a violet or a sunflower, depending on the splashiness of your inner feeling.

"You'd make a dandy lily of the field, Bird." Someone else laughed.

"What about a rose? One of the big red ones that you're supposed to come out smelling like?"

"I know about them all," he said to Joan. "Let me tell you about my family." His mother had outlived his father by fifteen years, and died in a nursing home with three million dollars in stocks. She loved her stocks, little hard-bitten old woman that she was, shriveled into her love of gilt-edged securities. The only thing she'd ever loved. Not his father and not him, not the ranch or the mountains.

Money, but not to spend. To hoard and gamble with, but not to spend. "It was gambling," Bird said. "And when she was going over that portfolio with her broker, she was having a real orgasm."

A couple of the women laughed uncomfortably. "Sounds like he hated her all right."

"Loved her money though, I'll bet."

"I used to visit her," Bird said. "Till she didn't recognize me. She always knew what was in that portfolio, though." Till it was mostly eaten up by her declining years and a tangle of lawyers trying to settle the inheritance.

"And where's all that money got to now?" Netta Gatlin whispered to her husband.

"She's got one of the fanciest tombstones in the cemetery," Bird said. "Bought a piece of eternity."

Fortunately, there were other passions.

But by now his listeners had lost interest, and the conversation narrowed to himself and Joan, who was sitting across from him on the leather couch. Though Bill was sitting next to her, he said very little. She couldn't tell if he was bored or just moody. The rest, those who talked about Bird over their morning coffee, as well as some of the neighboring ranchers from the area, stood in little clusters around the great living room of the Peacock ranch as well as in the study and another sitting room off to the side. They'd been discussing their various troubles and the causes: the closing of the mines, the poor grass and lack of rain, and finally the fire. For a time they speculated about various people who were leaving or might leave: Did you hear that so-and-so was going to Phoenix? Can't sell his house though . . . Never thought what's his name would leave.

Walter McKay kept looking at his watch, certain it had stopped or else that time itself had become defunct, taking some obscure revenge against him. The company of the mayor and his wife as they stood over by the stone fireplace was excruciating. Fortunately, he could distract himself with the burning cedar logs, for though it was June, it was cold enough there in the mountains to have a fire. To Walter's mind, only logs burning in a fireplace and enough alcohol to float him along could possibly make the evening bearable. He spent some moments admiring the pelt of a white polar bear mounted over the fireplace, thinking that the bear had the best of it. The whiskey radiating within and the pleasant warmth of the fire without made him think how good it would be to get back to L.A. Only a few more hours to suffer through the isolation and the boring small-town mentality. Then off to Albuquerque. He was already in the midst of a dissolve away from this tiresome party and into a scene on a crowded sunlit boulevard, one Walter McKay walking into a good restaurant on La Cienega; Patty, his latest, at his side. Prime rib, tender, juicy, and rare. His mouth watered.

He looked around blearily. The mayor and his dumpy wife were still there. In the very midst of these people, he was beginning to forget them. Even Bill. And Joan? He'd leave Bill to figure that one out. As if he deserved some kind of revenge for having thought up the idea in the first place.

In his early youth, Bird was telling Joan, his passion was the earth, and he'd wandered into the mountains fishing the streams, hunting deer and elk, brown bear and bobcat, rabbit and squirrel and quail. He could stalk an animal like an animal itself and knew the country so well he could find his way without a compass. He couldn't remember a time he hadn't known it. He'd been on the track of nearly every living thing you could think of. He called her attention to the bearskins on the walls and floors, some from his hunting in Alaska.

It was a life she knew nothing of, except for one of her men, whose knife she'd stolen, who'd come home smelling of dirt and the fish he'd caught, his pores giving out a rank odor that didn't belong in the living room. She'd envied him, she realized now. Wanting a bit of rankness, whatever it led to—something wild.

He could still survive alone if he had to, Bird told her. As a boy, he'd been where Indians had lived centuries before, and had collected a basketful of axes and arrowheads. He'd found a cave scattered with animal bones and pots and atl atls. "Once I found a skull," he told her. "Brought it home and scared the bejesus out of my mother. I used to bring some of that stuff to school, only nobody had much interest. That was before your time."

Joan smiled and let it go at that. Why was he telling her all this? The truth or just a good act?

"I had stuff spilling over all the shelves of my room. The skull and the snakes were what got my mother," he said. "They had to go. Finally gave it all to the museum."

He'd considered going up to Albuquerque and studying anthropology. Only, his father had knocked that idea out of him.

And probably they wouldn't have let him do it anyway. His grades in math and science were atrocious. But he had no head for business, so his father gave up on him, sent him back East for a good time and gentleman's C.

"I should've been an Indian," he said. "Or a trapper. That way you could explore. Right now it's not all that easy."

"Maybe there are other pioneers," Joan said.

"You think so?" He waited, his eyes on her, as though she was going to say something interesting. But the idea had just struck her, and she couldn't think beyond the obvious.

"There are places I've never been," she said tentatively. "Things I've never done or thought." Did that make you a pioneer though? She didn't think so.

"The land on its own terms—I wonder if you don't have to go back to that." He seemed to be musing aloud.

The land. She'd never thought about it. Just looked around. Living with it, taking it for granted. Tourists went on about beauty and magic.

"And then?"

"Hard to say. Those two years I spent in L.A.," he said, looking at her. She knew he'd been there with Roselle. "I was looking for something then."

He didn't seem bent on trapping her. In fact, he'd all but given away his hand, she thought. Be wary, she cautioned herself.

He waved it all away. "A mess," he said. "I turned into a mess." Before that, though, off at school in the East, he'd discovered a new set of passions: drinking, gambling, and women. He drank, won and lost money like a mad fool, and followed at the heels of every pretty woman who looked in his direction. And thought he was having the time of his life. Came back home and swaggered in the bars in all his youthful arrogance, got into fights, and nearly killed a man. Almost got killed himself. "Guess I thought I had to be like the local toughs. Naturally, they begrudged me that role. It was all they had." But the madness ran in his blood, and it seemed he'd never come to the end of it. And he'd learned what it was to gamble your life.

Then something happened to him . . .

Before Joan was able to discover what, the dogs began barking furiously, creating a great ruckus in the yard. "Don't worry about a thing, folks," Peacock said, heading for the trouble. "Had a few skunks coming up close to the house lately."

But Joan rushed over to the window—an action as spontaneous as fleeing the room. She'd been given a moment's respite. If the others wondered at her crass display of curiosity, they could count it the license of a famous actress. She didn't have to care. Maybe that was *her* passion—curiosity—and one way or another she'd succumbed to it. Always had. For a moment, she reveled in the disturbance outside. Let her not miss another chance for discovery. Dogs and their prey? The conversation had lapsed around her, as though the eyes at her back were trying to see through her into the yard. A series of sharp commands finally silenced all but an occasional growl from the dogs. Joan could hear a rapid exchange in Spanish between a young Mexican she had never seen before and a short, heavy block of a man she recognized as belonging to the ranch. The young man's clothes were torn, and he keep feeling his leg, where one of the dogs must have bitten him. He'd been trespassing, she decided. Bent on robbery? He'd certainly picked the wrong night. Maybe he intended to climb into one of the upstairs rooms under the cover of the noise below. She was longing to find out.

The mayor, then some of the others, came up beside her and she felt a prickle of resentment that they should barge in on her private spectacle. The blocky man was gesticulating excitedly; she could virtually see his mustache quiver, while the culprit stared down at his feet. She saw Peacock wave him off, then start back across the yard.

"Young fool," Peacock said, when he came in.

"What happened?"

Peacock laughed. "Geronomio's gold, he thinks it's buried on this land." He shook his head. "I've heard dozens of stories about treasure around the hills—lost mines, Indian loot. Geronimo's gold, that's a new one on me."

"My God, Bird, I've been hearing that story for years," the mayor said. "How come you missed out on it?"

"Because it's so farfetched. You know any Apaches with gold? Anyway, fools abound."

"You're talking *farfetched*," someone said. "That's a good one, Bird."

Bird laughed. "Guess I wouldn't say anything wasn't true. You never know."

"Makes the world go round, Bird," Virgil Langtry said.

"You want me to get Ramirez?" the mayor asked him.

"Hell no. I gave him a shovel and told him to get to work. I'll even give him three meals a day and a place to sleep. That kind of enterprise deserves encouragement. He's got sixty thousand acres to dig up; it'll take him a while. Afterward I can plant a crop."

"Bird, you're something else. What if he steals something?"

"Looks more like a dreamer than a thief. Maybe this'll keep him out of mischief."

What idea would he come up with for her, Joan wondered. To save her from herself. No doubt he had one. The sort of man who looked at people and had an idea for them. And whatever it was, it suddenly occurred to her, they'd have asked for it. The notion both appalled and excited her. That was the trick to it. But didn't he ever get trapped himself? He'd always had the laugh, even though, from what she'd heard, he'd come close to losing his spread. And this round. She had no clue to what might be going on, but since the fire she'd had the feeling that all of them were somehow bound together, moving or being maneuvered toward some mysterious consequence.

She was exhausted. It had taken all her concentration to get through the conversation with him. Now she drifted casually to the other side of the room, still keeping an eye on him. Some woman had Peacock in tow and Joan was given the opportunity to clear her focus. The pleasant buzz the alcohol had given her had subsided, along with the liveliness she had called upon to get her through evenings like this; otherwise she tended to bite her nails and offend people whose only fault was being in her presence. But this was different. On the two other occasions when she'd found herself in his company, she'd felt the hairs bristle on the back of her neck. Now in his house, she listened to him as if to measure the distance of that threat. How close now? He approached her with an eagerness that struck her as neither sexual nor overly friendly. But he talked to her as if what he had to say was entirely for her benefit. The more he revealed of himself, the more uncertain she felt, as if it was a guise, a distraction. He knew her, in some unfathomable way.

Or was it simply that he knew Roselle, and by extension, her, even though he must suspect her? There was the unspoken past between him and Roselle that he merely alluded to. Undoubtedly, he had seen right through her from the beginning. His eyes were always on her. But why? At certain moments she was sure that if he held her gaze another instant all the truth would come pouring out of her, leaving her drained and empty. But if he knew, why would he want to play with her?

Something uncanny about the man: whenever he approached, Joan felt that he knew not only her secret but her innermost thoughts. He had all the cards, and she none. No, she thought, I can't let myself think that way. Anyway, what did she have to lose? What could possibly happen if she was unmasked? Humiliation. Let her laugh it off. The joke's on you, buster. Accuse her of being an accessory to Roselle's disappearance? Creating the deceit all on her own. But that was stupid. That wasn't what she was really afraid of. Rather, for her there was a private horror: to be unmasked meant to be nothing. So that when his eyes lit on her—yellow eyes deep like amber, with a keenness of expression that was both critical and introspective—it took all her will and nerve to hang on. Whether Peacock wanted to find her out, trap her, she couldn't say. If he knew, why did he keep it up unless for the sake of malice or play? For a man like Bird, malice would seem too commonplace. So let her cast her lot with play. But I can't be afraid of him, she thought. And since I'm not honest, I'd better play the game like hell. And enjoy it. If I take it at all seriously, I'm lost.

Because she suspected that, in his way, he was playing too. Why not simply grant that he was enjoying himself? Sitting back and watching the whole show and giving out that ironic laugh. Suddenly she wanted to laugh—at herself, at the whole situation. Okay, then, she'd have to rise to this occasion too, play it to the hilt. She thought the scene with Jessie had taken all her talent. Looking back, she couldn't even say she'd carried that one off by the skin of her teeth. For she'd misinterpreted her role at first: Jessie was asking for the saving illusion, asking for one genuine feeling she could die with—in effect was begging Joan not to strip herself bare.

Now what was at stake she could hardly have imagined before: she was playing for something beyond dear life, deeper

—for something of her own. All right, enter into it then with a play of wits, a delight, that is, if she was going to survive and maybe find . . . what? And he was a witty man.

She got up and moved to the fireplace, which took almost the whole side of the room, and ran her hand over the fieldstones.

"This is quite a home," she said to the mayor. "I'd forgotten how impressive it was."

"Yes," the mayor agreed. "I remember the wonderful dances they used to have out here. I came down for a couple when my folks were living up in Albuquerque. Did you ever get to any of them?"

"Only once, during Christmas," Joan said, "when he came home from college. He had half the town that time."

The man knew Bird, probably knew things about him she'd do well to know. But she didn't trust him. Something in his manner: a wily eye and an unsettling laugh. It reminded her of a snarl, the way his lips raised at the corners and his nose wrinkled up. She wasn't sure of the rest of the gathering either. Sometimes they caught one another's eyes like conspirators. She hated to think she might have something in common with them. She'd heard about something underhanded having to do with Bird's inheritance. Maybe Bird was too smart for them, just wanted them around to keep an eye on. Very likely they were decent in their way. She'd found people like them everywhere she'd ever lived: the large red-faced man who sold real estate and told off-color stories; the fastidious-looking jeweler with hands as delicate as a woman's; the bluff and sociable undertaker; the banker whose frown suggested time-consuming calculations and answers.

"A. J.'s been working on this house off and on since you left. Fixed it up a lot last time he was back. His ma pretty well let it run down, those years in the nursing home. Old woman wouldn't spend a dime on it. And nobody knew where old Bird was."

So he'd disappeared, leaving behind his patrimony. This handsome house: adobe in the Spanish style, set around a courtyard, wrought-iron balconies at the windows of the upper story. A pond and fountain at the center. Mexican tile in a kitchen that held both stove and open fireplace. In the living room, pre-Columbian dogs and birds on the shelves, and figures of ancient women with the smile of fertility on their lips. Stone and wood.

174

Indian rugs on the floors. And shelves of books everywhere. But what interested her most were the clusters of pictures crowding the walls everywhere she looked—old daguerreotypes and photographs, of Indians and pioneers, faces roughened by weather and short rations, toughened by the will to survive. A pretty face now and then: a woman in a dress she'd brought from the East to remind her of her womanhood. And the bright faces of children. Some thin and serious. Joan had stood in front of them trying to look into their lives. An era lived in every room, one room devoted to photographs of members of Bird's family, a determined and hard-eyed lot—even the women.

"His family's been here a long time," she observed.

"Before Chloride was a town," the mayor said. "Leading citizens, all of them."

"And will he be the last of them? Did he ever have a wife during all these years? I never heard much about him." Let her dig out what facts she could. All part of the game—anything that might give you an edge.

"Not unless he's got one hidden away somewhere," the mayor said with a little laugh. "Don't think old Bird would light long enough in one place to build a nest, much less fill it. Otherwise . . ." He shrugged. "I heard once after I came back to town he'd been in love with a girl out in California. You never saw him out there?"

"No," she said on instinct, a tightness in her chest. Roselle? But then, she thought, there's more than one girl in California. She couldn't afford to confess any link to him; it would just complicate matters. But should she, if it came to it, pretend to Bird she'd been holding back even as he was? Or did it matter?

"He certainly gets around, though."

"Yep. Hasn't stayed put a lot of the time," the mayor said. "I think he's got a saddle burr under his soul."

His wife had joined them in time for the last remark. She didn't even have to ask whom they were talking about. "Too much time on his hands," Netta said. "A woman would have taken care of that."

"Fixed him good," Curry Gatlin said, "like you did me?" He poked her, and she seemed halfway pleased at the acknowledgment. Bluff, hearty, and phony, Joan thought. Hollow at the core. And the wife? A bit of rubber. They deserved each other.

"I don't think such a woman exists for Bird," Joan said.

"At least she hasn't showed up yet. We kept wondering if *he* was ever going to turn up. Some folks thought he was dead."

"His mother died, and they had a time tracking him down."

"Where was he?"

The mayor shrugged. "Every once in a while he'll say something about Mexico or Europe. He doesn't act like it's any big mystery."

"There was a rumor . . . ," his wife began.

"Oh hell, Netta, there're lots of rumors." Curry Gatlin could get impatient with his wife. Joan wished he'd leave her alone.

The man generated rumors all round him. And possibly they only confused matters rather than revealing anything. Before they'd come out to the ranch, Joan had had two conversations, one with an old Mexican woman who helped with the cooking at the lodge and who'd cooked for the Peacock family when Bird was a boy. "A very strange man," she said to Joan. "He can talk to the dead."

"Who is this person?" she'd asked the owner of the lodge, who told her only that he kept to himself, his nose always buried in a book. And had fooled a lot of people with parlor tricks. The rest was nonsense, he told her. Odd, she thought, that he was so well known, yet when you tried to pin anybody down, they didn't know him at all. No wonder each had his own story, mostly shot through with inconsistencies, a great heap of rubbish, piling up over the years. He'd been away long enough that people could invent several different lives for him, endow him with enough arcane knowledge to earn him a fortune and make him a dealer in miracles. He'd gathered strange lore in his travels. He'd run guns for a rebellion in Africa. His face never changed, because he had the power to keep away old age. He had true cat's eyes. He could bedazzle and trick and undo you. He'd robbed men of their fortunes and could find gold whenever he wanted. Wonderful, Joan had thought. A one-man monkey puzzle. Maybe they needed him to be all things, to blame for their troubles and turn loose their imaginations on.

The mayor fidgeted while his wife pulled out her own collection of bits and pieces.

"It's just conversation, Curry," Netta insisted.

"And if they're all true, he'd have had the lives of half an army."

"Some people live more than one life," Joan said, thinking he was jealous.

"Well, you're the actress," Netta said, with such transparent flattery Joan had to smile.

"How is it we always get into this conversation?" Curry said.

"And a more cynical man you've never met," Netta said, for the sake of Bird himself, who had come up to join them.

"Talking about me, are you?"

"Speak of the devil. Just telling her what a rascal you are."

"Rascal?" He did not look amused. "Maybe you mean scoundrel?"

"Why, Bird," Netta said, putting a hand on his arm.

"You think I haven't known it, the eye of envy always looking on? The folks that wish your death?"

"Goodness, Bird," Netta said. "I hope you don't think . . . Why, you're making the shivers go down my back."

"I nearly lost my place," he said. "Understand there are those who wanted it real bad," he said. "Why is it a tax notice, not one but many, goes astray? And notices of public auction get stuck on out-of-the-way telephone poles?"

The mayor looked grave. "Things like that can happen to a man. Why, even your grandfather, who was a great man, Bird . . ."

"The town thought so, though he was a thief and a murderer."

There was an awkward pause. He was pushing them, Joan could see. Maybe that was part of his intention.

"Hell, they're dead," Bird said, with a laugh. "I can talk about them all I want. Only it's the living—and some in this room . . ."

"Be careful, Bird," the mayor warned. "Insinuations can be dangerous."

"How about facts?" Bird said with a look. The pause was awkward. "But then," he said, urbanely, "I'm being a miserable host and abusing the occasion. Let me get you another drink."

"I think we better be going," Netta said, her face tight. "It's getting late, and I don't like Curry to drive on these dark roads."

"Apologies to you, Netta," Bird said, taking her hand. "I had no business dilating on my troubles. Since they're all taken care of anyhow."

"Heartily glad to hear that, Bird," the mayor said. "Whatever happened, your folks did a lot for the town. Wouldn't want your domain to leave the family."

"Maybe that wouldn't matter so much," Bird said, "if things could be set to rights first."

They waited for him to explain.

"Sounds hard to do," Joan said lightly, but she meant it.

"Particularly when you've got an evil past."

"Let us know when you figure it out," the mayor said.

"We're all ears," Netta said, for in spite of herself she couldn't help being intrigued by the man.

Bird pointed to the pictures on the wall. "Maybe you listen to them, look underneath their lives, and dig out their secrets. Maybe things have been festering down there so long, they've filled up the hollows of history and are busting to come out."

"What are you honestly talking about, Bird?" Curry Gatlin said.

"Why, you have to listen to the voices."

"All right," the mayor said, taking him on, "whatever craziness that amounts to."

"So why don't we call them up," Bird said, "and let them have their say?"

"You mean some sort of séance—that kind of mumbo jumbo? You can't be serious."

"Never more serious in my life."

"Come on, Bird."

"I can't say it'll work. Maybe not everybody can hear. Even if you've got a roomful of voices."

"That's your way out of it," Curry Gatlin said. "Tricks."

"Come see for yourself," Bird challenged him, and turned to the others. "I invite you all to come back tomorrow night. Let the living meet the dead."

What is this? people wanted to know. A séance? Really. You mean he's really claiming he'll do it—to speak to the dead, or whatever? He just got us out here to pull something like that. You can't believe anything he does. But what for?—that's what I want to know.

"I'll have everything arranged, any of you who want to be in on it."

"Now it's like you're a coward if you don't come. Looking foolish. Before or afterward—or both. You coming back?" "Sure. Wouldn't miss it." "Well, not me; it's a trick. Believe me, it is." "I don't know. I think he can hypnotize you. Like a snake charms a bird. Some people can, you know." "Come on, I know salesmen that are better at it."

"What are you trying to find out?" Joan asked him.

He looked at her squarely. "Something real," he said. "And how to master it. Maybe only the dead know what the living are trying to think."

"Now you know why there're all these rumors about him," the mayor said jocularly. "Nobody knows what he's talking about."

The evening affected her strangely, like a recurring dream. She kept seeing the scene in the yard, only in her memory a crowd of people stood there, horses and dogs, perhaps a posse come after an outlaw. And the commotion in the yard was the capturing of their game. Only she couldn't remember who was the outlaw, and the posse couldn't find him either. She didn't know if she slept or dreamed this awake. She hadn't gone to bed immediately, but went round the room slowly, looking into the mirror with the carved walnut frame, picking up the perfume bottles on the dressing table, looking at photographs on the walls, an Indian pot, a painted horse from Mexico.

I am in this room now, she thought. There had been other presences, and she was adding hers, superimposing it like another layer of a palimpsest. But if she remained, those other presences might enter her mind, as if they too were there. Like Roselle. At times she wondered what was happening to her, if the boundaries were slipping away and two worlds were being fused into one.

She liked the room, with its bed built into an alcove, the little revolving table with books in it, the Mexican rugs on the floor.

"I wanted you to have this room," Bird said, as he was settling his guests the day of their arrival, taking her upstairs first to this room at the corner of the house, facing east. "You can see the sun come up, if you have a mind to—best view in the house."

The room was divided into bedroom and sitting room, furnished clearly for a woman's taste and perhaps by a woman's hand.

"It's lovely," she told him, admiring the carved headboard of the bed, and the old santo that stood in a niche created for it.

"A girl I loved," he said casually, "liked this room because of the shade from that cottonwood."

It was a trap, she felt sure, and if she'd revealed anything, he'd have won. But maybe he had anyway. Giving her a clue that could have been true or false. Something he'd made up to tease her with. She wouldn't give him the satisfaction of asking. That was the game. If it had been Roselle, he might have said, "You remember this room." But if it hadn't been Roselle, and she pretended to have seen it before . . . She was getting muddled. "Of course," she said, with a smile that could have joined them in a point of common reference.

"And did *she* as well?" She indicated a figure of a woman painted on glass, with a face set hard against circumstance, young but somehow burdened, trying to keep the world at bay. Struggling but without much joy.

"Great-Aunt Sarah? No, this was after her time. Sarah Bridwell,"—he stood musing over her likeness—"missionary to the Indians. Came to convert 'em and send 'em all to heaven."

"Did she do it?"

"No," he said. "Actually she hated the Indians, without knowing it. That's why she tried so hard to make them into something else. They killed her, of course."

"But it didn't help."

"It didn't improve her mind," he said. "No, not a bit. She's a reminder, though."

"Of what?"

"They killed her but she triumphed." He smiled sardonically. "She triumphed, or what she stood for triumphed, and other things got buried in the wreckage. And that's where they stay till somebody looks around and says, 'We need some of that if only we could figure out what it was.'"

"Only then it's too late." She guessed that was what he meant.

"Of course. There's all kind of scrambling—digging up the past, trying to bring something back to life."

"And do they?"

"Maybe, only I'm not sure. And it's never the same when you do. Because you keep moving away from the spot. I still haven't got it figured out."

No wonder the house was full of people—portraits painted on glass, photographs on the walls, and pictures filling old albums. Rooms overflowing with them. As if to invite their continued presence. No wonder he wanted to speak to the dead.

"Who are all these people?" she'd asked him.

So far he hadn't found the time to tell her. At that point he'd left her to make acquaintance with the room. To take her life forward. That was all before the gathering that evening. The next day they were going on an excursion to an Indian burying ground that had never been excavated. Meanwhile another print of the film had arrived and would be shown in the high-school auditorium. And tomorrow night they would speak with the dead.

She lay in the dark unable to sleep. Was it a gift, a special sensitivity, or a curse to be able to see ghosts? To always know the company that had kept there in the past? All places were haunted then, where people had lived, though you never knew their lives. The ground everywhere was drenched with their blood, and perhaps if you listened hard enough you could hear the cries of those who'd shed it. Oh, then you could never walk across the grass. And even when they were gone they continued to play in the drama. They killed her but she triumphed. What she stood for triumphed. For good or ill. You couldn't say which. It had happened. Played out their roles but continued to move us, sometimes like puppets.

She sat up. Do we live out the rest, their unlived lives? For herself or Roselle? Creating what people would believe in, Roselle come back to life, Roselle released.

Finally, exhausted, she fell asleep. Toward dawn, not quite awake, she was caught in that space between memory and desire, between the night world and the day, of nascent energies taking their forms, caught there for a moment as the scene of a hunt crossed her vision. No, it was the other way around. She had awakened to horses and dogs, the barking and the plodding of hooves. But in her head, they had been the sounds of celebration, perhaps in another world.

He was weary, too weary to think or to struggle against thought. Death. Insanity. Obsession. These had driven him to the barren edge of things, to where the next day seemed only a new shade in the darkness of a continuous night. He could go no farther. They had trapped him: Gomez dead from having no future, old man Fullmer caught in a whirlpool, his memory washed away into a deeper past, while his own life floated in bits and pieces, and Henry Martinez, his eyes only on the present, lit up by the fever of his lust. They had haunted him because they had found him empty in himself. They had entered his nothingness. Disease beyond cure, disease beyond his powers. He, the healer. Nothing for it that would suffice, let him tear his own life into bandage strips. And what life was that anyway—work to the point of exhaustion, a hasty meal, a few hours of sleep? All so that he wouldn't think about failure. *Linda, where are you now?*

Now their voices drowned out all thought—voices of despair and chaos and frantic expectation. They made a babble in his head he couldn't quiet.

There was nowhere to go. Not sunny Hawaii, nor any other blue Pacific isle. The ocean wouldn't soothe him; the lapping of the waves would only irritate him; *their* voices would only speak through them. And the light would be harsh and glaring. He wanted to forsake the company of men and go back into silence. If he could find it. Silence without words, without thought. He would go into the Wilderness. There let him consort with the animals: deer and squirrel, hawk and snake. If he wandered far enough, either his head would clear or he would fall into oblivion; it didn't much matter if he lived or died. For now he was confused about what was life and what was death: it seemed he carried only death in him.

He turned his patients over to another of the local doctors, with whom he shared emergency call at the hospital. He paid his rent a month in advance, had the utilities shut off, took his sleeping bag and backpack and drove to the edge of the Gila

Wilderness. There he rented a horse and a mule from the stock they kept at the Hot Springs. He didn't want to say when he'd be back, though he'd have to write something down for the Park Service. In his wallet he had a thousand dollars he'd taken out of the bank. This he put in the hands of the young woman who took charge of the stock, the sort who looked as though she could pick up any one of the animals and break its back across her knee. "If anything happens," he told her, "it's yours to keep." She looked at him strangely, like some kind of nut. "I'm a doctor," he said. "Frank Lucero." They'd heard of him out there. The young woman smiled at him and gave him back his wallet and told him it would be all right.

He hastened away with his horse and mule, with his stock of food, and got his permit to enter the Wilderness before they raised any questions. To the rangers, he represented himself as an experienced woodsman, though his excursions had been brief and limited. He had some memories of boyhood hunting and fishing expeditions that had taken them on foot into some rough country. Like Henry Martinez, his father had cooked trout on a spit over a fire, and he could remember lifting the spine from the delicate white meat. They'd fished for catfish in the Rio Grande, the great whiskered fish that moved over the bottom. Only this time he'd brought only hook, line, and sinker, the simplest of means. If he knew the way, he could have fashioned hooks from pieces of bone, set traps for birds and rabbits. It was useless to suppose he could feel his way back to that, or should. He had to enter the Wilderness as a civilized man, no way around it, and whatever he discovered, if he could discover anything, he'd count it a blessing. Maybe he needed to discover if he wanted to survive at all.

He'd taken maps with the various trails marked. He wanted one that wandered along the river. Once they started, he gave the horse her head, and the mare took him surefootedly down the steep slope where the trail wound in tight curves. They crossed the river, shallow but with some swift eddies. The Middle Fork. He noticed the damage created by the flood some time back, recalled it from before, when he and Henry came out. It looked like the river had gone wild, trees uprooted in its former path, some still with green leaves that would turn brown before long. How many times over the centuries had the river grown savage and swept things away, changed its course? No one knew where the Indians here had gone after their brief sojourn, what catastrophe might have sent them from their dwellings in the cliffs. Had they, he wondered, carried corpses on their backs? He carried three.

He had not waited for Gomez to be put into the ground before he left, though he had gone to a memorial that the Local 890 held for him. A large gathering: men who had worked with him in the mines and their families. Curiously, Jimmy Peralta, president of the union, took Frank aside, and confidential and insistent, delivered a long complaint. As though he'd found the only man to whom he could pour out his long-accruing grief. He was going to resign, he told Frank. He was fed up.

"They're comfortable now. Too comfortable. They've got their homes and their TVs. But they'll be hurting before they know it. They're not thinking about the layoffs. Wait'll they see how far their paychecks go then. Their wives will have to find jobs—if they can. Their kids will grow up without them."

What was he supposed to say? There'd been talk of a strike, but then the miners voted against it. "Why didn't they fight, then? They took what the company offered."

"I told them, I told them." He seemed too young for the frown of worry, the pained expression in his eyes. "They have to keep fighting, or the company'll walk all over them. They won't think. They gave in."

They should have fought harder, Peralta insisted, while a gnarled old man told how Gomez had stood on the picket lines during the long months of the Empire Zinc strike and how, when the women had taken over, he'd brought food around to the strikers: the great strike they would all remember, the one that brought the company to its knees. Scattered cheers came from the mourners.

Frank Lucero had found himself pulled in two directions as he stood in the sour breath of Peralta's complaint and watched the old man hobble away. He's going to have a breakdown, Frank thought. The man's agitation was like a swarm of bees inside him. This union had supported the strike over in Morenci. Months later, and thousands of dollars poorer, they'd been told they were out of order. That was Peralta's plaint. The miners caved in then. And that, said Peralta, in the heat of his frustration, made our men lose heart. That and the closing of the smaller mines, the talk of closing down the smelter. They gave in without a struggle. Scared.

"But if the fight was empty . . . ," Frank said helplessly.

"At least they'd have their dignity," the other hissed in his ear.

Dignity. Frank could see that he felt betrayed, useless. "What's this about the company?"

"Propaganda. They gave it out that they'd have to cut back or close. That scared everybody. But they own the operation in South America. They're the ones in control. If copper is dying here . . ." He shrugged. It was the company's fault. Company bosses, and workers as victims.

Perhaps those were the only terms in which Peralta could picture his world and understand it. Terms for the old drama that allowed you to know who your enemies were. And who were they now? Frank couldn't answer. Pull one filament of copper and you were in South America; pull another and where would it take you? Copper in the world, and all the things connected to it. Frank had nothing to offer him. He'd left him to his misery. And now he was glad to be carried along by the horse. Problems had grown too vast, the source too remote for any one mind to comprehend. Better to try to appease wind and rain. Men had taken the measure of gods and created unappeasable forces in the world of men. And the workings shaped the destinies of Gomez and Peralta. And of him, who had nothing now to hang on to.

He rode on, the reins lying slack over the mare's neck. The horse knew where she was going. They rode, crossing and recrossing the Gila where the canyon walls abutted the river so closely at times they had to pick up the trail on the other side. The mule, more surefooted even than the horse, followed at the end of a slack line. High on the canyon walls he caught sight of more symbols like the one he'd seen when he was with Henry: arrows and zigzags painted in red, circles and snakelike curves. Signs still pointing into the future though their meaning had been lost, placed there by the Indians who'd lived in the cliff dwellings high above the river in the caves where they'd built them with exact architecture. Ceilings blackened by the smoke of their cooking fires; holes in the floors where their round-bottomed cooking pots could be set without spilling. Tiny ears of maize left piled in the adobe storage bins. All left behind, the men and women walking into the mists of time.

He thought of them lying in their deerskins at night and waking to the light at the mouths of the caves, born again each day out of the womb of the earth. And of the men setting out to hunt, and the women to gather cactus fruit and berries and wild squash. And having ensured their survival for another day, perhaps lying in the sun that warmed the ledges and watching the hawks ride the thermals. Living and dying there like bird or beast.

Dignity? Was there any such word or notion for them? Maybe nothing more than the straightness of the back, the look in the eye. What did he know? He was entering as a stranger and alone, burdened with his corpses. The sun was halfway past the meridian. He could have gone farther, but weariness overcame him. He pulled at the reins and stopped. Then he tethered the animals, set up his tent, and brought out his food. He saw a spot of wetness on the wall of the canyon and found a little pool underneath created by a spring. Cool and clear. He cupped his hands and drank, then touched his face and forehead with the water.

She had stepped across a threshold. Curious how nothing seemed to hold her. Her past had fallen away and the future was up for grabs. Now that it was all a game and nothing mattered but the playing of it, she was free. Let her play, experiment, take her knocks if she had to, she was used to that. Come Peacock, come Bill, come Walter McKay. And you, too, citizens. You'll get your money's worth. She took her image to and from the mirror, played with her hair, her expression. It would carry her forward, whatever wave she danced on. She trusted it now. And it would demand the most from her. For she had to look past the threshold, where Peacock beckoned her into the unacted possibilities of herself. Now that he had seen through her, knew her for what she was—he had to, there was no way around it—she was drawn toward the mystery that lay on the other side, that she had never approached. It sent chills down her spine when she thought about it, when she caught his eye on her. But she must do it. But not by any of the rules.

He would take her beyond herself. Not by unmasking her. He seemed to regard her with a certain skeptical admiration: You've got this far. All right, let's see if you can go one better. What's for the future, Princess? Only you didn't get the future just by waiting for it. He was pretty hard-nosed. The past had to be settled yet.

"Those things they had you doing," he said to Joan. "All that Hollywood fakery. It didn't do you much credit." He shook his head, then confronted Bill. "And where were you in all that?"

"Trying to survive, find my way. You keep trying to get off the treadmill."

"Shit. Can't anything change?" Peacock demanded. "Things getting born and dying in front of your eyes. Can't they change? Soak yourself enough in what's been done; then can't you go leaping past? Instead of making out Joan Crawford and Bette Davis were great actresses, clinging to them," he said with contempt.

"Well, you're so big on voices," Bill said irritably. "Why do you hang on to them?"

"To get free," he said. "At least I'm trying. Only, first, as I've got it figured out, you listen. Otherwise they'll haunt you without your knowing it—sapping your strength. When I get it set up—the voice box—those voices you hear'll be coming out of the past. And you'll see what was lost. They'll speak again. Out of the ruins everything'll speak again. You see the pictures on the wall, all those pictures of men that lived once . . ."

Bill scoffed at the whole idea. "How do you know they'll tell you anything of value? Suppose it's only that things lost are better let go of? Maybe it's all husks and empty shells—failures."

"I grant you," Peacock said. "But you see," he said, contemplating the pictures, "they all carry their own idea, down underneath—what they had to be. We look at the face they put on it. And some of them never knew what it was. But it was playing under the surface and goes on playing . . . Most of us never know our own, let alone anybody else's."

They were standing in the hallway on the way to the living room. The face she studied was sensuous and a little grim, as though the woman had been caught there, not where she wanted to be at all. Joan caught Peacock looking at her and her face burned, she didn't know why. She turned toward Bill, but he was concentrating on another of the pioneer women. She felt momentarily unstrung, as if she'd been pitched into the middle of a second adolescence. It was a tough game, all right. She smiled, then gave a little laugh, as though he'd caught her in her confusion, but just for a moment.

She looked at him: Straight as a rod. Square of head, deep-lined brow that ended in a widow's peak. Everything hard and chiseled. The eye bright. The man who'd flown everywhere, cocked his eye, and seen all around him. And the passion that ran through him—that. That had to be. Driving him out of the world. In a way like Roselle. It had driven her out, Joan was certain, but she couldn't come back. When the impulse for life was too strong . . . And maybe it had been for her too. A misery that took her here and there looking for the story, made her want to act it out. Or to find the story to put into words, because if you didn't catch it, you'd have only your empty hands.

And Bird. Looking at the faces, looking into them and trying to make them speak, deliver up the secret behind them. So many dying with their secrets. To leave you with only their faces to look into. And beyond them, not even an image. She understood his desire, and the desire as well to look into the living face. Into hers, not to unmask her, but with the hope that what was in her face was . . . what?

"Maybe they've got only the weather to talk about," Bill said nastily, "the hotel conditions in the underworld."

"Or the clue to the future," Bird said unperturbed. "Speak to the missing part. Speak to the past you can't know, the origins. Trouble with this country is we've always tried to fight it—kill off the Indians and chop down the forest. Fight it like we're afraid of it, and that's why we don't know it."

"You're getting beyond me," Bill said.

"We've never known this continent. Not in the bones. Otherwise the Indian would live in us as well as those that came rolling across the prairies. Something's been forgotten."

"Well, I'll be interested to see what happens," Bill said skeptically. One more piece of the clutter. He was beginning to think he'd never get any of it sorted out. So this Huerfano, according to Bird, was quite a fellow, and the voices spoke to him from the other side. Right through the voice box. And if they listened, there might be a few squawks and moans that Peacock would acclaim as the wisdom of the past.

Joan had put aside skepticism, even thought, and stood as empty as a glass. Wherever this led, she'd go along; it was certainly more intriguing than anything she could have invented. She wanted a walk outside before dinner. But as she turned to go, Peacock said, "I want to show you something. I've kept it all these years. Thought I'd lost it, but it was down in the pile where I've kept all sorts of junk. I want you to see it."

"I guess I'm not in on this," Bill said.

"Afraid not," Peacock said. "This way," he beckoned her, leading her along the hall to a part of the house she'd never been in before. She thought it led to the storage rooms. He turned and they went down a stairway to another set of rooms. "This is where we'll set things up for tonight," he said, pointing to a door at his left. He led her to a small room on the right, opened the door, and switched on the light. She saw a picture of a young girl framed and hanging on the wall. It could have been herself. But what caught her attention was what it held of promise. Whether he'd seen it in her as well, connecting portrait to face, she didn't know. Or could it be that something existed in himself that only the face could give expression to? She didn't know. But she found herself drawn into the mystery of whatever it held of suggestion. And that was the game. The point where she'd picked it up to continue, meanwhile becoming she scarcely knew what. A sudden joy rushed through her.

She turned to Bird, who appeared to be waiting for her reaction.

"It's wonderful," she said. "It's just wonderful." She threw her arms around his neck. "I love you," she said.

He held her for a moment, then drew back to look at her. "I've been waiting to hear that all my life."

"So what do you think of Peacock's little scheme?" Lester Pruitt asked the mayor in the privacy of his office in the new city hall. "You actually going back there tonight?"

"Of course. Aren't you?"

"Well, I hadn't made up my mind."

The mayor laughed. "I wouldn't miss it for anything."

"You expecting something spectacular?"

"No, in fact, I'm not. I'm amused. I can see right through him. Since he's got people thinking he's got all the tricks in his bag, he can work up some little piece of fakery like the money machine."

The banker didn't appear as sanguine about the prospect. Eyes a bit bloodshot, a grimness at the mouth, as though his expression sat on top of gas on the stomach. He was tapping his fingers against the desk. "I've been talking to Leonard Spicer. I think Bird shook some things out of him, got an inkling we had something to do with the tax notices and all."

The mayor shrugged. "Let him prove it then; an inkling's not a set of facts. And there were too many hands plucking the strings. Thoughts never killed the cat. I told Spicer he better get out of here for a while. The main thing, Lester, is to hold still. The Mexican kids used to have an expression when I was in school," Curry Gatlin went on. "Whenever a teacher came along, somebody to pounce on you, they'd warn one another, 'Truchas.' Fish. Keep still like a fish in the water."

"You think it'll all blow over, then?"

"Sure. Let him do his fooling. Can't be any harm in it. He's got himself blown up like a balloon. Voices! Drunk on the past. There's no power in that. Vanishes before your eyes. Maybe he's just trying to compete with his granddad. Become a legend in his own time. Monkey tricks. But he's not got their gumption."

"I wish we'd been able to get hold of his place," the banker said. "You have to admit his coming back . . ."

"I tell you," Curry Gatlin said vehemently, "it's not over. If he doesn't stay put, who knows what'll happen? He can blow in, convince people he's got something special. But he can't grow wings on an elephant or cure what ails us. And after he whips his cape around, the facts are still there staring you in the face. The mine closing and the town in a bad way. It'll take more than Peacock to make a difference. More than a bag of parlor tricks."

In a way, he was talking about himself as much as Peacock. He was quite clear about where he stood. Something had happened to him in that fire, as he stood out there with the fire trucks and the exhausted men. Some part of him stood helpless, going up in smoke. Then he'd felt something stir inside him, right after that morning in the Cactus when Bird had gigged him. And when he gave his speech, he was filled with a new energy taking hold. It took that to rally them. It was his town now. He knew what it needed and how it ought to be defined. No Peacock could scare him now.

He still thought about the woman who'd come to him afterward with tears in her eyes, saying that he'd put new heart into her. That was a power. He'd never thought of it before, what he could do that way. Why, take something and get people behind you, seize their wills and take off running. He owed a lot to that fire, the way it put him in touch with the town. He'd take care of them, put the town back on her feet, old whore that she was. Yet her instinct was life. Maybe you could still call that the pioneer spirit: surviving, keeping up a settled place to bear the young and let things go forward. The woman's instinct and the woman's touch. But she needed a man to tell her what she was. Build church and school, tell her when to pray and when to dance. She was the instinct, all right.

"Come on, Lester. I need a cup of coffee."

"Me too, I didn't sleep worth a damn last night."

The trouble with Lester was that although he'd plunge ahead with the best, he had too much conscience when he faced the prospect of getting caught. If Bird could beat down Leonard Spicer, he could work up a court case—against him and Lester and the rest. But he wasn't going to sweat it. He had public opinion on his side.

They left his office and walked down to the end of the block, to the Cactus. The insurance man, the undertaker, a couple of others were there already, halfway through the first round. "Morning, Mayor, Lester. You look like you haven't got properly woken up yet."

"Too much on my mind," Lester said. "You know the Beatty place. The wife's been trying to keep it going since Clyde's been sick. Only she can't. Feel sorry for her."

"Damn shame."

"I hear you got a real party coming up," the insurance man said eagerly. He'd heard all about the doings out at Peacock's.

He and Bird had never met, Bird being off somewhere when he first came to Chloride. He hadn't been invited and was prickling with curiosity and resentment, felt he was being cheated of experience. He wished somebody would wangle him an invitation. He had half a mind to call the man up and say he wanted to come. He wanted to see Bird in action. Wanted to tell somebody he'd gone and been part of the history. But when he mentioned the idea, his wife scoffed at him. "Mind your own business, Bob Larson," she said. "That ought to be enough to keep at least one man busy." But he was tempted to anyway. He loved a good joke, and loved to tell about it afterward. By God, he'd call him up.

"My opinion," the furniture dealer said, "is you should forget the whole thing. Nobody's there, no audience. Everything fizzles."

"And miss the chance?" the insurance man said.

"Nothing to miss," Harry Monroe said. "His only fun is getting people fascinated enough to think there's something there."

"I'd invite him to do it in my place," the undertaker said. "Let him see what he can get out of old Gomez. Only I have too much respect for the departed."

The jeweler had no interest in games. Looking through his optical, he was held spellbound by watchworks so finely tuned that time spun around them without moving them, and all things lived in a continuing miracle, with nothing broken or wasted. All dark shadows having retreated in the face of a continuous noon that brought sun and moon together, with light opalescent as a shell. He roused himself, thinking he had looked so long into the intricacies of things he would never know the larger design of gold and silver and copper. Refinements were what he loved, and lost himself in. Yet all around him was the grossness of matter, the inescapability of force: lightning and thunder, flash flood and sandstorm, and mud, always mud. Strikes and depressions. Failure and death. His optical stopped with the works of watches, though behind it all, he knew, lay particles that resisted the most powerful microscopes. He was sure the dead had nothing he wanted to hear.

"The whole thing kind of tickles me," the mayor said. "He thinks folks are going to sit still for this latest shenanigan. Well, he's got the wrong moment and the wrong folks, and I want to go out there and see him blow it."

192

"You think he will?" the insurance man said, intrigued. "Think he'd overstep his bounds?"

"I know he will." The mayor winked at Lester. "But this round ain't gonna be his."

"I don't understand him," the undertaker said. "Never have. Considering what's in his family."

"Takes the spotlight off, maybe," the insurance man suggested.

"No, keeps it on," the mayor countered. "It's what he wants, seems to me. Go them all one better. Out-Peacock the Peacocks. If he went his own way, nobody'd remember them or him. They'd look at the pictures in the museum and think of fine, upstanding men that made the territory."

"What's wrong with that?"

When you looked at something through the light, Emmett Early thought, you saw all the broken parts: the broken stem, the spring gone awry. Better to have the shadows. Did it always do to diagnose the disease when you didn't know the cure?

"I don't know why he keeps taking out the family skeletons," the undertaker said. "Sometimes it's best just to get them underground."

"Part of his game," the mayor said. "That's his power." And what's yours? he could feel them asking. "Don't worry," he said. "Can't have a game with only one side playing."

Virgil Langtry came in then, eager-looking, as though he'd been in a hurry. "Morning, everybody." He pulled up a chair. "Just been over at the courthouse, and I heard some gossip." He shook his head, looked around at his audience with a certain relish.

"Well, come on. You got your suspense."

"Mortimer told me Bird was giving away his land—everything."

"Now, that I don't believe," the banker said. "Coming back from God-knows-where, fighting tooth and nail to keep it, then just letting it go. I won't buy it."

But they were set back on their heels. Just when they were organized for one set of reactions, Bird had turned around on them.

"Who to?"

"Wouldn't say."

"To the town?" the mayor conjectured: Bird stealing his

193

thunder and gathering everybody's sympathies. No, that wasn't like him, or maybe it was. He hoped not anyway. While they continued heatedly speculating on motives and recipients, he fought against a sinking in the chest. What he really wished was that the scheme he and the others had hatched could work out after all. With him in charge, naturally. It needed leadership. But for the benefit of the town after all. Tourists coming there in flocks, the whole economy beefed up. *Now folks, this is unique. You won't find the likes of it anywhere—not in the whole state. You think you got skeletons in your closet? See what we got here, just like a line of kings, all the worst of everybody under one roof. Take a look. But remember these men made our town what it is . . .* He could see the growing enterprise: a sure drawing card for curiosity and spending money. Beyond the guided tours and maybe the performance of a melo-drama in the courtyard, he could see racks of post cards and key chains and piles of T-shirts and pennants and posters. And other effects generating out of this piece of western Americana. Let's say some fancy gunplay and a simulated shoot-out at high noon. And more film stars. They could walk the streets of Chloride the way they did in Taos, build homes out in the hills.

"The town? Not likely," Virgil Langtry scoffed. "But I'd damn sure like to know who he's got in mind. Any kin hidden under the bushes?"

"Hell," the mayor said, "for all I know he could have fathered a whole line of brats. Wouldn't put it past him."

The insurance man was enjoying himself. If he had to be merely a spectator, then he could exercise his objectivity. The man was always a leap and a guess ahead of everybody. That was his genius. "He gave the town a museum," he said.

"That's right," the mayor admitted.

"What are you going to do, Mayor?" the insurance man asked, wondering if the news had brought a sudden doubt into the midst of things.

"He's going to spring something on us," Lester Pruitt said. "I can see it coming."

"In that case," Curry Gatlin said, "we can be on hand to en-joy it. He's just made it more of a challenge."

"What've you got in mind?"

194

"Well, let's not let the kitty out of the bag, as they say. Might wander off to the wrong places. Well, my friends, I have a few pressing matters to attend to between now and tonight," he said, getting up. "But don't fail to come. Who knows, we might get the thrill of our lives . . ."

Back in his office, Curry Gatlin tried to reach the police chief, but the line was busy. Waiting, he pondered. He'd been here in Chloride longer than Bird, if it came to that. Born and bred here, and except for the four or five years when his folks moved to Albuquerque and his stint in the army, he'd lived here ever since. It was more his town than Bird's.

And this is what it's come down to, he thought. They'd started out together, had even been friends for a time. Then gone along two different tracks. Now adversaries. It's the third time, Bird, he said to himself. And if I've got anything to do with it, it'll be the last.

First the Communist thing back in their youth, the towns-folk up in arms. The second touched him personally, when they'd tried to close Ginger down and make Chloride a clean town. She'd been off in Alaska with a fellow on a bear hunt, a beautiful time to put her out of business, now that she'd gotten behind in her security payments. So Ramirez said. But Bird had gotten wind of the news and called her in Alaska. Right over the loudspeaker in the hotel, he'd said, "Ginger, you better get on home. They're fixing to close down your whorehouse." He must have enjoyed that.

And he told her what to do. Seems he'd read about some re-former gone all soft about the plight of orphaned black children. It suddenly occurred to Ginger to turn her place into an orphan-age, she was so affected by the poor little children. A whore-house devoted to pickaninnies! The town decided to leave her alone.

"It's a good thing, Mayor," Bird had told him, head cocked, looking sly, "seeing as how so much of the city income . . ."

"What are you hinting at, Bird?"

"Your salary, Mayor. That police car that stops by her ranch in the valley every Friday, it doesn't go cruising out there for the scenery."

"I'm not going to argue with you."

"No need to. And don't forget the times I've seen the chief taking one of the girls to the upstairs of the city building."

What was he doing on her side anyway? Digging up the ground like a jackal to find its food just in the right stage of rottenness. Wouldn't cover up his own evil-smelling past. Pulled out people's secrets like dust balls from under the box springs. To get his laugh. It wasn't natural not to cover your dirt. Didn't show the right attitude. You had to know what was going on, Curry Gatlin was willing to grant, but then you looked the other way. To survive and get on with it. That's how the West was won. Drinking and gambling and whoring and killing. Gambling fortunes and gambling lives. Made the world go round and got the rest of us born. Grease for the wheels. And if Ginger missed her payments, who was she to complain? She had a good thing going, under the cover of respectability. And if she had to pay to keep heads turned in the right direction, that was part of the deal. And just then it was a good move for the town to clean things up. So who was Bird to interfere? There was a town after all, and if you allowed people to play in the mud, it was because it was convenient. Then other things became convenient. A few could get their ire worked up because of a whore, but not the majority. Everybody seemed to understand that but Bird.

He rang again. "Hello, Chief. I just wanted to know if you got the evidence from Martinez." The chief had. "Well, let him go. And tell him to keep his mouth shut if he knows what's good for him."

Digging for Geronimo's gold. That was a good one. He was surprised Bird would fall for such a thin trick. But maybe it was the smallest pebble that tripped you up at last.

"Now I'll tell you what I want you to do." He didn't have anything to pin on Bird, nothing that would hold up in court, but the marijuana growing on his land was an excuse. At least it would take a little attention away from the main show. The chief was agreeable. "By the way, I think we got things worked out for your boy." The chief was grateful. The warehouse where the kid worked had been robbed, clearly an inside job. The mayor knew because he'd taken the kid's wife on a little out-of-town excursion as his secretary, and she told him. Naturally, he'd pulled a few strings. Grease for the wheels.

Ramirez had been police chief for the town longer than Curry Gatlin had been mayor. People complained about the bribes he took, the girls he threatened if they didn't comply. "You want the job?" Curry Gatlin would ask them. That got them every time. You could count on Ramirez, and if the town was at least halfway decent, it was because he was doing his job—a dirty job.

When Curry Gatlin put down the phone, he leaned back in his chair, looked out and studied the weather. He sent the secretary for coffee. He felt better and could actually look forward to an interesting evening. Something was clear to him now that he hadn't really acknowledged before: why he hated Peacock. He'd always considered him a damned nuisance. And somehow tried to dismiss him when the man raised his hackles. But it wasn't that simple; something remained behind to rankle and fester under the skin. And he'd finally got it figured out.

Now it was as mayor of Chloride that Curry Gatlin looked down at him, the place he'd earned. The place he'd been elected to, with the role the fire had conferred upon him. And he knew this: it wasn't just Bird's tricks that got his goat. Far more serious than that. Bird stirred things up, unsettled people's minds with doubt and confusion just when they needed solid ground to stand on. A flock of turkeys that he just sent scattering. Not just a game: Bird was attacking a way of life, the one Curry Gatlin had always lived by. He loved the town, he realized, had always loved it. It was what he saw in the morning when he woke up and what he counted on being there while he slept. Creating the dreams of his future while it served as receptacle of his past. For the sake of enterprise and forward movement, you had to keep things moving, no matter what. That was his mission: what had stood concealed but had been before his eyes all along. Defeat the enemy and forward march. It didn't matter what grease it took for the wheels.

VIII   THE VOICE BOX

They came. Curry Gatlin and Virgil Langtry and Emmett Early, the jeweler, and Lucien Hake, the undertaker. They were all there with their wives. Except Lester Pruitt,
who was late or else had decided against it. Bill Brodkey watched
them come indoors from the mild night air edged with a slight
chill, enter the great living room, joking lightly: Netta Gatlin, a
woman with broad shoulders and a little neck and a tendency to
blink, and the jeweler's wife, tall and elegant, in a lace blouse
that teased the eye but gave nothing away, there being, Bill observed, not much to offer. Miriam, married to the undertaker, as
affable and voluble as her husband. And Gretchen, small and
mousy, who left sociability to the real estate agent. They liked
sports and local politics; they spoke of their kids and medical
problems. They admitted to having relatives with nervous break-
downs. But as Bill put the men together with their women and
tried to gauge their loyalties, their choice of breakfast food, the
quality of their living rooms and vacations, then paired them off
differently and found no solace in the exchange, he felt his
imagination go limp. He grew afraid. Pick up the threads of sociability and they petered out into the trivial. All the decency,
all the energy, and there it went into the same dreary round. The
loss of the world and the loss of force. He should have left with
Walter and Sally and gone back where he belonged, in the traffic
of failure and ambiguity.

What was Peacock up to anyway? Specious nonsense and
sheer bravado would carry him through. When the world cracked
at the seams and let through the whiff of sulfur and idiot laugh-

ter, then you found the crooks and the cranks and A. J. Peacock. Happy as dung beetles. Let there be some spot, Bill thought, a little space where he too could rampage with the freaks, twist ideas like pretzels, some Hyde Park of the mind, where he could join the crackpots and con men twitching at the edges of history. That or be bored to death.

Joan appeared to be at the edge of excitement, as if she was in on the secret. He looked at her sharply, through the eye of envy because she was clearly enjoying herself, as though the next turn of events would reveal only more of what she had gathered in already. He envied her for that, and for a hint of something that lay maddeningly beyond him. The sort of show she and Peacock put on for each other. Dazzling flights of repartee, in which he threw in the air a lamp, a red nightgown, a basket full of apples, tangerines, and grapes, and she responded with strings of lights in the shapes of flowers, each one going off in a sharp explosion. The air was filled with colors and bells and sirens and a roll of drums. All fluid and sparkling. They could have been lovers. They dodged missiles and deflected arrows, then rubbed together like silk, gave off static, and laughed.

Resisting, Bill knew that she aroused him, that in more ways than one he wanted her for himself. He was jealous of Bird. Who was maybe crazy. What did he want? He was wary of a man whose motives eluded him. Who was he anyway? Holder of the trick cigar lit by the trick match? Who promised to take you to the very dead.

The guests acted as though the whole thing were a lark, laughing uproariously at stupid anecdotes and drinking up Bird's liquor. The mayor appeared to be in his element, smiling out of a great store of goodwill, waving a hand with a cigar as he proved and approved, as though he himself were putting on the show. He'd greeted Bill like an old friend and was obviously courting Joan. Since she'd found her home again, he was sure she'd come back. Bill too. He had plans for the town; big things were going to happen. He gave them a significant look.

One of your amiable asses, Bill concluded. Trying to put out like Peacock, only he had neither the delivery nor the equipment, just the urge.

Meanwhile Bird was in and out. "Just a little longer," he

promised them. "Enjoy yourselves. Have another drink, Virgil, Curry. Just a few more adjustments." Then he was gone.

"Where's Lester?" someone asked. Nobody'd missed him before, but now everybody looked around. "He's coming, isn't he?"

"So far as I know."

Bill fidgeted. It had better be good, he thought. If a man set out to bedazzle you, he'd better come through. Or what? You hanged him? "Then how did you escape?" came the inevitable question. He had to laugh at himself.

"Can't understand Lester. He'll miss all the fun."

For now Bird came to fetch them, to guide them downstairs. The chitchat suddenly dropped into the silence that opens when what you have waited for, refused to take seriously but in some way dreaded, beckons. "You'll have to be a bit careful here," Bird said, standing in a doorway that led off the living room. "These stairs are narrow. Careful not to trip on the stones."

They slowly descended, a breath of coolness coming up from below, the smell of old adobe and stone closed off to the sun and air. Netta Gatlin tittered nervously. "You need hiking boots."

"What've you got here, Bird?" Curry Gatlin demanded. "You're sure it's safe down here for the ladies?"

"It's my own little hideaway, Mayor," Bird said. "Perfectly safe, especially when you don't want anybody bothering you. The walls were already here. Just had to make a few alterations."

The stairs, winding and narrow, led down to a large room, circular with adobe walls. "Like the Indians did it," Bird said, "with a place for the spirits to enter from the other world."

"Why, it's dark down here," one of the women said, as they came away from the brightness. Covered lights along the walls created a glow around them but left the center of the room mostly in shadow. "I don't recognize you. I don't recognize anybody," someone said, as their faces dimmed into the shadows. They moved like swimmers into the room. There already, standing where the light seemed to make a mask of his face, was the man Bill had often seen around the stables and grounds but had never more than nodded to—who seemed more head than body, almost as if he'd been carved out of wood. His mustaches were quite astonishing, seemed to quiver with a life of their own. The buttons of his shirt and the silver spangles on the sides of his britches glinted. His fixed purpose, Bill supposed, was to add one more element of peculiarity to the general mix.

He laughed to himself. Theatrically spooky. A western fun house. Where were the vents to blow up the women's skirts? Nothing you would take seriously. Nor did anyone.

"Spookier than the house of horrors," the jeweler's wife commented.

"Ghosts love it."

"Maybe they'd prefer to see where they're going."

"You're sure the ghosts'll turn up?" the real estate agent said.

"That's what you came for, isn't it?" Bird said equably. "Only first, before the voices, come the faces. But you've got to sit down and settle your minds. Too much agitation scares them away." They moved to the benches lining the room. "Now, if you'll look at the wall yonder, you'll see some of the people we might be meeting."

And then a series of figures began to flit in front of the wall, three-dimensional, as though they were looking at them in a holograph. "Chinese fellow who ran the laundry," Bird said. "Killed another Chinaman for his money but was never convicted. And that was the lawyer who got him off—for a price. Even though he knew he was guilty as hell. Went on to the legislature."

"How do you know all this, Bird?" the mayor asked. "Looks like you've been doing some research."

"I got my ways."

"And this is Mrs. Bonney, trying to take care of her two boys after the death of her husband. Died of tuberculosis and left them orphaned in the world. And there's the boy. A man told him he'd help him out by giving him some shirts and clothes he'd left in the Chinese laundry, and here were the tickets. Only here comes a fellow claiming the kid stole his clothes and has the sheriff throw him in the pokey. Escaped through the chimney."

Bill Brodkey was able to see through it immediately. First the hypnotic voice to cast a spell. He gets you in the right frame of mind. Oh, you'd see and hear anything then. Clever, he thought. He tried to hold himself so as not to drift away past the moment. Maybe the fellow could really invite you into another dimension. Only he had no intention of going there, not if he could help it.

"And now for the voice box," Bird said, in the same soft but insistent tone, like water murmuring over stones. "And Huerfano, here. The voices will speak through him. If the voice is too low, we'll ask it to speak through the box. There's a microphone inside to amplify it so that you can hear."

So that was the trick, Bill thought. And how obvious. Connect a microphone up to a recording device and there you are.

"But most of the time, the voices speak above the head and to the left of this man," Bird went on. "You can almost look at the point in the air where they speak. And now," he said, nodding to the gnome, who had taken his place on a small, low seat in front of them, "I must ask you to remain very quiet, very still—for only in the silence, in the stillness in the heart of the silence . . ."

So his voice caressed them like a feather, drawing them deeper into a space where they drifted, found it difficult to rouse themselves. Meanwhile, having taken his place in the center under a dull orange light that did not quite illuminate him, sat Huerfano like a grotesque infant. He was rocking slowly back and forth, a deep humming sound coming from his throat.

"Are you there, Mimi?" Bird said.

A child's voice, clear and high-pitched, said suddenly, "They are blocking the way."

"Who, child?"

"All of them."

"For the sake of what will happen here, you must let go your thoughts," Bird said, looking round to each of them, as though to connect each one with his gaze. Charisma, Bill thought. There's something to that. "And concentrate on the experience. Relax. Let yourself go."

They sat quiet, but Bill couldn't tell if they were going along with it. He looked around to see what state Joan was in, but she was sitting with her eyes closed, her face closed to whatever he was trying to read from her. He was alone, a stranger with these people. He felt disoriented, no longer sure of what to grasp. With a sigh, he let go of resistance, of thought. It no longer mattered to him where he was going. Dangerous, some part of his mind cautioned him. I'm tired, he rationalized. I can't fight anymore. Let it go. In the light of day, he would put it all back into place, if he could. He was just tired, he told himself, yet something, he knew, had taken hold of his will. He knew it and could no longer resist it.

"Deeper. We must go deeper," Bird said, lulling them.

"There is someone to talk to you, Bird," the childish voice said. "A member of your family."

"To me?" Bird acted surprised. "That's never happened before."

"The town, what does it mean to you?" A woman's voice sang out.

"I was born here," Bird said. "And lived its life."

"Answer me more."

"The town's a circumstance. But I'm part of it."

"In all ways? Both truth and lies?"

He gave a little laugh. "You must know me all right."

"I killed him, Bird." The woman's voice sang out again, a little to the left and just over the head of the tranced medium.

"Grandmother," he said suddenly. "Now, isn't that amazing? And they never found you out? You tricked him?"

You had to admire him for his sheer gutsiness, the mayor was thinking, hoping that Ramirez wouldn't break in on them too quickly. He was intrigued now and somehow lulled away from all fear. He felt his wife fidgeting beside him, eager for it to be over and to see Bird unmantled at last. The hoax had gone far enough; it wasn't Bird hypnotizing them, but his talent as a ventriloquist that fooled everybody. She wasn't taken in any more than he was.

"They're getting in the way," the child's voice shrilled.

"Well, Grandmother," Bird said, "is it really you?"

"I lured him down to El Paso. Trust me to know him, to know he'd go out for that last dollar, even though he never liked to leave the ranch. I've suffered for it, Bird."

"Just imagine," Bird said, as if it were all news to him.

"Well, that's a good one," Curry Gatlin said. "You've got the facts all right. You've got your past."

"Hush," said someone close to him.

"You know me, Bird," another voice said, "by name only. You're kin to me, but no Peacock, Bird. You're not your father's child."

"Well now, how's that?" the mayor exclaimed again, and slapped his knee. "Now are you satisfied with the facts, Bird?"

"Shut up," Bird said. "Wait . . ."

But it was already too late. A frightful noise had jerked the Mexican out of his trance—first the excited barking of dogs, then pounding on the door.

"Damn it to hell," Bird said. "What fool is that come to spoil everything? I'll go strangle the sonofabitch."

"Well, you got your facts, Bird."

"What the hell do I care about that?" Bird said furiously, unmoved by the noise, as he helped the medium to lie down on one of the benches. "Why, you've very nearly killed him," he said, kneeling down beside Huerfano. "You know what it does to a person to be wakened violently during a trance?"

Some of the group had risen to their feet, agitated, speaking just under their voices:

"You think something's happened . . ." "A bit of drama. He makes it up as he goes along . . ." "It was kind of interesting . . ." "Spooky, though . . ." "You think he put something in the drinks? My head feels funny . . ." "I didn't drink anything . . ." "Did you see something move right above the Mexican's head . . ." "He's got a tape recorder inside that box . . ." "It's all tricks anyway . . ." "What about the little guy . . ." "They're going to break the door in . . ."

"Go on and open the door, Bird," the mayor said, "before they break it in."

"So it's your doing. I figured as much."

"Hell, you can't call the shots all the time."

"Well, go on up," Bird said, to the mayor. "Go on. Let in your dogs. I'm not moving. They can batter down the door for all I care. Give them a little work for their pay. You called 'em, you let 'em in."

"Have it your way," Curry Gatlin said with a shrug, and went up the stairs.

"Stupid," Bird muttered. "Don't worry, friends, no harm will come to you. Your protector's here." Though whether he meant himself or the mayor was open to conjecture. "May as well stick around for the show." They stood uncertainly for a moment, then sat back down as if commanded by the look in his eye.

"Is this part of the game?" someone asked.

"They've got a warrant to search this place," Curry Gatlin said, when he came back with Ramirez and two of his officers. "They've taken over that marijuana you've got growing out there."

Bird laughed. "So that's it. Search all you like, boys. It's not my sport, but it's a good excuse. Am I under arrest?"

"Just don't try anything," Ramirez said. He nodded to the two young men with him, who went upstairs to begin the search, while Ramirez remained, a large, dark figure in his uniform.

"You going to throw me in jail, too?" Bird said, looking from Ramirez to the mayor. "You always were stupid, Curry."

"Maybe you just outsmarted yourself, A. J. I think your man put one over on you. Growing grass on your hill and revealing a few more items of family history than you bargained for."

"Just like you. You think a few facts change what's happened, what we've all had to live?" Bird said. "What a joke. You sitting there as smug as if you'd got hold of the cat's tail. And you haven't got a goddam thing. Lord, if you can't get any deeper, you won't uncover any more'n a dried-out buffalo chip. Facts! The truth runs deeper than that. Look at yourself. Betraying this town every chance you get."

"Betraying it! Why, everything I've done, I've done for Chloride. What've you ever done? Dug up the place for scandal. Sent people running ragged while you turn the place inside out. Bird's good turn . . . turn for the worse." The mayor gave a bitter laugh. "Standing there in the way of progress . . ."

"Well, just don't pretend you got rich off your salary. Every one of those pockets has got a silver lining."

"Prove what you're driving at."

"I can do it all right, if you want to go that far."

"Pot calling the kettle black, it looks to me," the mayor said. "There's more than one kind of fraud and one kind of liar."

"Your kind's better? I'll tell you this. Whatever's going to save this town will take more than your brand of fraud."

They'd moved closer together, and Ramirez stood by, waiting to do what he'd come for. The mayor hadn't given him the high sign yet.

"You think I don't know what's been going on?" Bird said. "Trying to get this ranch out from under me so you could traffic in the sensational. Is that all the imagination you got? Pull out any scandal, truck in any piece of violence, the biggest bribery, baldest lies, and turn them into headlines and cash. Sell it to the movies for big bucks." Bird swiveled around toward the rest, as though to accuse them too.

Netta kept waiting for Ramirez to step in before things got out of hand. Fury had drawn her straight up, and caused little white lines to form around her mouth. "Look at that, look at that," she kept muttering, looking around for moral support. The others weren't paying any attention to her. At first confused about whether they should stay or go, they were now absorbed in the battle.

Bill Brodkey was equally fascinated. The two men brought together as if for a contest that would decide everything, not with revolvers at high noon in the street but at the tail end of the evening, underground with a privileged audience—it was a morality play, an ancient drama. Nothing real and yet everything at stake. Or so it seemed. It's all a creation, it struck him. Whatever the meaning, it had emanated from their being, like fate. But what soil did it spring from? He glanced over at Joan, who appeared similarly rapt. No one will believe this, Bill thought. It belonged to gossip and scuttlebutt, things people talk about but refuse to believe. If nothing else, Peacock had style. Maybe it was all you could ask for. Walking through time with a flair.

"And this ranch," Bird said, holding out his arms, "that's been in my family for three generations now. You think it's all that important to me? I'll let you be witness, folks."

"Another trick?" someone murmured. "Is it going up in smoke?"

Ramirez, increasingly restless, moving from one foot to the other, was eager to get on with it. He didn't have all night. The mayor must have lost his senses; he'd let Peacock lead him on. "Okay, that's enough," he intervened. "You're being charged with growing marijuana on your land illegally."

"You've come all the way out here just to say that?" Bird said. "Been practicing long? Come on, Curry. Even you ought to do better than this put-up job."

"You better call your lawyer, Bird."

"If I call mine, you'd better call yours. Because mine has got a few things to say about what yours has been up to. And he'll not want to face a court case that'll land him outside the law for good. And what about you? I thought you had a hankering for the legislature. I told you I had evidence."

Curry Gatlin felt a pain in his gums. Things had gone blurry and were wavering in front of him. It wasn't right. Everything should have been on his side. All justice said so. But he was having to back off, and he couldn't, not in front of everybody.

"Wait a minute," Ramirez said.

"You wait," Bird countered. "Unless you want to make trouble for yourselves. Over this—and it's not even my property."

"What is this? Another hole to weasel into?"

"Roselle," he said, "come here a second." Startled, Joan jerked up from the bench. As she came up beside him, he pulled a sheaf of papers from the inside pocket of his leather jacket. She had no idea what was going on. The mayor was all bluff, she knew that much. And Bird had successfully called it.

"You see this?" Bird said. "It's a deed of gift for this ranch. And now it's hers," he said, putting the papers into her hands. "Already signed and notarized. Let her create a future out of it. What have you done, after all?" he said, looking from the mayor to the rest. "Despoiled everything, forgotten what you are, where you came from. You have nothing to gain from me. You're on her property now, and you've got no business here," he said to the mayor.

"Wait a minute, Bird."

"I don't have any more time. The moment's come. You've grabbed at it and it's slipped right through. Could've saved yourself the trouble, Curry. You'd have been glad to see me dead to get your hands on all this," Bird said. "The best you can do. You're all so jaded, so worn into the groove, you've lost touch. You can't think anymore. Nothing enters you. Everything stinks of death."

"It's not true," Curry Gatlin protested. "You've got me wrong, Bird," he said, almost apologetically. "There's been a misunderstanding . . ."

"That's right," Bird said. "You miscalculated how far you could push me."

"Bird," Curry Gatlin tried again, "we're messing things up. This has come to the wrong conclusion. And it's my fault and your fault. Think how we used to be friends. Why," he said, as if suddenly remembering, "there's a whole history here. If there's been a misunderstanding . . ."

The politician all right, Bill thought. He can turn on a dime in the middle of a tightrope. He'd been ready to write him off as a bumbling amateur. But that might be premature.

"You're mated to the spirit of destruction," Bird said, undistracted. "But life breaks through anyway—always has."

"The town needs you, Bird. And our own Roselle."

"Needs me?" Bird said, with a laugh. "You still want something out of me . . ."

"You can go on," Curry Gatlin said to Ramirez, as though in a gesture of magnanimity, a momentary aberration having been cleared away. "We can work these things out."

"I thought you wanted me . . ."

The mayor motioned Ramirez to the side, and for a moment there was a heated exchange. Until the police chief stalked out of the room. While the debate went on, Bird turned away and was leading Joan toward a door in the opposite wall. "Bird, where are you going? Listen, Bird . . ."

"I've got other places to go—other doors to open. And when I go through this one, it'll be a step into the future. Come on, if you're game for it. Who knows what'll happen. Why, you might never see me again."

Now what? Bill wondered. Impossible to keep up with him. Versatile. Whatever was coming off, he was determined to be in on it. He was going to watch it and follow it; that's all there was to it.

Seeing the police chief leave, the others began to move. "Hadn't we better leave?" someone said.

"You're free," Bird said, turning toward them. "By all means, go."

"Look, Curry," Netta Gatlin said, "can't we get on home?"

The mayor wasn't paying any attention to her. "Listen, Bird, we've got to settle this."

The fool! Was the man playing to the house, or had he come up with a nub of an idea? All eager one minute to strong-arm him; now, when he had nothing left, the mayor was trying to conciliate him. To Bill, it made no sense.

"Where are you going, Bird?"

"Into the Wilderness."

"He can't be serious," someone said.

"It's not real."

"We've only got a little space and a little time," Bird continued. "Only one more day." He spoke slowly, as if to test his words, paused, looked around once more, then continued:

"It's still there, waiting. My family, yours, everybody else's nearly, they've pushed it back, cleared it, killed off the life in it. The game and the Indians. It's just about gone. But you've got to enter it anyway. At least dream yourself into it and let it kill you or cure you."

"What are you talking about, Bird?" the mayor said irritably. "I was just trying to get us to shake hands before we went home."

The man's mad, Netta Gatlin was convinced. Bird, crazy as a loon. They ought to commit him. Why hadn't they arrested him if that's what they came for? Her husband was beyond his depth, making a fool of himself and getting the worst of it into the bargain. She was plucking at his sleeve. His speech had put grandiose ideas into his brain. And a compliment or two from people trying to make him feel good had turned his head. She'd hardly been able to live with him since the fire. And now he was trying to rise to new heights of grandiosity. Ask her: she'd tell you it was all a bunch of humbug. Only let it take him to the legislature. But for now, let her get him home and feed the cat and let go of this night of foolishness and misadventure. When she woke the next morning, the sun would be in the window and the mountains solid on the horizon and the smell of coffee in the kitchen. Real things.

"Let's go," she hissed. The others were lagging behind out of courtesy, wanting as badly as she to be done with it.

"Maybe you'll die there or maybe you'll find what you've lost," Bird was saying.

Mad. Mad. A fanatic. "How much longer?" Netta jerked her husband's arm.

"Right now it's a junkyard of dead lives and buried civilizations, and all that you can take from it is a little scandal with the smell of the winding sheet."

No one had been paying any attention to Huerfano, who'd sat up and was slowly rocking back and forth as though to return to the state from which he'd been so roughly aroused. The lights began to blink and to go out one by one, and gusts of air swept up and buffeted the walls and those in the room. "Some evil winds are ghosts departed from the dead," a voice complained.

"Let's get out of here," Netta cried. "Curry!"

"The lights . . . I can't see a thing. What's happening?"

A dance of shapes took up the darkness, as people tried to feel their way toward the stairs. But they bumped into those trying to follow Peacock: "We should never have come . . ." "How do we get out of here?"

"Put the lights on."

"They won't take you there," Bird said.

They saw a light playing above a doorway.

"This way," Bird said. "*This* is the way. Don't panic. Here— into the nick of time."

The walls seemed to dissolve into distances. They were no longer inside anything. Once again, Joan held on to his arm. She didn't know if she was flying or falling or what was being carried in the wind—last year's leaves or this year's pollen. It was as though the house were suddenly lifted away and they were carried beyond it to a point where light and darkness met and melted, not yet separated into night or day.

IX   MISE-EN-SCÈNE

He was at a loss. You can't create something out of nothing. But down there in the void of generation, what was the nature of possibility? The dance of illusion, the quirkiness of aberration, chaos? Chaos is in the world, he thought, lying behind every moment. Crack the instant like an egg and the dark rushes upon you but with dancing sparks, as when he'd rubbed his eyes as a child to make the colors dance before his eyes. Sparks of brilliance: blue, orange, white. Now too the colors had whirled around him, been taken up into the violence of entry, the rush of the outside in. Overwhelming. Light and sound seizing hold in the dark burst of confusion, taking him up, whirling him around, till he lost all sense of direction. Groping along, trying to keep his balance. Then to his knees, crawling, as though along a dark passageway, trying to find an opening. The light had deserted him. He might have been a slave crawling underground, the word *freedom* in his mind without his knowing what it meant. He felt his way, his ears and eyes intricate antennae for a new set of impressions. Then the darkness lifted and he stood up, outside under the stars. He stood unthinking, gazing into distances along vistas, as though he'd stepped through a doorway into a difference. Only half awakened.

His name came floating down like a loose garment that did not seem to fit: Bill Brodkey. Billbillbill. The name fell in a ringing, ringed him, captured him to a life of dubious ownership. Let it go, he thought. BrodkeyBill were you? Bill, oh WillieBill. Follow-oh, follow-ho, WillieBill. Wind singing, singsong, song of winging wind, winding-sheet, death and dark. Calling him, ringing him with changes and dangers? He broke into a sweat. Follow, follow.

The sound echoed in the wood, he heard hooting, he heard laughter. His name was in the woods and they were telling him to go get it. He was standing outside it.

Should he claim it, that life of dubious ownership? Should he want it? Or let it be, beckoned by a suggestion that pulsed beyond the borders of his name?

He stood outside. How had he gotten there? The darkness stirred with people he didn't recognize but might know, and whether the sounds he heard reached across the distances of space or mind he couldn't tell. A world inside his head, that was possible. Chaos there too. He paused, breathing hard. He'd been running, though he didn't know why, dodging in and out among the trees. He looked around him, dazed. Someone being chased? Himself? Running, always running, is that what he'd been doing? Driving himself so hard he never knew he could pause. Or was it Bird? The old Bird? Was he running from his death? Had they trapped and killed him? Or was he himself dead? Maybe he'd died and was living outside his life. His mind yielded nothing. Only the memory of shrieks in the darkness. Frightened women perhaps, the sound of weeping? He couldn't tell. He felt he was being watched, by dark presences slipping between the trees.

He tried to remember. His mind yielded an image: Bird and Joan heading toward the door, then a dark rush that could have seized them up like leaves, all of them, and blown them into nowhere in a shrieking chorus. But no, that was time rushing past the dark edges of matter, toward a stillness. People standing there, people moving—a doorway. Did they have to climb down a stairway? Bird beckoning. The Wilderness, he'd said. Pointing toward that. He had caught a final glimpse of the strange gnomelike man, who sat unmoved.

Chaos again. Noise and confusion. Clamor of voices, barking of dogs.

"Where the hell are we? Where did they go?"

"We're lost, I tell you, here in the dark. Where's the moon?"

"Watch where you're going. Bad enough with the tree roots."

"Watch it yourself."

"Why didn't you arrest them? Goddam frauds. Liars and frauds. Killing's too good . . ."

"I want to be home in bed. Oh, I want to be there, all warm under the covers."

"Where is he?"

"In a clump of bushes somewhere with that film star he's screwing."

"Just leading us on."

"Dark . . . my God, it's thicker than gravy. Probably makes it up as he goes along. Churns it out of a machine."

"Why didn't you arrest him?"

"He has to be down there . . ."

Then those voices faded and, as he moved farther away from the house, a dark rectangle beyond the trees, others rose up. More bursts of anger and frustration, dying protests. Then a resurgence.

"Oh, I've twisted my ankle. I can't walk. Oh, I can't. I'm going to stay right here."

"We've got to find our way back."

"I can't walk. I can't. I'll be a cripple."

"All we need. Carry her piggyback, goddam it. Stupid, dumb shit. From start to finish. Stupid, stupid."

"Voice box! Mighty power of invention."

"Letting him put one over that way. What've we got a mayor for?"

"Hear his voice?"

"What? You sure?"

"The owl there in the woods. And the answering whoo-whoo."

"Too perfect for owls. It's Indians."

"You're crazy. Just another trick."

"Listen."

— No one will hear it right. The century has tuned the ear wrong.

— Then you've got to listen hard. Catch the sounds beyond the ear.

— There's no going back. I can't hear the voices.

— Listen to silence then. We're overtaken by an absence. Shaped by it.

"Who said that?"

"Don't anybody look at me."

Voices. In his head too? Bill raised his own voice and called. Somehow Bird was in every part of the woods, his various voices leading away his stumbling pursuers or followers, imitating owl and dog. But Bill himself was lost. When he called out, the sound strained forward in the darkness even as his eyes did. He raised his voice and called again. "Bird, where are you?" *Shadow shaper, schemer.* An echoing laughter rippled through the tree-tops and dissolved, then the silence wrapped around him profound and unbroken. He listened beyond his ears and caught faintly the sounds of voices, distant, receding. He was alone.

Breathless and worn to the bone, that's what. Peacock was leading them all a merry chase through the woods. To discomfit them all. Then he'd disappear as unpredictably as he'd arrived, and the town would be left enough gossip for the rest of the century. Enough confusion, enough belief and disbelief . . . "My gift and your inheritance."

The night had deepened into a lavender dark, very still and clear with a crescent moon fixed in a brilliant slice, a star between its points. He was held breathless, the dark tops of the pines spiring up. Dark forms that breathed a presence, in sharp surround like spectators about to make a judgment. He wanted to reach toward them, win their favor, beseech their help and even comfort. Perhaps he should offer explanations: For you see, I haven't grown up as you have, and I haven't the slightest intuition . . . If I've stumbled into your territory, it's unwittingly, not to offend . . . There are no houses here. No lights, you see . . . And no matter where I turn, I go deeper. He continued to mumble. Not scared, really, but . . . Wandering alone all night in the woods. Perhaps he was giving insult. But it's all right, he temporized. It won't matter. He wasn't at all cold and the moon was out, fuller than he'd thought, a gauzy haze around it—as though the night would give him a month of moons if he wanted, in all their gradations. And the night was soft, a rich night, with a few clouds trailing across it like scarves. It's all right, he told himself again, at the same moment walking into a low branch that stung him across the face. My God, he whimpered. Surely they haven't turned against me.

He was alone—absolutely. Find Joan. It struck him that he'd

lost Joan. He couldn't imagine it. She must be in these woods as well, there with Peacock. He'd stood tamely by and watched her go. And now he had to find her. "Joan," he called, violating the silence, but the trees dampened the syllable, swallowed up her name. He couldn't shout. The state of his nerves was so queer, he was sure he was under a spell. I'm dreaming this, he thought. Making it up as I go along, but I'm here too. So how does that figure?

He wanted to hold perfectly still, listen for some kind of verdict coming on a breath of air. Would he be forever lost in these woods? Would he ever see Joan?

The owl hooted again, and he heard the answering hoot; then a faint vibration of the air became, as he stood listening, the throbbing of drums. The ground trembled too, and he felt the pounding of feet, heard the throbbing of the drums mingled with the chanting of voices. The sounds became words in his head:

> Our father, the Whirlwind
> Our father, the Whirlwind
> By its aid I am running swiftly—
> by which means I saw our father.

The drums and chanting became louder as the light grew brighter in the trees. Firelight. The figures of the dancers moved in the clearing beyond him, dancing faster and faster, till the only thing in his head was the rhythm of drums, and the words that first he heard, then let go of, as he was swept into the sound, then past it, forgetting everything:

> The dreamer rides the Whirlwind
> To meet the spirit gaze
> I circle around—I circle around
> The boundaries of the earth.
> Wearing the long-winged feathers as I fly.

Before his eyes cities and highways fell away from the continent and he was looking at its roots, burrowing underneath its stones. A thrill of terror went through him, as he saw himself emerge from underneath the streets and sewers, from the dust of ancestors not his, the ruck of ancient bones. Born out of the dust. Not a thought of his own. The chanting filled his brain,

215

and the rhythms of the drums and the pounding feet took over his blood. Caught, caught up, he might fly, into that brightness, that beckoning ecstasy.

Forgetting everything as they danced the new earth out of the old. Everything blown away and left fallow. Ready for belief . . . belief in something? Too dizzy to walk, he tripped over a stone. The pain in his leg combined with the dizziness in his head. Peacock's doing. The schemer. Hynotizing them. The explosion of lights had sent him there, dropped him out of time. Left his head floating on his body, and where his feet were he wasn't sure. Roselle must have disappeared in these woods, never to come back.

The beat receded. Yet he strained to hear the dancers. In the lavender light the land grew wild with movement. Riders on horseback, wagons bumping over the rocks. Prospectors and trappers. And women with their household goods. The women had come, to tame these woods and tame the men who tamed the land and the wild man who stood in the way. He looked down at a solitary grave with a wooden marker. Woman, he read; that was all. Anonymous, but living again in Peacock's realm. All of them there, he was sure, fallen out of time, caught in the dramas they had lived. "Everybody's trying to make a comeback," Bill murmured. Only the dead know . . . He tried to remember what Peacock had said. The dead are living . . . The living and the dead. He stumbled on.

The firelight shone on the wall of the canyon, illumining it fitfully as the wood crackled and the flames shot up. "It all begins in darkness," Frank Lucero said, and looked around without comfort, "and goes back to shadows." The brotherhood of shadows had nothing to say to him. Silent, without dreams, the figures moved back and forth. Women taking their pots of cornmeal and squash from the fire.

"Where shall I go?" Frank said.

"Not here. Deeper."

"And what shall I do?"

"Leave everything behind, the whole mixed bag. Create a new saga of the Indian."

He'd get back on his horse and go: day-night, day-night, day-night. And if the days are as dark as the nights . . .

Let's have a new saga of the Indian then, Frank Lucero said to the civilization at his back. But the blood's confused. God knows what's in it now, and you have to kick the beer cans out of the way to start down the trail. Hell, I don't know the language anymore. If it ran in my dreams . . . If—back past memory—I spoke the word . . . Would the rock break open, and the water gush forth?

Connections? Father, is that you lurking in the firelight? But how would I know? So long, One-of-Many-Fathers, heading west, into the glitter of the main chance. California, here I come—where the last lights dazzle off the edge of the continent and snowbirds settle in droves on the salt marsh gone forever. Catch you later, Ma. Sitting at the bar, waving her hand while she drinks with the men, throwing her arms around the freest spender. I see you, I see you.

So get away, get away, get away, kid. Bright boy like you going to sink into drink and nothin'-doing? School and the army and foreign parts, a toehold on the future. Med school, courtesy of Uncle Sam. Army doc. Delivering babies. All shapes and colors of squalling baby. All the mixtures of blood and virtue. Humanity's next round, the next gamble. Forward march.

The original track, forget it. Too late. An Indian saga without an Indian. Send him all the way to the sun, looking for the Father. Truck bumping over the dirt road. The old paths, only if you've been kept close—and even then . . . Maybe survive with the bingo game and businessman's savvy. And a snatch of ceremony back in the kiva. Old secrets whispered in the ear of a few old men far away from the century. Quarrel with the flush toilet and the four-wheel drive. The rest of the throng streams past, going in a hell of a hurry God-knows-where.

Poke around. What you can use, take. Difficult salvage, even if you've left behind the junk. My little black bag? With no feather or holy stone inside. And, you, Linda, plump cactus fruit; but *you* left *me* . . . not for getting drunk or beating you. Only because I worked myself to the bone. And brought home a tired skeleton without hope. What else is there?

Rolling off the spool of day-night, it came round to day, and the day was past noon, the sun pressing warmly upon him, both from overhead and in the reflected heat from the rocks. The brilliance surrounded him, hardening the landscape, and made him squint. See what you've got here: a man gone a little crazy. When did my backside develop such a fondness for the horse? Even the Indians had to learn once; first they ate him. He pulled up the reins. Stop, my friend. Enough for me. He'd come to an assortment of rocks and boulders that maybe had broken off from the cliff above. Nature breaking off a chunk of land for the hell of it. Little ones out of big ones. Scattering a bunch of rocks, a new chaos. The Old Mother, never done rearranging herself. Throwing herself into change. Making up her face. Un-making it. Changing the streams of her blood. Nothing is ever let be. And maybe's she got the push behind her: Now don't take it into your head to sit down and get comfortable. Feel a few shocks in the bones. Let out some fire and flood, turn a few rockslides. What's this about staying put?

Down on the ground, he felt the earth shifting under his feet. His head swam in the glare. "Not going to let me off either," he said, slapping the horse on the rump. Think of this. A cripple for the rest of my life. I'm working hard enough to do it to myself.

Get away, get away, get away fast. Craziness like a germ you can catch, a galloping virus. Head spinning, body shaking. Mind clacking around in the gourd. Running with the craziness like a man caught on fire, galloping on like a symptom. Plague! Plague! And what has harmed us, syphilis or the telephone, uranium poison or greed? Run from the craziness, run from death . . . Run. To wherever. And it is a long way off. But Death is right on your heels, laughing as he runs.

Live alone with the craziness, till you look in the mirror and see its image, and everyone flees including the lunatic. And where do you take your madness? Maybe he would come across the Gila monster, as they called him, hunted by the Forest Service so they could round him up and belt him off to jail. A man who wanted to live alone in the woods. You can't get lost, Frank acknowledged. The Park Service has done a trail for you. To wherever. But not to your father, the Sun. Maybe that is what it means to be lost.

He brought the horse and the mule to the river to drink and

stood watching a hawk ride the thermals, soaring above the sheer rock of the canyon wall, circling and disappearing. Something in that. Style, he thought. Galloping after the buffalo, shooting arrows, onetwothree. Dream about the perfection of the action, the life that is perfect in the dream when you have gotten rid of all the trash, kicked aside the last beer can . . . But that too belongs to the dream time, always in the beginning. I am trying to dream it again, dream myself again in the darkness of broad daylight.

His eye moved down the canyon wall, solid, formidable, with here and there a bit of grass or a knot of juniper struggling out between the crevices. A seed working into a little piece of dirt, dropped by a bird or the wind and making the gamble, against the odds. Wind blowing the hell out of the fresh shoot, the aspiring twig and once every season a drop of water seeping into the crack. Hanging on. The pure instinct—easier than thinking about it. *And then he changed into a hawk and could soar and kill with style. For each thing has to kill in the battle.* Except for rock; rock endures. In the beginning, there was rock. No, before that water. Everything comes out of that. This land he traveled once lay under the sea. Count the teeth, fossilized and green, of the shark mouth, great cave, endless maw. A wicked row. Brute appetite slicing the water with a dark fin. The fun begins in the depths among the sea-covered peaks. Waters receding, the mountains bare, wave after wave of rock, stinking with slime and seaweed, dead fish. Then his people emerging from the dark, through the four lower worlds to this. This world born to the eye. Not just the hawk's eye, or the lizard's eye, the woolly mammoth's eye. But the eye faint with the light of waiting experience. That eye, that awesome eye.

With his knife, he cut slices of colby cheese and unwrapped the hard crackers he had brought. Raid the store for the tickle in the belly. Give the man a cracker. *The saga has no hunt. The atl atl, the bow, even the rifle, hang on the wall. And the fishing line doesn't count.* Only the gut, with its craving. Could you say the rest was stone? Linda, when you left, there was nothing . . . only more work.

He took his food and climbed to the top of a large rock to eat, leaning against the cottonwood that grew to one side. Stone—

not much better than horse. My bones, he said, have been soft-ening for two centuries. *When the waters receded, when the sun had dissolved the waters and left the bare rock, the solid footing . . . the hardness of stone . . . the foundation . . . you had the beginning. The human eye: the first phase of the saga.*

The heat wavered before his eyes, as he tried to eat slowly, the gnawing inside him contesting with the heaviness that lay on top. Pit and stone. You do not go into the wilderness alone.

"So the youth, no longer young—that was his name, Youth-No-Longer-Young—rode forward, carrying on his back three corpses, all of stone, except for a blazing in their eyes. They would not be buried, for they cried out against him, and threat-ened to kill him. And the farther he rode, the heavier they be-came. Himself barely alive in the land of stone, he urged his horse forward, before his father, the sun, set and the land was left in darkness . . ."

His inspiration dulled, and he lay full-length on the rock, the river entering his listening, gurgling and murmuring over the rocks below him. He sat up, leaned forward, tried to settle his hams on a more comfortable spot. A red mark he had missed before came to his eye, a red zigzag high on the canyon wall. "Others had marked the trail before him," he continued, "then disappeared, and left their sign." Someone from that long-ago would have had to climb down from above on a ladder to paint it there; he saw no way of ascending the sheer rock. Up or down, it looked impossible. Painted there to outlive any memory of it, or meaning. "It meant nothing to Youth-No-Longer-Young. Nor to the people who made it, extinct now. Though perhaps the first to climb up to this world from the blind earth below, to live in the wind-carved caves, tending their fires, sleeping in their deer hides, the light at the cave mouth waking them: 'Ah, father. Again the dawn. We wake from inside our mother. Our prayers for the hunt—a deer, a rabbit, a prairie chicken. So we do not starve and our children can live.'

"Disappeared from the earth. Leaving nothing to tell him. And for Youth-No-Longer-Young, there was no sign, even though the Forest Service had left a sign also: 10 miles to Turkey Creek. And the corpses he carried, heavier than the three men alive, so heavy even the horse could barely move."

Something buzzed past his cheek with a drone that made him want to follow it into sleep. Drowsy and hot, he moved toward the shade.

"The ride was long, the day was hot, and Youth-No-Longer-Young felt the silence close around him. First he spoke to the horse: 'My friend, it is unlucky for you. You could have had a young and agile rider, a buffalo darter, an antelope hunter.' The horse sighed deeply, but plodded on, accepting fate. It was a good beast, ragged from hard times. Next he spoke to the corpses:

"'Gomez, amigo. You think you died for nothing?'"

You could let your mind flow into the play of light on the water, the dance of leaves rustling lightly in the breeze. Consciousness flowing back into the stream, leaving the light. It was tempting.

"'Yes,' the corpse answered huskily. 'All the work of my hands, all the words, what do they mean now? The world is changed. It has gone beyond me—beyond my hands, my voice. It's all over with me now. But why have you taken me, where are you going?'

"'You won't leave, damn you,' Youth-No-Longer—Spent Youth said." It was good to simplify these things. "The fool could only argue, he had no strength to fight a corpse. All he could do was keep to the trail, though he didn't believe in it. Despite the wear and tear on his horse, he could neither fish nor cut bait. 'Your life, see, the living thing, is larger,' he said to the corpse. The benefit of his knowledge: someone had told him this in the past, and he repeated it. He knew he had nothing to say for himself. He was trying to be sly. Tricky. If he could convince Gomez' ghost, argue him back to life, his load would be lighter. If the end was bitter . . . and there was nothing left, he would become one with the corpse and they'd stick in one great lump in the center of the path."

Which didn't seem far from the fact of the matter: the doctor dying with the patient. Only a stubbornness beyond his will bearing him on, the persistence of memory, haunting. During his last visits to Gomez, the room was full of people—old friends, cronies, who'd worked with him and drunk with him in the bars after the shift and bitched about the foreman and the company and who'd gone on strike and gotten old together with him. His daughter, Angela, who had come up from Deming, was there, and the boy who'd become the living testimony of the fire.

An important person, this kid, a witness who knew all about it and carried history in his head—who had been, as well, the savior of the cat. What a great event the fire had been, filling him up and setting him ablaze. In his whole nine years together he had never spoken so many words. To so many listeners. With each new visitor, Gomez would say to him. "Tell the story of the fire. See this cat . . ."

And the boy would begin. He loved the story so much, he told it each time with greater length and enthusiasm. A story that had no bottom and no end. The more he told, the more he saw. The fire spreading along the row of houses, catching the theater and the buildings, till all the town appeared to be blazing up. The people running along the streets, trying to save their cars, their possessions at the risk of their lives. Panic from the theater. The roar of the flames, the wail of the fire trucks.

The cat he saved till the last.

"A wonderful story," Gomez said. "You see how well he tells it."

Did the kid have a home? Frank had wondered. And school, had it too gone up in smoke? These things did not matter. The boy had his story, Gomez, and the cat—all he needed. Though the cat was half starved and every rib showed through its skin— no doubt it was abandoned before the fire—still it played with string, chased bits of paper, and slept much of the time on Gomez' stomach.

"Look, you see," Gomez said, "it won't let me move, that cat. My stomach belongs to him."

"Does your cat have a name?" Frank asked the boy, Ramon.

"Fuego," he said, "because he came out of the fire. And it's black and white, the color of burned things."

"Ah."

"But it's his cat," the boy said, nodding toward Gomez, "because he told me I could keep it here and feed it here. There is no place in my house."

Was he there for the sake of the story or Gomez or the cat? It

222

was impossible to separate them. When the boy left for a time, Gomez lay in a stupor and Frank could not tell if he was dead or alive. When the boy returned, the old man rose out of his dark hole and entered the room like a grandfather. Meanwhile the boy sat on his bed and the cat romped across the covers.

"You see, he likes me," the boy said. "But he will play for you, if you want."

Frank took the string.

"Young things are all the same," Gomez said, with a slight smile.

The boy. The cat. Doctor and priest standing by. Better the boy and cat.

Mother, Frank said, when I was born, they gave you tea of the root of the white daisy to speed delivery and spruce tea afterward. So you told me once. And about Grandmother, who knew all the herbs. Some she gathered and some she grew—onions, wild mustard, peppergrass, beeweed pods, sage, mint—for healing. She made brews of tansy, yarrow, and boneset to stem fever and ease pain. Long ago and with different knowledge. In the dimness of memory, perhaps from hearsay and invention, he saw his grandmother, watched her hands and how they came to know a plant. Touching it . . . The plant told her what it was, how it was to be used. Told her whether it was poisonous or if it was food for animals or birds and if it could be used by humans for food or medicine. And in the dimness of the past too was a medicine man with his sacred dance, the holy stone and feather. Even if he could go back to that . . . If it were possible . . .

Other routes. From thought to confusion. Shall we be clear about the relation of cause and effect? In the world in which it worked, nature had given many gifts. She had them to give: penicillin and laser beams and atomic power. A whole nexus with a little nucleus of assumptions. And that is what is given me, Frank acknowledged, the ground of my thought. But if you moved over or back a few steps and put yourself into a different relation to the forces, perhaps the same forces, what would happen then?

"'Look,' said the corpse, 'this is a story. You're wandering off the track. I'm lying here—and don't tell me it's comfortable—

while you get lost in your head. Take your foul-tasting concoctions and cure yourself. Better to get drunk.'

"'Better to turn against yourself?' Spent Youth argued. 'Better to pull your own body into the grave?' And the jaded traveler saw how the lifeblood had leaked away. He tried to look inside, look down into the dark place that lay behind the ghost's blazing eyes. And saw then a man being strangled by his shadow, an eerie light surrounding it."

Enough of it. The sun was beating on him, the heat circling him, and he sweated as if he were melting. He clambered down from the rock, stripped off his clothes, and threw himself into the river. A shudder of cold went through him. Gasping, he stood up for a moment in air that made him shiver. Then he submerged himself and swam a short distance. It hurt his chest to breathe, the water was so cold. He couldn't swim far, it was too shallow and too cold, but he caught hold of a rock at the center and let his legs float out behind him.

Then he stood up, waded out, dried himself off, climbed the rock, and sat naked in the sun. The cold had left him momentarily exhilarated.

"Old man," Frank said, in his own voice, "you came with me. If I am hollow and bare, and the shadow is inside . . ." He didn't know how to conclude.

Shadows of pines and juniper fell across the rocky wall of the canyon. The rock the sea had left behind, white with only sea slime and the stench left by the sun. Dying fish and breeding worms, the stink of receding waters. And the roar of heaving earth, great spurts of lava. Heat and steam and crumbling rock, attacked by wind and rain. He was tired. He gathered up his things and put them into his pack, retrieved the animals, and climbed back on his horse. Let him put his mind to only the simplest of tasks, guiding horse and mule through the branches that sometimes tangled them up so that he had to cut out the brush with his ax, setting up a tent, and cooking a meal for himself. None of it was easy. He could not keep his head clear. He went rattling on, unable to keep still.

"'But you fought, old man,' Spent Youth argued with the ghost, as he labored forward. 'You lived and fought . . .'

"'And look what happened,' the ghost insisted. 'Giants, stretching their arms across continents. Copper companies, the power of nations. What is a union anymore? What is . . .'"

"See this boy," Frank interrupted, startling himself. "Would you tell him not to live? Old man,"—Frank whispered—"what place have I come to? Nothing I remember. But I cannot carry your corpse any longer."

Before she knew it, her sense of things had dissolved, as though the pattern that held them together had been pulled apart, the lines blurred. More than the wind that drives straws into telephone posts, this wind could blow you out of the four directions. Lights played with her mind, threw her off balance. And she was choked by a sense of panic as the wind swirled around her, bringing to mind the night of the fire. She sensed the movement of people about her as she was propelled forward, as though a will lay in the center of wind. She was more conscious this time of being urged forward, had more of a sense that someone knew where he was going. "This way," Peacock's voice insisted. They were moving down a passage; they were in an open space like a cave, and it was very dark. She was visited by a breath of cold and something oppressive. Alone, they could have been at the end of the world, with no one, nothing else near them that lived and breathed. Everything's gone, she thought, as she fought down the desire to scream. There was something she had yet to trust. She had to do that.

Then they were outside under the stars, not far from the house. He led her past the stables and alongside the corral.

"Where are the others?"

"Oh, they'll be along directly," Peacock assured her. "We're all in it together." He gave a chuckle. "You bet we are."

"And Bill?"

"Him too."

"Where're we going?"

"Out here a space. Mind you don't lose those papers."

The horse pond glimmered in the moonlight as they took the path winding round it. How come I don't feel the cold now? Joan wondered. And the wind's gone. Things keep changing.

"I don't understand," she said.

"It's yours now," Peacock said, leading her into the trees.

"What am I supposed to do with it?"

"You'll know. You'll find out."

"I'm not what you think."

"Oh but you are," he said, pausing, turning to look at her directly. "Wonderful face with the light on it."

"But, you see . . ." There was a life she'd always sensed and been drawn to in her men, but it seemed it never got through the tangle of their limitations. Or through herself either. Always at half throttle. Or more accurately, half throttled. You could always sense it in someone else, the energy and the waste. The great secret that nobody told. Who knew how to do it differently?

"There's only a little time," he said. "The crack behind the instant, the dream time. Then you have to go back."

"Time for what?"

"Time for everything," he said. "Hang on to those papers. You'll need them afterward. Now carry on, past those trees." He gave her hand a squeeze.

"Where are you going?" she wanted to know. "Don't leave me here."

"I have to go back to the others. They'd sit out the night confused as a turkey flock and wander around for days with their eyeballs on strings. Don't worry."

"What do you mean, Don't worry? What are you doing? What am I doing? I don't understand this. I thought they'd be in their cars by now. Why haven't they gone home?"

"Easy does it," he said. "Save your emotions; you can use them better than that. They're looking for me," he explained, and laughed. "They'd like to strangle me if they could. Wandering around in the woods without knowing where they're going. They'll need a little rescue."

She couldn't blame them. What a fool, letting herself be strung around like this. What was he doing, giving her his house? It was all mad, she just wanted . . . "Oh, don't leave me," she cried. "The house," she said. She didn't want that. She wanted all the wonderful promise: him. Something had happened; she wanted it to stay as it was.

"It's yours now. Don't worry about me. Everything's gone like magic."

"I can't . . . ," she said. He gave her a little pat on the rump to urge her forward.

"Go on, now." And was gone before she could get her anger together and make a protest.

"Wait," she cried, and started to move in his direction, but the trees had swallowed him up. "Bird," she cried. "Where are you?" Behind her she heard an owl hoot. "Bird," she cried again. "Damn the man." It wasn't just disconcerting to be shuffled around in the dark, it was . . . She didn't like mysteries. No, the truth was she adored them. Only she wanted company. "Damn the man."

She thought she saw a faint light in the distance in the direction he had gone. I ought to be able to see the house from here, she said to herself. But she couldn't make it out. Would he have gone back there? No, the others were wandering in the woods too. She turned around. By now she'd lost all sense of direction. Lost. Jesus, what was she supposed to do about that? A man who'd just turn her loose in the woods with a pat on the backside and the deed to his house. What sort of man was that? She'd have liked to give him a piece of her mind, except that he'd put himself nicely in charge of it. Maybe I'll never see him again, she thought but prevented herself. It would make her miserable. But I'm lost, she said; nothing changed that fact.

She'd have to find the others—no better off then she. But how? Find her way at night in the woods. How absurd! Wild animals might attack her. Mountain lions, bears. Suppose she had to sleep on the ground. No protection. She was exhausted already. Damn the man!

The haze had dropped from the moon and the light falling on the trees defined the branches with a faint aura, brought a sheen to the outcroppings of rock. The air was velvety, soft with an edge of coolness, like the backdrop for a scene behind a scrim. And the night woods were both inviting and alien. She'd have liked to move as if she belonged there, would have been glad to

227

forget she had no place within the unseen activities of the woods, the night movement of animals and hunting birds, the converse of roots with the earth and the deep sources of water. She knew that fear shaped her breath, her efforts to see everywhere. She did not want to go on, but the faint light suggested that something waited not far beyond. Tentatively she moved forward, met by sounds she paused and listened to but did not recognize. Birds? Wild animals? For a moment she was sure she caught the neighing of a horse. But when she listened again she was sure she heard voices and what sounded like the banging of hammers. She couldn't believe it. But then why should she believe anything, even Peacock? An opening appeared ahead, with light concentrated in a clearing. Could it be she'd circled back to the stables? But she saw no fence or outbuilding. Both lights and people defined the clearing ahead: the glow of lanterns set at intervals and various figures, some running back and forth. In a moment she could see they were setting planks, fetching chairs and tables from a cluster of wagons.

When she came up, a man was barking out orders as he alternately waved his arms and rumpled his hair. People dashed right and left as though impelled by his voice alone. She saw that a rough stage had been set up, and off to one side a woman stood patiently while a young girl fastened the stays of her dress.

"Costumes? Of course, costumes," the man said to whoever had raised the question. "Otherwise it wouldn't be dress rehearsal now, would it? We need the table, can't do without it. Use your common sense, boy. And the doorway in front."

"Where's Margaret?" he demanded, jerking in one direction, then the other. "All this waste of time," he yelled. "Infuriating. Margaret," he bawled.

"Off there," somebody suggested.

"Well, get her on, get her on." His attention moved elsewhere. "Jack, are you there?" An assent came from stage left. "I want to start this bloody thing while we've still got the moon."

Some kind of play, it was clear, and they'd chosen this spot to rehearse. Several of the cast had come forward now in their costumes, the women in long-skirted calicoes, then men in buskins and breeches. Joan almost laughed: what an extraordinary rescue in the depths of the woods. More acting. She wondered where she could stand to watch without drawing attention to herself.

But the eye of the director was on her. "It's time you showed up," he said. "We're ready to begin."

The reprimand startled her. The man had taken her for someone else; it seemed to happen every time she turned around. But before she could explain or think what to do next, he had turned his back and was gesticulating wildly in another direction. "You just have to make do," he said in answer to a question about the staging. "Remember we've got to go on tomorrow, and we've lost the rehearsal unless we do it here. Damn for getting off the track. Damn for losing time. Things to plague a man."

He was mumbling now. "But it's enough," he consoled himself. "Everything we need . . . We've made do before." A hint of pride. "Stage. A few planks to do it, a doorway, table, chairs. Back to scratch, but doesn't it all start from there anyway?"

She lingered within earshot, both curious and eager to put in a word. "What is all this?"

He gave her a glance, rude and annoyed: she had no business worrying at his elbow. "Why aren't you in costume?" he demanded. "Just because you're not on yet . . . There, there!" He was by then yelling at a boy who had set a chair in the wrong place.

"Go. That's a good girl," he said, giving Joan a little swat, who bristled and was determined to set things straight. That was the second time, and it was twice too many. The liberty! "Now look . . ."

"Ah, Margaret," he said, ignoring her, reaching a hand toward an older woman coming up. "Let me kiss you, love. Such a bad day, dear, but I know you'll give it your best. You know how to create the mood. Your best blue mood. You always have to think about how Caleb's been on you: you've not been a good wife, not been doing the work of God you came to do. You know. All right, take it from Scene I," he called out.

"For God's sake, girl," he said to Joan, who was still underfoot. "Get into your clothes. What ever do you want? We haven't got all night. Over there." He pointed, and it seemed to her she'd better go.

Where he was, he could only guess. Not lost, for he could always find some branch of the river. Had lost all track of time, though. Taken into the flow of things moving past. He could not stop the minutes or hours. No longer did he know time. Now there was only light—and body. Light told him when to rise; his hunger, when to eat; and his fatigue, when to stop or sleep. Each dawning he climbed on the horse, traveled that day's country—around weathered red bluffs, through hills covered with mesquite and prickly pear, scrub oak and cedar, through the canyon of the river when he came back to it. He moved so deeply into the silence his voice was strange to him, as if it did not belong, and his horse seemed not some separate creature but part of him that moved like an instinct because his mind floated beyond him, filled with sunlight and trees or night and shadow. And even then he was not sure whether he was in daylight and dark or whether he looked down from some other vantage point where day and night were part of a dream.

He was not alone. Not only had the corpses come with him, but the town was there too. Every once in a while he caught a glimpse out the corner of an eye. He caught the voices of men, heard them gathering together a posse to go out and search for the Indians who'd killed Judge Collins. Heard the cry of a woman stabbed by her husband in a fit of jealousy. Caught the drumbeats of the Indians and heard the hooves of their horses as they headed off the reservation toward Mexico. And heard other voices he knew. But he couldn't move to the left or right. Something drew him deeper, against his understanding. He had to continue his saga. He would follow a single thread and leave the rest to his horse. Otherwise he would be lost altogether.

"The second corpse was even more dangerous than the first," he continued, "for it was more stubbornly alive, and the blaze in its eyes was the blaze of fever. For a long time it made Spent Youth carry him on his back. 'My friend,' it whispered, 'do not think we are so different. Believe me, it is in us both to be led. Don't you see her, right there in front of me, and behind you? Ah, beautiful. She beckons and I must follow.'

"'I thought it was gold you were after,' Spent Youth said. His back was caving in from the weight. 'You mean I'm carrying her too?' He could not even look around to see.

"'But, of course, you fool,' the voice said. 'You know me—and her. I look for gold everywhere. And when I harvest my field, the best of all cannabis, it will be like nuggets in the hand.'

"'What for, Henry?' Though Spent Youth did not say so, he could sense the shape that led Henry Martinez on, the woman who was the shape of all desire . . .

"Light as air, this corpse, yet heavy as the heaviest metal. No roots in the earth, but always leaning forward into expectation, leaning so far forward he must come crashing to the earth. Not a future exactly, nor a dream of the future, only the wild fever that had always sent men running and scratching, ready to blow out somebody's brains. All the conquerors . . dark-skinned and light. The fever and the hunger, and all of them devouring, devouring everything in the path. And now Henry, the poorest of the devourers, devouring himself. Behind him, Spent Youth knew, the corpse was eating his own flesh, his own arm. And when there was no more of him, he would devour whoever was standing near. He would eat himself alive that way, all the while he was a corpse. All the while gazing at the shape of desire. And Spent Youth was terrified for himself.

"'But don't you see,' the voice whispered, and Spent Youth caught again the blazing of the fever, and was held by it. 'Do we not travel for the same thing?'

"Spent Youth was unable to answer, for he did not know what he traveled for. He did not want to say he traveled out of his sickness, his fatigue. He did not believe the sun awaited him. It was an old story. 'I thought,' he said, trying as usual to defend himself, 'you wanted to get rich.' And with a turn of his head, he saw the shape that beckoned was a fatal woman. Maybe to him woman was only fatal.

"'Ah. Rich yes, money yes. Power yes. To buy life,' the corpse said, 'what else? What is life when you have no power?'"

Ready to rave himself, caught in the futility of words, Frank wanted to get down off his horse and lie on the ground until he became part of it. This weaving a net around himself, capturing himself with words, from words like the spiders' webs that held him for a moment, that you tore through, the strands still clinging to your hair and face—it was too much. Like telling yourself jokes and forgetting the punchline.

If only he were rid of them, the corpses of words. You see the day as the light that fills it and the night as the emptiness of it, as though a single vessel. And the light touches forms into the eye, and the night puts shadows into the mind. And one flows into the other. And then they are torn away like sheets of paper, and everything floats. I see them all here again. The town. The mayor ready to give his speech. They will listen. There's Langtry and Pruitt; he came finally. They've all come for a speech from the mayor. It's about progress, Henry. It's about new sources of wealth. That's what will save us, that's what they think.

Frenzy. Only frenzy, the town throwing itself into celebration. Whistling for the main chance, the new beginning. Roselle, come out of the shadows. People will look at you and not know what they want, only that they want it, yearn for it. Imagining things. Dreaming awake.

Ah, Linda. So what do you say? Frank demanded of himself. For when you looked at a woman, you imagined what could be, what you could be.

His own wife Linda held out her hand from the shadowy throng. He yearned for her plump arms and lovely breasts, the roundness of her hip. "Come to the river," he said to her, "and see your reflection there." She used to stand in front of the mirror after her bath, examining herself critically—until he came up behind her and put his hands on her breasts and kissed her neck. Until the end, when she would pull his hands away and frown. "I would kiss you now if I could put my arms around you. Oh, don't be angry, I know what is in your mind, and I can't help it, I can't help myself."

"You work, but you work for nothing. I can't stand it."

"What do you mean? I work hard. Everywhere people are sick, in terrible shape, dying."

"You think I don't know? But it's the wrong way. Like when we were up north."

"I don't want to think about it."

"No," she said, "you want to forget it isn't there."

What else was there to do? He saw them again, coming to him, the men who had been poisoned from working in the uranium mines and the children with lung diseases, poisoned by the air from the power plant, and the boys drinking themselves to an early grave. They'd come to him, and gone away no better, carrying their deaths.

"What could I do? Lack of money, no equipment. A losing battle."

"You live in the giving-up, in the sickness of the sick."

"Don't leave. Don't leave. If you go, what will be left?"

"'I won't leave you,' the corpse told Spent Youth familiarly, tauntingly, 'till you've wrestled me to the ground.'"

The bedrock of devotion. Everything else leaves, you've nothing else, but demons and curses. "And all the burdened, defeated hero could do was sit on his horse with his back straight, continuing in the direction of the horse's head."

He was going to make a speech, that's what they told him. And everybody'd be there, by jim and by gee. An audience the likes of which nobody's ever seen. Fancy that. He hadn't made it up. He'd been called upon. Throw your voice into the wilderness, they told him. This is your moment.

Oh, the sweet ripeness of it, the past about to break into the future. On the breath of mighty words. Well, he was the man for the moment, and right now he was rushing forward to meet it, ducking his head and moving straight along as though to butt the trees out of the way. He couldn't be late for destiny, not a man like him, marked for great things. And words to give a shape to progress, take a populace over the rim and onto the tide of history. Words ringing out, the pure power of human speech, his, creating the moment, this time, this place, the audience in his palm. Oh, the pure victory of the word, as he went on to the legislature, the Senate. Who knew what might lie beyond?

If only the rest, including his wife, wouldn't fret a man, hang on to his coattails and worry his forward stride. He kept hearing a nagging at his back, as Netta and the others behind him struggled to keep up. He'd left them to catch up as best they could, pulled along by his own straining eagerness, a gathering momentum. Wait, they called. Oh wait. But he plunged forward undistracted, undaunted. He felt movement all around him, as of wagons and horses and people on foot. They were coming to hear him. A great gathering to bring the folks together. A mighty congregation.

And he had to get there first, so as to give proper welcome in the tumultuous arrival. Stand there and feel the rising excitement, poise himself on the brink of the spectacular while faces looked to him and voices grew silent. As he went along, he rehearsed the speech he was putting together, repeated certain phrases over and over till they had the right rhythm. The power, he thought, the power. Words and the way you say them. The spell, the incantation. Let them feel the hypnotic effect. Bird, move over. You're not the only one in the rodeo.

If only the wagons wouldn't drive through his concentration, the neighing of horses interrupt, the powwowing of Indians make him lose his train of thought. For the future was to be created out of words. Words calling up a new world, words to create buildings and factories and cities and space stations. Conjurations of words. Powers and potencies. Strike with a word and let the water gush forth. Let the future move through him in a rush of words.

Everything was in the air, like a fireworks display. Rockets and catherine wheels of possibility. Sparks and colors. Scarves and flags of shining strands. "We are a great people": that would have to be in the speech. Think of what it took to settle the country. The pioneer spirit. He'd say those things again. Speak to the hard recalcitrance of things. Whatever the adversary, he'd go and do battle. There were heroes back then, those hardfisted gunfighters of the West who stood up to the threat and saved the town. The old spirit—stubborn, feisty, even ruthless. Oh, it took ruthlessness. You couldn't let anybody stand in your way. Knock them aside. The West never belonged to pussycats. "Stand up and be men": he'd say that. "And you ladies, stand behind them": he'd say that too. People had to be reminded. Strength and courage. The old stick-to-itiveness, as his fifth-grade teacher would have said. Great little woman. Now he'd open the door and let the words come gushing out. He was running toward inspiration with every step. Let the mind follow as best it would.

"Curry, you're going so fast." With a burst of effort, Netta caught up to him, gasping. "We're here. We're all here behind you."

"Wait up, Curry," Lester Pruitt said. "I've come for your speech after all. I'm with the town, Curry. The town above all. We've got to buy the future, boy. Break a leg, old friend."

The jeweler was out of breath, and it was too dark to see. The stars looked to be less than half a carat in the sky. The brilliance lay back in his own jewelry case. Only let him get home. His wife complained of torn stockings, snagged lace, her grandmother's at that. Mrs. Langtry said for her to wait till she'd sprained her ankle, then she'd have something to complain about. For she had to hop and limp along, putting her weight sometimes on her bad foot just to keep up with the others. And why wouldn't somebody wait and pay attention?

"Let me go on ahead," the mayor said, rushing away from the cumbersome pigtail of folks behind him. "Can't you see I've been called? Can't a man have a little time and breath and consideration when things are popping like corks? I've got to rehearse, dammit. It's an occasion."

"Don't leave me alone, Curry," Netta Gatlin pleaded.

"It's all right, hon," one of the women said. "You'll be proud of him, right proud. It's not all of us rushing to meet the future."

"He'll catch cold," Netta wailed.

As they headed toward the spot of light in the distance, she watched her husband disappear into the trees just beyond them.

Lanterns set at intervals in the clearing ahead of him illumine a little scene between the trees. Footlights. And Bill sees that a stage lies ready, a table in the center, a rude chair and a bedstead over by the side. Figures move back and forth. "Where's the washtub?" someone asks and a young boy flies ahead of his feet to one of the wagons.

"Get going," a large, burly man insists. "We've got a full moon, and she'll go scudding across the sky before we know it."

It's full now, Bill murmurs to himself, looking up. But not before. "You're putting on a play here?" he blurts out; it seems so wonderful and ridiculous. My God, he's walked square into the middle of it.

"What does it look like?" the director says, with a flick of his hand. He has no time for stupid questions. "And for every minute you're wasting," he yells at the crew, "you're wasting a dozen human minutes, one for everybody here. Now in five minutes you'll have wasted a whole man-hour . . ."

"Not to mention horse-hours," the prop boy puts in, his shrill voice coming from the bush.

"Somebody ought to thrash the lad," the director mutters.

Aside: "That's how the night goes. And there's so little time."
He turns to Bill. "They're like a bunch of strays. It's enough to
send a man raving, trying to get them all together. But here, let's
find something for you to sit on. We need an audience. We're
heading toward California and we have to camp tonight in these
woods. All right, ready up there?" Then turning back to Bill:
"We've got to get this rehearsal in. Short schedule as it is." He
sits down on a stool, motions for the young boy who's brought
the washtub to bring over a plank and a couple of rocks for Bill.

"Okay, Margaret. Places everyone. Put yourselves in the right
mood. They've traveled across the continent—been through
hell, remember. Just like today." Bill hears a sardonic laugh
from one of the actors. "No preparation for it, just taking their
knocks. Put yourselves back into the memory. Left behind their
homes and families, maybe never to see them again. And had to
keep their eyes on the mud and the rapids and the graves of
cholera victims. And all they've got is plains or woods, like us.
Not a log cabin waiting for them in this wild place. They've had
to do it all. Let that live in the characters. You've had experience. Let 'er go."

*Woman scrubbing clothes in a tub, pouring in kettles of hot
water that she has heated over the fire. An Indian girl helps her,
takes a basket of clothes out the door of the cabin, stage left. A
small boy sits playing on the floor. A baby sleeps in a rough
wooden cradle, stage right.*

WOMAN: [*Brushes back a strand of hair that has fallen in her
eyes, then wipes her eyes, perhaps from the steam, with the
back of her hand.*] I wish my dear husband would speak to
me. I don't know what I have done to displease him so. Oh,
and the children are vexatious this morning. [*Drags back the
boy, who has opened the door and escaped outside.*] I told
you to stay in. Now look. You've got mud all over you. [*Slaps
him. The child bursts into tears.*] I will weep myself. The girl
does nothing and if I don't keep my eye out every minute, she
runs off. [*Goes to the door and peers out.*] I knew it. [*Her
child has come up and buried himself in her skirts.*] Yes, yes,
it's all right. You're a good boy. [*To herself.*] If only they weren't
in motion and underfoot every moment. Oh, Caleb, what will

I do? You look at me with a frown and go off. And when will you return and in what spirit? I pray for you, for the children, for the strength . . . [*Puts her hand to her head.*]

"You see how it is," the director says to Bill. "It's hard to do a scene like this nowadays. To put yourself back into that perspective. Here she is, from a good family, warm, close-knit, but she'll tear herself away from all that. All fired up with religious enthusiasm. Wants to be a missionary. Convert the savages, change the world. Marries this preacher she's only been introduced to just so she can go at it, have her chance. Crosses a continent. Imagine. All for the sake of an idea."

"The risk," Bill says, appreciating it. "The courage."

"And full of doubt every moment. I've written it myself. Tough material."

"I know what you mean. I've written . . . ," Bill says, but the director ignores him.

"She's different, you see. She has a belief working through her. I mean, the others: dreams of riches, a land of milk and honey. You understand that. But these are bringers of light. Hah!"

"Do you believe in your own creations?" Bill asks him, but the director motions him to silence.

Man entering, slowly removing his hat. His shoulders slump, and he looks as if he is barely able to stand.

WOMAN: Caleb! I did not expect you back so quickly. What? Are you ill?

CALEB: I could barely ride. I had to turn back before I was halfway there.

WOMAN: Come, you must rest. [*Leads him over to the bed against the wall of the cabin, stage right. He sits on the edge while she pulls off his boots.*] It is too early for you to take up your duties. You're still not recovered.

CALEB: [*Sits there dejectedly.*] But Sarah, they will forget all that we've taught them. Already two Sundays have passed without a proper sermon. They were singing the hymns so well.

SARAH: [*Sighs.*] We do all that is humanly possible. I don't know, Caleb. Sometimes I wonder if I have the strength.

CALEB: This is the way you greet me—with doubt?

SARAH: [*Weeps.*] The children take up my time, the washing, the canning . . . chasing the cattle when they wander off. And when you're gone . . .

CALEB: I'm sorry, my dear. [*Takes her hand.*] I've been in one of my brown moods. I do love you. Please forgive me.

SARAH: [*Looks at him for a moment. Wipes her eyes, sits beside him, and puts her arms around him.*] You've saved me. Oh, you don't know . . . I thought I was abandoned, by you, by . . .

"She doesn't dare say it," the director says confidentially to Bill. "She comes that close to real despair, so close to the edge. But you see, if she says that word, if she really thinks it . . ."

"She's into the twentieth century," Bill says.

The director gives him an ambiguous smile. "God and a husband, the four corners of the world. We'll see. Only what a husband! One of the melancholy. When the brown moods overcome him, he takes it out on her. She happens to be there."

The director is enjoying himself, is growing expansive. The actors are on cue, doing well. He has an audience.

CALEB: Sarah, I'm so tired. Even when I sleep, I dream I'm on horseback.

SARAH: Here. Lie down and rest. You'll feel better when you've slept. First, some tonic. [*Fetches the medicine bottle and spoon, pours out the tonic for him.*]

CALEB: You're a good wife, Sarah.

SARAH: [*Helps him to lie down, watches as he closes his eyes. Then moves softly to the doorway. The door is open, the boy nowhere in sight, but she doesn't appear to notice. She looks out.*] They sing in such disgusting voices. How they murder the words. I think of Mr. Griffith leading the choir—so long ago. And we lifted our voices. [*Turns slightly, looks down at the floor.*] And the smell! I can't get close to them. The filth and the smell turn my stomach.

"Make it even stronger," the director says. "The disgust. Let's hear the end of that speech again. Wants to convert them," he says. "You see how she feels, but she can't face what she really feels." Bill sees a gleam of almost feral pleasure in his eyes, as though he has proved a point. "That's the rub." He nudges Bill with an elbow.

"But you must feel some sympathy. It comes through the writing, or at least the acting."

"Of course, of course. Poor misguided fools."

"Given the perspective of a later age," Bill argues, he's not sure why. "Or a powerful cynicism . . . If you're down inside . . ."

"You mean error rules everything? And the truth gets so twisted out of shape . . ." The director waves his arms as though to clear away a distraction. "But you want to feel kindly toward it. Is it all redeemed by the idea? Dedication. The rack and the thumbscrew for the sake of salvation. Tell me, tell me. Cherish all this good intention, is that what you're saying?"

"Who's saying anything?"

"I don't have time to argue. There's no time. It's their lives after all, the truth of their living them. Maybe that's the only truth. But then . . . Good, good." He is now speaking to Margaret.

SARAH: I think of the home I left. Mother and Father and dear Anne. Never to see them again. For this work that called me . . .

[*Softly at first, then more loudly, the drums begin to beat from the trees surrounding the clearing. Then there is the pounding of dancing feet.*]

How bright is the moonlight!
How bright is the moonlight!
Tonight as I ride with my load of buffalo beef.

"Trying to dance the buffalo back," the director says. "They're having a great hunt. All the beloved dead, the prairies high with grass—and buffalo. The new heaven and the new earth. Dancing it all back. Each step toward the immortal. Build up more on the drums."

SARAH: The savages! [*A shiver goes through her.*] Like children. They lie and tell you they'll give up their medicine . . .

239

"There's the stumbling block. Can't get them to give up their medicine. Power—and they hold on to it for dear life. Oh, they argue one side, promise on the other. She and Caleb wring endless promises from them. But they go back and chant their chants, keep their medicine, even if they do sing the hymns. It would have been interesting to hear the arguments among the elders, the tribe having it all dumped in their laps. Holding a new idea by the tail. One of the scenes I scratched." He shakes his head. "You can get too ambitious. Ruin the form."

"So what's the point?"

"There is none. They kill her for her pains. Look back and it seems inevitable. The whites have brought the measles that kill the babies. And white man's medicine does no good. And this white woman's children do not die. What are they supposed to think?"

SARAH: I was thinking of Mother's rose garden. When I was a child, I used to try to pick the buds open; I was so impatient for them to bloom. [*Looks down as though holding a rose in her hand.*] But when they opened, they were only mangled flowers, and I would weep at the slaughter I had made.

[*A woman elegantly dressed in a striped silk, with bustle and lace collar, moves across the stage, a troupe of men following her.*]

GYPSY: Let me take it then. I'll figure out something to do with it. Just let it bloom right here in my parlor. A rose will smell as sweet without any name at all; think of that. [*Laughs.*] And I don't have a name. My sport is my fame; I go all over, the Gypsy girl. [*Moves to the other side of the stage, while Sarah stares after her with a mixture of astonishment and loathing as the lights fade.*]

[*When the lights come up again, the scene is the interior of a parlor, with a piano of burled walnut in the left corner, a brocaded sofa with a large gilt mirror above it at rear center, a love seat at stage right, with occasional chairs and tables furnishing the room. A crystal chandelier sheds light on the scene. Gradually the room fills up as the girls enter the par-*]

lor, *descending from a staircase, rear left. Several men observe admiringly.*]

HANK: Gypsy, you're the one. I took a bath and trimmed my beard—got all gussied up for you. [*Holds out his chin for her inspection, then his hand.*] Even got the dirt out from under my nails.

GYPSY: [*Runs her hand over his cheek and tugs his beard playfully.*] Look at you. Almost civilized. Well, you'll have to behave and not wreck the furniture.

"Things have changed a little," the director says. "A mission and house, she left those behind. And others follow, of course: the way of progress. I could have done another scene, the Indians actually forcing their way into the cabin, tomahawking her and Caleb. That's the way it happened. The boy escaped—hid under the bed. Or had the screams offstage. Get a crowd all worked with the violence. But then they'd miss the point. Why overdramatize . . . even the truth?" Bill tries to make a comment, but the director plunges on. "You can see the town." He waves his hand, and Bill can make out through the trees the facades of a general store, a bank, and a saloon, along with several handsome brick houses. "I'm thinking the town ought to be in it more, but I haven't worked it out. Anyway this gal of ours is quite something, wouldn't you say?"

"Proud of your creation?" Bill says wryly.

"In a way," the director says, giving him a sharp look. "But she has a mind of her own. You'll see what I mean."

Girl of about twelve running into the room and up to Gypsy. The men look at her with some surprise: "What's she doing?" "Leary's kid, isn't it?"

LILA: My father's coming. He's found out I'm here. He's drunk again, yelling down the street. He's coming to get me. He'll beat me.

GYPSY: Don't worry, honey. Nobody can come in here and cause trouble while I'm running things. And I won't give you up. Now go along. Amy, take her into the kitchen and give her some of that cake.

[*One of the women takes her by the hand and leads her off,
stage left.*]

HANK: You gonna become a mother, Gypsy.

GYPSY: Can you feature it? [*Stands with her arms akimbo.*]
What am I supposed to do with her?

MAN: Show her how to be a woman. [*Laughs.*]

GYPSY: Sure, and let the town spit on her.

MAN: The boys treat you well, don't we, Gypsy?

GYPSY: Sure you do, honey. [*Leans forward and tweaks his
nose.*] Me with a kid? This is a house, not a home. Not that I
ever knew one, either.

HANK: You born on route, Gypsy? [*One by one the girls leave,
going upstairs with the men they've been chatting with, sitting with.*]

GYPSY: You might say that. A caboose was more home to me
than anything else I came across. And the fireman was kinder
to me than the son of a bitch who spawned me. At least he
paid for what the other took for nothing. The scum.

"It might as well be her kid," the director says. "Born out of
the same egg. The egg that contains the future."

"And what's that?"

"You're getting ahead of the plot." He signals for silence.

"But all this waste." Bill can't hold himself in. "I've tried over
and over. The actresses, particularly Roselle. And now she's
gone. She's got a double, but what am I supposed to do with
that? What about the other?" The actors on stage are staring at
him; he feels utterly fatuous.

The director scrutinizes him. "Nobody said there wouldn't
be agony." He turns, gives a little wave of the hand. "Come on,
come on. Hank, you're slow picking up your cue."

*Hank approaching Gypsy from the other side of the table, where
he has been standing, and taking her hands.*

HANK: Marry me, Gypsy. Mary me and leave this life.

GYPSY: What would I do that for?

HANK: I'll give you half my gold mine. Take you to San Francisco and show you the town. You can be high society. Fancy
dresses and . . .

242

GYPSY: You'd show me off, squire me around?

HANK: You bet I would. I love you, Gypsy.

GYPSY: And all the while the whispers around you: He married the town whore. Your wife. Only if I married you, I wouldn't be Gypsy anymore.

HANK: The town's going to close you down, Gypsy. All the respectable folks. Things are changing.

GYPSY: Bluster and foolishness. Some things never change. Besides, what would the mayor do for his salary?

HANK: Marry me, Gypsy. And forget all this. Haven't you ever suffered for what you've done, for what you are?

GYPSY: Every moment of my life, Henry Desmond. You think I'm only curled hair and decoration, a smile and a languid pause? Forget it? What would I be then? It's been my life. Become a blank? Lila! Lila! [*Stage begins to darken.*] Will this darkness be only night? A dawning? I'll give her the rose. I've had my fling, enjoyed it too, while the ladies of the town turned their heads the other way. A wanton woman—who spoke to the loneliness of their men. They created me. How else could I exist? Lila, come dear. The rose. We're all pioneers . . . [*Blackness.*]

A circle of light in the dark. Stones first. He chose them carefully, as though he might be judged on his selection. He made no hurry . . . all the time in the world. Stones with colors in them, stones of the right heft, stones that felt right to lift and carry to a clear space by the river, where he set them one next to the other in a circle. A friendship with stones. Good and solid, they stay in one place; you can count on them. Good stones. True and loyal stones. He stood back admiring his ring of stones. He rearranged them, looked them over again, then made a nest of twigs and small branches, struck a match, watched the fire take hold and the flames leap up. The warmth touched him —touched the sore muscles in his body, took thought out of him, and captured his eyes. Shifting reds and blues, the intensity of the white flame that grew firmer in the receding daylight. Fire filled the ring of stones.

Fire raging through the town, houses and buildings collapsing. The sound of something snapping, and a long cry. Broken, the slender line of connection, like a faith, unseen yet there. Soup kitchens, people standing in line for food. And Merle Fullmer in his bed, being conquered by Indians.

"Spent Youth was weary to the bone. So many days he had traveled, half alive on the back of his horse, corpses for company. He put food into his body, but it gave him no strength. It had gone to feed the corpses. They had left well fed. Now only one remained behind, and its strength was in raving. 'Indians,' he yelled. 'They're coming closer.' So strong was the corpse it nearly pulled him over the precipice as he rode.

"'Why do they torment you, old man?' Spent Youth asked the body beside him, alive yet not alive.

"'They never go away.'"

The rage of the unassuaged past? Rising up to overwhelm an old man while the fire raged in the heart of the town. The fire speaking through him. Never to be done with? Never to be just put aside and forgotten, even the things you thought were finished? Blood speaking from the ground, from all those trampled underfoot, even though the grass grew over them and the paintbrush and desert poppy bloomed. Still the voices confused you. You woke, set down by history, and furies raged under the crib. Shaping you. Old hates and alliances, powers and conquests. Here, the wild desert peoples, wandering and marauding, raiding in Mexico and all over Arizona. Embodying the cruelty of the desert itself, if that's what you called it, there being no name for the force that ruled both. Subdued in the push across the continent with the help of Indians who had known their ravages. Did it matter? The world had changed: the hole of the big mine dug into the earth, the smelter rising above it.

"'Don't you see,' the corpse said to Spent Youth, 'you have conquered us after all. You haunt our dreams, you beckon us, terrorize us, mystify us. Till all the knots come undone and I forget my name . . .'"

The old man lying there, caught up in lives not his own, voices swirling around him, more real than his own life. What were you supposed to do with that? He had watched the face stiffen, the body tremble, the eyes become fixed in his head. An old man quite alone with his terror. In his sleep he cried out, and if he could be said to waken, his speech was babble. Swallowed up, all his experience.

Something cleaves you open like a nut. Here in the Wilderness the darkness settled over Frank. The evening had grown still, everything pulled down into the darkness till he could make out only the trees at the top of the canyon. He put on fresh wood, so that the coals set the flames leaping again. Fire that had cooked for him and kept the flesh warm and would keep animals away. What fire had always done. Comfort of warmth and light. Enter the fire, embrace intensity at the center, and return. Look over the edge, down to where the old man wandered, only do not fall.

And that one moment he had seen him back in the hospital: the old man, who lay asleep, had opened his eyes, and the look in them was blank and calm. The final defeat? The old man looked around as though he were seeing the room, the walls for the first time. He stood up and moved slowly to the window. Frank drew a chair up for him. He looked at Frank, did not appear to recognize him, but sat down and turned his gaze outside. After that he no longer raved. Frank wasn't sure what he was looking at. The movement of light and shadow on the grass? Or merely staring into space? Whatever it was, it belonged to him, nobody else.

"Spent Youth said to the voice: 'I cannot know anything more, old man. At least you've found some place for your mind to linger. And I must move on.'"

He gave himself to the fire, to the night. He had not eaten that day and was not hungry. The night brought him its offerings.

A towering pine. Great branches in silhouette. He saw them in their perennial green, cones and needles falling to the ground. It rose pointing upward into the night, seemed to point to a single star out of the cluster. He drowsed with its fragrance in his nostrils.

A howl, perhaps of a coyote, penetrated his sleep. He listened for more, but it was quiet around him, the moonlight bright as dawn. The light beckoned him, some instinct urging him to get up. The night was weakening. And just ahead of him he caught for a long solitary moment a small herd of deer, does that stood stock-still in the moonlight, like white statues.

He ceased to breathe, afraid of startling them, and waited. They stood for a long time, as though they would stand there as long as he would, white in the mist that hung by the river—not altogether distinct. He had never seen anything like it, this gathering of deer, white deer. But he had seen it.

Then the deer slowly trailed up the canyon. It was as far as he could go. Whatever he had come for, this was what he would take back. He was not sure if he had dreamed the deer or actually seen them. But it did not matter. He thought about white deer. He had to imagine what they were like. Had to imagine the light he caught them in. Something still of night, but part of dawn. The circle of white. Ground like snow in the moonlight and deer ghostly, as though they'd put aside flesh and blood to become what he had seen, saw now. One of their changes. One of their secrets. Or his. For it belonged to him, his eyes had seen it, and it had formed the image in his mind. And though he didn't know what it meant to him, he knew he would find it again in his mind, something given. He could even call himself by it, in the way his ancestors had done: Frank White Deer. Part of himself, part of the secret he kept to himself and that made him.

He packed his gear, mounted his horse, and rode through the canyons, around the stones, the enduring stones. If he looked hard enough perhaps he would begin to see human features in them, expressions, and if he listened carefully, perhaps he would hear voices in the wind.

"It's the next part that's got me stumped," the director admits. "I've got most of it written in, a new actress and all. But I don't know her yet, what's in her. And the other stuff. It'll have to be impromptu . . ."

"You really make it up as you go along?"

"What else? Throw caution to the winds, do it till it comes right. I mean, you've got to have certain stock characters, creations that fit every time and place. Comedy, say. You know, kicks in the butt, pratfalls, et cetera. The audience eats it up, till everybody gets sick of the same old routines. Always works, though. So they sit there, snapping their fingers: Come up with something . . . entertain us."

"Comedy? Never tried it."

"All you have to do is live," the director says, slapping him on the thigh. Bill doesn't appreciate the joke, if that's what it is. "Hell, isn't that funny enough for you? Maybe we need a little background, and a change in tone. Comedy . . . why not? In a certain light, it's all comedy. Lights!"

On either side of the stage separated by screens, men and women in various stages of undress completing their costumes and gathering together at the front of the stage, chatting.

"Why, they're here too," Bill says. "Part of the play?"
"Just watch."

MAYOR'S WIFE: He's supposed to give a speech, and I can't find him.
VOICE: [*Comes from behind her back.*] He's off with the new secretary in a high state of political excitement. [*Young woman dashes across the stage. Man in complete disarray runs behind her. His pants fall down around his knees and trip him.*]
WOMAN'S VOICE: [*Sotto voce.*] Does Ella know about this?
WOMAN'S VOICE: At his age too. He's supposed to be cleaning up the town.
MAN'S VOICE: I'd say he was cleaning up all right. Making a right good show. But then if I were in his shoes . . .
MAN'S VOICE: You'd be in her pants.
MAN'S VOICE: I'd be panting all right. And so is old Wally, the gollywog. He should be younger and in trim. He's lost his wind.
MAN'S VOICE: And his pants. She'll have to run more slowly.

[*The girl comes round again, skipping lightly, sidles up to him, as he goes through some confusion about dressing or undressing, and tries to undress her.*]
MAN'S VOICE: Delightful.
MAN'S VOICE: Disarming.
WOMAN'S VOICE: Disgusting. Disappointing.
MAN'S VOICE: What do you want from her?
WOMAN'S VOICE: Something more original.
MAN'S VOICE: Nothing more original than that. It was the first thing on the list.

WOMAN'S VOICE: At least she's got him where she wants him.

MAN'S VOICE: That's original too.

GIRL: You mean you can make me a star.

MAYOR: Honey, you'll be a whole constellation. A rising talent. And I'll rise with you.

GIRL: [*Laughs.*] You'll have to catch me first.

[*He reaches for her, but she slips from his grasp, twirls across the stage holding the rose, holds it out with a flourish, twirls around in a dance, undulating her shoulders first slowly, then to an increasing tempo, shaking her hips, twirling . . .*]

"Joan!"

"Quiet. You'll break her concentration."

WOMAN'S VOICE: The show-off.

WOMAN'S VOICE: You're jealous.

WOMAN'S VOICE: Speak for yourself. [*Calls out.*] What d'you mean coming in this way? Where do you come off? Who d'you think you are?

[*The dancer pauses, gives a little insolent bump of the shoulder, then laughs.*]

LILA: My mother was a Mexican. And my father, who can say what he was? Passing through, looking for a little diversion. Following it across the desert like a mirage. Who can say? I was conceived on the wings of the passing moment. [*Snaps her fingers.*] Between here and there, in the nip at the half of next to nothing . . . and everything.

MAN'S VOICE: The whole works? The real thing?

LILA: Innocent, sweet girl and smutty little tart, down to the gutter from the top of the tree. Dark as the inside of a hippo's belly and fox-fire bright. Twisted as a monkey puzzle and straight as Mrs. Grundy's corset stay. I am a mixed bag.

WOMAN'S VOICE: [*Sarcastically.*] How inspiring!

LILA: Sheer inspiration. Moonlight madness. Mixture of sweat . . .

MAYOR: [*Rushes onstage, hastily buckling his belt.*] I'm supposed to give my speech.

MAN'S VOICE: She's beat you to it.

MAYOR: I am your humble servant. The welfare of the town being in my charge. And for the people to rally round . . .

WOMAN'S VOICE: What nonsense!

MAYOR: What about the fire? I put some spirit into you.

MAN'S VOICE: Still congratulating yourself about that?

MAYOR: You've turned against me already?

WOMAN'S VOICE: What spirit? The same tired phrases.

MAYOR: That's your gratitude.

MAN'S VOICE: Let him get it off his chest.

WOMAN'S VOICE: What about her?

MAN'S VOICE: She's prettier to look at.

WOMAN'S VOICE: His words don't weigh anything.

MAYOR: How do you know?

JEWELER: [Comes forward.] Here, try these scales. I've weighed gold and silver in my time.

MAYOR: Thank you, thank you. [Reaches inside for his speech.] Ladies and gentlemen, these are difficult times, and we stand under leaden skies . . . There. Weighty enough for you?

MAN'S VOICE: Like old plumbing.

LILA: Besides you interrupted me. I was speaking of moonlight, things conceived in moonlight.

JEWELER: At least some points for silver there.

MAYOR: Once in the days of the golden West . . .

WOMAN'S VOICE: A cliché. Don't let him get away with that.

MAYOR: . . . we rode forward into a new land, men and women facing dangers untold. But our hearty forebears, beset by obstacles . . .

JEWELER: Still lead. The scale won't even pick it up.

LILA: Moonlight madness—mixture of sweat and grasshopper juice and wet grass, the smell of babies' hair. That's what Lila's made of, made of. All that spawns the crazies and the fools, hunchbacks and gimp-legs—everything that leaps and walks, and I, who dance. Dropped out of the moment in the here-I-am of a new beginning and the don't-waste-a-second cry of Feed me, Love me—that gleam of possibility.

WOMAN'S VOICE: Surely that's worth some points.

MAYOR: What kind of nonsense? This game's gone far enough.

WOMAN'S VOICE: Take your lead and put it in your pencil. [Addresses Lila.] And where does that leave you?

MAYOR: We need to bring back copper, so we can hear the clink of silver.

JEWELER: Rubbish!

LILA: Only in the arms of circumstance. That's where I'm left.

MAN: [*Steps out of the dark at the back of the stage and comes forward.*] Will my arms do? [*Puts his arms around her.*] Catching at the copper dark. Knowing nothing.

LILA: They'll do. You want me, then?

MAN: As always.

LILA: For your bed and board. To bear your brats.

"You can't tell a thing about her," the director says, marveling. "She moves toward him even as she heaps on her contempt. What can a mere man do?"

"You don't think she's met her match?"

The director shakes his head. "Nothing's clear. It's all up in the air."

MAN: To live—to find my idea in you, reaching toward discovery, toward any gleam.

LILA: Hah! So that's it. Model my flesh in marble and try to breathe it into life. I'm sick of being somebody else's idea. My face keeps changing. [*Moves away from him.*]

MAN: And mine. [*Moves toward her.*] If only I can see yours in the dark. To catch that arrow of light to see by.

Bill turns to the director. "It's his voice. I'm sure of it now. He's onto her, I tell you."

"Of course he recognizes her."

"Of course. He knows she's not Roselle."

Looks at him as if he were dense. "Recognizes what she is."

Puzzled. "I seem always to miss the point."

"That she can play all the parts, even the ones that haven't been invented yet."

LILA: [*Dances around him.*] I'm here to tell lies. I've drunk from the Gila River and am no more to be believed. Sometimes I fool myself. [*He catches her.*] You love me, then?

MAN: [*Kisses her.*] Let's snatch our bit of time out of time. The

250

great catch out of the sea that covered these mountains. The great whale. Nothing less will do.

LILA: And from his fins make needles and pins.

And from his eyes cast your own surmise.

One your leg, two your leg,

Three your leg, roll your leg

Over me, come now, my love. [*Dances around him, as they walk toward the back of the stage and disappear into the dark.*]

"Joan, Joan," Bill cries. "Come back, Joan."

"Think you can use her now?" The director raises his voice, calling out, "Okay, everybody, I've got a few suggestions."

Joan comes forward, throwing off her wig. "So there, I've had my story."

"No," Bill says, "there's more. You're part of this town now." She looks at him.

"Listen. I've got an idea for a film . . ."

"Where's Bird?" the mayor says. "Where's the old devil?"

"Gone. Slipped away as usual."

"He has to come back," Joan says.

"Next time," the mayor says, "I'll get him. You'll see if I don't."